W9-BYA-786

Lovelock

TOR BOOKS BY ORSON SCOTT CARD

LOVELOCK

THE MAYFLOWER TRILOGY

BOOK I

ORSON SCOTT CARD
AND
KATHRYN H. KIDD

TOR

A TOM DOHERTY ASSOCIATES BOOK

NEW YORK

This is a work of fiction. All the characters and events portrayed in this novel are either fictitious or are used fictitiously.

LOVELOCK

Copyright © 1994 by Orson Scott Card and Kathryn H. Kidd

All rights reserved, including the right to reproduce this book, or portions thereof, in any form.

This book is printed on acid-free paper.

A Tor Book
Published by Tom Doherty Associates, LLC
175 Fifth Avenue
New York, NY 10010

www.tor.com

Tor® is a registered trademark of Tom Doherty Associates, LLC.

Book Design by Ann Gold

Library of Congress Cataloging-in-Publication Data

Card, Orson Scott.
    Lovelock / Orson Scott Card and Kathryn H. Kidd
       p.   cm.—(The Mayflower trilogy ; bk. 1)
    "A Tom Doherty Associates book."
    ISBN 0-312-85732-2 (hc)
    ISBN 0-312-87751-X (pbk)
    1. Interplanetary voyages—Fiction. 2. Women scientists—Fiction.
3. Monkeys—Fiction. I. Kidd, Kathryn H. II. Title. III. Series: Card,
Orson Scott. Mayflower trilogy ; bk. 1.
PS3553.A655L68   1994
81-'.564—dc20   94-605
                                        CIP

First Hardcover Edition: July 1994
First Trade Paperback Edition: February 2001

Printed in the United States of America

0 9 8 7 6 5 4 3 2 1

To our good friends the Childs,
particularly
Dennis, who has the right tool for suitors and sheep,
Carla, with a soft shoulder and a warm heart,
and Derek—welcome home

Contents

On Collaboration

Science fiction has a long, proud tradition of collaboration between first-rate writers, who, together, produce work that is different from—and sometimes better than—what either of them produces alone. My first exposure to the power of collaboration was Larry Niven and Jerry Pournelle's brilliant *The Mote in God's Eye*. I soon read both authors' solo work as well, and was surprised to discover that *Mote* was not just an average of the two styles. The result of the collaboration was a new "virtual author" who was neither Niven nor Pournelle. Neither could have produced the novel alone.

Since those days, however, a new kind of "collaboration" has sprung up in the science fiction field. I realized this when a book packager approached me with the idea of putting together a series of "collaborations." My job would be to come up with a plot outline and some basic world creation for a science fiction novel. Then a young, unknown (i.e., desperate) writer would be engaged to do the actual word-by-word writing. I would have approval of all chapters and could reject any of them or ask for whatever changes I wanted. I could nominate my novice collaborator, or the packager would be glad to find someone for me. This would be good for the young writers, said the packager, because the commercial value of my name would get them far more exposure than they could otherwise hope for. It would be good for me, because it would help keep my name constantly before the public and would bring in some extra royalties without my having to do all that hard work.

Needless to say, this was a flattering proposal, not least because I was not then and am not now convinced that my name has any particular commercial value. American Express has not yet called me to do one of their TV ads. Naturally, to have a packager treat me as if the mere presence of my name on the cover of a book would guarantee sales was heady stuff. Also, I'm lazy. I keep wishing somebody else could do the work of writing my books. And wasn't this sort of thing right in the tradition of the Renaissance artist's workshop? An apprentice writer, learning from the (ahem) master even as he helps take some of the burden from the master's shoulders . . .

The trouble was, as a reviewer in those days for *The Magazine of Fantasy & Science Fiction*, I had actually read some of these collaborations and reviewed one of them in print. The one I reviewed happened to be the first in Isaac Asimov's "Robot City" series, and Asimov's young collaborator was no novice—it was Michael Kube-McDowell, who had already published his own Trigon Disunity trilogy to much critical praise and reader enthusiasm. Imagine my surprise, then, when the resulting novel turned out to be far below either writer's standards. It was as if neither writer felt responsible for the quality of the product. If he had any misgivings, Kube-McDowell's unconscious could always whisper to him, Hey, it's Asimov's story, not mine; and Asimov might unconsciously say, Oh well, I didn't really write it anyway. Whatever the reason, the result was pretty thin. And in the months and years to come, I found that Kube-McDowell's and Asimov's "collaboration" was the *best* of these master-apprentice works.

I didn't want to do that.

But I *did* want to do something like what Harlan Ellison depicted in his great collection *Partners in Wonder*. His project, back in the 70s, was to collaborate with other leading sf writers on a single story each. He talked about each writer composing first drafts of various sections and then passing them to the other for rewrites. Each had to show respect for the other's work—but also could freely expand upon or reshape what the other had done. It sounded like a wonderful process, akin to the experiences I had had in theatre back at the beginning of my career, where playwright, director, and actors all push and pull on the story to give it a final shape that none of them could have produced on their own.

So instead of agreeing to the packager's proposal, I began to think of a writer whose work I admired, and who could do things with fiction that I didn't know how to do. There were obvious choices within the field, of course—I would have loved to see what John Kessel and I might produce together, or Nancy Kress, or Karen Joy Fowler. The trouble was that I was pretty sure they wouldn't be interested, and I'm just shy enough that I didn't have the courage to ask. (One of them has since made it very clear that my instinct was correct, and there would have been no interest.) And outside the field of science fiction, the chances were even slimmer. I didn't think Anne Tyler or Harry Crews or Tom Gavin or François Camoin or John Hersey or James Clavell would want to collaborate with me on a science fiction story, let alone a novel.

When I stopped fantasizing, I realized that I *did* know one writer whose work I admired and who was doing things I didn't know how to do; and best of all, I knew she wouldn't laugh in my face when I proposed the collaboration. Kathy Helms Kidd had been my friend since back in the days when she was a reporter for the *Deseret News* and I was an assistant editor at *The Ensign* in Salt Lake City. I had been a witness at her wedding to Clark Kidd. And I had goaded her into writing a Mormon novel to help me launch my small publishing company, Hatrack River Publications. That first novel of hers, *Paradise Vue*, has gone through three printings and has given a new shape to Mormon publishing—it's been fun to watch other publishers come out with novels clearly attempting to imitate Kathy's inimitable humor and incisive truthfulness of vision. They always fall short; and Hatrack River has prospered.

Since then Kathy had written other excellent books for Hatrack River, and was also working on a mainstream novel, *Crayola Country*. She had strengths that I couldn't match, among them her natural humor; her ability to create a whole community of quirky, fascinating people; her deft handling of pain. I wanted to see what the two of us would produce through collaboration. So I proposed the idea, and we began to develop a storyline, starting with the basic premise of "small towns in space."

We talked it back and forth during the days I was hiding out with her and Clark while I worked on another novel (I often have to change environments to kick-start a new project). Neither of us can remember which of us thought of the ideas we ended up keeping. But at the end of the process, we had characters and situations that we, at least, found compelling. The story had grown larger than the original concept—the small towns are still there, but while the story takes place within those small towns, it is not really *about* them. Instead, our narrator, an enhanced capuchin monkey named Lovelock, had graduated from observer to protagonist, and the novel you are holding in your hands was born.

The process we worked with was a true collaboration. As you read this novel, you will have no way of knowing which of us wrote the first draft of any chapter; in fact, I don't remember myself anymore, except that my impression is that we each did first draft on about half. And both of us felt free to make changes in the other's work. We each had respect for the strengths the other brought to the project and valued each other's contributions. And we both felt keenly responsible for the quality of the outcome.

The trouble was, we knew perfectly well that in today's publishing climate, when sf readers saw that this book was by Orson Scott Card, whom they have probably heard of, and Kathryn H. Kidd, whom they have almost certainly not (since her publications have been in another genre) these readers would naturally conclude that this was another of those master-apprentice "collaborations," and therefore not likely to be very good.

Well, we can't be sure that you'll think this novel is good—though *we* do, or we wouldn't have sent it off to be published. But we wanted you to know that whatever flaws this book might have did not result from having a junior writer do the real work on an outline written by the senior one. This is a true collaboration from beginning to end.

Ellison also warned that collaboration, when done well, isn't easier than writing alone—it's harder. Twice as much work for half the money, is the way I remember him putting it. I mentioned that to Kathy at the beginning of our project, and we both laughed. It would be different for us.

As in so many other things, Ellison was right. But you don't collaborate in order to save time or avoid work. You collaborate in order to create a story that neither of you could have created as well alone.

(Just think, Kathy. We only have to do this two more times.)

—Orson Scott Card
Greensboro, 16 September 1993

Lovelock

CHAPTER ONE

LEAVETAKING

If I had known what Mayflower held for me, I might have stayed in New Hampshire. Even if I had been dragged screaming from our clapboard house, I could have hidden myself before we ever got on the space shuttle. Carol Jeanne would have searched, of course, and for a long time. But she would never have found me, and, as much as she would have mourned my loss, eventually she would have left without me. There was a new world waiting for her—to observe it, understand it, and transform it. The playground of her dreams. What was love compared to that?

I had already lost her; I should have known. Who can compete with a new planet for a gaiologist's heart? But at the time I was too naive to understand anything that mattered. In those days my devotion to Carol Jeanne was so strong that even if I had known what would happen on the Ark, the terrible things I would do, the frightening course my life would take, I still would have gone with her, gladly. It didn't occur to me that I could live for a single day without her. What would a little murder have mattered to me then? I was besotted.

From the moment Carol Jeanne received her invitation, there was no doubt that she would accept it. I also welcomed the move to the village of Mayflower on the interstellar Ark. A great adventure; *she* was so happy I couldn't help but be delighted myself. And there was a personal benefit: the artificial atmosphere of the Ark would be warmer and brighter than New England's.

Because I was Carol Jeanne's witness, she and I were so close that the two of us were almost one individual. On the morning we left she awoke me first, before she got her own husband out of bed.

"Lovelock," she whispered, leaning over my pillow. "Are you awake? It's time."

I was instantly alert, but I lay in bed with my eyes closed, knowing she would put her hand on my forehead to awaken me. Her touch was so gentle.

"Lovelock! I know you're awake. I can feel you trembling."

I couldn't help that; my body always gives me away.

I raised my hand and squeezed her finger, the way I always greeted her in the mornings. When I opened my eyes, she was smiling.

"That's better, you wretched little slug. We'll be leaving soon. Make yourself some breakfast; I'll get everyone else out of bed."

I lay in bed for a moment or two, as Carol Jeanne went to awaken Red. It was a thankless task, because Red was a heavy sleeper, lethargic and snappish in the mornings, thinking only of himself. Usually Carol Jeanne let him awaken himself after we had gone to work. In his own sweet time, he'd rouse himself and then make breakfast for Lydia and Emmy. At the end of each day, when we saw him after work, he had transformed himself into the perfect husband and father. I always suspected that Red's real personality was the early morning one, when his guard was down and he was nasty and irritable. But even if the nice evening self was a fake, I still gave him points for trying.

I heard Carol Jeanne awaken him in the next room, but not as tenderly as she had awakened me moments before. She knew the difference between us. Red grunted a reply and stumbled toward the bathroom. Sounded like a morning I should stay away from him for at least an hour. I went to the kitchen and tore open three bananas for breakfast.

When I returned to the sleeping area, both the girls were awake. Emmy, like all human babies, was completely useless and incompetent, even now that she was old enough to walk. She was wet, but instead of taking her soggy diaper off, she just stood there crying, doing nothing to help, nothing even to *cooperate* as Carol Jeanne struggled to get her into fresh clothes. Humans are born so stupid; but that's the script their DNA has prepared for them, so I didn't blame Emmy. In fact, as a cool, dispassionate observer, I couldn't help but notice that most of the difficulty was caused by Carol

Jeanne's incompetence at dressing her own child. As much as I loved Carol Jeanne, I had to admit that Red was a better mother than she was. Red could have soothed Emmy in a moment, and in the meantime he could flip clothes onto a child as fast as he dealt cards; Carol Jeanne, on the other hand, made everything twice as hard as it needed to be, and every sound that Emmy made only exasperated her more.

I may be a witness, but that doesn't mean that I'm not allowed to help. I distracted Emmy from the task at hand, entertaining her with meaningless chatter and funny faces. Almost at once the little girl forgot her discomfort. "You are my hero, Lovelock," said Carol Jeanne. If only she had really believed her own words.

The older daughter, Lydia, wasn't as easy to pacify. "Lovelock's watching me get *dressed*," she complained when I turned my attention to her. "He keeps staring at me. Tell him not to look at me."

"Tell him yourself, Lydia. He isn't staring. He's only being friendly."

I didn't understand this human obsession with privacy and modesty. What—did Lydia, in her little prepubescent brain, suppose that I had some interspecies hankering for her neotenous, immature body? I knew where I wasn't wanted. Turning my back on Lydia, I reached for Emmy. She held out her arms for me. I clambered into her clumsy embrace and held my breath as she hugged me with dangerous enthusiasm. The real benefit of this was that it always made Lydia crazy with jealousy when I let Emmy hug me.

"I want a hug, too," she wailed.

"Please don't get them competing with each other, Lovelock," Carol Jeanne said. "Not today."

I scrambled out of Emmy's hug and climbed over Carol Jeanne to get to Lydia, who was reaching for me with a look of coy triumph on her face. Poor child—she thought *she* was the one manipulating *me*. Once enfolded in her false little embrace, I permitted myself an audible sigh. Carol Jeanne was usually oblivious to how much I endured for her sake, but I still tried to help her notice. Already I had heard Red grumble, Emmy cry, and Lydia whine—and Red's parents weren't even awake yet. Not for the first time, I wished that Carol Jeanne and I were going to the Ark without the rest of her family. If I could have thought of a way to do it, I would have.

As Carol Jeanne clumsily took care of the girls—setting them at the table, where they splashingly ate their cold cereal—I settled myself in a corner to do my job: recording how Carol Jeanne spent her last morning on Earth. I thought it was appropriate to see that she dressed herself only after her children were dressed and ready to go, ate only after her children had eaten. The leading scientist of her time, and still she placed her children before the weighty concerns of her work. Thus did the greatest of all gaiologists humbly act out her natural role within the species. She had said it herself, once: Gaiologists must always recognize that they are part of the living organism, never an outside observer, and never, not for a moment, impartial or unbiased about anything. To help her make her point, I never recorded Red doing these family chores, even though he was the one who usually did them. Why should I have? He had his own witness, didn't he?

Even though the children hardly understood what the Ark would mean, they had caught on that something exciting was happening, which made them jumpy and quick to whine—not my favorite trait in human children—but the adults were no less jumpy in their own way. They were grieving in silent, unconscious ways—grieving for the place, for the house in New Hampshire, for all the possessions they were leaving behind. Fortunately I lack the genes for that sense of bonding with inanimate objects. I'm as territorial as the next primate, but when I change territories I don't get sentimental about the one I abandoned. I can pick up tools and use them, I can make almost any place into a nest, but I never think of it as being part of myself. Therefore I am freer than they are.

Certainly *I* didn't have to stand around looking at things the way Red did, as if he were trying to preserve their images in his pathetically limited memory. What did he think his witness was *for*? And when Red's father, old Stef, came out of his bedroom, still zipping his fly (was this an old man's way of reminding us of his manliness?), he was already babbling on about memories of the house. Fortunately, he didn't expect *me* to answer him and therefore I didn't have to listen.

The most obnoxious mourner was, of course, Mamie, the she-human who gave birth to Red. At least Stef's chatter showed that he had mastered the rudiments of speech. Mamie went around *touching* everything, caressing it, as if she thought that by stroking the pewter tea set on the dining room buffet she could wake it up and entice it to tag along with us. Touching, grooming—that's a primate behavior that I indulge in. But I'd never groom a metal pitcher.

What annoyed me most about Mamie's touching things—besides the fact that everything she did annoyed me—was that the things she was touching so possessively *weren't hers*. Somehow she had managed to extend her sense of territoriality to include things that belonged to Carol Jeanne, or to Red and Carol Jeanne together. It betrayed the way she really felt about this house: In her own mind, she was no guest, but rather the secret owner of it all.

Including the people. She thought she owned them, too. I had once tried to explain this to Carol Jeanne, but she refused to listen. I think she knew that I was right, but she simply didn't want to be disloyal to Red by listening to somebody saying bad things about Red's dear mother. Thus, out of love, do humans force themselves to love even the barnacles and parasites that attach themselves to their beloved. We lower primates have a more sensible approach: We pick the parasites off and eat them. Our loved ones are relieved of the annoying little bloodsuckers, and we get a little boost in our dietary animal protein.

"I wish I could have taken this," sighed Mamie. She was caressing the sofa in the living room. Only six months ago she had complained about how uncomfortable it was—the opening move in the game of getting Red to buy another one just to please her. Another test of her little boy's love. Now, of course, the sofa was precious. "The thousand-pound limit seems so meager," she said. "Poundage should be allotted by a person's age. Young people just haven't put down so many roots."

Tentacles, I think she meant.

I waited for someone to point out that Mamie was already taking much more than her thousand pounds. She had appropriated most of Stef's and Lydia's and Emmy's poundage—and a little bit of my pathetic fifty-pound allotment, too. She was taking *all* the weight allotted to Red's witness, Pink the pig. I imagined that most people who went off-Earth didn't leave with as many possessions as Mamie was taking. Actually, most people *on* Earth didn't have as many possessions as she was taking.

But no one corrected Mamie; no one put her in her place. Red apparently thought his mother was perfect, Stef had been hammered into submissiveness many decades ago—probably within the first month of their marriage—and Carol Jeanne just didn't like confrontation. So everyone treated Mamie respectfully as she drifted from room to room, leaving oily fingerprints and sickly-sweet perfume on everything. Carol Jeanne wouldn't have appreciated it if I compared Mamie to a dog marking its territory, so I kept that observation to myself. Besides, the comparison wasn't really fair. Among dogs it's not the bitches that do the marking.

With all her mourning over things she hadn't owned anyway, Mamie wasn't leaving behind anything that couldn't be replaced. Carol Jeanne, on the other hand, was leaving her sister Irene, who was an irreplaceable resource. Even I could understand her feelings of desolation; in those days, I would have preferred a death sentence to separation from Carol Jeanne.

Of course no one but me even guessed at her feelings. What did Red know about siblings? He had never had one. As for Stef, well, I had a secret suspicion that he regarded all relatives as something to be endured when they were present, not missed when they were gone. Mamie was taking with her all the people that she owned, or at least controlled. Only Carol Jeanne had a real reason for deep grief and regret—and only Carol Jeanne had enough self-control not to display her feelings the way the others did.

At last breakfast was over. The small carry-on bags were packed, mostly with spare clothes and toys for Emmy and Lydia, or the banana chips Carol Jeanne always carried to feed me when fresh fruit or monkey chow wasn't available. The *real* luggage had already been shipped ahead to be weighed and examined. So when the time came, the departure was surprisingly quick. A last look at the house, and then everyone clambered into the boxy-but-comfortable Nintendo Hoverboy, the driver revved the engine, and we bounced into the air and were gone. I thought of the months of winter remaining in New England and was glad to get away, but of course Carol Jeanne and Red held hands and both of them got misty-eyed. Seeing that, Mamie began to sniffle and quickly pulled Red's attention away from his wife. I imagined poking my finger into Mamie's eye; *then* she'd have something to cry about. I glanced at Stef and saw a faint smile on his lips. I wondered if he had the same fantasy. His was probably more elaborate. He had lived with her longer.

The trip to Boston was nothing special, scooting over the same roads that Carol Jeanne and I used to get to the university. The road surface was clear of snow—the constant hover traffic blew the snow off as fast as it ever fell. Instead, the snow was piled so high on either side that only the tops of the trees were visible. It was like driving through a tunnel.

Inside the craft, the scenery was much more interesting. Lydia kept asking if we were almost there. Emmy, ever the one to find a physical metaphor for her feelings, soon got carsick and vomited on the floor, raising an interesting smell and soiling Mamie's shoes. I wondered if Emmy's aim had been deliberate. If so, she might grow up to be worth keeping. Mamie pouted for the rest of the trip.

When we got to the airport, I considered it my duty to find Irene. So I stood on Carol Jeanne's shoulder and scanned for Irene's powder-blue habit; she was never hard to find. When I spotted her, sitting in a patch of warm sunlight near the windows, I hooted softly a couple of times and pointed.

"There she is," said Carol Jeanne. "Lovelock found her." As if any one of the others understood how much it meant to her to see Irene this last time.

With me sitting on her shoulder, of course, Carol Jeanne was as easy to spot from a distance as Irene was in her habit. We hadn't gone two steps toward her when Irene stood and raised her arm in salute. At that, Carol Jeanne lost all restraint and ran toward her. I knew enough to climb down from her shoulder and cling to her back, out of the way. Out of sight. Carol Jeanne and Irene would be more free with each other if I was invisible. But I could see and hear *them*, for this was one of those moments I was there to preserve.

A big, showy embrace—and then the two of them were suddenly shy. Neither knew how to say farewell. Neither was willing to be the first to cry.

"Come with me," Carol Jeanne said. "We can find you a place."
I knew that she did not expect Irene to change her mind. It was her
oblique way of begging Irene to forgive her for leaving.

Irene only shook her head.

"I know your covenant is for a lifetime," said Carol Jeanne, "but
don't you think you can serve God out there, too? Don't you think
people will need you there?" And then, her voice breaking a little,
she added the words that were hardest to say. "Don't you think *I'll*
need you?"

Irene smiled wanly. "I'm going to live the years that God gives
me, in the place where he put me."

I could see that Carol Jeanne took that hard, as if it were a criticism of the colonization voyage itself. I knew Irene well enough to
understand that she didn't mean it that way, but that was how Carol
Jeanne heard it because of her own sense of guilt about leaving her
sister. "If God created a universe where relativity works," said Carol
Jeanne, "you can hardly blame us for traveling to the places God
put within our reach."

Irene shook her head. "I know you're doing what you were born
to do, Jeannie. Just because I can't bring myself to leave doesn't
mean that when I'm old, I won't be glad to think of you out there
somewhere, still young and happy and looking forward to your life's
work. Maybe God meant you to stretch time and travel to the stars
and live for centuries after I'm dead. Maybe I just don't want to put
off my climb up Jacob's ladder." She made a try at laughing, but it
was a feeble chuckle that fooled no one. And because Irene had
actually mentioned death, Carol Jeanne finally lost her compo-
sure—not completely, but enough that tears started to flow.

Irene raised her arm and put her left hand on Carol Jeanne's
shoulder. The flowing sleeve of her habit looked like an angel's wing.
This was the last time the two sisters would touch each other, or
see each other, or hear one another speak.

"After all, Jesus himself chose not to cheat death," Irene added.

Irene had meant this innocently—hadn't she tied her life to Jesus?—but again, Carol Jeanne interpreted her words as criticism.
"We aren't *cheating* death, Irene." Her voice sounded hesitant and
unconvincing. "My life will be no longer than yours. It will only

seem longer to me because you could have gone with me and you didn't."

Irene looked away for a long moment. When she faced Carol Jeanne, there were tears on her face, too.

"Don't you think I *want* to stay with you?" she asked. "You're the only people I love—you and Lydia and Emmy. Even Lovelock—in a way, he's family, too."

That was nice.

"But my work is here. And as crazy as it sounds, I feel as if God is here. Even though I know that he'll be with you too, I wouldn't know how to find him out there. I can't leave God, not even for you."

Carol Jeanne answered quietly. "It was unfair of me to ask."

"But I'm glad you did," said Irene. "It will comfort me when I'm lonely for you, knowing how much you wanted me with you."

They embraced, so suddenly that I couldn't get my tail out of the way. In a way, then, Irene's arm included me in the hug. I looked at her face—only inches away from mine, now—to see if she noticed me. She did: She opened her eyes, and despite her tears managed to wink at me and smile a little.

I put my hands on her cheeks and gave her a wide-mouthed kiss on the lips. She kissed me back, squeezing her own lips together as though she were kissing a small child. Then she lifted her arm enough that I could pull my tail out of the embrace.

Carol Jeanne must have taken that release of pressure as a sign that the embrace was over; she started to pull away. But I could not let that happen, not so soon. I scrambled to their shoulders and held them together, my hands firm on their shoulders. They laughed at me as they renewed the embrace, but I knew how soon their trembling turned from laughter to silent weeping.

I held them together there until I could see Mamie bustling over, no doubt to "cheer them up." I knew Carol Jeanne would not want to be caught so emotionally exposed, so I chattered softly. She took the cue—probably without even realizing I had given it—and pulled back, drying her eyes on her sleeve. Irene, of course, had a handkerchief. She was prepared for emotion; Carol Jeanne was always taken by surprise.

Then I turned around on Carol Jeanne's shoulder and glared at

Mamie. She looked at my bared teeth and for a moment seemed to catch on to the idea that her intrusion might not be welcome. At least she paused in her headlong rush.

Oblivious to Mamie, Carol Jeanne spoke again to Irene. "I guess I can't expect you to write."

"I can, the whole time you're in solar orbit. And I'll pray for you, too, all my life. Of course, a few weeks into your real journey, I'll be dead of old age. Then you'll be on your own."

"On the contrary. Then you'll watch over me. Then I'll know you're taking care of me, protecting me."

"It's the saints who get to do that," Irene said. "But wouldn't it be wonderful if I *could*? I'd watch over you, and Lydia, and Emmy, and even Lovelock, until you joined me in heaven."

I chattered at that—the particular sound that I knew they interpreted as laughter.

"God knows you," Irene said to me. "Don't you doubt it."

I had my own ideas about what God, if he existed, must think of *me*. If he had wanted creatures like me to exist, he would have arranged for it himself. There was no one like me when Adam was naming the beasts. If there was anyone like me in the mythical Garden, it was a certain talkative snake.

"Light a candle for me," Carol Jeanne said.

"I'll light enough candles for you to keep the church warm in winter."

Mamie, of course, was suffering greatly, being in the presence of a connection between human beings that she didn't control. "Oh, you two mustn't be so sad," she said. "You can talk to each other for *months* by phone, until the voyage actually starts."

They gave no sign that they heard her.

"Good-bye," said Irene. "God bless you."

"I love you." Carol Jeanne barely whispered the words, but I knew that Irene felt them, even if she didn't hear them.

By now, Stef and Red had brought the girls along, and Mamie seized the opportunity. "Your pretty little nieces want to say bye-bye to Auntie Irene," she said. "You mustn't make them sad, now, with all these silly tears."

Only then did Carol Jeanne and Irene pay attention to the rest of the family. Irene hugged Lydia and Emmy as Mamie thrust each of them toward her; despite Mamie's orchestration of the scene, Irene's love for the girls was real, and they had always adored this strange creature who had no children to love but them. Irene's embrace of Red was more clumsy, but only because *he* felt so awkward hugging a nun; she genuinely liked Red, and he liked her, too. Then she shook hands with Mamie and Stef.

"You're such a dear thing," said Mamie. "We'll all miss your little visits so much."

Stef said nothing, but nodded to Irene as he shook her hand, as if to say that he understood her grief and approved of the strength of her commitment, even if he didn't share her faith.

Irene turned again to Carol Jeanne. But, having said their good-byes, neither said another word to the other. They only embraced once more and silently broke apart. Irene raised her fingers in fare-well as the rest of us moved away from her and headed for the tram that would take us out to the spacehopper on its extra-long runway.

Carol Jeanne stoically refused to look back, but that's what I was for. I sat on her shoulder, my hand in her hair, and watched Irene every moment until she was out of sight. I knew that in a few weeks or months, Carol Jeanne would ask for the memory. I would have long since stored the scene on the Ark's master computer, exactly as I saw it; she would play it out on the holographic display of her terminal, zooming in for a close-up of her sister's face. Then she would see what I had seen: Irene smiling, waving, then bringing her hand to cover her eyes as she wept.

CHAPTER TWO

OFF EARTH

The shuttle was just like the suborbital space cruisers that ran the one hour intercontinental express routes. The same fetishistic cleanliness. The same simple opulence that made you think you were flying to meet God instead of just going to another conference. Except that this time, instead of rising up out of the thick part of the atmosphere only to descend later over New Delhi or Zanzibar or Porto Alegre, we would go all the way up to Grissom Station.

People took the shuttle to Grissom Station for only three reasons. Half were tourists with so much money that they thought it was worth the expense of this flight just so they could look down at Earth from a window in space instead of the much larger and clearer view through a two-meter hi-def on the wall at home. They got bored in a few minutes and spent the week till the next shuttle getting drunk or laid or underfoot.

Most of the others were serious people bound for the moon or Mars or the asteroids—scientists, engineers, or half-crazy high-tech manual laborers who would work in low gravity for five years and come home with enough money to pay cash for a Tokyo apartment or a Pacific island and they'd never have to work again as long as they lived, which might not be all that long after the damage that the time they spent in low gee did to their bodies.

And then there were the people like us, the craziest of all, collecting ourselves at Grissom so we could take the long voyage out to the Ark, in its perpendicular orbit, now only a few months away from its launch point at its farthest point from the planetary orbits. We arkoids, as they called us on Grissom, were the ones who were going to leave the solar system. If we found a habitable planet and established a colony, we'd never come back. And if we gave up and headed home, relativity would have made centuries pass on Earth—we'd come "home" to a planet that had passed through so many changes we'd probably recognize nothing at all.

Two hundred years ago Britain was still trying to wipe out the African slave trade, Spain had just lost her American colonies, and Russia and the Ottoman Empire were still maneuvering for control of the Black Sea. Ships were still made of wood, steam was the hot new technology, and no one in the world had yet heard the triumphant sound of a toilet flushing. What would Earth be like two hundred years from now?

Maybe they would have found a way to give speech to people like me. Maybe, in the name of progress, the world would be filled with mentally-enhanced capuchins, baboons, possums, pigs, and dogs, all eagerly and obediently doing everything their creators demanded of them. All the work of the world being done by brilliant little beasts; all the information creatively stored in our oversized genetically-engineered brains.

Two more centuries, and humanity would finally have got what they coveted all along: slavery without shame. No, they were *enhancing* the lives of their little beasty servants.

But I'm getting ahead of myself. My thoughts didn't go that far at the time. I was naive; my real education was still before me. All I noticed as we boarded the Grissom-bound shuttle was the way the other people looked at us. Rich tourists and serious travelers alike, they sized us up immediately: a family with two small children, a couple of old people, and a monkey. None were particularly happy to see us. I knew what they were thinking: The children will cry, the old people will jabber and whine, and the monkey will probably pee on somebody.

How right they were.

We started out well enough. Lydia was sitting with Red—to my relief. The child was so odious to me that I even preferred sitting next to Emmy and watching the inevitable diaper changes. Human feces, especially baby ones mashed into a diaper, are so repulsive. There's nothing you can *do* with them, they stick to everything they touch, and they stink. Besides, at three years, the child should have been toilet-trained long before. I suspect her "accidents" were only attention-getting devices, oft repeated because they were so successful. But despite the attendant odors, at least Emmy had her pleasant moments; Lydia was a spoiled, petulant creature whose every breath was more offensive than a thousand of Emmy's diapers.

With Red and Lydia sharing one another's company, Mamie and Stef were left to sit by themselves. Pink was nowhere to be seen—she had been sedated through her little piggy snout and placed in the cargo hold, which was where she belonged. Red had tried to trot her up the gangplank like a regular passenger, but the shuttle crew banished her to the hold like a pet. I knew Red resented the fact that Carol Jeanne got to keep *her* witness and he didn't. But then, Red was no Carol Jeanne. And Pink was no *me*.

Carol Jeanne and I had flown on suborbitals—subbos—a dozen times before, and I had the routine down pat. There was always a little bit of fuss at the gate, as they examined her letter from the ISA authorizing her to bring her witness inside the cabin; they were always impressed that somebody (never *us*) was paying full fare for my seat. Then I'd coast into the cruiser on Carol Jeanne's shoulder, hop down when we got to our seat, and put myself in place on my seat. The attendant would bustle up, inspect my harness, and then attach it to the human-size lap-belt. They always made sure that the fasteners were all where I couldn't reach them—as if it wouldn't be enough just to *tell* me to keep them fastened.

This time was no different, except that instead of it being only me and Carol Jeanne on the two-seat row, Emmy's presence forced us to sit on the three-seat side. Emmy had the aisle seat and Carol Jeanne was between us. There was no window on the wall next to me—there was so much white heat on reentry that giving the passengers a view would cause panic on every flight.

My harness held me tight enough against the seat that I couldn't reach the in-flight magazine. Carol Jeanne remembered, though, and handed it to me. An attendant noticed it.

"He's acting just as if he were reading," he said, delighted at my antics.

"He *is* reading," Carol Jeanne said.

"But he turns the pages so fast."

"He reads about two thousand words a minute," she answered.

I looked up at him and grinned. Humans always think my smile is cute, until they see how sharp my teeth are. He went away.

Takeoff was takeoff. It felt like we traveled three kilometers on the ground before we finally shambled up into the air. And then, once we were aloft, the pilot laid us on our backs and climbed straight up—or so it felt. I could see across the aisle where Mamie and Stef were both gripping the armrests—they'd never flown on a subbo and the harsher movements were unnerving them a little. I knew something they didn't know—that the initial climb was nothing.

When we reached twenty thousand meters, the pilot came on the loudspeaker and warned us to face front and not to attempt any movements during the boost. I usually follow instructions to the letter, if only to win Carol Jeanne the tiny reward of having the flight crew tell her at the end of the flight that I was such a *good* little flier. This time, though, I couldn't help a moment of disobedience—I had to lean forward and steal a glance at Mamie and Stef. Sure enough, her eyes were pressed shut and tears were squeezing out of the corners. Mamie Foxe Todd was having a new experience, and she didn't like it a bit.

"Sit back, Lovelock," muttered Carol Jeanne.

She had been checking on me. It was nice to be reminded that she was looking out for me almost as carefully as I always looked out for her. And she was right, too. Leaning forward and turning my head to the side hadn't been a good move. It gave me a queasy little ache at the back of my head. The genetic enhancements that enlarged my head enough to hold my expanded brain and the digital interface weren't fully matched with enough extra strength in the cushioning and support mechanisms of my neck and skull. I get headaches fairly easily, and with the stress of the climb out of the atmosphere, moving and turning like that had given me an instant nausea headache. And because we were boosting clear up to orbit, the stress went on and on. Smart move, Lovelock, I thought. A little bit of gloating at Mamie's fear, and now you get to feel icky for the rest of the day until you sleep it off. My arms were so immobilized that I could barely hold the magazine, so there was no way of freeing my hands enough for me to pinch the pain away with acupressure.

In the seat behind us I could hear Lydia complaining about not being able to play during the boost. For once Red was actually being firm with her—he did firmness about once a year—so with luck she'd hold still and we wouldn't have to put up with Lydia sick, which was even more annoying than Lydia healthy.

Finally the boost let up, and we went from sharp acceleration to free-fall in an instant.

I could hear the panicked whimpering from across the aisle. I didn't even have to look.

"It's just low-gee, Mamie," said Carol Jeanne. "You get used to it in a few moments."

"We're falling!" Mamie insisted.

"That's how it feels," said Carol Jeanne.

"We'll be just fine, dear," said Stef. "People do this all the time."

"This is just awful," said Mamie. "They ought to do something about this. People like us shouldn't have to put *up* with this."

If only I had a voice, if only I could make words, I would have answered. These are laws of physics, Mamie, and even the bodies of people with genteel upbringing react to the sudden absence of gravity. The only way to spare you the discomfort would be total anesthesia, and most travelers prefer to arrive at their destination awake. But for *you*, Mamie, total anesthesia is more of an aesthetic statement than a medical procedure, and we'll be glad to provide it whenever you request.

Wordless, I could only save up my comments for the next time Carol Jeanne and I were alone together. She'd shush me, of course, but not until she laughed. Carol Jeanne found Mamie almost as funny as I did. She did not understand how deep my feelings about Mamie really were. So I never mentioned to her how much I looked forward to Mamie's funeral. Carol Jeanne was too kind-hearted to feel genuine malice toward anyone, no matter how they deserved it. I've never had that deficiency. Malice is one thing that even wild stupid capuchins do fairly well, and I was the enhanced model.

I didn't wish Mamie dead, actually. I just wished her *gone*. But since there was no chance of her ever letting her dear boy out of her sight for more than a few hours at a time as long as she had a breath in her body, death seemed the only way we'd ever be rid of her.

Mamie was absolutely transparent—to me, at least. She pretended to be so well-bred that she hardly noticed Carol Jeanne's international renown—fame was just another burden that people of "our" class have to bear. Yet she clung to every scrap of reflected glory that she could get hold of, all the while resenting the fact that it was her Catholic-born daughter-in-law and not her dear little white-bread boy who earned all the attention. So she was always sniping at Carol Jeanne, even though everything that Mamie valued in life came because Red had married so well.

In the seat behind us, Lydia was talking again. "Is this free-fall? Can I fly now?"

"Not till we get to the Ark," said Red.

"And probably not even then," said Carol Jeanne. She was unfastening her seat belt and getting up.

"Mommy's getting up!" cried Lydia. "Why can't I?"

"Because Mommy's been in low gee often enough that she knows how to move around without smashing her head on the ceiling or putting her elbows into other people's faces," said Carol Jeanne. She was standing in the aisle now, holding on to the handgrips, her feet hooked under the edge of the seat. "I thought I saw Dr. Tuli in the gate area," she explained to Red. "If it's really him, he'll be on his way back to Mars and I'd like to talk to him."

"You haven't seen him in years," said Red. "It's not as if you'll have a chance to get the friendship going again *now*."

Red was right, actually. Since we were leaving the solar system and never coming back in anybody's lifetime, why bother performing friendship maintenance with people who were staying behind? It was as pointless as visiting people with terminal illnesses. But human beings do *that*, too.

So Carol Jeanne went forward, hand over hand on the seat grips, as smoothly as the attendants, her legs trailing behind her gracefully.

"Mommy's flying!" cried Lydia in delight. "Emmy, can you see that?"

Emmy, of course, was not interested in whether or not Mommy was flying. She only noticed that Mommy was *gone*, and so of course she began to cry. This was perfectly understandable. After all, Emmy was not yet a sentient being. She could hardly be expected to understand that Carol Jeanne would soon return.

"Emmy's crying," said Lydia.

There was no one within three rows who was not keenly aware of this, of course. But then, Lydia's own hold on sentience was none too firm.

"I know she's crying," said Red. "But her mother will be back soon."

I knew Red. He had no intention of doing anything to quell Emmy's noise. He thought it was perfectly all right. If he let the crying go on, Carol Jeanne would hear and come back and deal with it. Even though he was better equipped for motherhood than Carol Jeanne, he was perfectly willing to let the kids jerk her around when it made things go his way. I had seen this pattern a thousand times. A ringing phone, a doorbell, the stove timer going off, a crying child—if Carol Jeanne was anywhere near, Red would simply pretend that he didn't know anything was happening until she dropped what she was doing and came to handle it. *Then*, when the situation was well in hand, he would say, "Oh, I can do that." To which Carol Jeanne would always respond, "Don't worry, dear, I've got it taken care of." It was a marriage made in heaven. Carol Jeanne never even realized she was being had. After all, Red did all these things whenever she was away, which was more often than not. But her absence made her feel guilty, and I think in a way she really *was* glad to have a chance to do those little jobs that made her feel as though she were as connected to her family as a traditional stay-at-home mother.

So the crying continued. But apparently Carol Jeanne was far enough away—or so engrossed in conversation—that she couldn't hear it. Other passengers were looking around now, glaring at Red for doing nothing to quiet Emmy down. Red, of course, was reading and paid no attention.

Mamie noticed, however. As she had said so many times, she detested being made a public spectacle. Actually, of course, she *loved* being a public spectacle. It was *negative* attention that she hated. At the moment, it was her dear boy who was getting all the loathing glances; therefore she had to do something to turn away all that disfavor.

"What are you doing?" asked Stef.

"Unfastening my seat belt," said Mamie.

"You aren't experienced in low gee," he said. "You shouldn't be getting up."

"I have to take care of my precious little unhappy girl."

At that moment her seatbelt came loose and she tried to stand up. The force of her movement immediately launched her straight toward the ceiling at high speed. She screeched and managed to get her hands up fast enough that she didn't knock herself unconscious on impact. Instead she rebounded into the aisle, clutching desperately at the handgrips on the aisle seats. She caught one, but had no idea of anchoring herself by hooking her feet under the seats. So the angular momentum spun her around the handgrip. If she had planned any of this it would have been a brilliant stunt, and even as an idiotic accident I had to admire the fact that despite her age, her reflexes were still pretty quick and she was strong enough not to lose her hold on the handgrip despite all the twisting and wrenching.

By the time the attendant got there to rescue her, she had managed to get herself into Carol Jeanne's seat, and she dismissed the man rather coldly. "As you can see, I'm simply here to comfort my precious little granddaughter." As far as Mamie was concerned, her athletic adventure of a moment before had never happened. No doubt her memory was already edited to show her moving with perfect grace at all times. Even when her muscles were sore tomorrow from the wrenching, I knew Mamie wouldn't connect the stiffness with her acrobatics, because the acrobatics never happened.

As for comforting Emmy, however, that was not to be. Emmy wasn't fully human yet, but she could certainly tell the difference between Mommy and not-Mommy, and Mamie was definitely in the not-Mommy category. The crying continued without slackening.

"You dear child, there must be *something* I can do with you," she said. There was now an edge to her voice. Patience was wearing thin. After all this trouble to get across the aisle, it would hardly do if she were shown to be ineffectual as a grandmother. So she cast about for anything that might distract the child and put a stop to the crying. After giving up on the in-flight magazine, Emmy's teething ring, and the vomit bag, Mamie cast her gaze in another direction.

"Emmy, dear, would you like to play with Mommy's monkey?

I'll even let you feed him. Now, where did Carol Jeanne put that bag of treats?"

I'm a witness. I'm supposed to observe. And when Mamie—who had never willingly touched me before in her life—decided that I might be useful in solving her little dilemma, my first thought was to bite her hand if it came anywhere near me. Since interfering with a legally registered witness was a serious crime, no one ever sued or even struck back when I bit them for trying to touch me. Still, this wasn't a stranger, this was Carol Jeanne's mother-in-law, and if I bit her we'd probably never hear the end of it. So I hesitated.

As she fumbled around with the straps and buckles behind me— she wasn't very good at figuring out how things fastened or came apart—I began to think of several reasons why Mamie's idea was actually a very good one. Emmy always responded well to me, and I enjoyed playing with her. Even though her style of play was to try every possible way to kill me with her bare hands, she had about as much dexterity as an oyster and so I could always get away. I knew that within moments, Emmy would be laughing with delight. That would allow Carol Jeanne to continue her conversation without interference, and she would appreciate it. If it also happened to make Mamie feel just a little bit more tolerant toward me, so much the better.

That's what I was thinking at the time. What never crossed my mind was the fact that I was no more experienced in freefall than Mamie. After all, I had been kept harnessed in my seat on every subbo flight I'd taken. But why should I have expected to have any problems? All my experience told me that if something required balance and dexterity, I could do it a hundred times more easily than any human. Freefall was just another physical challenge, and of course I would handle it easily and naturally, making humans seem clumsy by comparison.

And maybe it would have been that way, if it had all depended on dexterity. Certainly I have *that,* and my enhancements have, if anything, made me even quicker and sharper. What I hadn't reckoned on was how freefall would make me *feel.* Primates have invested a lot of evolution in learning how to swing through trees. Only a handful of species—humans and baboons, mostly—got back down out of the trees and learned to hoof it like cattle. We tree-swingers are the ones who developed binocular vision—the front-pointing eyes that define the primate face. They gave us the ability to judge exactly how far to leap to reach the next branch, and when and how to grasp it with our agile fingers and nubby little opposable thumbs. It's the perfect setup for amazing acrobatics.

The trouble is that all of it depends on a very keen sense of gravity: exactly how much we weigh, how far we'll go on a leap, and how far downward we'll drift in midair. Humans and baboons don't need to be so aware of where *down* is. Their biggest challenge is standing up without falling over. We tree-swingers absolutely depend on our sense of down-ness or we'd die on the first jump.

In freefall, no direction is down, yet every movement feels like falling.

Harnessed to the seat, my understanding of this point was wholly intellectual. Now, when Mamie opened the seat straps, I understood freefall on an entirely different level. I wasn't stupid the way Mamie had been. I kept my grip on the armrest, the strap, Mamie's sleeve, whatever it took to keep from flying off into space. The trouble was that as soon as I started moving, my brain instinctively rebelled against the information it was getting.

Sure, I was holding on to solid objects—but that couldn't override the horrifying sense that I couldn't find *down*. For humans, *down* comes as much from visual cues as from the little water tubes in their inner ear—if something *looks* like down, it's pretty much down, no matter how it feels. But for me, well, I'm used to hanging upside down and swinging any which way. Visual cues mean nothing. And with my inner-ear balancing mechanism giving me the clear information that I was plunging to my death, it didn't matter *how* tightly I held on to things. I panicked.

At first, panic meant that I froze, gripping even more tightly—one hand on the armrest, one on Mamie's sleeve, and one foot on a strap. My other foot and my tail were both flailing around like crazy, probing for something else that could be grasped. My foot found Mamie's fingers.

Her eyes widened. My grip was not subtle. And I was involuntarily making my panic face—teeth bared, eyes wide—which humans invariably interpret as anger. She thought I was attacking her.

"What are you doing?" she whispered. *"Let go of me."*

She yanked her hand away. Now, since my right foot and my left hand were gripping her finger and sleeve, and my left foot and right hand were holding on to much bigger, harder-to-grip objects, it was inevitable that instead of tearing herself free of me, she merely tore *me* free of the seat. She was waving her arm around, with six pounds of panicked jungle creature clinging to her finger and sleeve. "Let go, you filthy little devil!" she screamed.

Now I was holding on at only two points, and to make things worse she was flailing me around. What I had felt before was only the first stage of panic. Now I was in the second stage, and compared to this, the first stage was mere anxiety. All my sphincter muscles released at once, demonstrating the fact that the term *going apeshit* has a literal meaning. With every wave of her arm, monkey turds and monkey urine were being flung out in every direction, personal souvenirs of the trip for the hapless passengers who witnessed my degradation.

All I knew at the time was that I was no longer the only one screaming. Within moments, others were trying to grab hold of me, and I reflexively grabbed their fingers and clothing, their hair and ears and noses. I lost Mamie at once, and began scrambling insanely from person to person. Since many of them were also losing control in freefall, it became quite a dangerous situation; at one point the man I was clinging to smashed into a wall, and if I'd been hanging on in a slightly different position I might have been crushed.

It only ended when Carol Jeanne caught me. She was calm—always, in a crisis, that's the one thing you can count on, that Carol Jeanne will be the cool one, methodically doing what's necessary. She plucked me out of the air—none too gently—and immediately tucked me, leaking urine and all, under her blouse, where she gripped me tightly.

Immediately, as soon as I was completely restrained, I felt safe again. The panic subsided. All I could think about was relief; all I could do was pat her, stroke her, groom her in gratitude. What this felt like to *her* I have no idea. After a few minutes I was able to move a little, and—with her arms still pressing on me, confining me—I twisted to peer out of an opening between the buttons of her blouse.

The attendants were getting people settled down again. One of them was sweeping the air with a powerful vacuum cleaner tube, sucking up free-floating urine drops and spinning turds—little dry ones, nothing like the disgusting things that humans make, though you'd never guess it from the way they were all dodging them and shuddering. Others were passing out moist towelettes to passengers who were wiping at their faces, their hands, their clothing, trying to clean themselves.

Carol Jeanne was moving now, returning to our seats. I wanted to explain to her what had happened, but there wasn't a notebook handy, and her computer was in the stowed luggage. So it wasn't from me that she heard an accounting.

Mamie was still sitting in Carol Jeanne's seat, wiping Emmy down. Emmy, of course, was having a wonderful time. She had found the whole episode very entertaining. "Monkey poop!" she cried. "Monkey wet! Lovey-law fly!" I, of course, was Lovey-law. Technically I had not actually flown, having never let go of one person till I had a good grip on the next, but since the people themselves were flying around the cabin, I thought Emmy's words were a fair summation of what had happened.

Carol Jeanne, however, wanted a more specific accounting. "Who let Lovelock out of his harness?" she demanded.

With Mamie sitting in Carol Jeanne's seat, there was really only one possible candidate. But Mamie looked up at Carol Jeanne, her face stern with righteous anger, and said, coldly, "I was trying to take care of *your* daughter, whom you had abandoned here. With Emmy sobbing her little heart out, I could hardly be expected to watch out for your monkey at the same time."

So that was Mamie's story—*she* had nothing to do with my being loosed from my restraints. I waited for someone to point out the obvious—that the harness and straps were arranged so that I could not possibly have gotten free on my own. I wasn't surprised that Stef said nothing—he hadn't lived this long without knowing better than to contradict Mamie in public. Red, on the other hand, had actually argued with his mother from time to time over the years, and she had even backed down now and then.

But when he opened his mouth, it was not to tell the truth. "Apparently they have good reasons for confining *most* witnesses to the cargo compartment," he said.

The liar! *He* knew it was all his mother's fault, but he let me take the blame anyway. He did it solely out of jealousy. I was Carol Jeanne's companion—the one who shared every waking moment of her life with her. She told me her secrets and developed her scientific theories with me at her side. Red was only good for breeding, and if my little monkey appendage had been bigger I gladly would have donated myself to Carol Jeanne for *that*. He was as useless as yesterday's oatmeal, and everyone couldn't help but know it. Now he grabbed his chance to get even. I snarled at him, but he ignored me.

Only Lydia offered something like the truth. "Can *I* play with Lovelock? Grandma let *Emmy* play with him. She was going to give Lovelock a treat. Can *I* give him a treat? Can I?"

"Nonsense," said Mamie. "Of course the child doesn't understand what happened."

"He can't get loose by himself," said Carol Jeanne.

"Well, then, we *do* live in an age of miracles," said Mamie. "You can't be suggesting that *I* would voluntarily come anywhere *near* the creature." My heart sank. Since Mamie was well known to recoil from any contact with me, it was quite possible that her lie would be believed. In fact, Mamie sounded so truthful, so *injured* by the whole notion of being at fault for anything, that if I hadn't known better I probably would have believed her myself.

I think the secret to Mamie's skill at lying is that she never tells a lie that she doesn't believe with all her heart, at least for the moment it takes to tell it.

I shouldn't have been surprised at any of this. Not that she would lie, nor that her lie was believed. But I *was* surprised. I guess it had never occurred to me that she would lie so outrageously when the consequences were so dire to someone else. I was the only one who would pay the price for her lie. Once they believed that I knew how to get loose from my harness, there was no hope of my remaining in the cabin with the people. I would inevitably spend the rest of the voyage treated as cargo, like Pink. It was a miserable punishment and I didn't deserve it.

But what did that matter to Mamie? I was only an animal, and she was a *human*. In fact, as *she* saw it anyway, she was the most important person in the world, the person whose comfort, whose dignity, whose any passing whim mattered more than the life or death of any other living soul. If she had confessed to having set me loose, she would have had to endure another hour of resentment from the rest of the passengers—people that she would never see again in her life, who would all be dead of old age by the time we were a year into our interstellar voyage. And she could have assuaged most resentment with a quick, sincere apology: I'm sorry, I had no idea that letting the monkey loose would cause such a problem, please forgive me. But such a simple condescension was impossible for her. Mamie Foxe Todd, *apologize?*

The attendants were apologetic but firm. "I'm sorry, Dr. Coccio-lone, but your witness will have to be removed from the cabin."

Bless her, she tried to keep me. "I'll be with him the whole time," she said. "It won't happen again."

"I'm sure you're aware that the situation here was extremely dangerous," said the attendant. "I have no room for maneuvering here. If I let the monkey remain in the cabin now that we know he can get free of the harness, I would certainly lose my job and could possibly go to jail."

"If you must," said Carol Jeanne. She was not one to insist when there was nothing to be gained by it. Into the hold I would go—we both knew it.

Mamie didn't have the decency to stay out of the situation she had created. "Where *is* the little fellow, anyway?" she asked.

There I was, peering out of Carol Jeanne's blouse not half a meter from Mamie's face, and right at her eye level. It was too good an opportunity to miss. I screeched and lunged at her.

She screamed, of course. To have me suddenly appear right in front of her face, teeth bared and reaching for her with my long arms—well, she would have been surprised and frightened under any circumstances. But I'd like to think that her fear was also partly the result of guilt and shame for having made me bear the brunt of her lie. I'm not above taking petty revenge.

Naturally, Carol Jeanne gripped me all the tighter. "You're being very bad, Lovelock," she said. But she didn't punish me. She didn't say the painword. And that told me that she must have known the truth, that she must have sympathized with my plight, and she was only going along with Mamie's lie in order to keep peace in the family.

You can always let the monkey suffer in order to keep the family from quarreling. Thus did I learn my first lesson about our mutual loyalty.

I spent the rest of the voyage in a box. As boxes go, I suppose it wasn't a bad one—plenty to eat and drink, a soft floor, a bright light that I could turn on and off myself, and a few books to read. But I don't care what you do to a box, it's still a box.

My only consolation was that after we got to Grissom Station and transferred to Ironsides, the interplanetary shuttle, *they* all had to ride in boxes, too. Unlike the Ark, which would offer us kilometers of interior space, Ironsides was cramped in size and packed tight. There was no way to handle a hundred passengers and all their belongings during a month-long flight, even though acceleration and deceleration gave us an almost constant artificial gravity. Instead everybody was catheterized, drugged to the gills, and packed in "slumber chambers" that were suspiciously like my own little casquette. We would all be equals on *that* voyage.

CHAPTER THREE

The Ark

During the long month when Ironsides made its journey to the Ark, I dozed, then woke, then dozed again in my box. I preferred the dozing; when I was awake, all I could think about was my humiliation in the subbo, as if it had only just happened. Was this going to happen to me every time we went into freefall? On the Ark I'd be free to roam—except at the changeover points, when they'd *have* to lock me in a box or strap me down, just to keep me from engaging in revolting behavior. Each time I would be reminded of my weakness. Which was bitterly unfair—most of the time it was the humans who revolted *me*, and no one locked *them* in boxes or strapped *them* down.

I knew that my feelings of persecution were absurd. I wasn't being persecuted in particular. I simply belonged to an oppressed species. Which, on Earth at least, included every species that wasn't human. Most nonhumans didn't mind, of course. Most nonhumans didn't even *know* they were being exploited, domesticated, dominated, and spiritually annihilated by the master race. Only I and a handful like me.

If there *was* anyone in the universe like me. Or was I, I wondered, alone? Was I in fact the only thinking entity that existed? Were human beings nothing but imaginary tormentors spawned by my own self-hatred? And if I only came to accept my hairy little self for what I was, would they then go away—or turn kind, or even loving?

Did Pink have wings?

In such moments of despondency, I remembered that there was one who cared for me. The only thing that kept her from coming to me, from opening the door of my miserable cave and setting me free, was the fact that she too was locked into the prison of human customs and laws and so she could not save me. But she *would* come. I clung to that hope, and perhaps that was why I kept my sanity.

Or, more likely, my sanity was never at risk, and all my mad half-waking thoughts were merely the products of the drugs that dripped into me to keep me artificially calm during Ironsides' interminable voyage.

At last I felt the ship movements that told me that Ironsides was jockeying into position at its final destination. I knew from my advance reading that Ironsides would come to rest against the outer surface of the cylindrical Ark, held in place by powerful magnets. The passengers would be herded into the transfer carton. A vast door would open in the side of the Ark and a long mechanical arm would reach out, pluck the carton like a louse off the skin of the Ark, and draw us into the hungry mouth of the cargo bay. How very like *me* the Ark behaved.

Was that jarring our impact against the Ark? Soon they would come for the humans, draw them out of their casquettes, and then she would come, in turn, for me.

Unless she forgot me. Unless she carelessly waited for them to unload me with the rest of the luggage and deposit me in her quarters like her library and her lingerie. Unless she still hadn't forgiven me for having brought disgrace upon her in the subbo.

It was a miserable half hour that I waited, if it wasn't half a day.

Or a minute and a half. For Carol Jeanne *did* love me. She knew that I must be filled with fears and dreads and insecurities and shame. In her immeasurable compassion she must have practically *flown* down into the hold to retrieve me, to open the door and give me light again. What a scraggly, sweat-soaked, stinky, trembling little primate I must have been, and yet she didn't hesitate to draw me close and let me cling to her neck, to her hair, climb all over her shoulders and arms, holding tight and then rushing to take another hold, to reassure myself that she was unchanged. Touching her body was my homecoming; soft, warm skin, the salty perfume of her confinement, the sound of her voice and its sweet vibrations in the thin bones of her cheeks, the warmth of her breath on my face, the wind of it in my eyes—my world had been restored to me. After my time in the box, Carol Jeanne's body seemed as infinite as the universe. I could have explored her until I died and I would never have grown weary of it.

At last, though, my ecstasy grew containable. I stopped my compulsive scampering and settled down to normal grooming. I was sure of her; I was myself again. Then she knew that she could take me to join the others.

Passengers and witnesses alike were herded into the transfer carton. Mamie never seemed to learn that the first one *on* a one-door conveyance would be the last one *off*, so she ran interference for us to be the first aboard the transfer carton. Then we were packed in by all the other families who boarded after we did, squashing us toward the corner farthest from the door.

Mamie seemed oblivious to the fact that she was the cause of her family's discomfort. Instead, as the bodies of strangers were pressed closer and closer against us, she sniffed with a tight little grimace on her face. She had a point. Humans become very rank after long confinement in boxes, and while each person was completely used to their *own* smell, everybody else's smell was exquisitely rancid. I enjoyed it—a delightful rush of olfactory variety after the sterile sameness of my own box—but the humans all seemed to be shrinking into themselves, trying to move away from everyone else simultaneously. And there was Mamie, sniffing with disdain at our malodorous boxmates, as if her own sweat were an expensive perfume. Not to mention the faint odor of Emmy's vomit still clinging to her shoes, not that anybody but me could pick up those old traces. If Mamie could only smell herself as *I* smelled her, she would probably die of disgust.

The transfer carton locked itself firmly against an inside wall of the docking bay, and the doors opened. It seemed to take forever for the people in front of us to move out into the open. And then, when we finally were able to move, it turned out it wasn't "the open" that we were bound for. The whole group was being herded down a corridor and into a large elevator. To go up or down? The person in charge was French; therefore she felt no need to explain anything to anybody. Not even whether the elevator was going up or down. She simply kept intoning—mostly in heavily accented English, but now and then in French, Portuguese, and phonetically memorized Japanese—"Please move as far to the back of the elevator as possible."

Mamie's pushiness was finally rewarded: As the last people out of the transfer carton, we were the last people onto the elevator—upward, as it turned out—and so when the elevator came to a stop we were the first ones off.

After all those months in canisters in space, it was a glorious sight. You could see for kilometers, and the landscape was green. Not the green of New England, with its endless woods, because the Ark was all fields and bushes. More like Iowa without the hills. Wyoming without the antelope. There *were* some trees, but they all grew in neat rows. Orchards, and dwarf ones at that. There was no hope of finding a *real* tree. The Ark hadn't existed for enough years to grow a tree to thirty or forty meters. But when I saw one of those pathetic dwarf orchards not far off from the elevator, I found myself hungering for the feel of rough bark against the palms of my hands and feet.

It took only a few moments, though, for the first relief at the largeness of the space inside the Ark to wear off, and then all we could see was the strangeness of it. There was no sky, though a bright "sun" shone above us. There was no horizon. Instead, far in the distance, the land curved upward before us and behind us, as if we were in a broad valley, except that the "mountains" on either side got steeper and steeper, and then sloped outward until they met in an arch overhead. If we looked up, shielding our eyes from the "sun" glowing in the middle, we could make out the fields and villages above us. We could imagine the people walking around up there. Impossibly, they did not fall toward us, screaming. When I vertiginously imagined *them* to be on the ground and us to be dangling in the air above them, it made no difference; the spin of the Ark held us tightly to its inner surface.

The curving, along with the greenery, stretched before and behind us in a band no more than a couple of kilometers wide. To either side there was a vast greyish-blue wall, crisscrossed with inexplicable lines. Each wall made a huge wheel, with the giant skeletal legs of a tripod rising like spokes from the rim of each wheel, meeting in the middle to hold the track on which the "sun" pere-grinated at the center of everything.

It was like being inside a vast tuna-fish can. All the greenery and all the people were on the curving wall, while the bottom and the lid of the can were nothing but metal sheathed in plastic the color of a dismal winter sky.

But that was only for now, while the Ark moved in orbit around the sun—the real sun, dear old Sol, whose happy little photons had given sight to every creature that ever opened its eyes on God's green Earth. To keep us from having to live in perpetual freefall, the Ark was spun around and all the soil and people and buildings clung to the curved wall of the tuna can. That was orbital mode. It was the way we lived in orbit around Sol, and it was the way we would live again when at last we reached our new star system, as we waited for Carol Jeanne and her crews to prepare our new planet for human habitation.

There would be two other phases to the journey—acceleration and deceleration. The voyage itself. And for those, everything would be different. There'd be no spin at all. Instead, the sense of "gravity" would come from acceleration, and all the soil and the villages and orchards would be moved from the curving wall to the flat circular floor. There we would live, bounding happily through life at about a fifth of a gee, until we reached the midpoint of the trip. Then, once again, everything would change, as the soil would be moved from the bottom to the lid of the tuna can, as deceleration put our "down" in the opposite direction.

Those changeovers—from spin to acceleration, from accelera-tion to deceleration, and from deceleration to spin again—would be brutal. Tons of soil plunging from one surface to another in a vast avalanche, clouds of choking dust that wouldn't settle for days. No one could live through it.

Fortunately, we wouldn't have to. For the curving wall of the Ark—the wall that seemed like the ground to us right now—was really a wheel-shaped building several stories thick. In huge cham-bers were stored the embryos of millions of animals, along with all the nutrients we would need to sustain human life during the voy-age. In much smaller rooms, the humans had their offices, their computers, and the tiny rooms where they would huddle during the cataclysms of changeover.

When the Ark was being designed, there had been some talk of the wastefulness of maintaining the huge open area with its greenery. Why not pack people into a ship designed more like a vast Ironsides? If they don't like it, sedate them and let them sleep. The voyage was only a few years, anyway, right?

But wiser heads prevailed. The goal of the voyage was not simply to get to another planet, it was to form a viable human colony there. The open farmland and villages had very practical purposes. In the fields, the people would learn the skills, the customs, the calendar of farming. And by living in villages instead of apartments, with country lanes instead of corridors leading from house to house, the people would form stable farming communities long before they reached the planet where those communities would have to work together to create a second human world.

That was the theory, anyway—to use the voyage as one long rehearsal, to create the colony as a society before they had to make it a physical reality on what might turn out to be a hostile planet. After all, what good would it do to save money by building a cheaper Ark, only to have the colony fail because the people were all strangers to each other?

That was why the Ark was subdivided into villages, their citizens grouped according to general categories of compatibility. By necessity and recent international custom, English was the common language of the Ark, but within the villages there were many languages; all would be preserved in the new world.

Dividing communities by language made sense to me. But it was a typical human absurdity that, after language, the next most important set of divisions was religious. Muslims, Buddhists, Catholics, Jews, Hindus, Espiritistas: All had their own villages. Those groups with too few practitioners to maintain villages of their own—Baha'i, for instance, and Sikh, animist, atheist, Mormon, Mithraist, Druse, native American tribal religions, Jehovah's Witnesses—were either thrown together in a couple of catch-all villages or were "adopted" as minorities within fairly compatible or tolerant villages of other faiths.

The whole thing struck me as absurd. Why didn't they simply limit the colony to rational human beings who were above the petty concerns of religion, and spare themselves all these meaningless dogmas and hostilities?

The answer, of course, was that they couldn't have found enough *rational* human beings on planet Earth to fill the Ark. A man might be a brilliant scientist, but he was still a Hindu, and there was no hope of him living peacefully with a Sikh; or he was a Jew, and the Muslims would allow him only second-class citizenship at best. A certain woman might be the greatest gaiologist in the world, and perfectly rational, but she had grown up Catholic, and so her Episcopalian mother-in-law would always look down on her and "her people."

Even most of the "rational" people—the ones who claimed not to have a religion—were just as chauvinistic about their irreligion, sneering at and ostracizing the believers just the way the believers treated nonmembers of their own groups. It's a human universal. My tribe above all other tribes. That's what religion *is*—another name for tribalism in a supposedly civilized world.

What about me? I felt no tribal kinship with the other witnesses. Certainly not with Pink, but even as I became aware of other wit-nesses—Carol Jeanne was not the only colonist important enough to merit bringing her witness—I felt no particular kinship with them. Yes, we were all victims of an oppressive system, but that mattered far less to us than our deep bonding with our owners. Carol Jeanne was my tribe. It was from her that I drew my identity, it was around her that I built my hopes, it was in her that I had my life. What was another witness to *me?* I could look at them and pity them for their helpless devotion to an unworthy human. But my feelings for Carol Jeanne were different. She was *not* unworthy. She was deeply good, brilliant of mind and generous of heart, and she loved me. Our bond was stronger than blood, than religion, than language, than marriage. It was the bond of selfhood. I saw the world through her eyes, and she through mine. We—almost—were the same person.

We were a village in ourselves, no matter that officially she was going to belong to an arbitrary clumping of effete Christians called

Mayflower Village. She would be a Catholic among Congregation-
alists, I a low-order primate among Presbyterians; we belonged only
to each other.

That was what I thought of as I looked out onto the scenery of
our new home, the flat farms and clotted villages of the Ark.

The other people emerging from the elevator milled around,
rubbernecking like country tourists on their first visit to the big city.
Only instead of looking up at skyscrapers, they were looking up at
overhead farms.

Someone had tried to brighten up the arrival area with some
nasty orange flowers. They were probably meant to look pretty. Instead they looked garish, and a little weary, too, as if the effort of
trying to make this place pretty had worn them out.

Mamie surveyed the terrain, holding a hand above her eyes to
shield them from the sun orbiting on its track above us. Then she
sighed. "Did I survive all these years only to end up in Kansas?"

"Curves a little, for Kansas," said Stef. It was as close as he ever
came to contradicting her.

"What are we supposed to do now?" asked Mamie.

"I'm hungry," said Lydia.

"I'm thirsty," said Emmy.

"I'm hungry *and* thirsty," said Lydia.

"No, *I'm* hungry and thirsty," said Emmy.

"No, *me*," said Lydia. "I said it first!"

"No, *me!*" screeched Emmy.

Did they really think that only one of them would be permitted
to eat? Red's genes must have been extraordinarily dominant.

But the decision about what to do next was taken out of our
hands. Bearing down on the herd of people and witnesses was a
massive woman, big and busty. When she walked, the weight of her
breasts pulled her posture out of alignment. She looked like the
masthead on a ship, straining forward against the wind.

She carried a placard in front of her, hand-lettered with the
word *Cocciolone*. Unless there were some other Cocciolones on the
transport, she was looking for us. Red raised his hand to get her
attention. He might have called to her, but Mamie touched his arm
and said, "Don't be vulgar, Red," and so he merely held up his hand,
not even waving it.

The woman with the sign finally noticed him. He beckoned— not a *bit* vulgarly—and she bore down on us like a steamship.

"My Mayflower people! I knew I'd recognize you the minute I saw you," she said as she approached.

Of course, thought I. We look like a slice of Wonder bread on a platter of lentils and beans.

"Are you our guide?" asked Mamie, moving forward to meet the woman with the sign.

"Why, I suppose I *am*. Your guide, your nursemaid, and your first friend in the village, I hope." She lowered the sign. "I'm your Mayor," she said. "But don't be intimidated, my dears. I wasn't elected, and the title doesn't mean a blessed thing. Penelope Frizzle's the name. It's pronounced the way I said it—PENNY-lope. Puh-NELL-o-pee sounds so—*ex*cretory. And you must be the Cocciolones." She pronounced the name as if it rhymed with "bones." She was obviously as cavalier with other people's names as she was with her own.

Then she saw *me*. "What a cute monkey! That must be one of your witnesses."

She reached out a hand. Constricted by gaudy rings, her fingers were as bloated as sausages. I was tired. I couldn't stop my reflexes. I bit her.

"Lovelock!" Carol Jeanne was furious. "Trab!"

It was the painword. Immediately I felt that terrible scissor grip on my testicles. I fell from her shoulder and rolled into a ball on the ground, whimpering. As luck would have it, another family was called by *their* mayor as I writhed in the dirt. They stepped right over me as if I were a turd on the ground, compounding my shame.

As she always did, Carol Jeanne relented the moment she saw my agony. Rescuing me from the stampede of human feet, she picked me up and stroked me, holding me close until my trembling stopped. I confess I enjoyed this enough that I made no effort to hasten my recovery.

When I opened my eyes again, I was glad to see a small drop of blood on Penelope's outstretched finger. Still, she obviously wasn't hurt too badly. Even though she held her finger ostentatiously in the air for sympathy, everyone ignored her while Carol Jeanne comforted me.

"The beast is obviously enjoying all this sympathy," said Penelope. "It will probably bite me again, just to get all this attention."

I bared my teeth at her. Just a flash, you understand.

"Now it's threatening me!" cried Penelope.

"Not at all," said Carol Jeanne. "Monkeys bare their teeth to show fear. He's afraid of you."

That's what ordinary monkeys mean when they bare their teeth, and it's my natural way of expressing fear, too—but I'm an enhanced capuchin, and so I'm clever enough to use that grimace for other reasons as well. I thought it was wise to let our mayor know that despite the punishment, and even without Carol Jeanne comforting me, I'll bite anyone who tries to *handle* me like that. What do they think I am—a *pet*?

"Well," said Penelope, suddenly beaming with a brand-new just-for-us smile. "It's all for the best. You can be sure I'll *never* forget my first meeting with the Cocciolones!"

"We're the Todds," Mamie said, tight-lipped. "*Cocciolone* is my daughter-in-law's *maiden* name."

"Then you *are* the very ones I'm looking for. My! You're such an attractive family." If she was being ironic, you couldn't tell from her voice. Nobody in our family was especially attractive at the moment.

"It's sweet of you to say so," Mamie said, accepting it as a compliment instead of sarcasm.

But now that Penelope knew which of our group was *the* Cocciolone, she hardly noticed that Mamie had spoken. Instead she planted the mountains of her bosom directly in front of Carol Jeanne. "So *you're* Carol Jeanne Cocciolone. All those brains, and beautiful too. Just like those *lovely* children. They're so pretty they *must* be yours."

They certainly weren't *my* children, and since Mamie's childbearing years were centuries behind her, of course they belonged to Carol Jeanne. But Lydia and Emmy *were* lovely to look at; even I had to admit it. They looked just like Carol Jeanne in miniature, and Carol Jeanne was the fairest of all.

Carol Jeanne ignored the compliments, though. "We're all pretty tired and dirty right now," she said. "It's been a long trip."

"And you smell a little *stale*, too," Penelope said. "Everybody does, when they first come out of the box. But we can't do anything about that at the moment. We barely have time to get you to the funeral."

"Funeral? What funeral?" Stef's Adam's apple bobbed when he talked. His voice sounded dry.

"Haven't you heard? I thought *every*body knew. The chief administrator's wife died three days ago. Mayflower gets to host the funeral. It's one of the blessings we get for having the chief administrator dwelling in our village."

"We didn't know there was a funeral," Carol Jeanne said, her voice low and respectful, "but we really didn't know the lady who died. Can't we go somewhere and rest until it's over?"

"You can't be serious." Penelope's chest quivered when she talked. "It would be an affront to *everyone* in Mayflower Village. People will be here from all sixty villages, and Mayflower has to feed them *all*. Though I suppose you're so important that people will overlook it if you don't do your fair share."

"We want to do our fair share," said Carol Jeanne. "But we just got here, and we're—"

"That's why it's such a wonderful opportunity for you, coming to the funeral. It's the best way in the world to meet the community. You'll be one of us before nightfall."

"That's a great idea," Red said.

What kind of husband was he, to undermine Carol Jeanne's effort to get them out of this? I hissed at him.

"Lovelock, *hush*." Carol Jeanne sounded annoyed. But I knew she was as irritated at Red as I was.

Penelope ignored Carol Jeanne and me; apparently she only noticed the existence of people who agreed with her. "Of *course* it's a great idea," she said. She seized Red's arm in the iron grip of intimacy. "I can see that you're going to be a great success in Mayflower village, Mr. Cocciolone."

Mamie cut in, her voice as cold as liquid nitrogen. "I told you. Cocciolone is Carol Jeanne's maiden name. She uses it professionally, but the rest of us are *Todds*."

"Oh," Penelope said. "You did tell me that, didn't you?" She gave Mamie her sweetest smile. Only her words revealed just how toxic that smile could be. "Did you know, my dear," she said to Mamie, "that when I first saw you folks I just *assumed* that *you* were Carol

Jeanne Cocciolone. It just seemed to me that this sweet girl here was too *young* to be the world's greatest gaiologist. While *you* were the only one who looked *old* enough to have worked with James Lovelock himself."

I hooted with laughter.

Carol Jeanne silenced me with a touch. "I'm afraid I never had the privilege of knowing James Lovelock himself. I studied under *his* student, Ralph Twickenham."

Penelope brightened. "Oh. Our English village is named Twickenham. They're very high-church. Is it the same Twickenham?"

"Probably. Twicky is pretty famous."

"Carol *Jeanne* is pretty famous," Red broke in. "The American Catholic village applied for the name Cocciolone, but Carol Jeanne said she wouldn't come with the Ark unless they named their village something else."

"It's all for the best," Penelope said. "*Assisi* sounds so much nicer, doesn't it? There's that business about St. Francis feeding the birds, and Assisi is so much easier to *say*, don't you think?"

I hissed again. Penelope glanced at me and tucked her fingers safely behind her back.

"Anyway," she added, "the whole village has been waiting for you. They'll be so excited when they see you at the funeral. Imagine our good fortune, to have the chief administrator and the chief gaiologist in the same village. What a lucky coincidence!"

"My son Red is going to be quite a contributor to the voyage, too," Mamie said, putting her hand on Red's shoulder to indicate who he was. And then, to make sure the mayor understood how important he was, she made sure Penelope noticed his most important status symbol. "*His* witness isn't half so much trouble as the monkey. See?" She pointed at Pink, who simply stood there, looking piglike.

"A pig," Penelope said, her voice flat and unenthusiastic. "How nice." After the briefest glance at Pink, she turned to Carol Jeanne. "Tell me, Dr. Cocciolone," she asked deferentially, "what do you think of the Ark?"

"As Mamie pointed out when we got here, it looks like Kansas, with a curve," Carol Jeanne said. She had never had a particular fondness for Kansas, but Penelope puffed out her chest with pride as if it had been a personal compliment.

"Kansas, but the air smells like dirty underwear," Stef added. He spoke softly, under his breath. If he hoped Penelope would hear him, his wish was granted.

"Those are the flowers, my dear—nasturtiums. The smell's more concentrated here on the Ark because we have an artificial atmosphere."

I hopped down from Carol Jeanne's shoulder and landed squarely on a nasturtium plant. I picked the smallest flower I could find and ate it, but it tasted much better than the humans around me smelled. Except for Carol Jeanne, of course. It would have been disloyal for me to admit that Carol Jeanne smelled just like all the other humans around me, so I didn't. Not even to myself.

Stef looked at the orange flowers as if willing them to go away. "Clunky looking things," he said.

"Oh? I think they're pretty," said Penelope. "Soon you'll hardly notice the smell. Besides—we also grow lilies of the valley here, and *they* smell just like perfume." She didn't add that they're as lethal as cobra venom. That's a human for you. When they leave Earth to start a new world, they take their poisons with them—just to make the new world more exciting. I wouldn't have been surprised to learn they carried black mambas in the embryo banks, on the theory that the snakes could eat whatever pesky rodents inhabited the new planet.

She dusted off her hands officiously and said, "Well! We've chatted here long enough. You'll want to be going to Mayflower now. The tube is down this ladderway."

"Ladder?" asked Mamie, aghast. She hadn't climbed a ladder in her life. She had always *hired* people to climb ladders. I suspected that even as a child, she hired the servants' children to climb trees for her.

"Up and down change around here," said Penelope. "Ladders are the only practical way of getting from level to level without using up valuable space on stairways that would end up being on a wall or the ceiling for half the voyage. Besides, since we're never more than two-thirds of Earth-normal gravity—much less during the actual voyage—ladders are really very easy. We're all light on our feet around here."

"*Still,*" said Red, "using ladders is pretty confining." He looked pointedly at Pink. Pink was pretty agile; she was a *small* pig, and her enhancements made her about as clever as a pig can get. She could climb stairs and hop up on furniture, but she couldn't handle a ladderway. The people of the Ark should have mentioned the ladder thing before they let Red bring his witness. Or maybe they did, and Red insisted on bringing Pink anyway. Only someone clinging desperately to every shred of personal status would have insisted on bringing into space a witness without functional feet or opposable thumbs.

"There *is* a lift," Penelope said, turning her most helpful face toward Red and Mamie. "For *heavy* loads." Since Pink hardly qualified, the remark seemed vaguely pointed at Mamie—and from the look of faint disgust on her face, Mamie didn't miss the barb, either. It was pretty absurd, coming from Penelope; although Mamie was round, she was small enough that each of Penelope's breasts probably outweighed her. Penelope was obviously a person who didn't like having to change her plans to accommodate other people.

She led us to another elevator, a small one designed for people instead of cargo, and we crowded inside for the trip downstairs. Then she led us to the tube platform. It took only moments for a car to arrive. She seated us efficiently and pressed the name of our village, Mayflower, on the destination board. There was a pneumatic sound as the magnetics were turned on and the car lifted itself from the floor. Then, smoothly, it slipped through the network of tubes, choosing its own way at each intersection.

As we glided along, Penelope cheerfully pressed ahead with the urgent business of becoming our dearest friend. "Now that we're settled down," she said, "tell me about yourselves. Of course, I know all about *you*, Dr. Cocciolone."

Carol Jeanne interrupted. "Please, no titles. Call me Carol Jeanne."

Penelope pounced on the name and played with it like a cat. "Carol Jeanne it is, then," she said. "Such a lovely name, Carol Jeanne. I'm so glad we're going to be friends, Carol Jeanne."

After bestowing a winning smile on Mayflower's newest celebrity, she turned to Red, who was holding Emmy by a lock of hair to keep her from wandering. "Now, Mr. Cocciolone, what should I call you?"

"He's Mr. *Todd*," Mamie corrected. "Redmond Eugene Todd. We call him Red. Carol Jeanne is *Mrs*. Todd."

Poor Mamie. Didn't she realize that Penelope was only goading her?

Penelope and her breasts ignored Mamie. "And what do you do?" she asked Red.

"I'm a family counselor." Red always looked proud when he said that—as if he had a real job, doing real work. Being a family counselor seemed as useless to me as going to church—it was just a way to pander to emotions instead of focusing on what was really important. Nevertheless, Red was probably good at it; he was one of those touchy-feely humans who communicate with hugs and pats on the back, forever clucking over strangers and telling them, *I* understand. Humans loved him for it.

Penelope looked as unimpressed with Red's occupation as I was, though. "Inside or Outside?"

Red was obviously confused. "I usually consult with people in an office, if that's what you mean."

"You don't even know about Inside and Outside?" Silence was all the answer she needed. "Outside is up on the surface, where the sun shines, where the crops grow. Where we *live* and farm. The *villages*. And Inside is down here, in the closed spaces, where we *work*. Our *jobs*. It's as if we all lead double lives. Our Inside life, where we work with people in our profession, just like an office building on Earth, and our Outside life, where we live with our fellow villagers."

"And family counselors specialize in Inside or Outside work?" Red asked.

"The Outside counselors are called by the chief administrator of the Ark to serve each village," said Penelope. "People go to them when they have village problems. Being an Outside counselor is the greatest honor a person can have—except being the Mayor, of course. Only the most compassionate people in the village can be called to a job like that."

"Then our Red will be an Outside counselor, of course," said

Mamie. The woman took the bait as eagerly as a trout sprang for a fly above the pond back home, and I was disgusted at how easily Penelope reeled her in. "He's the most compassionate person I've ever met."

"Indeed. That's interesting news—I hadn't heard that Mayflower's counselor was due for replacement." I don't believe I imagined the smirk in Penelope's voice, but to her credit she kept the smile from her lips. "The scientifically trained family counselors are Inside, of course, in offices. But I always think the Inside counselors are for when people are, you know . . . what's the word—"

"Clinically ill," said Carol Jeanne.

"Crazy," said Penelope at the same moment. "Whatever. You go to a village counselor because you want to talk with somebody you can trust. You go to an office counselor because your supervisor thinks that your problems are interfering with your job. It's so sterile and frightening."

Red tried to look cheerful, though no doubt he was seething at her primitive attitudes about therapy. "I'm an Inside counselor, I guess. I'll work for personnel. No doubt in an office."

"Well, how interesting," said Penelope, apparently completely oblivious to the fact that she had just insulted his profession. But I was sure that she had known all along that he was one of the "sterile and frightening" ones.

Dismissing Red, she turned her attention to Mamie and Stef. "And you—what are *your* names, and what do *you* do?"

She looked at Mamie expectantly. I was actually looking forward to what Penelope would say to put Mamie in her place.

"We're Red's parents," said Mamie. "I'm Mamie Foxe Todd, and this is my husband, Stephan Brantley Todd. Everyone calls him Stef."

"*I'll* call him Stephan," Penelope said, speaking to Mamie as if Stef were incapable of speaking for himself. "*Stef* sounds like a bacterial infection. And what do you do for a living?"

"We don't do anything," said Mamie. "Stef is a man of means, so it's not as though he ever had to have a *job*. Of course he'd be retired anyway. He's *much* older than I am . . . he's sixty-three."

I waited for Penelope to raise her eyebrows at that. Stef didn't look like he was anywhere near sixty-three. He could have passed for seventy-five, and an old seventy-five, at that. Years of living with Mamie had beaten him down until he was shriveled inside himself, as though he had retreated into his very skin to escape her venom. But Penelope saw none of that. She smiled coquettishly at Stef and patted his forearm. She was *flirting* with that decrepit old fossil, and Stef responded. He smiled back, and years fell off his face. Once, centuries ago, he had been a handsome man.

Mamie cleared her throat. Mentioning Stef, she had relinquished her place as the center of attention, and she wanted it back. "Of course, I've *never* worked at a paying job, though I've done a great deal of volunteer work. I expect to continue with that sort of thing here, and Stef will no doubt putter around the way he did at home."

Penelope dropped her hand from Stef's forearm and knitted her brows. She checked her clipboard computer as if for reassurance. Then, obviously not learning anything from the computer screen, she snapped the clipboard shut.

"That's not good news, I'm afraid," she said. "That's definitely not good news. Everyone here has to work, both Inside and Outside. It's in the Compact. Don't you remember?"

"What Compact?" Mamie asked blankly.

"The contract you signed before you came here, of course."

"*That* thing? All I did was sign it. It was very long."

"You didn't read it?" Carol Jeanne asked.

"You didn't *read* it?" echoed Penelope. The skin tightened on her neck, and her mammoth breasts jutted forward like warheads. "The Compact is everything. When you signed it, you agreed to work Inside and Outside. This is a working community. We can't afford to have drones. Fair share, that's how we live. Everybody does their fair share, and gets their fair share in return."

"What else did we agree?" Stef's voice sounded drier and thirstier.

"My goodness! There was so much of it, I can't possibly remember. You'll have to go back and read the Compact. I can promise you one thing—you signed it, and you're responsible for keeping your end of the bargain, whether you knew what you were signing or not."

There was an uncomfortable silence. Emmy started whimpering, and Stef held out his arms to her. She climbed on his lap and stuck her thumb in her mouth. Almost immediately, she fell asleep.

Carol Jeanne looked out the window at the blank tube walls gliding lazily by, and Red stroked the top of Lydia's head. Only Mamie was unintimidated by Penelope. She stared at Penelope's chest for a long moment, watching it rise and fall the way some people sit and watch the ocean waves. Then, as if she had made a conscious decision to be pleasant, Mamie's expression softened.

"Tell me about Mayflower," she asked brightly, using the sing-song tone she usually reserved for Lydia and Emmy. "Tell me all about where we're going to live."

Penelope was obviously unaware of the effort that Mamie was making. "You read all about us when you chose the place you wanted to live," she said. "We're just as the prospectus described us."

"I didn't read the prospectus," said Mamie.

"I didn't, either," Carol Jeanne admitted. "Other than the legal papers I signed, I didn't read any of the specifics. I've been so busy planning our agenda once we reach the new planet that I haven't had time to think about the Ark. I'm afraid I left all those decisions to Red."

Carol Jeanne blushed, as well she should have. Red had never made a rational decision in his life. The truth was that she had left the reading to *me*, and so apparently I was the only one in the group to know what we were in for. Carol Jeanne knew that I would fill her in on anything she needed to know, as soon as she needed to know it. At least, that's what I'd do as soon as I got a clipboard or a computer so I could communicate fully with her.

Penelope looked disgruntled; then she swelled up importantly and took a deep breath. "Well, I'll have to tell you about it myself. First of all, we're Presbyterian here."

Mamie sniffed. "There's not a Presbyterian in the bunch of us," she said. "*I'm* Congregationalist, and Stef and Red and the girls are Episcopalian. Of course, with a name like Cocciolone, Carol Jeanne just *has* to be Catholic." Mamie treated it as if it were an old family joke. But her smile was tight. Lines radiated from her mouth like legs on a spider.

"Mayflower is a compromise, Mother." Red said it patiently, as

if he had explained it a hundred times before. I'd heard him say it
so many times that I wanted to throw feces at him whenever I
heard it again. When I read the specs, I knew at once that Carol
Jeanne should live in the village of Einstein, with the people for
whom science was life, not just a job; or in Mensa, with the god-
less heathens. There would have been fewer distractions that way.
But no, Mamie had insisted on living among Christians. Her
brand of Christians, of course—or as close to her brand as she
could get.

Mamie smiled indulgently at her dear boy. "Of course Mayflower's a compromise, Redmond. I'm very happy with it."

Penelope smiled, too. "You'll be even happier the better you get
to know us," she said cheerfully. "We're pretty open-minded here.
Presbyterians are tolerant folks. All religions are the same, anyway,
as long as they're Christian. In fact, we even have three Jewish families who live with us, because Bethel Village is too Orthodox for
them, and there are also some Mormons because nobody else
wanted them. They have their own services, of course, but otherwise
you'd never know they belonged to a cult."

"How interesting," said Mamie, plainly uninterested. It did not
particularly please her to know that her village was one that included Jews and fanatics. She had never in her life had to associate
with such people except when they served her in such roles as lawyer, store clerk, or maid.

Penelope didn't catch Mamie's sarcasm. "Actually, I think most
people agree that Mayflower is the best village of all. For one thing,
the chief administrator lives here. That gives the village a certain—
prestige, if you will—that the others don't have. It makes Mayflower—well, there *is* no capital city on the Ark, but if there were
one, it would be Mayflower."

"Oh?" Mamie's mouth relaxed into a tentative smile.

"And now we have the chief gaiologist as well. People would *kill*
to live in Mayflower. Oh, the parties we'll have!—after the mourning
is over, of course. I hope Cyrus marries again soon."

"Cyrus?" Stef asked, sounding more tired than curious.

"The chief administrator, Dad," said Red. "It's his wife's funeral
we're going to attend." Red sounded as if he were looking forward
to it.

"It starts in just a few minutes," Penelope said. "Mayflower is directly ahead. We should be stopping right . . . now."

With timing that was either a lucky coincidence or the result of diligent practice on Penelope's part, the tube settled onto its wheels the moment she finished speaking, and in moments we came to a stop. The doors opened, and Penelope herded us onto the platform. We wouldn't reach our house for seven hours, but in some sense we were finally home.

CHAPTER FOUR

Odie's Funeral

When we finally saw the village of Mayflower, nobody was more surprised than I was. We had flown all those miles away from Earth, only to boomerang home again. Except for the weather, we could have been back in Temple, New Hampshire. The photographs in the prospectus hadn't prepared me for how like Temple the villages on the Ark would be.

Mayflower hadn't been patterned after our home town, of course. It's just that both Temple and the village of Mayflower had been designed, centuries apart, to look like any small town in New England. The elevator up from the tube disgorged us onto a town square just like the one in Temple. There was a grassy commons in the middle, with white buildings all around. One looked like a general store. Another could have been a post office, though that was unlikely. All that was missing was a Revolutionary War cannon in the center of the town square—that and a big clock that tolled the hours. There was even a church on the far end of the square, as white as every other structure in the village.

There was one difference, and that was a big one. All the buildings were inflatable. All of them looked puffy and impermanent. I knew that inflatable buildings were vital here—all structures had to be designed so they could be removed and stored for each change-over, and then quickly put back in place when the soil had been restabilized. Even so, the overblown structures reminded me of nothing so much as Penelope's breasts. This place would be heaven for an unscrupulous person with a pin.

As I clung to Carol Jeanne's neck, Mamie was the one who blocked my line of vision. Her mouth opened and closed, just like the gaping mouth of a goldfish in a bowl. I knew she was going to say something when she got her breath.

"Good grief," Mamie said finally. "The buildings all look like *balloons.*"

"They're *cartoon* houses!" cried Lydia.

"*Our* house won't look like that, will it?" asked Mamie.

"Oh, you're such a tease," Penelope said. "Of course it will. The prospectus explained all about it . . . but you didn't read that, did you? I keep forgetting. I never heard of anyone else who came here without reading it."

"I had more important things to do—packing up our household. And saying good-bye to all my friends."

Red had handled the packing; all Mamie had done was point and command. And what friends was she talking about? Mamie had acquaintances by the score, but none of her country club peers would be so gauche as to have *friends*. Their primary entertainment was getting together in groups and saying vicious things about whoever wasn't coming or had just left.

The corners of Penelope's mouth turned up just a bit. I already knew she had a sarcastic streak in her, and I rather liked her for it. "Just think," she said, "you'll *never* have to say good-bye to any friends again as long as you live."

Mamie looked at her sharply. "What do you mean?"

Penelope was all innocence. "Why, because we'll all be together *forever*. One big happy permanent family."

"Mamie treats *all* her friends just like family," Stef said. Did Penelope get the double meaning of that? Mamie certainly knew *something* was wrong with what he said—she gave her husband a withering look. But Penelope's smile only broadened.

Lydia pulled on Red's shirt, as desperate for attention as her beloved grandmother had been. "Are we home already?" she asked. "When is breakfast? Why do all the houses look like cartoons?"

"They're balloon buildings, Lydia," Red said. "People blow them up just like balloons."

"Oh, wouldn't we just wear ourselves *out* with puffing if we did!" said Penelope. "No, there's an air vent inside every house, putting out the gentle air pressure that keeps the structures standing."

"It sounds very drafty," said Mamie.

"Cool and refreshing, most people think," said Penelope.

"What if the ventilation system fails?" asked Stef.

"Oh, Stef, must you ask worrisome questions in front of the children?" asked Mamie.

"There's a semirigid structure built into the walls. You can always get out, and there's always enough air to breathe. But that was a *very* good question." Penelope patted Stef on the arm. Stef smiled wanly—he knew that whatever happened in this quiet catfight between Mamie and Penelope, he was going to pay for it later.

Since we couldn't escape the funeral, we trudged toward the church behind Penelope. Trudging was only a state of mind on the Ark, because the lower gravity lightened our steps. In fact, it lightened everyone's steps so much that practically everyone stumbled several times.

"It's physics," Penelope explained cheerily. "We still have the same mass, even if we don't have the same weight. So you hurtle along with as much force as you ever had, and gravity won't help you slow down. Your children will doubtless bump into walls a lot till they learn how to stop. It's another benefit of inflatable walls—you can't get hurt bumping into them."

I inspected the village as we crossed the town square, and I was amused to see that every one of the dwarf trees that made up the orchards and beautified the landscape here and there was neatly contained in a pot. Portability was the word of the day. There'd be no spreading chestnut trees large enough to shelter a village smithy, unless the potters here had exceptionally large potter's wheels.

People were still flowing into the village church that faced the town square; the funeral hadn't started yet. The closer we got to the church, the more it looked like a parody of the ones in New Hampshire. The inflatable church had an inflatable steeple, as functionless as the steeples back home. A lot of trouble had been taken to make Mayflower as homelike as possible, but in my opinion humans who were that susceptible to homesickness should have stayed on Earth where they belonged.

Outside the church was a table, stacked high with clear packets of some sort. A woman sat behind the table, looking officious.

"Oh, it's you, Penelope," she said when we approached. "I'm sure *you'll* want to spread the word about Odie Lee."

"Oh my, yes!" Penelope extended her sausage fingers, and the woman handed her a strange object encased in a clear protective sheath. It looked like a flower, with a green stem and filigree leaves. But at the top of the stem, the flower was a puff of tiny white threads that looked as if they would scatter at the slightest provocation.

"Those are dandelions," Stef said, wheezing dryly.

Mamie giggled. "You actually brought *weeds* to the Ark? Even out in the country we had exterminators. I haven't seen a dandelion in years."

Penelope shook her head vigorously. "These may be dandelions, but here they're not weeds. They're a very useful flower. Glory village grows them for the leaves. Nothing is better than a mess of young dandelion greens. Plymouth village grows dandelions for the yellow flowers; you can make a delicious wine from the blossoms. And the bees like them, of course." She bounced her sausage hand on Lydia's head a few times; no doubt she meant the gesture as a love pat. "*You* like honey, don't you, you sweet thing? That's why we need dandelions—so the bees can make honey for *you*."

Lydia looked at her as if she were crazy.

"I'm afraid I still don't understand what dandelions have to do with funerals," Carol Jeanne said.

It was interesting to see how Penelope deferred to Carol Jeanne. She delighted in needling Mamie, and she enjoyed flirting with Stef—though whether that was because she was attracted to him or simply wanted to annoy Mamie it was impossible to tell. But when Carol Jeanne asked a question, everything changed. Penelope immediately became sincerely deferent. Apparently she knew her place in the hierarchy, and wished to ingratiate herself with the Ark's chief gaiologist. She almost stammered when she spoke to Carol Jeanne. Either she really was in awe or she was very good at simulating it.

"It's a little custom we've developed here," said Penelope. "I hope you don't think we're too silly. It's a way of—I don't know, sharing with each other. Giving the dead back to the world. Releasing the soul to flight. You'll see how it works. All the villages do it—it's an Ark thing, not just in Mayflower."

"Will *we* need dandelions?" asked Carol Jeanne.

"Oh, I don't think so," said Penelope. "I mean, you don't even *know* Odie Lee! How could you possibly spread the word about a *stranger?*"

Carol Jeanne said nothing, but I knew what she was thinking: If Odie Lee is such a stranger, why are we at this funeral at all?

Penelope herded us inside the church, holding her dandelion packet as carefully as she would a vial of liquid nitroglycerine. "Sit here," she whispered. "No! There's a better spot up in front." She opened a path for us through the congregation milling in the aisles. We had to file along behind her as she loudly announced, "Move aside, please! We have important guests here. The Cocciolones just arrived. Please make way for the Cocciolones."

Necks craned to see us. Carol Jeanne was embarrassed, of course; she hated the trappings of celebrity, and having Penelope call out her name like that was excruciating. But Mamie loved it. Oh, she didn't like it that Penelope identified everyone by the Cocciolone name, but having all eyes upon us, people straining to catch a glimpse—that was heaven. Carol Jeanne might be trying to disappear, but Mamie strutted down the aisle like an ocean liner surrounded by tugboats. *She* knew how to look important. Anyone glancing at us would naturally assume that she was the celebrity among us.

Penelope scooted down to the center of a long pew, sat, and patted the wooden bench next to her so we would sit with her. One after another, we found our places and took a seat. Pink squealed once and Red lifted her into his lap, so she could see. I never had to interrupt Carol Jeanne's thoughts for petty help like that—but then, it didn't much matter whether Red's thoughts were interrupted or not.

"Look! A monkey!" It was an ugly little girl on the row in front of us. "Have you ever seen such tiny black hands?" She had buck teeth and her nose looked squashed, like someone had used her face for a whoopee cushion. I estimated her age at eleven or twelve. Closer to sentience than Lydia or Emmy; she was mature enough to keep her remarks to a whisper, though of course I could hear her easily.

The boy next to her, no doubt her older brother, turned and looked. "There's a pig, too," he said. "They must be witnesses."

She got a look of disgust. "Of *course* they're witnesses. You can tell by the i/o ports in the back of their necks. That's where they hook up to computers." She craned her neck for another look at Pink. "Besides—who'd let a pig into church if he wasn't a witness?"

He rolled his eyes and faced front again. "Who'd have a *pig* for a witness? That's the stupidest choice I've ever seen. They should have gotten two monkeys."

I knew on the spot that these were bright children, charming children, and buck teeth and squashed noses were not altogether ungraceful features.

"Whoever they are," said the girl, "they must have just left the ship. They smell like they haven't bathed in a month."

Observant children, logical children. I hoped Carol Jeanne and Red had overheard their comments. Everyone stank, but I was cute. I was practical. I was a perfect witness. On the other hand, Pink couldn't even hop up on a crowded bench without help, and she squatted on Red's lap as precariously as if she were on a tightwire. I chattered at the children and made faces; the boy soon realized he was being patronized and stoically faced front, but the girl kept stealing glances at me. I stood on my head. She smiled. I waggled my hips. She broke up laughing and her brother jabbed her with an elbow.

Carol Jeanne relaxed into her seat as I performed. She knew what was going on, but she didn't mind. I think she felt that regular people would be less in awe of *her* if they liked *me*.

All too soon, a scrawny old man revved up the synthesizer, and the service began with a rousing Protestant hymn. As mourners chirruped to the music, the star of the funeral—the dead body herself—was wheeled up the aisle on a cart. She was round and healthy looking; she didn't look sick enough to be lying there dead. The way she was rolled up to the front of the church, she looked like a rib roast at a prime rib banquet. Carol Jeanne would have appreciated that observation, and I wished again for a clipboard.

Everyone sat reverently through the invocation. I groomed Carol Jeanne while the heads were bowed.

The minister plunged right in at the end of the prayer, not even stopping for a breath between "Amen" and the opening remarks. "We're here for a sad but glorious occasion." He did a remarkable job with his facial expression; he looked both mournful and exalted, all at once, like a medieval painting of a saint. I imagined him practicing in front of a mirror all during his years of study in the seminary. "Odie Lee Morris was our chief administrator's wife. If that had been her only accomplishment, people would have honored her, for she was a gracious accompaniment to that good man all her life."

He paused for this profound idea to sink in. The man was a philosopher, a poet of the quotidian. "But the praise of the world meant nothing to Odie Lee," he continued. He also had a remarkably large and active Adam's apple. "From the moment she set foot on the Ark, she *devoted* herself . . . to *others*. Here was a woman who never worried about herself. Despite her poor health—and we who knew her are well aware how much Odie Lee suffered—she spent her life administering to others' needs."

The minister bowed his head for a moment. His Adam's apple quivered in indecision, waiting for a cue to begin dancing again. "But enough of my humble words." His tone had changed. He was through with the ministerial part, and now he was master of ceremonies. "I will speak of no particular creed or doctrine. Odie Lee lived as a Christian—an exemplar of Christianity at its best—but she belonged to all of us in the Ark, Christian or. . . " The words *pagan, heathen, heretic,* and *infidel* no doubt crossed his mind. " . . . non-Christian. Now it's time to let the people who loved her spread the word about Odie Lee. Form a line here, to the left of the podium. Take your turn. Everyone who wants to speak will have a chance."

Immediately, dozens of people stood and walked to the front of the church. The seated audience buzzed with approval at the number of people who were queueing up.

"You can tell how important Odie Lee was," Penelope said as she stepped over us to get to the aisle. "Usually, only a few people spread the word. Today, we may have as many as fifty." When she reached the aisle, she followed her bosom to the podium, where she got in line about twenty people back.

When the crowd had settled down, the minister beckoned to the first woman in line. She stood at the microphone and carefully took the protective dome off her dandelion.

"I'd like to spread the word for Odie Lee," she said. "Odie Lee was an angel in human form. She and her prayer partners were the first to help me when my husband Hyrum was down with prostate cancer. I'll never know how they even found out we needed help, but she and the prayer partners were at my door, bearing food and leading us in prayers. That's what I'll remember about Odie Lee."

When the speaker ended, she stood motionless at the podium. Then, hesitantly, the crowd murmured, "Spread the word!" Timidly, the woman held the white flower in front of her mouth and, filling her cheeks with air, blew mightily on it. Immediately the puffball disintegrated; white threads scattered in all directions. Many of them landed on the inert form of Odie Lee that was lying on its cart under the podium. Others were carried aloft by the air currents, and they flew haphazardly across the sanctuary.

One cluster of filaments landed on the head of a man two rows ahead of me. I leapt from Carol Jeanne's arm and scampered over the shoulder and lap of the little girl directly in front of us; she gasped in delight. Standing on the back of the next pew, I reached up and picked the piece of white dandelion fur from the top of the man's head. Several people turned to watch me, smiling or frowning or pointing, but I ignored them. I was only interested in the projectile. I carried it back to Carol Jeanne and held it out to her, but she shook her head and patted the crook of her arm for me to lie next to her there.

I settled next to her body and inspected my find. The white portion was as soft as down. I tickled my nose with it. Then I reached up and tickled Carol Jeanne's nose with the featherlike strands. She looked down at me and smiled.

Attached to each filament was a pale brown seed. *That* explained it. Once I saw the reason for the buoyancy of the white threads, there was nothing for me to do but discard the fluff and eat the seeds. There was no substance to them, though; they were dry and tasteless.

The next voice from the podium was so loud and tearful and discordant that it piqued my interest. "I was a prayer partner of Odie

Lee's," the woman said. "She was always the first to know who had a problem and lead the prayers on their behalf."

I heard another woman's voice mutter in the row behind us, "That's because her husband couldn't keep his mouth shut." Someone shushed at her. "Cyrus told her everything we ever said to him in confidence."

"Liz, *hush!*" another voice hissed.

Liz hushed. Not that many humans could have heard her anyway—she spoke very softly. Nevertheless, her words intrigued me. Maybe this Odie Lee wasn't the saint that Penelope and all these other people thought she was. I wriggled up and peered over Carol Jeanne's shoulder to get a look at Liz. She was a fairly attractive woman, very skillfully made up, with not a hair out of place. The bull-necked, overmuscled man sitting beside her had to be her husband. From the rigidity of her pose, she did not like it when he hushed her.

She looked down at me—not moving her head, not varying that perfect posture—and stared coldly at me until I turned back and looked at the podium.

"Spread the word!" the crowd was murmuring, more confidently than the first time. A puff, and the dandelion seeds were propelled across the church. The prayer partner, a young and tearful woman, marched down the aisle to her seat.

"I was another prayer partner," the next woman said piously. "Odie Lee always told us who to pray for, and why they needed our prayers. She always took a dinner to the family and told them we were praying on their behalf."

"*Pry*ing on their behalf is closer to it," Liz whispered behind me. "She was only twisting the knife."

I couldn't help looking at Liz again—and this time everything had changed. It was her husband who held a rigid posture, staring coldly straight ahead, and Liz seemed much more relaxed. She even smiled at me. What kind of war was going on between these people? Why did people like that stay married, when life was a bitter contest between them, a wrestling match that never ended?

"Spread the word!" the audience commanded the tearful young woman. Each time the audience gave the command, they spoke a little louder. By the end of the service, they'd be hoarse.

This time, the speaker's breath missed the mark. She had to blow three times before the dandelion stem was clean of white fuzz. She was red with exertion or embarrassment when she left the podium to return to her seat.

When Penelope reached the podium, she told the crowd that Odie Lee was the most honest person she had ever met. "In fact," she said, "Odie Lee often recognized people's predicaments before *they* did. How often she mourned because they couldn't face the truth! Odie Lee prayed with them and counseled them until they recognized their problems and turned to God for help."

I waited for Liz to respond to Penelope's testimony, but she held her tongue. Of course, she knew we were with Penelope, and she knew I was listening to her, and she certainly knew that witnesses reported on what they heard. She could not have known that Carol Jeanne and I were not Penelope's friends—that Carol Jeanne was going to laugh with me about Liz's comments when I reported on them later.

When Liz remained silent, I turned and watched Penelope take a mighty breath and scatter her dandelion all over the church. Then, having caught the drift of what people were going to say about Odie Lee, I slept through the rest of the service. I could always skim through the rest of the word-spreadings when I did my memory dump later.

After a mournful closing hymn and a prayer, Odie Lee's corpse was wheeled out of the sanctuary. I hopped over Carol Jeanne and Stef and Mamie and Lydia and Red to see the procession. Sitting on Emmy's lap, I watched the cart bearing Odie Lee roll up the aisle and out the door. The dead woman's body was covered with white dandelion filaments. A disproportionate number of them had landed on her chin, leaving her with a dandelion beardlet. Odie Lee didn't look like the kind of woman who would enjoy having a goatee.

"Where's she going?" Emmy asked me. It was a good question. They certainly weren't going to bury her.

When no one answered her quickly enough, Emmy turned up the volume. "WHERE'S SHE GOING?" Heads turned, and I abandoned the screeching Emmy to sit with Carol Jeanne.

"Daddy doesn't know," Red said, and the answer seemed to satisfy Emmy. It didn't satisfy Mamie, though. As soon as we left the church, she pulled Penelope aside.

"Where *did* she go?" Mamie asked.

"I assume you want to know the final destination of her *mortal* remains," Penelope said.

"Of course. Where's the cemetery?"

Penelope raised one eyebrow. "There's no cemetery on the Ark," she said.

Red tapped Mamie on the shoulder. "What she means," he explained, "is that people who die on the Ark are jettisoned into space. It's like a sea burial, only people are launched right into heaven."

Penelope lowered the first eyebrow and raised the second. I wondered if she was aware of the tricks her eyebrows were doing, or if the brows moved up and down as an unconscious stupidity gauge. Red was almost as dimwitted as Mamie.

"That's a romantic idea," she said, "but it's not at all sensible. Every object in space is a potential weapon. Sure, the odds are against a ship hitting Odie Lee, but if one did, the collision would be fatal. We don't jettison anything from the Ark."

"Then you bury them," Mamie said. It was a statement, not a question.

Penelope rolled her eyes. "*You've* been underground. That's where the tube runs. That's where we have our offices. I'm not sharing *my* desk with a corpse. Not even with a saint like Odie Lee."

"What, then?" Good grief! The woman was dense.

"It's like they say in the Good Book. 'Ashes to ashes . . . '"

I accessed my computer files under Bible, and I didn't find "ashes to ashes" anything. But I was hardly surprised. Christians will say any old thing and if they claim it's in the Bible, everyone nods wisely and accepts every word of it. That's because nobody *reads* the book. They believe it—but they leave it unstudied and unread. Of course, there are scientists like that, too—the ones who accept the orthodoxy of the past without ever looking at the evidence themselves. But people like that never change the world; they move through it invisibly. Carol Jeanne questioned *everything*, and as a result she had transformed her field. And soon enough she was going to transform a world. She was living a life that was unfathomable to people who assumed that every cliché in their heads came from the Bible and was therefore not to be questioned.

Mamie didn't care about the source of the quote—it was the idea of cremation that bothered her. "That's barbaric!"

"It's a simple necessity, practiced in many places back on Earth," said Penelope. "It was also fully explained in the prospectus."

"Nobody's burning me."

"You won't exactly be burned," said Penelope cheerfully. "*Rendered* is more accurate. We'll break you down to your component elements and recycle you. We'll use you to fertilize plants and do all *sorts* of other things. It's only the unusable parts that will be cremated."

"That will *never* happen to me." Mamie was near tears, and I almost felt sorry for her. Almost.

Penelope smiled sweetly. "You signed the Compact."

"*That* was in there? That I could be—incinerated? Recycled? *Rendered*, like a bar of soap?"

Penelope smiled and shrugged—a slow, eloquent, voluminous gesture. "We'll almost certainly wait until you're dead."

Mamie turned in fury at Stef. "Why didn't you tell me that!"

Because you wouldn't have listened, you poor dimwitted woman—certainly not to Stef. Of course I could say nothing, but I knew this pattern very well. *Red* was the one who had studied the Compact and decided not to tell his mother about cremation, and even Mamie must have been well aware of that. But since she could never be angry with her dear boy, it was Stef she turned on. Poor Stef. She never gave him the slightest power or influence over her, but held him responsible for anything that went wrong.

"I'm sorry, dear. I don't know what I was thinking of," Stef croaked.

"My goodness, Stephan! Your throat sounds as dry as sandpaper," Penelope said, immediately solicitous. "We *must* get you something to drink."

Never mind that it was Penelope's fault that they hadn't even been able to get a drink before the funeral. She was his rescuer now, in more ways than one. "If it's not too much trouble," he murmured.

"No trouble at all," said Penelope, beaming. "We were going to the kitchen anyway. Once people have seen Odie Lee's display, the next thing they'll want is food."

"Odie Lee's display?" Red asked.

Penelope only dismissed them with a shake of her head. "Oh, you'll have plenty of time to see it," she said. "Right now all of us Mayflowerites have to help with the meal." Then she looked down at Pink, who was dozing in Red's arms. "Of course you can't take a pig into the kitchen."

"Pink is a witness," said Red, wearily. "A heavy witness, in fact."

"Well then," said Penelope, "I'll bet we can get someone to take the pig home for you."

Red considered for a moment. I could imagine the internal debate. On the one hand, Pink, unlike the children, would be perfectly all right at home by herself, and she *was* tired. But on the other hand, it would be a confession that what Red was doing here wasn't important enough to be witnessed. Of course *nothing* that he did was important enough to be witnessed, but that was one bit of reality that he wasn't ready to face yet.

"Pink *is* tired and I really can't carry her around," said Red. He looked at the lazy little swine in his arms and she winked at him. "Yes, Pink would like to go to the new house."

"Why don't we all go home with Pink?" suggested Carol Jeanne.

Penelope looked at her with an ingenuous expression. "Oh, what a good idea. I'm sure people will understand. Everyone else in Mayflower is helping with the funeral, but the chief gaiologist's husband's *pig* is sleepy so of course she had to go home—"

Red intervened quickly. "Don't be silly, Penelope, of course we'll stay and help. But who are you going to have take her? Pink isn't a pet or . . . or an ordinary animal."

No, Pink was a walking doorstop.

"One of our young people—oh, Nancy!"

Nancy was a horse-faced girl whose every movement betrayed the fact that she thought she was even uglier than in fact she was. Her shoulders slumped and she seemed to shrink as she walked, as if she hoped that if she became unobtrusive enough she would entirely disappear. Of course her very ungainliness served only to call more attention to her, but I have learned that human adolescents never understand that the best way to avoid notice is to behave normally. Though in Nancy's case, there was no need for her to disappear. When she looked up and smiled she seemed to be a very nice person. Very trustworthy. No sign of the hostility that most human teenagers have when an adult calls their name.

"Mr. Cocciolone's witness needs to be dropped off at their new home," said Penelope. "You know where their house has been set up, don't you?"

"Oh, yes," said Nancy. "It's right up the street from us." ·

"Then you wouldn't mind running the pig home for him, would you?"

She wouldn't mind. She bundled Pink into her arms and took off briskly.

"But won't the door be. . . " Red's voice trailed off.

"She'll be just fine," said Penelope. "And your poor pig looked so tired." She spared a glance at me. "I'd suggest sending the monkey home, too, but I don't know who would dare to handle an animal that *bites*."

Damn straight, Penelope, thought I.

The social hall was connected to the sanctuary by a gravel path. The mourners were grouped in the large room, apparently viewing Odie Lee's display. We bypassed that as Penelope led us to a large, square kitchen where a cluster of volunteers were slopping food on reusable plates. Everyone was taking the food outdoors and sitting on the lawn or on benches to eat it.

I stood on tiptoe on Carol Jeanne's shoulder, clutching her hair for balance as I inspected the fare. It was such *human* food—overcooked and overspiced and hopelessly carnivorous. There wasn't so much as a grape that was fresh. I wouldn't be eating at *this* meal.

"Who has the punch?" Penelope boomed. "I need some punch. We have a thirsty man here." She found a cup of fruit drink and gave it to Stef, ignoring the rest of our group.

"I'm thirsty," Emmy wailed, eyeing Stef's empty cup.

"I'm hungry," said Lydia. "I'm supposed to have food right *now*." Lydia was always so charming when she imitated Mamie.

Penelope looked at them like they were roaches. "What are *children* doing in the kitchen?" she asked rhetorically. Everyone knew she had led them there. "Joan, be a dear and take them off to the nursery." Then Penelope bent down and blasted Lydia cheerfully with her foghorn voice. "There are little snacks for you in the nursery, darling."

A tiny blond woman, not much taller than Lydia, stepped down off a stool and wiped her hands on the towel she wore around her waist. Then, without speaking a word, she took Lydia and Emmy by the wrist and led them from the kitchen. Emmy's wails sounded like a siren diminishing in the distance. "Daddy!" she howled.

"You'll be fine!" Red called after her.

I felt Carol Jeanne's muscles stiffen under me. It took me a moment to realize why she was angry: Emmy had called out for her father, not her mother.

But why should that bother Carol Jeanne? She had made her choice. Red was the childcare man, the family therapist; she was the scientist, the worldshaper. *Her* children were the countless generations of every species, human and otherwise, that would grow up on our new world. These two genetic accidents that had come from her womb were Red's children—they were all he'd ever create, so why shouldn't he be closer to them than Carol Jeanne was? I didn't understand her.

"Now, everybody's squared away!" Penelope said, obviously pleased with herself. "We have some new kitchen volunteers to do their fair share today," she announced. "These are Carol Jeanne Cocciolone, and her husband Red, and his dear mama. The handsome one is Stephan, who is *far* too young to be Red's father." This last was said with a coy smile. "Carol Jeanne, why don't you and Mamie go out and collect the empty plates? We want everyone to see our handsome new citizens. Red and Stef can stay here and help wash the dishes—these dear men won't mind doing the obscure, difficult work that no one ever sees, will you?"

Penelope was a genius at this, I could see. It was important for Mayflower colony's prestige to have Carol Jeanne as visible as possible, while Penelope simply wanted Mamie out of the way. Mamie stupidly grabbed at the lure; she picked up the plastic tray and bustled importantly away, smiling attractively at everyone within eyeshot.

But as far as Carol Jeanne was concerned, Penelope couldn't

have made a worse suggestion. Carol Jeanne shunned public appearances. She nuzzled me with her chin as I perched on her shoulder. It was one of the ways she bought time.

Finally she said, "I appreciate the offer, Penelope, but I don't smell good enough to be seen by the public. I'd love to wash dishes, though."

"Dishes? You're Carol Jeanne Cocciolone. *You* don't wash dishes."

Heads turned. Carol Jeanne's name was already famous on Mayflower. She blushed.

"Of course I wash dishes," she said quietly. "I didn't grow up in a house with servants, and the dishes never washed themselves."

I knew, and Stef knew, and certainly Red knew that he did most of the dishwashing in our house back on earth—but Penelope didn't know that. The color deepened on her cheeks. "Of course," she said, making a quick recovery. " 'Whoever would be the greatest among you, let him be the servant of all.' Isn't that just like you?" Penelope was hardly in a position to know what was "just like" Carol Jeanne, but because the comment saved face for her, no one contradicted her. "You wash dishes here with us for a while, and then I'll take you around to introduce you—fair enough?"

Freed of Penelope's orchestration, Carol Jeanne found a place at a sink and washed dishes. Red and Stef ended up drying dishes and wiping up counters and whatever else Penelope commanded; somehow, the moment she entered the kitchen, she was the overseer and everyone there accepted her assignments.

I stayed with Carol Jeanne, drying the silverware and glasses and platters as she finished with them. As always, we worked together with grace and precision. We settled into such a comfortable rhythm that I was soon oblivious to the activity around me. A grating human voice brought me back.

"I *said*, is that monkey touching our plates?"

I looked up to see a tall ugly treetrunk of a woman who had apparently suffered from crippling acne in her teens. I recognized her, though—yes, she had been sitting beside the children on the row in front of us at Odie Lee's funeral. She had a squashed-in nose, so there was certainly a genetic connection between her and the children. She lacked the buck teeth, but no doubt orthodontia had played a role in that. It was impossible to think that the children's father could have contributed to their ugliness. No one else's genes would dare interfere with this woman's reproductive process. The children no doubt looked at their mother's complexion, realized what lay ahead of them in adolescence, and contemplated suicide.

I bared my teeth at her, and she stepped back.

"He's not a *real* monkey, Dolores. He's a witness." Penelope jumped in before Carol Jeanne could defend my cleanliness. "You'd better watch yourself around him," she added in an undertone. "He bites."

Dolores took another step back. Already, the only two people I had officially met on the Ark were wary of me. I didn't want to make people think less of Carol Jeanne, so I set the platter I was drying aside and did a somersault on the counter. I was trying to overcome this woman's aversion to monkeys by being unbearably cute and nonthreatening. It didn't work, though.

Carol Jeanne understood, and let me off the hook. "Lovelock," she said, "doing dishes is such repetitive work. Go out where people are eating and observe for me, would you?"

She gave me a banana chip—as if I needed a bribe to escape *that* little domestic scene. But I used the treat as an excuse to play my monkey role to the hilt, begging with outstretched hands and a hopeful expression for the tidbit that she so generously bestowed on me.

I stood at attention on the counter, bowed deeply, then jumped up and kicked my heels together. Definitely a vaudeville move, but it had the desired effect—the *other* women in the kitchen laughed in delight, and even Penelope smiled. Of course, Dolores's curled lip didn't relax a bit. Her disgust was impenetrable. The name *Do-lores* is Spanish for "pains," originating no doubt as a reference to the pains of Christ, but I thought it was the perfect name for her.

I leapt from the counter, clung for a moment to Carol Jeanne's upper arm, and then, on impulse, took a flying leap at Dolores, landing on her shoulder. Penelope shrieked, but Dolores barely flinched. "Get this animal. . . " she began, but then I leaned up and kissed her—a dry kiss—on her scarred and pitted cheek. I was almost certain that no one in her life, not even her husband, had ever kissed that cheek.

It was perhaps too much to hope that my kiss would make her realize that she, too, had been a victim of prejudice, and that her bigotry toward me was therefore unjust; it would be enough if the gesture touched her emotions a little bit and softened her loathing toward me. This was part of my job, after all. To make sure that Carol Jeanne always looked good to other people. That naturally included helping dispel negative feelings toward her witness.

I jumped from Dolores's shoulder. To my surprise, my trajectory didn't work as I'd planned—instead of landing in the kitchen doorway, I found myself heading straight for the doorjamb, and barely recovered in time to hit it with my hands and feet instead of my head. I rolled on the ground, trying to look less clumsy than I felt. What could possibly have thrown me off?

Idiot, I thought. The Coriolis effect. The Ark was spinning, so of course when I jumped free of all objects connected to the ground, the Ark moved under me and I didn't land where I'd expected. This was the first time since arriving here that I'd tried a serious leap. It was obvious that it would take some practice to learn how to get around. That reminded me of my terrible experience on the shuttle, when we were in freefall. I never wanted to lose control of myself like that again. I'd have to find a way to practice that, too.

Of course, everyone thought that hitting the doorjamb was part of my vaudeville routine, so there was more laughter as I left. Fine, that was fine. Open, happy laughter meant that humans weren't afraid.

Outside, people were scattered all over the lawns, eating and talking cheerfully. It really was a social occasion; any mournfulness left over from the funeral was apparently confined to the hall where people were viewing Odie Lee's display. I was curious—I wanted to see what that was about. But Carol Jeanne had told me to do my observing where people were eating, so that was where I went.

People noticed me, of course, but they quickly dismissed me as a harmless animal and went on talking. Everyone knew about witnesses, and if they'd thought about it they would have realized that anything they said in front of me could and probably would be repeated. But it was in their nature to dismiss me as nothing more than an animal, which was fine with me—it made my job easier.

Most of the conversations were dull enough—gossip, silly

things. I didn't stay long with any of them. Carol Jeanne would glance at them as I uploaded them into the computer. Then I'd search the Ark's database, identify all the people, and index them so that later, if she needed to, Carol Jeanne could look them up and see them in conversation. It was a kind of spying, I supposed, but indexed recordings were about the only way a famous person like Carol Jeanne could possibly keep track of all the people who would expect her to remember them. Carol Jeanne told me once that it was for this that she finally decided to get a witness in the first place. She had no idea at the time that we would become such good friends.

I felt as though I had listened in on a thousand conversations, when finally I came upon the two children who had sat in front of us at the funeral. They were playing. Or rather, *he* was playing, by turning his dirty plate upside down and flipping it out so it flew like a Frisbee.

"You'll break the plate!" the girl insisted.

"Haven't yet," he said.

"But you *will*."

The plate landed face down on the lawn, and he sauntered over to pick it up. "I'm just wiping it off in the grass, see?"

She ran ahead of him. "I won't let you do it!"

He ran, too, but she had too much of a head start. She got the plate. He lunged for it, but she ran and held it out of reach. "It's mine!" he shouted.

"It belongs to the village," she said. "We can't make more, not for another whole year."

"It's not going to break, but *you* might," he said. "Give it back."

"If this dish breaks Mother will never let you come to anything grown-up like this again."

"Good," he said. But the mention of his mother stopped him cold. The running was over. "You can't just take stuff that belongs to me and keep it away."

"It doesn't belong to you," she said. "And I'm saving you from getting your stupid self punished."

"I don't want to be saved."

"Then you're as stupid as you are ugly."

"Look who's talking."

Since they *were* both quite ugly, it was almost painful to hear them talk like this. I liked them—probably because they had liked *me* when they first saw me in church. So I intruded myself into their little scene, scampering in between them. I did a little imitation of their quarrel, taking each part in turn, chattering in fury and waving my arms in a crescendo of argument. Then I put my hands behind my back and strutted away, nose in the air. They laughed. I turned, took a bow, then allowed the bow to topple me over into the grass.

"Look at that," the girl said. "How do they train him to *do* that?"

"They don't *train* him, stupid," said the boy. "He does it because he wants to. He's a witness. He's probably smarter than we are."

A very perceptive boy.

"Besides which," said the boy, "he probably recorded everything and he'll tell on us later."

I jumped to my feet, stood at attention, and very solemnly shook my head.

"See?" she said. "He's not going to tell on you."

"Then *you* will."

"Will not."

"Will so."

Again I bounded between them, and pantomimed taking a punch at an imaginary opponent. Then I became the opponent and pretended to take the punch, flinging myself backward into the grass. Again they laughed.

"I think he doesn't want us to fight," said the boy.

"Why should *he* care?" asked the girl.

I shrugged eloquently.

"I wish he could talk," said the boy.

"They can read and write," said the girl. "If we had a computer, he could type."

"How come you know so much about witnesses?"

"Because I'm going to be famous someday and have one," she said.

He shook his head in disgust. "Listen, pinbrain, that was something that happened on *Earth*, where we will never in our lives go to again. Where are they going to get a witness for you here?"

She looked dismayed. "Don't they just *make* them?"

"Sure, with really complicated crossbreeding and genetic splicing and who knows what else."

"So what?" said the girl. "We have embryo banks here. Millions of animal embryos. I bet they have some that could become witnesses."

"Fine, maybe," said the boy. Clearly he didn't believe it.

She turned her back on him. "What's your name, monkey?"

"He can't *talk*," said the boy.

"Maybe he can act it out," she said. "I bet he can act out *your* name."

The boy blushed with anger. "If you make any jokes about my name I'll kill you."

"It could be worse," she said. "Your name could be *Dick*."

"That's it," he said. "You're dead!"

He lunged for her, and because they were both sitting in the grass, she couldn't get away. I was afraid he was really going to hurt her, because he *was* angry. But instead he tickled her. She laughed and screamed for him to stop, and I understood that this was humiliating for her, that she hated being tickled, so it was a punishment after all—but at the same time, he could have hit her, and instead he chose this far less violent way of acting out his rage.

In fact, the way they rolled and tussled on the ground stirred something in me. Feelings that I had never had with Carol Jeanne's and Red's children. Maybe they were too young. Maybe Mamie's influence had made them so prissy that they could never really *play* like this. But watching the way these two ugly children played, seeing how they loved and bossed and tormented each other, I felt a gnawing hunger. Not for food or water. I didn't realize it at the time, but soon enough I understood: I was hungry for childhood. It was one thing to strut and perform for people. It was something else to *play* with them. I was supposedly an adult, and yet I still had that child-hunger.

For a moment, I let it get the better of me. Seeing how he tickled her, I couldn't—or at least didn't—stop myself from leaping onto his back and tickling *him*. He was distracted enough that in only a moment *she* was on top, tickling him, so that he couldn't concentrate enough even to get me off his face.

"Not fair!" he howled. "Two against one!"

"That's right," she cackled. "We're cheaters! But that's better than being *Peters!*"

That was too much for him. He roared, flung me off his face, and went after her again. But this time when he caught her, she had had enough. "I'm sorry," she said. "I'm sorry, I take it back, I didn't mean it."

"I don't make fun of *your* name," Peter said.

"There's nothing to make fun of," she said. "Diana is a perfectly ordinary name."

"Oh yeah?" he said. "She was the *virgin* huntress." He looked as triumphant as if he had just called her something obscene.

"Of course I'm a virgin," Diana answered contemptuously. "I don't even get a period yet."

"Don't talk about that," he said, excruciatingly embarrassed.

"Period period period," she said. "Blood and cramps and little eggs rolling down tubes. *Fertilization.*"

He covered his ears. "You are *sick!*" he said. "You are deeply disturbed."

"On the contrary," she said, triumphant at last. "I'm simply a woman, and not ashamed of it."

"I'm going to take my plate in and see if Mother's finished so we can go home," he said. He got up and started looking for the onetime frisbee.

When he found it, it was broken into two halves.

"I told you," she said.

"It didn't happen from playing Frisbee," he said. "You must have stepped on it."

"Because *you* were chasing me. And besides, I didn't step on it. I would have noticed."

"Then you rolled over on it."

"If I did then that's what you get for tickling me," she said.

"You're going to get killed."

"Oh really? *I'm* not the one who has to hand Mother a broken plate."

They were heading for the kitchen. I was completely forgotten. But no sooner did I think that than Diana turned around and looked at me. "Are you coming or not?" she asked. "My mother was looking for your owner. Mother's a botanist and she's going to be working with Dr. Cocciolone."

Oh, great. The bark-faced woman was going to be around a lot. Just what I hoped for.

"He doesn't have to come with us," said Peter. "He can do whatever he wants."

That was the second time Peter had said I could do whatever I wanted, but I was so naive then that I didn't give it a second thought. Of *course* I was a free agent, bound to Carol Jeanne only by my love for her and hers for me. But that was why I went with them—not because I had to, but because it was time to see if I could make myself useful to the creature whose life meant more to me than my own pitiful existence.

There was still a mountain of dishes when we got to the kitchen. It looked like there were hours of work left to do. And Carol Jeanne looked so tired. Not to mention poor Stef, who was drying dishes now. Red was nowhere to be seen. Penelope and Dolores were putting dishes away—working very slowly, because they were so busy talking. All of it was gossip, talking about people, not a single intelligent idea to be heard.

Carol Jeanne had been imposed on long enough. It was time for somebody to put his foot down. And since it wasn't likely to be Carol Jeanne or Stef, it had to be me.

I bounded up onto the counter. I was already getting better at allowing for the Coriolis effect, so I landed pretty much where I wanted to. And then I splashed across the wet counter and stood directly in front of Penelope's bosom and Dolores's skin and *screeched* at them at the top of my lungs. They looked at me in horror. I bent over, flashing my little pink butt at them, and wrote in the water, "DONE." The letters stayed long enough to be read— I know they read the word, because Penelope's lips moved—and then I stalked over to Carol Jeanne, splashing angrily with every step, and began to pull her away from the sink by the sleeve. Of course I wasn't strong enough actually to move her—I only skidded on the water on the counter—but the symbolism finally penetrated the thick skulls of the gossiping grotesques who had trapped her there.

"Oh, you poor dear," said Penelope. "We've been *so* thoughtless, keeping you here so long when you haven't even been to your house yet."

I was afraid that Carol Jeanne's martyr syndrome would kick in and she'd insist on staying until the job was done, but at that moment she looked at Stef and saw the hope on his face and so she smiled at Penelope and said, "I've enjoyed helping, but you're right, I *do* need to get home."

I hated hearing her talk like that—she was already picking up the oversincere intonation that Penelope always used.

"You just wait half a minute and I'll take you," said Penelope.

"Please don't bother," said Carol Jeanne. "You've got too many responsibilities here for us to take you away. It can't be a secret where our house is, can it?"

"No," said Dolores, "just ask anybody and they'll tell you. We're all very excited that you're here." She didn't *sound* excited. She sounded how you'd expect a talking tree to sound—bored out of her mind.

"It was so nice meeting you—and all the others who were working here in the kitchen today—"

"Let's go," said Stef. I'm sure he saw a ray of hope that he might actually get away from Penelope today, and he didn't want small talk to delay the happy moment.

I climbed up to Carol Jeanne's shoulder.

"That monkey really looks out for you," said Dolores.

I could have been wrong, but her tone suggested grudging respect. Maybe having her around wouldn't be as unbearable as I had feared.

At that moment, though, Dolores saw the two half-plates in Peter's hands. She went rigid but said nothing. Instead she fixed him with a terrible glare. He carefully, shamefacedly laid the fragments on the counter. "I was playing with it and I broke it," he said. "Diana warned me not to and I did it anyway."

I was astonished at this—the way he took full responsibility, the sheer courage of it. But there was still something terrible and frightening in the way his mother said nothing at all. Just continued to glare at Peter, unmoving, until he left the room, Diana tagging along after him. I had never seen anything like it. The woman really *did* become treelike in moments of stress.

Or perhaps she merely saved her fury for later, when they were home. Yet nothing in Peter's and Diana's behavior had suggested an inordinate fear of their mother. Her glare of death might well be the entire punishment Peter would receive. I suspected that it was probably more than enough.

Once outside the kitchen, Carol Jeanne straightened up, as if a huge weight had been taken from her shoulders.

"I think I love your monkey like another son," said Stef. "He just saved my life."

Carol Jeanne chuckled. "He does look out for me."

We were in the social hall now, and the crowd around Odie Lee's display had thinned considerably. Carol Jeanne was looking toward it, but I knew that she probably didn't share my curiosity about it. Nor was Stef likely to speak in favor of examining Odie Lee's detritus. I was disappointed—I wanted to see what a dead human would choose to have put on display at her own funeral.

My wish was granted by an unexpected fairy godmother. As we stood there, looking toward the display, a familiar voice spoke up. "It's like a little prayer chapel. The shrine of the Blessed Odie Lee, patron saint of hypocrites."

It was Liz, the woman who had sat behind us during the funeral. She was without her bull-necked husband, and apparently she had sized up Carol Jeanne and Stef as people who would share her caustic attitude toward Odie Lee.

She was right. Carol Jeanne gave her a warm smile (the first unforced one she had given anyone but me today) and said, "I must be a terrible cynic, but I was sitting there in the funeral thinking how grateful I was that I wouldn't have to meet this Odie Lee."

"The post-Odie Lee era begins today in Mayflower," said Liz. "The year one, P.O.L. New calendars for everyone." She held out her hand. "My name is Liz Fisher. My husband is—off somewhere. Would you like me to give you the guided tour through Odieland?"

"I'd love it," said Carol Jeanne. "My name is—"

"Carol Jeanne Cocciolone. Peloponnesia has been shouting your name all day—how could I miss it?"

"Peloponnesia," echoed Stef, with a chuckle.

"Sorry, my pet name for Penelope," said Liz. "But when you look at her, I just can't help but think of peninsulas. Can *you*?"

Carol Jeanne laughed out loud. Several people looked at us. "Oh, no, I mustn't laugh," said Carol Jeanne. "People will think I'm—"

"Disrespectful," said Liz. "Don't worry—I won't say anything to embarrass you at the display. Besides, I don't have to. No one but Odie Lee would ever think of arranging her own audio-visual This-Is-Your-Life. It speaks for itself."

It did indeed. Odie Lee had carefully planned every detail of her own funeral display. She must have known she was going to die. No, she must have *hoped* she was going to die. She must have craved death and this final burst of martyrdom, the way Carol Jeanne craved chocolate and Red craved salt. Funeral displays weren't customary on Mayflower; this was Odie Lee's own idea and her own passion, although from the worshipful way others were looking at it, I had no doubt it would *become* a funeral tradition from now on. The display was magnificent in its tackiness. If I had the ability to blush, I would have done it, out of humiliation for Odie Lee. I was grateful that we weren't of the same species.

There was an arrangement of insipid sayings that she had hand-sewn in *X*-shaped stitches on fabric. These framed sayings surrounded a bigger tapestry, which was a crude reproduction of Odie Lee's own face. It, too, was sewn into fabric with the curious *X*-shaped stitches. Even dead, Odie Lee didn't look as lifeless as her needlework image. The idea of someone sewing her own likeness into fabric was faintly nauseating. A portrait of the artist in threads.

Other crafts dotted the exhibit. There were pottery bowls in shapes that roughly approximated half-spheres. There were watercolors of landscapes that looked like animals, and animals that looked like scenery. Odie Lee apparently fancied herself an artist.

Then we got to the photographs: Odie Lee knocking on a front door with a hamper of food; Odie Lee holding hands with a group of other women, their heads bowed in prayer; Odie Lee kneeling at a bedside, praying again, as she gazed upward with a supplicating expression on her face. All the things that people had praised her for at the funeral were on display here, and Odie Lee had posed for the pictures. I imagined her looking through the photographer's proofs, picking out the pictures in which she looked most beatific as she humbly loved her neighbor as herself.

Even more nauseating were the refreshments. Odie Lee had

cooked fudge and nut breads and cookies and candy in anticipation of her coming death. They'd been frozen or vacu-packed or set aside on a shelf, waiting for Odie Lee to die so they could be served at her funeral. Now they sat on a table next to the funeral display, not six feet from Odie Lee's coffin, labeled with a note (in Odie Lee's own calligraphy) admonishing visitors to "Just Take 1, Please!" How long had she been dying, anyway? Why couldn't it have happened sooner, before she cooked the fudge?

I assumed that what killed Odie Lee must not have been contagious, since most of the food had been eaten. No doubt it was lip-smacking good, and just as pretty as the picture in the recipe book.

The most interesting part of the display—even more interesting than Odie Lee's own body—was a holo image of Odie Lee, giving her final words-to-live-by sermonette to those who had come to see her dead. Her assumption must have been that others would be eager to learn how to live as selfless a life as she had. Here was a woman who was brazen in her humility.

With organ music in the background to accent her words, Odie Lee's holo told us she hoped we would be as holy as the photographs had already shown her to have been. "Visit the sick," she said. The holograph dissolved to a scene of Odie Lee bent over a child's sick-bed. "The Savior taught us, 'Feed my lambs.'" And now we saw Odie Lee whipping up a batch of fudge—perhaps even the same fudge that sat on the table beside us.

I don't know how long the holo loop would have lasted. I had a morbid fascination that made me want to see every minute of Odie Lee's shame, but I was overruled. The small silent woman who had led the children off to the nursery so long before came into the hall, carrying Emmy in front of her as gingerly as if she had just taken her from the oven and was trying not to get burned. A pungent smell filled the room; Emmy had outlasted her diaper.

"Oh, dear," said Carol Jeanne. "Where's Red?"

The woman said nothing, just held Emmy out in front of her.

"Poo-poo," said Emmy, pleased as punch.

"You can set her down," said Carol Jeanne. "She can walk."

"Better not," said the woman—the first sound I had heard her make. "She's oozing."

It was true. Carol Jeanne reluctantly took her younger daughter, handling her even more carefully than the nursery teacher had done.

"Oh, let me do that," said Liz. "It's only a little mess, that's all—but I know how it is when you just got out of the box from Ironsides, it's too much to handle all at once." And in no time there was Liz, holding Emmy perfectly easily, even affectionately, never mind what was oozing onto her bare arm. "Let me lead you home. Where's the other one? Didn't I see you with two daughters?"

"I don't know where Lydia is," said Carol Jeanne. "Or Red either, for that matter."

I noticed that she didn't mention Mamie. Stef didn't remind her, which either meant he was tactful or he was hoping to lose her forever in the crowd. "I'll go retrieve Lydia," Stef said. "You go on ahead—I'll round up the others, too."

"The house is easy to find," said Liz. "Head down the lane straight across the square from the church—that way." She indicated the direction with a nod of her head.

"Got it," said Stef, and he was gone.

As we left the social hall, Odie Lee's voice followed us, saying, "Suffer the little children to come unto me, for of such is the kingdom of heaven."

Once we were outside on the square, Carol Jeanne must have realized that she was actually letting a stranger carry her child for her. "I really can't let you carry Emmy all that way," she said.

"Don't be silly," said Liz. "We walk everywhere here, for the exercise. And walking in low-gee is hard at first—you don't want to fall while carrying her, do you?"

I remembered all the tripping and stumbling on the way over here, and had to agree with Liz. It made sense for her to carry Emmy. It was practical. But it was also decent and friendly and it was the first kindness extended to us here that didn't seem to carry a price tag.

"Liz Fisher?" Carol Jeanne said. "Did I get your name right?"

"Oh yes," she said. "I'm nobody, though, so don't worry about remembering—I'll remind you whenever you ask."

"Oh, you can't be *nobody*," Carol Jeanne began.

"There I go again," said Liz. "I don't *mean* to sound self-deprecating. I'm really not—I have a perfectly healthy self-image. I just happen to know that my skills are more along the lines of typing very fast and raising children well. It's my husband who's the one that was needed on the Ark. He's an orthopedist. A very good one— he was the specialist that NFL team doctors called in for the tricky problems. He'll be really vital to the colony when we get onto the planet."

"We'll *all* be vital."

"Well, *I* know that. I daresay my mothering skills will be at least as important as his doctoring ones. But I understand the world well enough to know that I'll never be particularly noticed for what I do. It's really all right with me. When I say I'm nobody, I'm actually rather proud of it. But Warren hates it when I talk like that. He says it makes me sound mousy." Liz laughed, lightly and easily. "Warren and I don't get along too well. He used to like it when I made smart remarks, for instance, but now he's always hushing me. Ever since we got on the Ark, everything I do is wrong. Isn't that silly? I'm the same person, doing the same things. Except I don't shop at the mall anymore."

I thought that Carol Jeanne might be getting bored with all this. It was really empty prattle, wasn't it? Just a woman gossiping about her own life. But the woman was carrying Carol Jeanne's leaky papoose, so she couldn't very well *seem* uninterested.

"I imagine just being on the Ark changes people's attitudes and relationships," said Carol Jeanne. "I remember my husband saying that it was a likely problem—a lot of people wouldn't respond well to how small this world would be. Social claustrophobia, he called it."

"Is your husband a scientist, too?" asked Liz.

"Not at all," said Carol Jeanne, revealing her opinion of Red's profession in three short words. "He's a family therapist."

"Oh," said Liz.

"I wish I could tell you that he's good at it, because it sounds to me like you and your husband might need one. But I honestly have no idea whether Red is a good therapist or not."

Liz laughed nervously. "Don't his patients *tell* you whether he's good?"

"I've never met any of his clients," said Carol Jeanne. "Or if I have, I don't know it. He never tells me who they are or anything about them. I have never once heard a single fact about any of them, or a single story." She flashed a smile at Liz. "I thought you might want to know that."

So Carol Jeanne *had* heard Liz's remarks during the funeral—especially her comments about how Odie Lee's husband told her things that he had learned in confidence. Carol Jeanne was assuring Liz that she could trust Red.

In fact, I realized now, Carol Jeanne was drumming up business for her husband. That would be good for her *own* marriage, if Red got a client right away, so that he could feel needed and important on the Ark. Sometimes I didn't give Carol Jeanne enough credit—she had noticed a way she could help this woman and her own husband at the same time, and I hadn't even had to suggest it to her.

CHAPTER FIVE

The Apple and the Coconut

We crossed the town square at a fast clip. Liz walked with the speed and precision of a drill sergeant. Carol Jeanne trotted to keep up with her, occasionally turning to see if the others were yet in sight. When she finally glimpsed Red, she waved for him to follow. I turned around to watch their progress: Mamie leading, Red just behind, Lydia trailing after him, and Stef bringing up the rear. All were weary. A sorry-looking parade.

Just as Emmy's diaper reached critical mass, Liz stopped in front of a puffy white house on a street lined with little potted trees.

"This is it—and not a moment too soon." She led Carol Jeanne up the plastic sheet of sidewalk to the house. She opened the door without a key, and when I looked more closely I saw that there was no way to lock the door. Apparently privacy wasn't regarded highly here. Everyone in Mayflower would have full access to our lives and our possessions. Carol Jeanne apparently didn't notice that; I predicted that when she did, locks would magically appear on our doorknobs.

Inside, the house looked more like a tent than a permanent structure. The floor was covered with carpet that could be rolled up and taken away when the house collapsed during changeover. No plumbing tied the structure to the ground, either; I soon discovered that toilets and sinks and showers were placed around the periphery of the house and supplied by water tanks whose portable pipes snaked house to house above ground, ready for disassembly.

The walls were made somewhat rigid by tightly inflated ribs, but the real structural strength came from a continuous jet of air that caused the house to have more air pressure inside than out. The slight but constant whooshing of air filled the house with whispers and sighs.

Somebody had already unloaded our furniture inside, dumping it unceremoniously in whatever room seemed to be appropriate. The dark mahogany pieces jarred with the airy puffed walls of the house. Liz picked her way through the maze of chairs and sofas to reach the nearest bathroom, ignoring our strewn possessions in her haste to get Emmy's diaper under control. No sooner had she entered the bathroom than she shrieked. Then we heard the patter of little feet as Pink scurried like a roach out of the bathroom and down the hall. Apparently Nancy had gotten Pink safely home, and she had immediately taken possession of the toilet seat, just as she had back in the house in New Hampshire.

Carol Jeanne and I entered the bathroom to find that Liz had already recovered from the shock of meeting Pink. The bathroom was too small for Carol Jeanne to get close enough to help with anything. But Emmy *was* her child. So she hovered behind Liz, looking attentive as Liz dealt efficiently with the dirty business.

When Emmy was clean, Liz handed the child over to Carol Jeanne. Only then did Liz wash the ooze from her own arms. Miraculously, she had gotten none of the mess on her clothing.

"Well *that's* done," said Liz. "The air smells sweeter already. *I'm* not any bed of roses, I'm afraid, but that's what children are for."

"You're good at this," said Carol Jeanne. "I assume you have children?"

"It's like I told you at the funeral—motherhood is the only talent I have. Not that it's a particular virtue, of course. It's the irresistible hunger of every living creature, to reproduce."

I suppose Carol Jeanne must have had that hunger herself, once, but seeing what Lydia and Emmy turned out to be was no doubt a lasting cure for any reproductive hunger that might pop up in her these days.

"And of every species," added Carol Jeanne. "Sometimes I think the reproductive drive in individual creatures is merely an expression of the species' overall hunger to fill every available space. In which case individuality is merely an accident. Nature doesn't care about individuals."

"Ah, but nature cares whether *we* care," said Liz, "since our children would never survive to adulthood if we didn't. That's what the rules of nature are like, I guess. Even if it doesn't taste good, you bite down hard."

"Bite down?"

"On the apple, Eve. On the apple." Suddenly Liz laughed in embarrassment. "But this is so silly of me, standing here prattling about nature with the one person in all the world who understands nature best!"

"Maybe you understand more, because you think you know less," said Carol Jeanne. I knew that Carol Jeanne did not believe this for a moment, but apparently she liked Liz, or was at least grateful for her help, and so she took a bit of thought to making Liz feel more at ease with her. No doubt Carol Jeanne was grateful just to have someone in Mayflower that she could stand to talk to at all. The other women we had any kind of acquaintance with—Penelope, Dolores, and the dead Odie Lee—were monstrous, and life in Mayflower was beginning to resemble the fifth ring of the Inferno. So if Carol Jeanne flattered Liz a little, who could blame her?

"I understand children, and that's all," said Liz. "Warren's a good orthopedist, but he isn't good enough to have gotten us here if we didn't have bright and therefore desirable children. *You* remember the Compact. Only people who have had at least one child and are still capable of having more can come here, and preference is given to people whose older children test high. Warren and I make good babies, and his skill was certainly *useful*, so here we are."

I caught a glimpse out the window of Mamie bustling up the street. I chattered and pointed, and Carol Jeanne looked out in time to see Mamie stop, give the house a once-over, and frown. Liz followed Carol Jeanne's line of sight and smiled inscrutably.

"There *are* exceptions to the rules about child-bearing age, of course, like your parents."

"My in-laws," said Carol Jeanne.

"Some people were important enough to the success of this project that the rules were bent just a little for them." Liz smiled. "Nobody minds. We would have been glad to have *you* even if your witness was an elephant and you had had a hysterectomy and you brought *four* old people along with you. Your being here means that *our* children will have a better chance of survival in the new world."

Yes, well, Liz might feel different after she really got to know Mamie.

Red passed Mamie on the street and a moment later appeared in the doorway, with Lydia in tow. "Is Pink all right?" he asked Carol Jeanne.

"She owns the bathroom already," she said.

Mamie burst through the door and paused, panting like a Saint Bernard as she struggled to catch her breath. She appraised the living quarters in one glance, and as soon as she could breathe well enough to close her mouth she pursed her lips.

"Where are the movers? They can't just *leave* things here. When are they going to finish the job?"

"There aren't any movers on the Ark," Liz said cheerfully. "The folks in Materials Management must have unloaded your things to be nice to our chief gaiologist. Most people just find a big carton in front of their house."

Mamie sniffed. "If they had been *nice*, they would have put things where they belonged instead of *dumping* them here. Where's my room?"

"I don't think that's been decided yet, Mother," said Red. Lydia whimpered and clung to her father's hips. "But I'm glad if Materials Management set up the children's beds. Wherever they are will be good enough for a nap."

To Mamie, though, this clearly meant that if she acted fast, she would get her pick of rooms. Stepping around boxes and over chairs, she made a beeline for the hallway connecting the bedrooms.

"The houses aren't much," said Liz to Red and Carol Jeanne. "But since everybody has the same basic amenities—"

Mamie was already back, scowling. "Clearly the people who arranged this furniture had no understanding of the way we need the house set up," said Mamie. "Can you believe they actually brought your office furniture *here* to the *house*, Carol Jeanne? As if we could afford to spare one of the four bedrooms for an office, when you'll no doubt have a perfectly good one in the . . . Inside? Is that what they call it?"

Liz smiled cheerfully. "This is the largest house available on the

Ark. It's supposed to be reserved for families with more than six children. You have two couples and two daughters. Normally that would mean three bedrooms, so I expect that Carol Jeanne here is like the chief administrator and has the extra bedroom specifically so she can work at home, too."

"*You don't understand.*" Mamie fixed a withering gaze on Liz. "I don't share a bedroom. I never have. Do they expect Stef to sleep in the kitchen?"

"I think they expect him to share a room with you," said Liz, clearly amused. I liked the way she stood up to Mamie. If only someone in the family would ever do it as well.

"Stef makes *noises* in his sleep," said Mamie icily.

"Well, your domestic arrangements are your affair," said Liz. "But my understanding of the rules here is that if you aren't using the fourth bedroom as an office for the chief gaiologist, then you'll be reassigned to a three-bedroom house. Two couples, two children, three bedrooms." Liz smiled benignly at Mamie. "I understand your problem, though, Mamie, and I think you can resolve easily enough. They have excellent sleeping aids in the pharmacy. Including earplugs, gentle soporifics, and white-noise generators. Though I think you'll find that the air pump puts out plenty of white noise all by itself."

"No doubt the monkey will get to sleep in the office," said Mamie, glaring at me. "*It* will have a bedroom all to itself."

"If Lovelock sleeps in the office," said Carol Jeanne, "so will Pink. Pink makes noises in her sleep, too."

I was quite sure I was the only one who heard Stef murmur, "So does Mamie."

I loved it when I heard stirrings of rebellion in the poor hammered man. I didn't understand yet why I had so much sympathy for him, but I delighted in his occasional snide remarks, even if they were never loud enough to hear.

"I think it's time for me to head on home," Liz said. "You're tired and you need time to get settled in. I can't believe you were so conscientious that you actually came to the funeral. Nobody expected you to come, but everyone I talked to was impressed that you did."

So . . . nobody expected us to come. I could feel Carol Jeanne seethe. It was a good thing that Mayor Penelope Frizzle was not present. Carol Jeanne had a tendency to blurt out very angry remarks when she found she had been lied to.

"We wanted to be part of the community from the start," said Red. But I could see that he was angry, too.

"Well, you don't need company now, when it's naptime," said Liz. "My house is two doors to the right of the church, if you want anything. Look for me in the directory under Fisher. Warren and Liz Fisher." With a cheerful wave she disappeared.

"Let's hold a public hanging," said Carol Jeanne. "If there's a rope strong enough to hold our beloved mayor."

"No, Penelope was right, even if she was a bit manipulative," said Red. "It was a good thing for us to show up, even if it was hard on the kids."

"It was hard on me, too," said Carol Jeanne.

"Well, I think it was a lovely thing," said Mamie, following her pattern of trying to look virtuous whenever she could do so at Carol Jeanne's expense. "I wish I could have known that lovely woman. The whole funeral service was so lovely. I hope I can have such a lovely funeral."

If only I could have spoken.

"I want a *lovely* nap," said Stef. "I'm afraid it will be noisy, though."

"Yes, it's all fine for you," said Mamie. "You can joke about it because you never hear the racket you make. Besides—you all know I abhor clutter. If we don't put the furniture in place, I can't *possibly* sleep."

"Do what you like, Mamie," said Carol Jeanne. "The rest of us are going to bed." She carried Emmy into the room where the children's beds had been set up. Red hefted Lydia into his arms and carried her in afterward. I saw Stef bringing up the rear, leaving Mamie alone in the front room.

Beds and linens were not part of the furniture allotment we had brought with us. Instead, standard-issue inflatable mattresses lay on the floor, covered with sheets that had been washed so often that the floral pattern was faded to the point of near-invisibility. It took only moments to get the girls undressed and tucked into bed, and they were asleep immediately, almost a miracle in itself. Then Carol

Jeanne headed straight for a bedroom that had a large enough bed for her and Red to share, and I scrambled around the room, identifying the packing boxes and scratching on the one that had Carol Jeanne's nightgowns. But she didn't hear me. She, too, had fallen asleep at once, wearing her street clothes.

Red was not so lucky. Ever the dutiful son, he went into the front room and, with Mamie directing thoughtfully, he moved furniture back and forth until she was satisfied. I heard them going at it as I prowled the rest of the house.

Pink was asleep in the office, right on Carol Jeanne's chair, of course. I was tired myself, but I couldn't pass up the chance to accomplish a few things in privacy. I found the box with the computer equipment, opened it, and pulled out the cable that I used to link my own i/o port with the computer. Then I found the little electronic trinket that I had slipped into the box back in New Hampshire, when Red wasn't looking. It was an adapter for the computer end of the cable, turning it into another witness connection. I plugged myself into the cable and slipped the other end into the port on the back of Pink's neck. I'm deft and Pink is sluggish, so she didn't wake up. I activated the useful little snoop program that I had downloaded from one of the computers in the Witness Training Center back when I was a mere lad, and perused Pink's memories.

Poor thing. She'd had a miserable, humiliating trip from the time she left Earth. People kept treating her like an animal. And she didn't even get to pee all over them first.

But I was looking for something else. Sure enough, Nancy had got Pink to the house while the workers were still carrying in the furniture. And even though Pink was too stupid to know the implications of what she was seeing, there was one little bit of business that caught my eye. Pink had been dozing in the office when she opened one eye to watch one of the movers open up Carol Jeanne's computer and quickly replace one of the control chips with a larger chip that had a tiny antenna on it. Apparently someone wanted to be able to monitor all of Carol Jeanne's computer activity.

It took me only half an hour to open up the computer, figure out what the chip was doing, sever two of the pins that connected it to the motherboard, and connect them together with a short length of wire I cannibalized from elsewhere in the computer. Now nothing would be routed through their little chip unless I made the computer send it there.

Then I wrote a small program to ride on top of the operating system and feed scrambled keystroke and data information to the parasite chip. It would monitor computer activity, all right—but it would give them no readable information about the content of Carol Jeanne's activity.

With that job finished, I had to figure out who was doing the spying and make a guess at why. I used the computer to access the Ark photo directory. It took a while, since I had no idea of the name of the man who had done the doctoring job on Carol Jeanne's computer, and he wasn't an employee of Materials Management. That in itself was no surprise—Materials Management had a couple of administrators and then relied on duty-hours "volunteers" to do the actual labor. But it meant that I had to look at picture after picture after picture until I found him. Fortunately, I have excellent powers of recognition and I was able to cycle through the directory far faster than any human could have done.

The chip doctor was a man named Pavlos Koundouriotes. His official job title was Assistant to the Director of Physical Fitness Training. That was the department that ran the mandatory exercise program. The whole department was probably a front for the secret police—it would give them a cover and explain why they worked so hard to remain stronger and faster than anybody else. Officially, discipline was handled in each village by two elected constables. But of course the administrator would have to have his own police to watch out for signs of trouble. In a place like the Ark, with so many ethnic groups mixed together, it would be absurd to trust in good will and volunteer constables to keep the peace. Resentments were bound to grow here and there; there would be incidents. The chief administrator had to have somebody keeping watch for plots and troublemakers.

So there was a good chance that the little broadcast chip was not directed against Carol Jeanne in particular, but rather was a routine precaution taken with all the privately owned computers on the Ark. If that was the case, then there was no chance that they would have time to monitor everything that was done on every computer on the Ark. But they might have a program that scanned all

the computers they were monitoring to find anomalous patterns—
and if Carol Jeanne's computer seemed to be putting out completely
random keystrokes and datafiles, that might call attention to itself.

So I went back into the little program I had written and revised
it. Now, instead of randomizing keystrokes and datafiles, it would
cause the parasite chip to capture and broadcast excerpts from
Carol Jeanne's published works. It would look like language, and
probably wouldn't flag the alarms in the monitoring program. Until
and unless someone specifically looked into Carol Jeanne's computer activity, she would have privacy.

In the meantime, I'd check the computer every day for the first
week to see if my doctoring of their parasite chip had been discovered and tampered with. If the first week was OK, then I'd only
check once a week thereafter.

Why did I do this? At the time it couldn't have occurred to me
that I could have any motive but Carol Jeanne's protection. Yet now
I wonder if perhaps I already had an unconscious understanding
that sometime in the future my own survival would depend on my
being able to use Carol Jeanne's computer without anyone else
knowing what I was doing. There was no earthly reason why Carol
Jeanne would ever need to protect herself from the chief administrator's snoops. The whole expedition depended on her ability to
understand the biosystems of the new planet and find a way to fit
human society into it without destroying anything crucial. The security forces would do anything to protect her and nothing to interfere with her. *She* would never need the privacy I had created for
her.

But *I* would.

I didn't know that then. I didn't know anything. And yet I must
have known it all. There are depths to me that no one has glimpsed,
not even me.

"What is that monkey doing?" demanded Mamie from the doorway. Apparently the furniture had finally been set up to her satisfaction.

"He's doing a memory dump," said Red.

She whispered to him, "I have always hated the thought of that
thing snooping through the house when *we're* all asleep. Sneaky,
prying little dwarf. It has such tiny *hands*."

Did she think I couldn't hear her, just because she was talking so softly?

"He's doing his job," said Red. "Even for an enhanced capuchin, he's unusually conscientious. One of the best they ever produced. It was quite a feather in Carol Jeanne's cap when Lovelock was assigned to her."

"It keeps touching her," said Mamie, her voice getting nasty. "Very possessively. Like a lover."

Red said nothing.

"Like an obscene, filthy, dwarfish, black, mute, vile, satanic lover," said Mamie.

"Monkeys groom each other," said Red.

"And pigs rut," said Mamie. "But I don't see Pink doing that with *you*."

"Mother."

"If I were a man I wouldn't tolerate that little lucifer touching my wife."

Lucifer. Light-bringer. A term for an old-fashioned match. What an apt choice of epithet, O thou aging bitch, thought I.

"Mother," said Red again. "His hearing is very good. He probably hears everything you're saying."

"That's fine with me," said Mamie.

"And everything he hears, he tells to Carol Jeanne."

"Then maybe when he tells her this, she'll realize how disgusting it looks to decent people, to see the way that monkey is with her."

"Lovelock isn't her lover," said Red. "But he watches her all the time. He knows things about her that I'll never know. So yes, I'm jealous, but not the way you're thinking. I'm jealous because I can never love and understand my wife as well as her witness can."

Mamie chuckled grimly. "Since men never understand women in the first place, I'm not surprised."

"Yes, Mother."

I could hear the resentment in his voice. She must have said things like this to him all his life, and he didn't like it—but he also knew enough not to argue with her.

"Men are so cocksure of themselves, but they always run rough-shod over women's tender feelings," said Mamie. "Your father has never had a moment's compassion for me. And you're hardly any better."

"I'm sorry you feel that way, Mother." Another ritual phrase.

"I don't mind," said Mamie. "It's a woman's lot in life. We work and serve our men, and in return we get more and more demands and no understanding."

He said nothing.

"You always liked her hair long," said Mamie, resuming the attack on Carol Jeanne. "But she cut it for the monkey."

"She cut it because Lovelock kept getting his hands tangled in it when he groomed her."

"The monkey is more important in her life than you are, Red. You pretend not to mind, but I know it bothers you."

"Go to bed, Mother." I heard him walk away from her and go into Carol Jeanne's room.

Immediately I disconnected from the computer and leapt straight toward Mamie, who was still standing in the door. She gave a little screech and backed out into the hall. I ignored her and headed on into Carol Jeanne's bedroom, where Red was just sliding his shoes off.

Behind me I could hear Mamie muttering—loudly enough that I suspected Red could hear her perfectly well. "It just goes to show you that certain kinds of people are not that far removed from the jungle."

I slept then, because I was at least as exhausted as anybody else. And I dreamed. I'm sure that my dream was triggered by what Liz had said to Carol Jeanne, about every creature having a hunger to reproduce. I dreamed of myself as a parent, but absurdly enough I saw myself as a *human* parent, with a smooth stupid hairless baby who couldn't even hold on to my fur. And the baby in my dream was large, so that I couldn't pick him up, but had to drag him along the ground. And when I climbed a tree and jumped from one branch to another, the baby was so heavy that together we dropped like an overripe fruit; the baby splatted horribly on the concrete floor when we landed. I was surprised that there was concrete in the jungle, but when I looked around it wasn't a jungle anymore after all, it was a cage, with humans all around me, looking disgusted at the oozing mess that had been my baby. Only now it wasn't a human baby, it was a little capuchin, and its skull had split open in the fall and it was dead. I felt a terrible grief well up inside me and I kept yanking at the dead baby's arm, trying to get it to wake up. Finally the thought came to me: This is a really terrible dream, and I really ought to wake up and end it. And so I did.

I was trembling. It had seemed so real. I lay there in my temporary nest among the stacked-up boxes, thinking, What will my child be? Enhanced like me, or simply an ordinary stupid capuchin? How many of the genetic changes they had introduced in me were actually present in my gametes, to be passed on to my children? Did any part of what I am depend on specific *in utero* treatments that caused me to overdevelop in certain ways? I would have to look into this before I sired a child.

And then I came fully awake and realized the absurdity of what I was thinking. A child? What was I thinking of? I was a witness. There was no room in my life to have a child.

No room in my life. But why not? Didn't every creature have a hunger to reproduce? Even if it *was* only an expression of the species' will to fill all available space.

Only what *was* my species? I was no monkey, not anymore. As far as I knew, I was one of a kind. And as for having a family, Carol Jeanne was my family. Carol Jeanne is all I need, I said to myself, over and over. But instead of the happiness that normally filled me at the thought of belonging to her, I was overcome for several minutes by an ineffable sadness. I did not understand what was happening to me, but I knew that it would not make me happy, and I wanted it to go away. And, that time, it did.

Dear stupid diary,
Peter and I met a monkey at the funeral. It's a witness and it was very cute and very smart. Peter says it's nasty because its little weenie is hanging right out in front of everybody but that's because all he thinks about is weenies right now except when he thinks about breasts. I think it's a great monkey and I'm going to make friends with it. Nancy got to go in their house to take

the man's witness there, which is a pig. Next time Nancy tends us I'm going to get her to tell me all about their house. She's the chief gaiologist and the most brilliant person in the Ark. I read about monkeys in the encyclopedia as soon as I got home from the funeral and I wonder if this one throws turds and masturbates all the time like those monkeys we saw in the zoo in San Francisco or if witness monkeys are more like people. I'm going to find out all about him and be his friend and Peter won't know anything about him or be his friend or anything. I wonder what his name is.

We arrived in Mayflower on a Sixday. That meant Carol Jeanne would only have Sevenday at work before having her first community workday, which in our case was Eightday, and then Nineday was our household Freeday. So Carol Jeanne would have only a single day among civilized scientists at work before she had to spend two days in a row in the dreary village of Mayflower.

As Sevenday dawned, Carol Jeanne sprang out of bed and fixed generic cold cereal from the cupboard for the few family members who were awake to eat it. Then, clutching a map that had been left us by an anonymous benefactor, she and I escaped the house.

The design of the Ark didn't allow for penthouse offices. Everything looked alike, contributing to the egalitarian atmosphere. Carol Jeanne's lab and office suite were no more impressive than those of any of the other scientists aboard the Ark. And for once, Carol Jeanne was treated like a scientist instead of a celebrity. After brief hellos, the other scientists returned to their work as quickly as they could. They knew that they would have plenty of time to talk to Carol Jeanne when their work brought them together. But it was their work they loved, and *her* work they admired her for, and so why not get more of it done? Besides, the rest of them had been working together for months. They had developed their own routines, and Carol Jeanne's arrival to take the reins would not cause a disruption in their work habits unless she insisted on it. Which was not her style.

Carol Jeanne let herself in at her office door—which *had* a lock in the form of an I.D. panel—and inspected the sterile furniture inside. Her office library and paper files had been moved here, just as the furniture in our house had been transported. But some moron had tried to *unpack* Carol Jeanne's important books and papers, strewing them everywhere, and now it would take her days to put things back in order. Or—and this was pure paranoia on my part—someone had examined all the papers, perhaps had even photographed and inventoried them.

"What a *mess*, Lovelock," she said angrily. "Why couldn't they have just left everything in the boxes? Stupid. Well, help me restore my files to their proper order—you'll remember it better than I will."

Before we could get well started, someone knocked on the door and then entered immediately, without waiting for Carol Jeanne's permission. He was short and square and brown. Carol Jeanne wasn't a tall woman, but she was several centimeters taller than *he* was. Sitting on her shoulder, I could see that his black hair was thinning on top. I could tell he was a vain man: he wore a mustache, a feature whose only functions are to stroke the vanity of the wearer and to catch little droplets of anything he drinks. And his teeth were so white that he could probably flash messages for kilometers using the light reflected off them. But there was a joy in his face and an ebullience in his step and mannerisms that I've seen in few humans. I knew at once that he would either be very exciting to have around or else an unbearable bore. Everything depended on whether he was intelligent along with being so happy. In my experience, happiness and intelligence didn't come together in the same people very often.

On *his* shoulder was an apricot-colored cockatoo, his witness. A cockatoo was a good choice for a witness, I soon learned—as good in his own way as a monkey. His claws weren't as flexible as my hands, of course, but he was dexterous enough to be able to operate a simplified computer quite rapidly. And he had one talent that I would have given up a thumb for: power of speech. His enhanced voice was birdlike, of course, but he was no imitative parrot. He spoke as intelligently as I would have if I had been able to talk. I envied him; at the same time, I liked him. Equally important, I liked a man who was practical enough to choose such a useful witness.

The stranger carried a coconut in his left hand and a machete in his right. Bowing low, he set the coconut on the floor of Carol Jeanne's office and, before she could protest, he sliced the coconut in half with a deft stroke of the machete. One coconut half landed upside-down, and he wiped up spilled milk with a handkerchief he produced from his pocket. An errant shard had flown across the room, and the cockatoo took flight to retrieve it. He picked it up off a desk with one claw, balancing on the other as he pulled coconut meat from the shell with his beak.

The other coconut half remained upright and full of milk. The stranger held out that half to Carol Jeanne, who accepted the offering in bafflement.

"What is *this*?"

"This is the ceremony of the coconut—my means of welcoming you here. I am Neeraj Bhushan, chief xenobiologist."

"Yes, I know your work. I didn't realize that you also had a thing with machetes and coconuts."

He laughed lightly, as if her words had been a joke instead of a jab. "Back in India I would have thrown the coconut to the floor to break it. Here the coconut only bounces. Welcome to the Ark."

Carol Jeanne didn't return his smile. She glared at him for a moment before setting the coconut half on her desk. "I don't *like* coconut," she said. She liked it well enough. She was lying to show her displeasure.

He apparently was oblivious to complaint. "No matter. Ramanujan will eat it. The welcome is the important thing. I trust you had a safe journey."

"I'm *here*. Anything that goes seriously wrong in space kills you."

"So I see." He reached up and caught my eye, and his smile widened. He bowed his head in greeting to me before returning his attention to Carol Jeanne. "A witness with hands. I was so torn, choosing between a witness with a voice and one with hands. Does he find his speechlessness an inconvenience?"

He moved his fingers in an incomprehensible mishmash of signs that were directed at me. I automatically recorded his gestures; later, when I looked up tables of sign language, I was able to interpret them. "Hello, friend," his hands said. "I will enjoy working side by side with you."

Neeraj was the first human being who treated me as an equal, but because I had not been taught Ameslan, I didn't recognize the kindness that he offered. Instead I extended my hands, palms up, in the universal human gesture that means "I don't understand you." That is, when it doesn't mean "I'm stupider than you think."

"I don't use sign language with him," Carol Jeanne explained. There was a touch of impatience in her voice. "He understands everything I say, and he can write up his reports and point things out on the computer. If he could speak, he'd be chattering to me all the time and I'd have to keep looking at him to understand what he was saying and then I couldn't be doing anything else, could I?"

I had never heard her explain this before. I had been kept from learning sign language because I might talk too much? Well, pardon me. The more I thought about it, the more it bothered me that she felt that way. Didn't it occur to her that perhaps *I* might want to be able to speak and have someone understand me?

"I know," said Neeraj. "At the training center they discourage new owners from trying to work with sign language. But I thought all their reasoning was specious, didn't you? I suspect that the real reason they don't want the witnesses with hands using sign language is because then there would be no way to distinguish them from mute humans. And if they are indistinguishable from mute humans, how are we entitled to treat them as slaves?"

I felt the stiffening of the muscles in her shoulders. Carol Jeanne was angry. But why, I wondered? He hadn't said anything against *her*. Besides, I wasn't her slave. I was her friend.

A friend that she had decided to deprive of speech because it might annoy her. Suddenly *I* was angry, and to a degree that took me by surprise.

"That is absurd," said Carol Jeanne. "Enhanced animals are hardly slaves. Whatever extra capabilities they have been given, they were given in order to serve particular functions. Like shoeing a horse to make it a better beast of burden."

Neeraj smiled and nodded. "Yes, yes, I am aware of this line of reasoning, and it has many constituents."

I might have detected the glint of irony in his voice, had I not been fixated on the phrase "beast of burden."

"Besides, Neeraj," said Carol Jeanne, "I never had time to learn Ameslan. *Your* witness speaks aloud, so I can't imagine why *you* bothered to learn it."

"I had a deaf colleague for several years, and I found that she had more interesting things to say than any of the people I knew who had voices. So I was well rewarded for learning to sign. Perhaps your witness—what is his name?"

"Lovelock."

"Ah—yours is named after a scientist and mine after a mathematician. Perhaps your Lovelock would be a charming conversationalist as well."

She laughed. "He throws dung, Neeraj. That is eloquent enough that speech would be gilding the lily."

For a moment I was overwhelmed by rage. I leapt from her shoulder to the top of a file cabinet, and at once felt myself squeezing out a small turd. I caught it in my hand, and only then did I realize that my anger was directed at Carol Jeanne. At my friend.

No, my master.

The person I loved best in all the world.

My owner.

It didn't matter which she was. I couldn't possibly throw a turd at her. My conditioning was against it, for one thing. And I loved her desperately and was deeply ashamed of having let myself even contemplate doing such a derisive, offensive thing to her.

And yet my anger toward her was unabated.

So I jumped from the file cabinet down onto her desk, and gently laid the turd into the middle of the pool of milk in the middle of her coconut half.

"Lovelock, that was disgusting," she said. "Now no one can drink the milk."

"Such a pity he can't talk," said Neeraj.

I looked up at him. For a moment, Neeraj's merry face looked sad. Then he smiled at me. "I will communicate with you, Lovelock, according to your custom. But someday I would love to understand your sense of humor. I have a feeling that the turd in the coconut is a punchline of some kind, and I regret that I didn't get the joke."

I liked Neeraj already. I stared into Carol Jeanne's face, hoping she'd download the scene later and see exactly how much Neeraj's kindly countenance contrasted with her flared nostrils and downturned mouth. To emphasize the difference, I stood underneath her giant face and looked up into it. It was a horrible perspective. Carol Jeanne would hate seeing the still of it on her computer screen.

Finally she managed to force a smile at Neeraj. "It was awfully nice of you to greet me, but I do have to get to work. Somebody has made a mess of this office, I'm afraid."

"So I see. Would you join me for lunch?"

Not in *this* lifetime, I was quite sure. After all, Neeraj had just proven himself to be much more compassionate toward Carol Jeanne's witness than Carol Jeanne was herself. Not someone she would enjoy spending time with, I was sure.

"Not today," she said. "I really do have to work. Thank you for welcoming me." Carol Jeanne escorted him to the door and shut it firmly behind him.

"What a pompous little man!" she said when the two of us were alone.

I glared at her.

Which was fine, since she was glaring at me, too. "Lovelock, you're supposed to be on my side. That business with the coconut milk made it look as though you agreed with his absurd remarks about witnesses."

I bobbed my head up and down in agreement. But she was already sinking into her chair, not looking at me. For the first time I realized how often she didn't even bother to look at me to see my reaction to what she said. I saw how very little she cared about understanding my thoughts and feelings.

Which was as it should be. I was a mere witness; *she* was the genius whose works and words needed to be so constantly recorded. Why should she look at me, to try to understand my wordless words?

Carol Jeanne laughed, oblivious to what I was thinking. "Can you believe a scientist owning a *machete*? And there's coconut milk splashed *everywhere*. And he's head xeno; I'll have to have meetings with him all the time. Here I thought that all the horrible people were in Mayflower village. I'll have to barricade myself in here, or I'll end up grabbing his machete to use it on him."

How could she be so wrong about Neeraj, to think this man was anything like Penelope?

"You organize the files, Lovelock, and I'll see if the staff has provided me with the reports I asked for before I left Earth. I think I'll schedule a staff meeting tomorrow, and tell them where to go from here."

I scrambled over to the computer keyboard and typed: "Not tomorrow. Workday."

"I forgot. I have a Workday, then a Freeday. Two miserable days trapped in Mayflower doing insignificant things with annoying people, when I have work waiting for me here."

"Liz," I typed. "You liked *her*."

"There's only one Liz. Everyone else is a Penelope or a Dolores or an Odie Lee."

"Odie Lee's dead," I pointed out.

"Her husband isn't—and I'm not so sure Odie Lee is, either. Those holo images could play for years. By the time we land on Genesis, there's going to be a whole generation of people who worship Odie Lee. Probably pray to her and have communion by eating fudge made according to her recipe."

I rolled onto my back and pantomimed laughing uproariously. It was just like old times. I was her perfect audience. Except that even as I laughed for her, I felt a sick remnant of my anger in the pit of my stomach.

She laughed at my laughter, but then sighed. "It's going to be a long trip," she said, but she didn't look at me for a response. She was already immersed in her role as chief gaiologist and ruler of everything within her reach.

After that we passed the rest of the day wrapped in our own thoughts. Most of the time was spent organizing her office. Carol Jeanne pursued this activity so single-mindedly that she never left her suite—not even to find food for us. She ignored her rumbling stomach and my plaintive looks, unwilling to venture into the hall. Could she really fear Neeraj so much?

But just because she didn't want to leave didn't mean I was trapped there. I took a break early in the afternoon and carried the coconut half to the toilet, where I poured out the milk and the turd. Then I rinsed the meat of the coconut and ate it ravenously. It was delicious—*real* food, not that miserable Purina Monkey Chow that was dear lazy Carol Jeanne's idea of a perfect diet for me, mostly because it could be poured into a bowl. Neeraj must have used part of his weight allotment to bring coconuts with him from Earth, and it really was generous of him to share. If Carol Jeanne wanted to pretend she didn't like it, *I* didn't have to go along.

When I was full there was still plenty of coconut left. I brought it back to her office and put it at the back of one of the more lightly loaded file drawers. Carol Jeanne looked up only long enough to say, "Don't forget you put that there. I don't want it to rot in there and start to smell."

But I wouldn't forget. I'd eat it all, and not share any of it with her.

The day ended slowly. Carol Jeanne stayed after the others went home, only leaving when the voices in the hallway had died. I didn't know whether she was avoiding seeing any of them or was simply reluctant to return to Mayflower.

We took the tube to Mayflower. People looked at us discreetly, staring when they thought we wouldn't notice, but of course I noticed. They'd be used to us soon enough.

When we arrived home, we were late enough that our welcome was less than cheerful. Red must have got back from work early—how many clients could he have on his first day in the therapy biz here on the Ark?—and was on the larger sofa, reading *The Little Engine That Could* to Emmy and Lydia. The girls barely looked up when Carol Jeanne opened the door, and Red didn't glance away from the pages of the book to smile at his wife. Not that he needed to look at the book. The girls had made him read it so often that he must have had the wretched book memorized by now.

Red might have been silent about Carol Jeanne's late return from her first day at work, but Mamie was not shy about speaking up. "Here's the queen of the Ark," she said, "back off the throne to visit the peons. How *good* of you to come."

But Carol Jeanne did not rise to the bait, except jokingly. "It *was* good of me, wasn't it? Tell me—if I'm the queen, can I sit here and let you wait on me?"

"I *did* wait on you all day," Mamie said. "I fed your children and dressed them and *baby*-sat them, too, because their mother left them without anyone to care for them."

"We'll figure out the day-care situation soon," Carol Jeanne said.

"And in the meantime I left them with two adults. They were hardly unsupervised."

"Oh, of course," said Mamie. "Why don't we just put the children in cold storage during the day?"

"In case anyone cares," said Red, "I found out that the preschool is over at the church. They can start on Tenday."

"I *hate* preschool," Lydia said. Her voice was as cold as Mamie's. "I'm *not* going back."

"Your daughter was terrorized at that preschool you abandoned her at back in New Hampshire," Mamie said. As if Red hadn't also put her there.

"Terrorized isn't what I'd call it," Stef said. He was the only one in the room who had smiled when Carol Jeanne entered the house. Now his contradiction earned a glare from Mamie.

"They locked her in a closet, didn't they?" said Mamie.

"It was an office, not a closet," said Stef, "and Lydia *had* hit a kid over the head with a chair."

"It wasn't my fault!" cried Lydia. "I *hate* you, Grandpa!"

Finally Red spoke up. "Lydia! Go to your room!"

Wailing, Lydia staggered off to her room to suffer in melodramatic solitude. Emmy, inspired by Lydia, began to scream at twice the volume. Red stood up to carry her out of the room, but paused long enough to speak coldly to his wife. "It would have been nice if you could have managed to come home on time on your first day."

"I had a lot to do," said Carol Jeanne, equally coldly.

"They've managed for all these months without you," said Red. "But I'm sure that everything was on the verge of collapse until you arrived." He stalked out of the room, carrying Emmy's siren howls with him.

In the relative quiet, Mamie remembered Stef's earlier offense. "Someday perhaps I'll understand your sadistic streak, Stef, but today I don't."

Stef sighed.

"Bringing up that business with the chair, when you *know* that Lydia was provoked by that horrible child."

"There were two adult witnesses who said that the boy was playing quietly by himself and hadn't done anything to Lydia."

"Maybe not that *day*," said Mamie. "But you're always so eager to blame women for everything. It could *never* be the *boy's* fault, oh, no, it's always the female who wasn't *patient* enough, while the boy is always perfectly innocent."

Stef got up and walked out of the room.

"That's right, Stef, walk away from the truth, walk away from everything. There are people in this world who stay and face things, and people who are always running away from the truth or staying late at work while other people take care of their families for them."

Now that Mamie had come back to listing Carol Jeanne's offenses, it was time for us to leave. We heard her still grumbling behind us as we walked down the hall.

Just another wonderful night in the Todd household.

Only this time, instead of automatically thinking how obnoxious Red and Mamie were, I found myself thinking that Carol Jeanne could easily have gone home on time, since there wasn't a thing she was doing those last ninety minutes that couldn't have been done in a week or a month. There was no commuter traffic to avoid here on the Ark, either. To Red it had to look as though she were deliberately staying away from him. And, if he thought so, maybe he was right.

Well, why *should* she hurry home? She was a genius, living in a household full of inferiors. Except me. I was the only one in the household who understood her work and her needs and her very *soul*.

When we walked into her office, Pink was asleep on her chair again. Carol Jeanne sighed, but I knew my duty. I jumped down to the chair, bouncing it enough that Pink opened one eye. Seeing me, and knowing me as she did, she immediately stood up and started to shamble off the chair—but not fast enough to avoid me. I rammed my longest finger right up her nostril. She *hated* it when I did that. With a squeal, she bounded from the chair and out of the office.

While I got to work, cabling myself to the computer and dumping the day's observations into memory, Carol Jeanne sat back in her chair with a sigh. "Oh, Lovelock," she said. "Lovelock Lovelock Lovelock."

Apparently my name had become her mantra of the moment.

"Two days before I can go back to work. I've got to get myself out of this Workday business. Look it up and see if there's any way I can do that."

Yes, I understood her needs. But if *I* ever had a child, I wouldn't leave it for my spouse to raise, or total strangers.

If I ever had a child. Where did *that* idea come from? That stupid remark of Liz's yesterday?

And to be critical of Carol Jeanne—I had never thought of her so caustically before. What was happening to me?

Bite down hard.

CHAPTER SIX

FREEFALL

My role as Carol Jeanne's witness kept me at her side during her waking hours, but at bedtime she removed me like a pair of shoes. If I had come equipped with an off switch, she would have turned me off when she went to bed at night. Or maybe she wouldn't have bothered. She had no use for me when she was asleep, and therefore it didn't occur to her that I might have a use for myself.

And during those first few days on the Ark, I shared her attitude. Carol Jeanne was my life. When she was asleep, there was nothing for me to do. My own thoughts bored me, unless they had some reference to her. My single-mindedness might have been programmed into me genetically or it might have been a natural consequence of my love for her. The result was the same: I was only alive when I was serving Carol Jeanne.

Or was I? On Earth, I had slept when Carol Jeanne slept. But for some reason on the Ark I could not sleep. I was agitated. I was unhappy. I told myself at the time—I believed it, too—that I was upset because my loss of self-control during weightlessness had caused embarrassment to Carol Jeanne. Null gravity would happen several times during the voyage—just before launch, at changeover, and again when we reached our destination—and I was determined not to lose control of myself. I had to train myself, for Carol Jeanne's sake.

Or so I told myself. But it was never true.

For Carol Jeanne's sake? Why couldn't I have realized that as far as Carol Jeanne and my creators were concerned, I had already *been* trained? Like a computer program, I was supposed to endlessly play out the same activities until the end of my life. After all, ordi-

119

nary monkeys live out the same pattern over and over again, and they're perfectly happy. It didn't occur to them that by juicing up my intellectual abilities, they were also making me hungrier for knowledge and accomplishment. I was no longer a happy jungle monkey, but they refused to know that. No, I was supposed to be content to learn only the data that I acquired in service of Carol Jeanne. I was definitely *not* intended to embark on a program of self-education. After all, I was a tool. In a metaphorical sense, Carol Jeanne had bought a hammer; she had no need for it to learn how to be a saw. So from the start, no matter what I told myself at the time, my night activities were not for her. They were for me.

And there was another reason why I should have realized that my whole enterprise was bogus: There was no chance, after what had happened on the shuttle, that I would be left unrestrained during null gravity. If Carol Jeanne didn't have me strapped down tight, others in authority would see to it for her.

Why didn't that obvious fact enter my mind at the time? Now, thinking back, I can clearly remember how single-minded I was about my plan to train myself to endure weightlessness. Why? Did I already know, at some level of unconsciousness, that I would *not* be restrained during one of the passages through null gravity? Did I realize that this could only happen because I was no longer Carol Jeanne's single-minded servant? Did I already know—perhaps because she compared me to a beast of burden—that I meant nothing to her? Was my loyalty already leaching away?

I must have known all of this. Or why else would I have been so careful to conceal from her what I was doing? Why else would I have refrained from telling her about the parasite chip they put in her computer? Keeping secrets was the beginning of freedom. There was now a place in my own mind that did not belong to Carol Jeanne.

I had always told her everything. That was what I *did*. Telling Carol Jeanne everything was built into my conditioning back at the monkey factory, as the human trainers charmingly referred to the witness training facility.

My conditioning. Maybe that was what I was avoiding, by lying to myself. At that point, if I had consciously realized what I was already planning to do, if I had admitted my rage, my feelings of betrayal, then my conditioning would have kicked in and I would either have suppressed those feelings or gone mad.

(I must consider the possibility that in fact I did go mad. That I am crazy now.)

However I talked myself into it, here is what I did:

I waited until all the lights were out in the house and the whispering had subsided. Then I lingered an additional half hour, until I was sure my human family was unconscious. Only then did I wriggle out of bed and hop to the open window. My training program was under way.

Despite the unfamiliar terrain of the Ark, I had no trouble finding my way at night. The "sun" went to its night setting promptly at 2100 hours, dimming so the humans could sleep, but staying alive enough that people could still get around without extra outdoor lighting. During all our years on the Ark, no one would spend a moment in utter darkness outdoors.

I had already memorized the whole floorplan of the Ark. The sun was supported by two immense tripods, one extending from each of the two flat sides of the cylinder of the Ark. Once we were in flight, one of the tripods would rise from the floor, and the other would hang down from the ceiling, meeting the sun in the middle. But since we were still in solar orbit, with our false gravity coming from spinning the Ark, the future floor and ceiling rose up like canyon walls on either side of the ground. And the three legs of each tripod reached from one of those walls, starting about forty meters from the ground.

In flight, our pseudogravity would come from acceleration and deceleration, and there would be no region of null gravity. But now, with the Ark in spin, the higher you climbed up those canyon walls toward the tripods that held the sun, the less you weighed.

Everyone knew this, but they also knew that attempting to climb up there and fly would be stupid in the extreme, because the moment you had nothing to hold onto, you would drift toward the rim and would have no way of stopping yourself. The air currents had several shifting layers of turbulence, which would throw you arse-over-teakettle—that's why even hang-gliding and parachuting were forbidden. But the worst thing would be landing. When you hit the ground or one of the walls, you would *not* be going at the same speed or even in the same direction as the spin of the Ark. In short, you would hit the ground as if you had thrown yourself from a speeding car, and with no control.

I wasn't going up there to fly. I would end up as a monkeyburger in notime flat.

No, I was going to climb the canyon walls toward the tripod, and then climb a leg of the tripod toward the sun, not so I could fly, but so I could make myself terrified and sick. Greater love hath no primate than this, that he puke up his guts for his master.

(I don't feel insane. Terrified, yes, and lonely, but not insane.)

No place on the Ark was far from one of the side walls, and I reached it soon enough. Behind the wall that would someday be the floor, there was a three-meter space through which the transportation tubes and sewers ran, though of course they would not be used until we were in flight. Behind the other wall, the one that would be the ceiling, ran the ventilation system, and since this wall would never be a floor, it served that function whether we were in orbit or in flight.

If I could have got inside either crawl space, the climb would have been much easier. But those areas were strictly off-limits to all but the qualified maintenance workers, and I had not yet added lock-picking and other such subterfuges to my repertoire of skills. So for me, reaching weightless regions required an outdoor climb on surfaces that weren't designed for climbing.

Which was fine, I thought. I'm a monkey.

What I'm not is a spider, and that's what it would have taken to climb the ceiling. No handholds, nothing. Just air vents here and there, and the nozzles that sprayed rain. There was an access door near the foot of each leg of the tripod, but that was no help to me.

The wall-that-would-be-a-floor was better. It was laced with the drainage pipes. But those pipes were specifically designed *not* to be climbable. After all, they didn't want children plunging to their deaths. I'm a good jumper, but not four meters, not from the ground.

So I didn't jump from the ground. I found a potted tree that was near enough to the wall, climbed it, and took a flying leap. I even remembered to allow for the Coriolis effect. Unfortunately, I didn't remember it until I was already on the ground, breathless and dazed from having slammed into the wall half a meter from where I had intended to end up. But on the second try, I found myself clinging to one of the soil drainage pipes.

I had thought to get up near the sun, but on this first climb I didn't even reach the leg of the tripod. Huge as the Ark is, it's small enough that you don't have to climb far up the wall before losing most of the centrifugal effect of the spin. Well, not so much losing it as having it change. Down on the ground, I couldn't feel the rotation, only the sense of gravity. But up on the wall, I began to get a sense of motion. I also began to feel lighter and lighter. I began to lose my sense of where down was.

For every gram of body weight I shed, I lost an equivalent amount of fearless determination. Panic rose in my gullet, and I found myself baring my teeth in abject fear. Eventually my hold on the drainage pipe gave me absolutely no sense of security: Up didn't feel like up anymore.

I could feel the world spinning around me, and I had no idea where down might be. I could fall in any direction. I screeched in terror. I saw my own tail, floating in the sky above my body. The sight of my tail in a location where it shouldn't have been threw me into a frenzy. I lost my grip, just for a moment, but long enough that I began to slide along the pole. There was still enough centrifugal force to draw me inexorably toward the ground. And soon my drifting turned to skidding down the pipe much faster than I had ascended. Fortunately, this began to restore my sense of down, and I was able to regain enough presence of mind to hold onto the pole so I didn't drift away from the wall. I slowed my fall as much as I could, but when I hit the ground, I was dazed and out of breath.

I lay panting on the grass for several minutes before daring to sit up and scrutinize my person. The friction of the slide down the drainage pipe had rubbed patches of fur from the insides of both my arms. There was a little abrasion on my chin, too. I was stiff and sore all over.

The only thing I could think of was: Carol Jeanne will notice. Carol Jeanne will realize that these injuries happened while she was asleep. But here's how twisted my perceptions were at the time: I thought she would panic at how close I came to dying. I thought she would care. I told myself that the reason I was afraid to let her know how I got these injuries was to keep her from needless worrying about me. I loved her so much that I had to keep her from knowing of my dangerous sacrifices for her sake. Oh what tangled webs we weave.

It was apparent that I couldn't conquer null gravity all at once. I could only subdue weightlessness by degrees, going no higher up the wall until I had achieved mastery of the gravity lower down. But I *would* triumph over weightlessness. Perhaps I was a genetic construct trained to be dependent on Carol Jeanne, but I refused to be tied by terror of natural laws. *I* refused. *I* would not tolerate this limitation on my abilities.

Was it this hunger to improve myself that lifted me from clever beast to anguished person? Was this what you wanted me to do, Gepetto?

If I cleaned myself up, maybe my superficial injuries wouldn't be so noticeable. I went in quietly through the front door of the house—thinking kind thoughts of the designer who had not thought locks were necessary—and bathed in the kitchen sink, sudsing myself with dish soap until my fur was free of blood. Stef was snoring in the living room and Pink huffed her way through little pig dreams under the kitchen table—neither woke up. Good thing I wasn't a burglar. Since I had only abrasions and burns, the fluffiness of my fur after I dried myself served to conceal everything. Only if Carol Jeanne looked closely would she notice anything. And I knew Carol Jeanne well enough to know that she didn't look closely at anything that was not part of her research.

I cleaned up the kitchen, then crawled into bed, exhausted from my nocturnal endeavors. I didn't need as much sleep as a human, but I was accustomed to Carol Jeanne's hours. My body craved slumber, and my wounds needed time to heal.

But I couldn't sleep. My inadequacy tonight on the wall was only the most recent in a series of failures, each of which reinforced my lifelong suspicion that I was indeed inferior to my human companions. Even Mamie handled null gravity with more aplomb than I. After all, it wasn't *she* who spewed fecal matter and urine all over the subbo. Nor was it Mamie who lurched and bumped into things in the low gee environment of the Ark. The children bounded around oafishly, of course, but they did that on Earth. I, who had once been deft and physically sure, was now incapable of even the most modest of athletic achievements.

Carol Jeanne's computer screen bathed the room in bluish light. It was a beacon that finally lured me from my cot. Once again my body had failed me, but my mind was still intact. Even though I couldn't navigate in null gravity—yet—there was a world on the Ark that didn't depend on physical agility. I need only access the computer banks, and nothing on the Ark would be hidden from my view.

The computer was connected to a node of the network that linked all the computers on the Ark. I entered my password and dived into the communal memory banks, skimming the files for interesting information. It never occurred to me that I was looking for something; but my unconscious mind was my guide, and I was attracted only by information that would later become vital to my survival.

That first night I found the entire blueprints of the Ark—much more complete than the cursory layout that was part of the Ark's formal prospectus. It was in a restricted-access region of the network, but I had worked with this networking software before and I knew all the back doors. I downloaded the files into my own memory banks and moved on. If I had thought about it, I would have realized that I now had access to the crawlspaces of the Ark. But at the time I simply thought they were interesting and worth loading into my direct-access digital memory.

But I wasn't done yet. An inventory of the Ark's contents caught my attention. It detailed everything that had been brought aboard the Ark from Earth—right down to the last stick of furniture that Mamie had so carefully chosen to accompany us into space. I was more interested in the communal inventory than I was in personal possessions, however, so I skipped through the files until I found the materials Carol Jeanne and I would need to develop an appropriate new ecological system when we reached our new planet, Genesis. I opened the files of the seed bank and scanned the inventory of dried seeds and frozen embryos.

The quantities were enormous, partly because there was a hefty failure rate in the process of reviving frozen embryos. This was why humans were not frozen—a two-in-five success rate was not acceptable for human beings.

But it was acceptable for capuchin monkeys. I found a cache of fifteen hundred frozen capuchin embryos, never guessing that this was what I had been looking for, that it was the need to know this that had kept me awake. At the time all I felt was a bit of pride that my species-of-origin was valued enough to be included in the new world. There could be an admirable colony of capuchins.

Right then, for just a moment, there flashed into my mind a picture of myself as the alpha male for a troop of monkeys. I pictured myself displaying aggressively at young upstart monkeys and watching them hoot and retreat and finally run from me. It made me laugh silently. And then I imagined myself with the most valued female of the troop when she came into estrus, and . . .

And I found myself trembling with desire.

What I would give to be the alpha male for a group such as that one!

Naturally, my body responded to the desire, and just as naturally I reached down to touch my rather formidable generative organ.

It was as if I had stuck my finger in an electric socket. A sharp pain raced through me, and I found myself on the floor, trembling with fear and horror.

Only then did I remember what they had done to me—to all of us—in the monkey factory. Young capuchin males, as with most monkey species, masturbate whenever they think of it, which is often. But this was disgusting and distracting to humans, and therefore we who would be witnesses, we who would be privileged to consort with the master species, had to be trained not to do such nasty things. The I/O implant they gave me, my connection to the world of digital information, was also my whip. When it recognized that I was doing the Bad Thing, it gave me a dose of what the painword gave me.

The conditioning had been so effective that in all my time with Carol Jeanne I had never once even begun to touch myself, had never even become aroused while awake. And the punishment was so painful and brutal that, in its absence, I had blocked the memory of it out of my mind. Until now, lying on the floor.

They thought of everything, those clever lads and lassies in their lab coats with their bowls of monkey chow and their painwords. I had to be shaped into a socially acceptable little monkey-toy, so sexual pleasures were off limits to me. Stupid brute monkeys in the zoo could dandle their little weenies to their heart's content, but I could not so much as touch mine, even when my master was asleep, even when I was completely alone.

I could never be an alpha male. They hadn't castrated me because a certain amount of aggression in a witness was desirable. They had simply built in a whip to keep me in line.

Weren't they thorough, these people who created me? They didn't miss a trick, did they?

So why wasn't I made immune to the disorientation of null gravity? They were so busy fixing things to keep me from being annoying; why didn't they give me the power to fly in space without panicking?

Because they weren't thinking of what *I* needed, that's why. They were thinking only of the needs of my master, my owner, the object of my undying affection, the *only* love I would be permitted to have in my life.

Be fair, I told myself. They didn't know you'd be going into space.

And then I thought, Why *am* I here in space? Because Carol Jeanne decided to go. She consulted with Red before she made up her mind. She even talked it over with Mamie and Stef and her sister. She and Red discussed the needs of their children, too. But not once in their discussions did Carol Jeanne or Red ever say, "I wonder if the pig and the monkey will be happy there." They worried about whether other people would accept our presence, but it never crossed their minds to wonder if *we* would want to go.

The trainers at the monkey factory never asked us, Would you mind terribly if we took away all possibility of sexual satisfaction? Carol Jeanne never asked me, Would it bother you if I took you away from Earth and carried you off into a place where you will live in terror of null gravity?

They didn't have to ask me. Because they had manufactured me as surely as if I were an armoire. You don't ask the furniture what it wants, you just arrange it in the room and use it till it wears out.

Furniture might be so precious that Mamie, for instance, couldn't imagine living without the familiar pieces. But that doesn't mean the furniture has rights.

Well, just because somebody created you doesn't mean you're not alive. When they make furniture they kill the trees first. But they didn't kill the monkey. I'm still real, no matter how they changed me.

They gave me powers of thought and memory far beyond anything natural evolution would have given me, but that doesn't give them the right to decide the meaning of my life as if I were some *dream*. *I* decide the meaning. If my life is a dream then it's *my* dream, *I'm* the dreamer.

I'm the dreamer, except in the midst of my dream they intrude, they hurt me, they stop me from dreaming of—dreaming of what? Dreaming of the most fundamental urge of all life, to reproduce myself. They have cut me off from the great cycle of life. I am not part of Gaia because I have no power to add my genes to the ongoing story of my species. I *have* no species. I have been stolen from myself. I am the property of someone else, and when they took away my own dreams, they didn't bother to give me any new dreams to take their place. Carol Jeanne has no dreams for me. And I'm not allowed to have any dreams for myself.

Maybe I didn't think of all of this that night. I've had plenty of time since then to brood, to refine my sense of grievance. I can't remember now exactly which thoughts I had that night. But I know this: That was the night, sitting there in front of the computer, thinking of sex, that I realized that I would always be punished for daring to want what all life fundamentally wants, that I had been deprived of the most basic of all rights, the right to reproduce. Even amoebas have the right to copy themselves.

And as soon as I realized how wrong it was, what they'd done to me, a whole lifetime of suppressed resentment flooded through me. For a few moments, I was insane. I was filled with only one thought, one desire, one will: An infinite, inexpressible *no*. I rejected them. I rejected their power over me. And in that madness, I did the one thing that they knew I would never do. I disobeyed them, knowing full well how much pain it would cost me. I touched myself again.

This time the pain was so great that I think I blacked out for a while. I woke up on the floor. But I remembered, and the rage was undiminished. So I did it again. And again. Never has anyone suffered so much agony. But as long as I was conscious, during that long, long night, I refused to obey them. I would rather suffer the pain than to comply with their decision to make a eunuch of me.

It was light when I blinked open my eyes. I was exhausted, as if I hadn't slept at all, as indeed I hardly had. My small injuries stung, but more important was a kind of spiritual numbness, a bitter ennui. My mouth tasted like a metal canister. My limbs trembled when I tried to move them.

I was lying under the desk. In the kitchen I could hear the sounds of breakfast. I didn't bother trying to distinguish words. It was enough to hear the atonal music of the children whining, Mamie stentoriously proclaiming her decisions on this or that, Red murmuring weak-willed responses. Silence from Stef.

And from Carol Jeanne—what?

I heard nothing from her. And suddenly I was filled with panic. Carol Jeanne was gone! She had already left home! My madness last night had kept me awake so late that I overslept and she left without me. Or worse—somehow she knew the evil things I had done and thought, and now she rejected me, she no longer wanted me with her!

I dragged myself out from under the desk. I found several hard pellets and a pool of urine—I really *had* lost control last night. I thought of the raging beast I had been and I was filled with self-loathing. I was unworthy of Carol Jeanne. She deserved a perfect friend, not a self-pitying rebellious jerk-off animal who slept the night in his own wastes.

Pink had wandered into the room during the night; when I slid out from under the desk, she got up, came over, and sniffed with contempt at my feces. I picked one up and made as if to jam it into her nostril. She bared her teeth at me—as if she could ever be quick enough to bite me! Except that maybe today she could—I was shaky. I nearly fell over. I felt as if someone had wrung my body out and left me barely moist.

The housing people had been thoughtful enough to stock the bathroom cabinet with basic cleaning supplies. It took me only a few minutes to wipe up the evidence of my shame on the office floor. It really annoyed me that Pink had a record of the scene, but my guess was that Red wouldn't bother looking at memories of *me*. In his narcissism, he would skip right by until he found himself.

I bathed quickly, this time in the tub instead of the sink. Then I went looking for Carol Jeanne.

She was in the kitchen. She hadn't left after all. She had simply been silent. So I hadn't overslept all that badly.

All my efforts to hide my injuries were in vain. Not that Carol Jeanne would ever have seen them. I simply hadn't counted on Lydia's powers of observation.

"Lovelock has a bobo," she said, pointing at the scrape on my chin.

Carol Jeanne set her breakfast aside and held out her arms to me. Obediently I scampered into her embrace.

"You *are* hurt," she said, puzzled. "Whatever happened to you?"

Rolling my shoulders upward in an elaborate shrug, I jumped from her shoulder to the kitchen counter, and there on the kitchen computer I typed, "I cut myself shaving." Carol Jeanne laughed when she read the words on the monitor. As she laughed I furiously tried to think of some plausible lie, but to my surprise there was no follow-up question. The joke was enough.

This was a sign of respect, I told myself. She recognized my little joke as a request for privacy, and so she didn't ask any further questions.

But even as I insisted to myself on the most generous possible interpretation of her indifference, I knew in the back of my mind that I was lying to myself.

So there *was* some residue from the night before. For now, when the conditioned lies and rationalizations came to mind, I recognized them for what they were. Yes, I still made up the stories that depicted Carol Jeanne as a perfectly loving and caring master. But I no longer believed them, not completely. The doubt was now alive in me, awake in me.

"Lovelock, I need a report on the status of each individual's work," said Carol Jeanne.

An assignment! She still wants me, she still needs me, she still loves me!

But also: What is my injury to her? All that matters is that I can produce the data she needs. Let the slave bleed, as long as he doesn't spill any of it on the printouts.

And this, too: Have I been conditioned to receive her every command with joy? Just as there is an implanted pain response that is triggered by forbidden actions, is there also an implanted pleasure response activated by her orders?

Is there any part of my soul that they have left alone?

Even as I thought this, I scampered to the office and plugged in, filled with excitement and joy at the project she had assigned me. Never mind that I hadn't eaten yet. Never mind that I hadn't slept enough. Never mind that I was still weak and trembled with the memory of pain. I was filled with joy at the chance to serve my mistress, and I hated it.

I scanned the status reports that each of the scientists in her project left on the network at the end of the working day, and organized them into an easy-to-read chart. It was an absurd thing for her to have me do—it would have taken her no more time to call up the status reports herself than it would take her to read my report. She was wasting my time, but what did she care?

In the kitchen I could hear Red saying, "You're not going to be able to spend much time on your work today, Carol Jeanne. This is our Workday, remember."

Carol Jeanne muttered her answer, but I was so keyed in on her voice that I heard her clearly. "Waste of my time."

Oh, well excuse *us*, O Mistress of the Universe.

I trembled at the audacity of my own thought. I dared to criticize her?

Yes, and in doing so I sounded just as judgmental and petulant as Mamie.

So what? Carol Jeanne sounded like Mamie, too, thinking that she should be exempt from Workday because she was so special.

Red seemed to see the similarity, too, for he was talking to Carol Jeanne in his "Now, Mother," voice. "It's important for the overall stability of the colony that we have these significant rituals of egalitarianism."

Carol Jeanne wasn't in the mood to be patronized. "I'm aware of that, Red, and I agree. I just think they might have let me have the first week off, to get up to speed in the project."

"Maybe they think you have years and years ahead of you, so there's no rush now. While the Workday projects won't wait."

I finished my report and tagged it for Carol Jeanne's work-waiting queue, with first priority. Anything I tagged for her was automatically first priority. Thinking of that, I was filled with pride.

Was that, too, a product of my conditioning? Was any part of myself still natural and unprogrammed?

This was getting to me, I could see that. My judgment was being distorted, badly. Carol Jeanne did *not* sound like Mamie, not even for a moment. It really *was* true that her project was of vital importance, and it was absurd for her not to be exempted from Workday this week so she could move in and establish herself in the scientific community on board the Ark. Just because I now understood my true relationship to Carol Jeanne did not mean that she was always wrong. She really *was* a genius. And there really *were* thousands of young scientists who would give anything to be able to work with her as closely as I did.

Anything? Would they give up any hope of sex or reproduction? Or would they think that was a monstrous price to pay? They would condemn even the idea of it. No human being is worth such a sacrifice.

Unless you can get a dumb monkey to do it.

In exactly what sense was I smarter than Pink?

My job was done. And when I got back into the kitchen, so was breakfast. Except for a miserable little bowl of monkey chow and a lousy segment of dried grapefruit.

A message was coming in on the kitchen computer, and Red was reading from it. "It's our Workday assignments," he said. "Dad's going to the fish hatchery. He's due there in a half hour. We'd better get him out of bed. Mom, they want you at the pre-school with the girls."

Mamie groaned, but Red shut her up with a wave of his hand. "You've always told people how good you were with children, Mother. Now you get to demonstrate it."

In my new clarity of mind, I realized that this was not like Red, to respond to his mother so sharply. Something was different about him. Was he taking charge of his mother, just a little?

"Here come *our* assignments," he said. "Carol Jeanne, you and I are going together. They want us at the cannery. We'll have to hurry—all the assignments start at nine."

"Do we *have* to go?" Lydia asked.

"If there were any justice in the world—" Mamie began.

"We all *get* to go," Red said to Lydia, ignoring his mother. He turned from the monitor to encompass us all in a beatific smile. Carol Jeanne, Mamie, and Lydia scowled at him in unison. "That's why we're awake for this voyage instead of sleeping through it—the Ark will only succeed if we all work together."

Maybe Red was right, but his exaggerated enthusiasm didn't win any converts. Carol Jeanne stood to clean the cereal bowls from the kitchen table. Emmy left the table and ambled toward her bedroom; Lydia followed, probably planning to torment her. Even Mamie sniffed at her son and then scurried away to rouse Stef from bed.

After getting directions to our respective assignments, Carol Jeanne and I left the girls with Mamie and went to the cannery with Red. I was pleased with our assignment. Processing food with heat and steam was so archaic that no one on Earth had seen a cannery in more than a generation. But on our new world we would need a way to preserve food without refrigeration. Working in this cannery would be even better than going on an archeological dig, because instead of delving through potsherds we could experience firsthand how humans used to provide for themselves before being freed by technology from such primitive rites.

There was only one cannery on the Ark, a fair-sized plant that was easily accessible by tube from any village. Red led the way as if he had been living on the Ark for years.

We found the Mayflower contingent sitting in a corner of the cannery waiting room, waiting under a handmade sign that said MAYFLOWER. The first person I saw was Penelope. I wondered if she made the Workday assignments. From what I had seen, it would have been typical for Penelope to delegate Mayflower's celebrity to the task that she herself would be doing.

"Do you see Liz?" Carol Jeanne whispered. I climbed atop her head and surveyed the Mayflower group, and although I recognized dozens of people from Odie Lee's funeral, Liz was nowhere to be found.

"It figures," Carol Jeanne said when I shook my head no. "There's one rational person in Mayflower, and she's off doing something else." I tapped Carol Jeanne's watch, but she only shook her head. "Liz isn't late, Lovelock. She won't be here. We'll just go off in a corner and work by ourselves."

Carol Jeanne was right about Liz, but she over-estimated her ability to hide in a corner. There *is* no corner on an assembly line. Everything in a cannery is done communally. Our project this Workday was stewed tomatoes. The humans donned aprons and tucked their hair under scarves or caps. I was warned to stay away from the line lest I shed into the food. There was a long-winded recitation of safety rules and an even longer-winded generic Protestant prayer for our safety. From the expression on Carol Jeanne's face, I could see her thinking: Weren't they carrying this communal religion thing a little far? But it was religion that supposedly bound Mayflower together, so no doubt we'd still be praying long after we knew the routine well enough to skip the safety lecture.

During the prayer I scanned the room. Everything was mounted on tracks; there were identical tracks on the wall-that-would-become-the-floor. All the tables and equipment were clamped to the tracks. At changeover, curved tracks would be inserted between the floor tracks and the wall tracks, and the equipment would be rolled from the old floor position to the new. The power sources were located near the corner, midway between—the equipment wouldn't even have to be unplugged.

We gathered around huge vats of boiling water, where Penelope demonstrated how to blanch tomatoes by dunking them in the water just long enough for the skins to burst. We took our stations around the vats, blanching tomatoes and then discarding the skins. We dug out the stem ends with paring knives and threw them into troughs of running water at our feet. Then we quartered the pulpy remains and put them in giant kettles to simmer.

I say "we," but the word is woefully inaccurate. As a witness I was allowed on the cannery floor, but I was not allowed to handle the food or even the utensils that touched the food. I was meant to stay in a corner, probably, but I rejected that advice and stayed with

Carol Jeanne. I perched on her shoulder, fanning her and keeping strands of hair tucked under her scarf and out of her eyes.

Even my presence was too much for some people. One of our co-workers was the hatchet-faced Dolores, whose loathing had made Odie Lee's funeral dinner such a delight for me. Half the tomatoes on the conveyor belt weren't as red of countenance as the sweating Dolores. The steam that permeated the cannery was hot enough to color even her scarred epidermis.

Whenever Carol Jeanne bowed her head over a tomato, Dolores curled her lip at me. I thought of producing a little jewel of a pellet to throw at her, but I didn't want to be permanently banned from food processing areas. So I waved and blew a kiss to her instead. She didn't bat an eye. She had appointed herself as the cannery's capuchin watcher, and she observed me vigilantly to see that I kept myself away from the food. As soon as I realized what she was doing, I knew I could torture her cruelly with just a little bit of effort. Changing my position on Carol Jeanne's shoulder to give me a little more leverage, I dandled my tail as if to caress the pulpy fruit. I held it over tomatoes, less than a half-inch from their surface, as if that prehensile appendage had eyes to admire their redness. I never got close enough for Dolores to sound the alarm, but I made sure I was *always* close enough that an alarm was imminent. Dolores moved closer so she could keep an eye on me—a maneuver that no doubt delighted Carol Jeanne.

For her part, Carol Jeanne assiduously tried to keep her distance from people, choosing the farthest vat of water to blanch her tomatoes and then coring and peeling them at the far end of a long table. But her efforts were futile. In case anybody had not known who Carol Jeanne was, Penelope told them. During breaks, men and women gathered around Carol Jeanne as if she were calling numbers at a bingo game. As they worked, they smiled at her and tried to include her in their conversations. But they were soon chilled by her tight-lipped smiles.

The more Carol Jeanne withdrew into herself, the more animated Red became. He organized a group of volunteers to run the onions through the chopper, and then he absorbed the worst of the onion fumes by positioning himself closer to the chopper than anyone else. Why had he taken the most odious task in the process upon himself? Because he knew it would endear him to the community. I realized his plan at once. Carol Jeanne might have unassailably higher status on the Ark, but Red could easily best her in Mayflower village, and it was Mayflower where they actually lived.

I had to give Red credit. He understood Carol Jeanne enough to know that her introverted personality would put her in the worst possible light. He also knew his psychology well enough to know how to make himself shine by contrast. He even *sang* as he worked, onion-tears running down his cheeks as he bellowed an aria from *The Barber of Seville*. The others were delighted. Even *I* was impressed. Red was actually good at something. Good at sucking up, that is, not singing.

Poor socially-obtuse Carol Jeanne actually thought that his singing was annoying people, and told him to hush up. The only result was to provoke other people to glance at each other and raise eyebrows or wink. Poor Red, they were thinking. She might be a genius, but she was a harridan wife with no sense of fun. Poor Red, poor wonderful fun-loving generous-hearted Red. Thus even Carol Jeanne's ineptness helped Red win a place in their hearts. I could hear the gossip already. *She's* as stuck-up as you might imagine, but the husband, Red, *he's* a gem.

When the onions were chopped, Red and his disciples diced celery together. Red abandoned *The Barber of Seville* and launched into a chorus of songs from ancient Broadway musicals—*My Fair Lady* and then *Camelot*. A few of the others were Broadway buffs, and joined in on the refrains. I noticed that Red managed to include "How to Handle a Woman" and "I've Grown Accustomed to Her Face," which subliminally—or perhaps quite openly—made the others think of him as a patient man dealing with an impossible wife. He was really sneaky, and I found myself admiring him for the first time.

Admiring him? I should have been outraged. This was my beloved Carol Jeanne that he was hurting.

Then I realized with relief that the very fact that I was not automatically sympathetic to Carol Jeanne in this little domestic contest meant that I had found one of the boundaries of my conditioning. I might get a rush of pleasure from my implants whenever I complied with one of Carol Jeanne's commands, but I wasn't forced to think loyal thoughts all the time, and I wasn't punished for sympathy with her rival. The implant couldn't read my thoughts or feelings—it only responded to my actions. After all, I didn't get the pain response the night before until I actually did something physical about my generative thoughts. And my pleasure came from the physical act of complying with Carol Jeanne's command. They might enslave my body, but they could not control my mind.

Of course, that might mean nothing more than the fact that they didn't think my mind was worth controlling. As long as my body did their bidding, what did it matter what I *thought?*

The women who had first surrounded Carol Jeanne soon abandoned her to join the excitement at Red's table. This would normally have been a boon to Carol Jeanne, but she was not stupid. She was only too well aware that she had been weighed against Red and found wanting. People withered around her, but Red inspired those same people to work harder and more happily. I knew that even as she did things that put people off, Carol Jeanne longed for their acceptance. She just didn't know how to go about winning it, and none of her natural responses helped. It was the bane of her life, her inability to connect with groups of people. Her extraordinary success as a scientist had made it unnecessary for her to win people over—they all spent their time trying to win *her* over. But on the Ark, she couldn't remain with scientists all the time. Being in Mayflower village would be almost like high school again. Poor Carol Jeanne. You didn't know what you were in for when you dragged us all onto the Ark, did you?

After the ingredients had been simmered together, the workers dished portions into vacu-board containers to be sealed. Only then did we break for lunch, a spartan affair served in reusable nylon sacks to each of the unpaid workers. Each sack contained a sandwich, an apple, a cookie, and a carton of milk. Carol Jeanne was not given an additional lunch for me, so she bequeathed me half her apple. It was hardly a satisfying meal.

Red's new friends congregated around him during the lunch break, just as they had on the cannery floor. This was more than Carol Jeanne could stand, so she hurriedly ate her lunch and then wandered off by herself to inspect the cannery.

The cannery was a massive structure—but, because of the structure of the Ark, it was long and thin, exactly as tall as it was wide. There were fully a dozen groups processing batches of food, although tomatoes were apparently in season right now. Steam hung low in the building, and it occurred to me that Pink must be having a hard time in the artificial heat. Then I realized I hadn't *seen* Pink since the process began. With no means of dissipating heat from her body other than rolling in cool mud, which was hardly available here, she must have excused herself to wait outside for Red. Once again, Pink had proven her uselessness as a witness.

We continued our tour of the plant, watching as quality control experts analyzed the contents of vacu-board containers to make sure the processing had gone well. Then we tried to enter another room, but that door was locked.

"You can't go in there. It's the extraction room," said a voice behind us. I turned to see that Penelope was less than two paces to our rear. She must have followed us, unless she had learned the art of materializing wherever she was least welcome.

"That's nice," said Carol Jeanne primly. And then, a little more politely, "What's an extraction room?"

"Guess." But Penelope's command was rhetorical, and she continued without waiting for Carol Jeanne to proffer a hunch. "An extraction room is a freeze-dry chamber. We *do* have modern technology here—the cannery is just to teach us all how to work together."

I waited for Carol Jeanne to correct Penelope. The purpose of the cannery was not to teach humans how to cooperate. It was a practical endeavor, designed to provide cheap food storage until technicians could plumb the resources of our new planet and modernize our lifestyle—perhaps generations after landing. Only a dolt like Penelope would expect to land on Genesis with all the conveniences of modern life. But Carol Jeanne missed her chance to humiliate Penelope. She only smiled that tight, constipated smile, and we ambled off on our own again.

After lunch, we returned to the cannery to start the whole process afresh. This time, people automatically looked to Red as the team's leader. At first Penelope furrowed her brow in disgust, because *she* was the alleged commander of Mayflower's little group.

But even Penelope succumbed to Red's charm. He flirted shamelessly with her, as he did with all the women, drawing her into his circle like a trout hooked to a lure. Penelope responded by calling Red her "mascot," pretending she had sanctioned Red as community cheerleader in the first place. The afternoon's work passed swiftly once the territory was divided between them.

Not everybody could work at Red's table; not everyone could stand around the same tomato vat. Red's area filled up first, and then the adjoining vicinities. Enough workers were assigned to Mayflower's group that eventually even Carol Jeanne was surrounded by people—people who would rather have been singing with Red.

Carol Jeanne ignored their conversation until it became painfully apparent that some of the words were directed at her. People weren't talking *to* her, of course; nobody was brave enough for that. But a group of women, led by Dolores of the crimson face, began speaking in the pointed undertones that invited eavesdropping.

"We have to do *something* about them," Dolores said. "It's not *fair* to give drones a free ride while the rest of us work."

"You're right about that," said a woman standing next to Dolores around the vat. She was soft and round and fluffy of countenance, but her words were sharp. "I'm not about to give people a free ride just because they're old."

Dolores snorted. "I don't think *old* has anything to do with it. They only let any of these old people get on the Ark because they live with celebrities."

"Even if they *do* live with celebrities, they're *still* old," said a skinny woman whose most prominent feature was an Adam's apple the size of her nose. "There's not too much you can *do* with 'em."

Good old Penelope. She had spread the news of Stef's and Mamie's unemployment far and wide.

Carol Jeanne blushed. Her skin never attained the cardinal red of Dolores's complexion, but the words obviously upset her. She didn't like confrontation, and it was especially hard for her to defend Mamie and Stef when she detested Mamie so much. But the women had issued a challenge, and Carol Jeanne was never one who could ignore a gauntlet once it had been thrown down. You don't get to her kind of stature in the scientific world by being a mouse.

She ripped the skin from a tomato, cored it, and quartered it, bruising its flesh in her anger. Finally she said, "I agree with you completely. But what *should* we do with my in-laws? The only thing I've thought of so far is to jettison them from the Ark and let them die in space. That'll do the trick, won't it?"

The woman with the big Adam's apple swallowed hard. It's quite possible that she hadn't realized that the old people they were talking about were linked to the illustrious Cocciolone. She was obviously embarrassed. "I don't think we were talking about your in-laws. We were only talking about drones in general."

"Oh. I'm glad to know there are *other* drones who live with celebrities. Give me their names, will you? I want to send sympathy cards to their families after they've been locked up to starve because they're too old and feeble to do their fair share."

Even Dolores backed down then. Like most cowards, she was only brave until she was confronted. "Of course we don't want to *hurt* anyone," she said. "We just have to find something for them to *do*."

But Fluffy didn't retreat. "Drones use up as many nonrenewable resources as productive people. If they can function at all, they can at least do sanitation work, and if they're truly so feeble and incapacitated that they can't even do that, they should be put to sleep and recycled."

"How practical of you," said Carol Jeanne. "It's such a good idea to wring the last drop of work out of people and then off them when they're too old. How old are *you*, by the way?"

Fluffy, who looked to be at least a million years old and counting, said, "*I'm* still productive."

"Oh, yes," said Carol Jeanne. "Producing gossip and ill-feelings at quite a remarkable rate." Oh, she had a mouth on her, when she cared enough to use it.

Fluffy turned her back on Carol Jeanne.

But I knew—and I'm certain that Carol Jeanne knew—that Fluffy was right. Old people should never have been allowed on the Ark. And they really *did* need to become productive, if only because, if they weren't, they would never truly belong to this self-consciously pioneering society.

With the argument silenced, if not settled, Carol Jeanne retreated to the private world where she had always spent so much of her time. Even as her hands skinned tomatoes or stirred the stewed tomatoes as they simmered or filled the vacu-board containers with the soupy contents of the second run of the day, her eyes were empty and her mind was elsewhere. I observed the scene for her, filing conversations away and watching people as it was my wont to do.

I noticed that while Fluffy was as vindictive as her remarks to Carol Jeanne had indicated, Adam's Apple seemed like a decent enough sort. She had apparently been drawn into the conversation because drones were a subject of worry for her, rather than because she wanted to antagonize Carol Jeanne. I focused on Adam's Apple several times during the remainder of the day as she did little, decent things, such as lifting heavy pans for people who were frailer than she was, or taking a glass of cool water to an older woman who appeared to be suffering from the heat. But if Adam's Apple hoped that Carol Jeanne wouldn't judge her solely by the one bad experience, her efforts were in vain. Like a true introvert, Carol Jeanne never seemed to notice. On the other hand, she didn't really care about the argument, either. Not caring is the next best thing to forgiving, isn't it?

At last the quality control team assured us that the second batch of stewed tomatoes was good. We were free. Although I had only perched on Carol Jeanne's shoulder throughout the day, being forbidden to handle the foodstuffs myself, I was still exhausted and bruised from yesterday's misadventures in low gee and my venture into the wonderful world of excruciatingly painful autoeroticism. I was sorely ready for a rest.

Rest wasn't on the agenda, however. Workday customarily ended with a community picnic, one of the many obligatory functions that held a township and its people together. When we walked up the ladderway from the tube, it seemed for a moment as though a mob had gathered and was rioting. Thus we learned that Mayflower's workday picnic was not a sedate affair.

If Mayflower had a population of 500, at least 499 of them were crammed into the town square. Children played games on the lawn. Mothers spread tablecloths on the ground for their families, and workers piled platters of food on the long banquet tables. I climbed atop Carol Jeanne's head to get a better view of the food and was rewarded with a beatific vision. There were hundreds of bananas in a crate—a lifetime supply of them. If they had brought exactly 500 bananas to the picnic, I predicted that at least a dozen humans would go without their banana ration today. After my sorry lunch at the cannery I estimated I could eat nearly two bananas for dinner. The other ten would be stored away for future retrieval.

I saw Stef sitting underneath a tree, wearily leaning against the pot that held the roots. The spindly maple offered scant shade, but Stef appropriated what little he could find. He looked tired and old; the trip across space had drained him, leaving a fragile old man where Red's father used to be. I didn't know what task he had performed at the fish hatchery on this Workday, but he was too old and feeble to have made a good job of it.

"Do you see the children?" Carol Jeanne asked Red.

"Not yet," he said.

"Lovelock, help us find them," she said to me. "They're probably feeling pretty lost in this crowd."

I thought: My, but we're maternal, aren't we? What about *my* children? They're *really* lost, aren't they—since they can never be conceived.

When I didn't instantly obey, I began to feel deeply anxious. My conditioning kicking in. Better get to looking for the bratlings.

"They're not lost," said Red, rather sharply. "They're with Mother." The change in him was remarkable. No longer the jocular, hardworking, fun-loving, hail-fellow-well-met singing suck-up who had dominated the cannery session, Red was now testy and tired. I wanted to suggest to him that if he needed to relieve tension, he could find nothing more satisfying than to kick a pig.

But I had a job to do. I stretched upright on Carol Jeanne's shoulder, balancing myself with a hand atop her head. My vision was acute, but human children all look alike to me, especially when all I can see of them is the tops of their darling little heads. I had better luck scanning the crowd for Mamie. *She* was easy to find, dressed as she was in a garish orange dress. She was busily ignoring Lydia and Emmy, asserting her status by giving orders to workers around a banquet table. Lydia and Emmy clung to the hem of her skirt, looking forlorn.

I directed Carol Jeanne to the little girls, but when they caught sight of us it was Red they wanted.

"Daddy!" Emmy's voice was a screech.

"*Daddy!*" Lydia and Emmy seemed to believe that the person who screamed the loudest was somehow superior. This time, Lydia won the prize.

They let go of Mamie's skirt and hurried into Red's arms. He smiled just a little *too* broadly, and I thought uncharitably that Carol Jeanne and Red were in competition as surely as their daughters were, and *this* battle, for the hearts of the children, Red had won.

Carol Jeanne shared my sentiments. She tensed the muscles in her upper back, a sure sign of her anger. She smiled briefly, scrutinizing the throng as if she were looking for witnesses to her humiliation. Sure enough, Emmy's and Lydia's shrieks had attracted some attention, even over the hubbub of the multitude. Several Mayflower women were watching the tender scene between Red and the daughters who loved him better than they loved their mother.

This was a spectacle I had witnessed more than once before. Only now, as Carol Jeanne smiled and turned away, did I understand that the tug of war wasn't really over the affection of Lydia and Emmy at all. Carol Jeanne didn't necessarily want the children to love her best—she simply didn't want anyone else to realize it. When the children ran to Red, she looked to others like a failure of a mother. She didn't like to fail at anything, especially in front of spectators.

"Liz," said Carol Jeanne. I thought she wanted me to look for her, but no. She said Liz's name because she had seen her.

Liz was spreading a tablecloth on the lawn, being observed by a passel of children and a man whose similarity to the children was so strong he could only be Liz's husband. The man was strong and dumb-looking—football material if I'd ever seen it. Then I remembered his connection with football was not as a player, but as an orthopedist for football teams. He folded his arms before him like a coach standing on the sidelines, letting Liz do the work as he supervised her progress.

"The cloth isn't straight over here," he said, making no effort to help align it.

"I'll get it in a minute. I can't do the whole cloth at once."

"We can't eat on a cloth that's crinkled up like that."

"I *said*, I'll get it in a minute."

Carol Jeanne stood beside the little panorama, waiting for Liz to notice her and say hello. But I'd already seen enough marital discord for one afternoon, so I chattered in her ear and did the food gesture, practically cramming, my whole arm down my throat.

"Go ahead and eat," she said to me.

"We plan to," said Liz, laughing. "Hi, Carol Jeanne."

The surly expression on her husband's face immediately changed to a happy, crinkly smile. Sometimes humans make me sick. I ran down to Carol Jeanne's elbow and hopped to the ground.

The crowd was thick enough that I put myself in a dangerous situation, scampering over the lawn because there weren't enough trees to make my progress in the air. But the scent of bananas was heavy in the breeze, drawing me as inexorably as the sight of Liz's brute of a husband pushed me away. I dodged human feet and playing children as I made my way to the banana cache.

There was a commotion in the center of the common, and I halted my progress long enough to shinny up a tree and investigate. Red was at the center of the noise. He had commandeered a gaggle of children and was beginning to lead them in a game I didn't recognize. Parents stood around in a loose circle, watching as their children intently focused on Red to learn the rules of the game. Just as Red had won followers at the cannery, he was repeating his performance here. Apparently the cannery wasn't an isolated battle. He had a major campaign in mind. He was going to be the best-loved man in Mayflower, and if Carol Jeanne looked drab and unpleasant in comparison, well . . . she *had* her career, after all. Red didn't have to worry about *her*.

From the tree I was a short run away from the banana pile. I hid behind a table leg, waiting until the workers on the food line were distracted by conversation. Then I reached into a barrel and pulled out a large banana. I climbed a tree with my prize and ate it quickly; nobody molested me. My success emboldened me, and I took two bananas the next time, hoping to hide them for future consumption.

I hurried toward home, planning to hide my treasures in a tree near the house and then return to the food line for more. As I approached the outskirts of the common, I spied the children I had met at Odie Lee's funeral. My first impulse was to detour around them, accomplish my mission to hide these bananas, and get back to steal a half-dozen others. But my curiosity took precedence over my instinct for survival, and I chose the tree Peter was leaning against to hide my stash.

Neither Peter nor Diana heard the leaves rustle as I scaled the tree. I balanced my bananas in the crook of a branch and lowered myself through the foliage until I saw their faces. Diana had tears on her cheeks. As Peter stood above her he chewed an apple, apparently oblivious to her misery. I'd observed adolescent males enough to know this was only a pose, however. I already knew from watching the two of them together that Peter did care about Diana, even though his concern remained a secret even from himself.

Diana wiped her nose with the back of her hand. Her words were unintelligible for a moment, but then I did hear the end of her complaint. "She hates us. She always has. You *know* she doesn't want us here."

Peter took a bite of apple and barely chewed it before swallowing. He scooped up a dribble of juice from the apple skin with a forefinger and then sucked the juice from his fingertip. Then, "She doesn't hate us, Diana. We're not Hansel and Gretel, all right? How often do I have to tell you that?"

"But she doesn't want us here."

"Maybe not."

"Then why did she fight so hard for us? We could have stayed with Father, if we'd known. At least, *I* would have."

"Not me," said Peter. Then, noticing Diana's crestfallen face, he added, "And I would have brought you with me, Virgin Huntress. You can't go to another world by yourself. At least, *I* can't. It wouldn't be any fun."

"*Mother* wanted to come alone."

"That she did. But she really doesn't hate us. Sometimes when people mess up their lives and want to make a fresh start, the way they do it is to go somewhere nobody knows them. You can be a different person, because nobody remembers the mistakes you made or how nasty you used to be. It's just like erasing a computer's memory. Once you reformat the memory drive, nobody knows what used to be there; all they care is what's on the drive now."

What a compassionate attitude he seemed to have toward his mother. I wondered how he really felt.

Diana put her hand on Peter's knee. It was the first time I'd seen her touch him with tenderness, and she looked like a miniature adult. "Peter, what happened to Dill Aaronson wasn't your fault. That hovercar came out of nowhere. You were lucky you weren't killed too."

"We aren't talking about *me*. We're talking about Mother. Back on Earth, Mother always rubbed everyone the wrong way. She didn't mean to; she just didn't know how to be nice to people."

"She still doesn't—or haven't you noticed?"

"That's the point, Diana. We are who we are. We can change habits, maybe, but our character is as much a part of us as our fingerprints. Mother is Mother; she'll never change. But she didn't know she wasn't going to change when she left Earth, and that's why she wanted to leave us behind. Some people want so much to start over again that they'll do anything—even leaving their families behind on Earth, if that's what it takes."

Diana took a lock of hair and held it in front of her face, frowning as she inspected the ends. She singled out one strand and bit it off, throwing the end to the ground before she looked for another damaged hair. Then she said, "You can't be right. Not about Mother. All she had to do was tell us to stay home, and we would have done it. Even you."

"But she's our mother. She had to fight for us. What would people think?"

"She didn't have to fight so hard."

Peter shrugged.

"Father's dead by now," Diana said. "If we'd stayed home, we'd be dead too."

"Not yet. Time won't *really* change until the Ark takes off. *Then* Father will be dead. Then *we* would have been dead. I don't know about you, but I don't *want* to be dead. I want to be on the Ark, going to a new planet that nobody's ever seen before. I wish Father had come with us, but I'd rather be here with Mother than back on Earth with him."

"I'd rather be here with Father, and *Mother* back on Earth."

What a wise and perceptive child, I thought. Most children don't come to understand how loathsome their parents are until they're *much* older. But Dolores had made her daughter into a precocious mother-hater rather early in life.

"And I'd like to be grown-up and handsome and rich," said Peter. "Wishes are a waste of time, Diana. They only make you unhappy."

Diana sighed. She opened her mouth to say something, but a rustling in the tree branches drew her attention. I looked upward to the source of the noise, barely in time to dodge a banana that had slid loose from its hiding place and was toppling to the ground.

My presence thus betrayed, I had no choice but to make an appearance. I somersaulted out of the foliage, landing squarely atop Peter's head. Peter yelped and Diana laughed. Temporarily their misery was forgotten.

"What were you doing here?" Peter asked.

I concealed my face behind my hands. *Hiding, of course.*

"Why didn't you come out in the open?"

Gestures couldn't convey that my presence would have ended the conversation, so I pantomimed an elaborate shrug. *I don't know.*

"It would help if we had a clipboard," Peter said. "We can't talk to him without a clipboard."

Diana rolled her eyes. "Sure you can, stupid—unless that notebook you keep in your pocket is for decoration." She turned to me. "Peter thinks he's Mr. Scientist. He's got a notebook welded to his rear end, and he writes all his important discoveries in there. *I* think the notebook is empty. The only discovery *he's* made is that Carolee Engebritson has breasts."

Peter leapt at Diana. Unless I intervened, they'd be rolling on the grass within moments. I wasn't in the mood for playing, so I ran down Peter's back and pulled the notebook from his back pocket. I leapt with it to a lower branch of my banana tree, and the sudden movement knocked my remaining banana to the ground.

As Diana had suspected, the notebook was empty of important discoveries. But there was a pen on a string attached to the spiral binding, and I uncapped the pen to write a note.

Sticking my tongue firmly between my teeth—my helpless-hardworking-monkey pose—I wrote, "Help me get bananas." It wasn't *War and Peace*, but there wasn't much else I could say. I didn't know how to erase Diana's anguish. If Peter was right, Dolores really *didn't* want her children with her in Mayflower, and there wasn't an easy solution for that.

Diana giggled. "You already *have* bananas, silly. They're all over the ground."

"He wants more," Peter said, and I bowed in agreement. "He wants *zillions* of bananas," he added, and I put the notebook under my armpit as I clapped my hands.

Diana and Peter were so malleable that I didn't have to do anything from then on but sit in the tree and wait for them to return with armfuls of precious cargo. I was gratified to see that they were smart enough to choose bananas of varying degrees of ripeness. I'd be able to return to the hiding place for days, feeding myself as each fruit reached its peak of goodness.

Peter was wedging one of the last bananas into the crotch of a tree branch when Dolores cleared her throat from below him.

"Peter! You are too old and too big to be climbing trees. Do I have to watch you *every minute*?"

"Yes, Mother. I mean, no, Mother." The child's countenance withered, so much that if I had estimated his height then I would have guessed him to be several inches shorter than my previous approximation. He shoved the rest of the bananas aside and jumped from the rim of the tree pot, and I hid behind the tree trunk to spare Diana and Peter from an extra dose of Dolores's wrath.

Diana wasn't so easily intimidated, however. "But *Mother*—we were only playing with—" She winced as Peter pinched her from behind, but she lamely finished with, "—the tree."

Dolores sighed. "I'm sure you've had an enlightening time, but I'm ready to go home. Have you eaten?"

"Yes," said Peter, even as Diana said, "No."

"Then get a plate, Diana. Peter, since you lied about it, you'll go without. Come on. Let's go home."

Hiding behind Peter, I pulled a banana from my store and slid it down inside his trousers, hooking the stem over the waistband. He would have *some* dinner tonight, no thanks to Dolores, and what he ate would doubtless be more palatable than the overcooked mess I'd seen on the picnic tables.

I found Carol Jeanne and spent the rest of the evening with her. She had left Liz to her own family and stood at the periphery of the crowd that Red had drawn to himself. By now, Red's followers constituted a group of at least fifty humans who were so gullible that they mistook his extroversion for brilliance and goodness. He was particularly attractive to the children of Mayflower, who constituted a wave of humanity around his knees.

None of the adoring parents noticed how Red gave Emmy to Carol Jeanne for diaper duty, or how, when Lydia got cranky or tired, he shunted her off to Carol Jeanne too. The only comments I heard were murmured compliments, as parents asked each other the identity of the fascinating newcomer who was so good with their children.

I was glad when the sun dimmed and Carol Jeanne took me home. I was already in bed, fresh from the memory of her goodnight kiss, when I remembered that my day was not over. Despite my exhaustion, the sun's null gravity beckoned me. My most important task of the day was yet to begin.

I was going back up the wall tonight. If I could master my responses to null gravity, I could master anything. Maybe even the pain of fatherhood.

We saw the monkey again today and stole bananas for him and he put a banana in Peter's pants which looked really stupid from behind, like he had dumped a load in his underwear, but he never has a sense of humor about his own personal appearance so I only mentioned it a couple of times.

I still wish I was on Earth. The only good thing about the Ark is Peter and the monkey. If I was older I could babysit for the Cocciolones or whatever the dad's name is. He's such a barfhead. Making stupid jokes and talking to me and Peter like we were brain dead. Of course the other kids ate it up because they're all dumb as a thumb, Peter's the only person here worth talking to. Peter and the monkey. I wish he could talk. I bet Nancy will be their babysitter. I wonder if the monkey wanted the bananas so he can run away from home. But that's stupid because if you ran away, you'd still be on the Ark! I wish I could run away. Hide on the last Ironsides trip home, so they couldn't send me back. I wish

I wish I wish. If wishes were fishes I'd stink like a fishmarket, Peter says, because all my wishes are getting old and rotten and I need some new ones. All right, I wish *Lovelock* could be my monkey. I'd steal fruit for him all the time and Mother would never know.

Of course Lovelock probably wouldn't want to be my monkey anyway. Why should he? I'm probably going to grow up to be just like Mother and who would want to belong to me then?

CHAPTER SEVEN

REBELLION

Pink and I might have been the only slaves in our household, since
we had been purchased, but that did not mean that everyone else
was free. During the weeks that I struggled to break the shackles of
my conditioning, others, too, found that our new life on the Ark
might provide an opportunity to slip out of bondage. We were no
longer in the same society that we had lived in before, and therefore
we could no longer fill the same roles. What had been bearable before might be unbearable now.

I had only been at the business of climbing the walls for a few
days when I was startled out of my exhausted sleep one morning
by Emmy's shrieking. "Bees!" she cried. "Bees! Bees!"

I had visions of a swarm of Africanized bees stinging her to
death, which did not seem an unmitigated tragedy. But the quiet
reaction of the adults told me that it was no emergency. I got up
and loped into the kitchen, where Emmy was jumping up and down
in front of the household computer. Sure enough, there were bees
pictured on the screen. It was a little animation program, apparently sent to our house over the network. A sort of message.

And not a very subtle one, either. When I arrived, Red and Pink
were already in the kitchen with Emmy and Lydia, and soon Carol
Jeanne, Mamie, and Stef emerged from the back of the house to see
what was going on. The animation was simple enough. A flower
appeared somewhere on the screen. Worker bees discovered it,
swarmed over it, and then flew back to the hive. On top of the hive
were two sleeping bees. The workers came and deposited their
honey inside the hive. As if it were a translucent tank, we could see
the hive filling up with honey. Then the worker bees flew off. Im-

mediately the two sleeping bees woke up, flew to the hive entrance, and drank the honey until the hive was empty again. Then the hive sank out of sight and a new flower appeared.

After about three flowers, however, there was a change. When the workers came back to find the hive empty again, they picked up the two sleeping bees, carried them off, and dropped them in front of a giant human shoe, which came down hard and squished them. As the workers flew back to the hive, buzzing happily, a message crawled along the bottom of the screen: "Drones are thieves, but they can't steal the workers' honey forever."

"Where did you get this silly program, Red?" asked Mamie.

"It isn't a program," said Red. "It's a message."

"You mean somebody *sent* this to us?" said Mamie. "But they didn't even sign it. What does it mean?"

Could she really have been so oblivious? I think she expected everyone to protect her from the nastiness of the message, so that she didn't have to admit that she understood.

Stef answered her, and his voice was not nice. "This message is from one of our neighbors," he said. "Someone who thinks that nobody should be excused from working as long as they have their health. Someone who thinks that it's a shameful thing for you and me to do nothing."

"Well, that's envy," said Mamie. "Envy is an ugly thing."

"I know something uglier," said Stef.

His words hung in the air, unanswered.

Finally, Carol Jeanne said, "Lovelock, I expect you to track down who sent this message. The network surely has some way to trace the mail."

"Pure nastiness," said Red. "This sort of thing is what tears apart fragile communities. It has to be stopped."

"Just what I think," said Mamie.

"Well, it's not what *I* think," said Stef.

"Oh, so you think vicious anonymous hate mail is civilized behavior?" asked Mamie witheringly.

"I think what's tearing apart the community is the insistence of some people that they're above work," said Stef. "Well, *I* don't think I'm above work. There are jobs I could do."

"At *your* age?" said Mamie. "What have you ever done, except call your broker about your investments and go to board meetings once a year where you rubberstamp the decisions of *real* businessmen? There's not much call for that *here*. We are not the kind of people who do the kind of work that is required in this little . . . village."

"Maybe you're not," said Stef. "But I am. Even if it's only permanent sanitation detail, I can do it."

"Don't be absurd," said Mamie. "We didn't come here in order to sink back into the lower classes."

"No," said Stef. "We came here so you could continue to coast on the achievements of your daughter-in-law."

"That is so offensive it's not even worthy of—"

Stef, having left such thoughts unsaid for so many years, must have been unable to stem the flow of words. "Well, Mamie, you miscalculated. This is a society that values people for what they accomplish, and not for whom they're related to. You should have stayed on Earth."

"And lose my son and my grandchildren, all taken away into space?" Mamie's voice trembled.

"You're both making too much of this nasty little anonymous message," said Red, trying to make peace.

"This nasty little anonymous message only forces the issue," said Stef. "I've put up with complete indolence long enough. Whoever sent that message is right. It's an offense against everything that this Ark is supposed to represent, to have Mamie and me be completely unproductive. And I, for one, am bored out of my mind with nothing to do."

Mamie answered with immediate contempt. "It's not *my* fault if you have such poverty of imagination that you—"

"It's not my poverty of imagination that makes my life intolerable," said Stef. "It's you."

I was astonished but also delighted. I had never realized that Stef had it in him to say such a thing.

Neither, for that matter, had Mamie. She gasped. Her face reddened. "How can you say such a cruel, heartless—"

"Heartless is insisting that I be as lazy as you," said Stef, "and earn the contempt of everyone around me when it's completely unnecessary. You only keep me home to feed your vanity, so that you can be the only woman on the Ark whose husband doesn't have to work for a living. Well, I have news for you. I *want* to earn a living. I always have. And now I'm going to."

"No you're not," said Mamie. Her voice was savage. This was as angry—as desperate?—as I had ever seen her.

"I'm going today to find an assignment they're willing to train me for."

"Perhaps you should think about this for a while," offered Red.

"Shut up, Red," said Stef.

"There!" cried Mamie triumphantly. "Is this what we've come to? Rudeness and hate! Low-class behavior!"

"That's right," said Stef.

"You don't even care that you are becoming . . . *common!*" Obviously it was the cruelest thing Mamie could think of to say.

I looked at Carol Jeanne and saw that she, too, was enjoying this. In fact, she could hardly keep from laughing.

"Yes," said Stef. "That's exactly what I intend to become. A common man. A regular ordinary citizen of the Ark."

"Well, I won't have it!" cried Mamie. "You can't do this to me! You can't drag me down into the *muck* with you!" You would have thought he had proposed group sex with a flock of diseased sheep.

"I'm not dragging you anywhere," said Stef. "You can stay home and hibernate if you want."

"No husband of mine is going to—"

"That's really your choice," said Stef.

"So you're leaving it up to me?" said Mamie. "Good. You're not doing it."

"No, Mamie," said Stef. "I mean that it's your choice whether I do it as your husband or not. But I *will* do it."

"You will *not* do it! I forbid it! You made a solemn covenant with me!"

"For richer or for poorer," said Stef. "In sickness and in health. Well, I stayed with you through a lifetime of sickness. Now I'm poor, just like everybody else."

"Not me!" said Mamie. "I am not poor, I will never be poor, and if you insist on living like a poor man then I'm done with you."

Stef turned to Red. "I've been reading the Compact, as I should have done long ago. I hereby declare myself to be no longer a member of your household. I'll be in bachelor quarters for the time being, and I'll petition to have myself associated with another village. I'll be packed and out of here in an hour."

"Father, you don't have to leave," said Red.

"You don't understand," said Stef. "I *want* to leave."

"You're just trying to make me do what you want, you manipulative, controlling, dictatorial . . . *man!*" cried Mamie.

"Not at all," said Stef. "I'm just sick of sleeping on the damned couch." He walked out of the room.

Mamie, red-faced and furious, looked back and forth from Red to Carol Jeanne. "And you're just going to sit there? You're just going to let this happen?"

"I've been reading the rules of life here," said Carol Jeanne, "and he has a perfect right to go if he wants to."

Mamie curled her lip and turned away from her. "Red, this is our *family* here. This is your father who is going to humiliate us in front of everybody by making this silly family tiff a public matter. The gossip will be dreadful. You've got to *talk* to him and get him to see reason."

"I'll do my best," said Red.

"What do you mean?" said Carol Jeanne. "Stef's not the one who's being unreasonable."

"I can't believe I'm hearing this," said Mamie.

"Carol Jeanne, please let me handle this," said Red.

"Your father wants to do what is required of every adult male on this Ark—have a job. And you're going to ask *him* to see reason?"

Mamie squared off for battle. "Stay out of family matters that don't concern you, Carol Jeanne."

"Excuse me," said Carol Jeanne, "but I'm a part of this family."

"Maybe it's all right for Cocciolones to walk out on their marriages," said Mamie, "but *Todds* don't."

"I think the evidence at hand indicates that Todds *do*," said Carol Jeanne.

"Carol Jeanne," said Red. "Drop this discussion at once."

"Let her talk," said Mamie, confident because Red was so clearly on her side. "Obviously family means nothing to her."

Carol Jeanne rose to her feet. "If family meant nothing to me, Mamie, then you wouldn't be here, because the only reason I allowed you to follow me into the Ark and continue to live in the same house with me was because I care about family. If you weren't my husband's mother I would never even have met you, because I have never wasted my time going to the kind of parties where people like you show up to fawn over celebrities. Yet I've had you in my house and endured your whims and your snobbery and your vicious comments about Italians and Catholics and Cocciolones because I love Red and because you are the grandmother of my children. So don't tell me that I don't care about family."

It was a speech that was about seven years overdue. I jumped onto Carol Jeanne's shoulder and applauded and hooted.

Mamie looked from Carol Jeanne to me and back again, and then burst into tears and fled the room. I continued hooting and clapping. The tyrant had been pulled down from her throne.

Red was not taking it well, however. Since he couldn't argue with anything Carol Jeanne said, he struck back the only way a coward like him could think of. He reached for *me*.

What he had in mind I'll never know, because Carol Jeanne caught his arm before he could touch me.

"Don't," she said.

"That damned monkey is laughing at my mother!"

"Don't you ever try to lay a hand on my witness again," said Carol Jeanne.

It was an interesting choice of words. She didn't call me Lovelock or even "that damned monkey." She called me her witness, which meant that she was reminding Red that the law absolutely forbade anyone to interfere with a witness doing its job. It was an outrageous thing for a wife to say to a husband—it was reducing him to the intimacy of a stranger. I loved it.

"You had no right to interfere between my parents," said Red.

"I didn't interfere."

"You took sides!" Red insisted.

"So did you," said Carol Jeanne. "The difference is that I sided with the man who was asking nothing more than to live with dignity as a full citizen of the Ark. And you were siding with the woman who was using her connection with me as a way of raising herself above other people, which is foolish and self-destructive and I kept waiting for you to say something, for you to do *anything* to get your mother under control and you never did, not even when your father was walking out on her because he couldn't take her psychotic hunger for control any longer."

"Psychotic?" said Red contemptuously. "Stick to your own discipline, Carol Jeanne. You don't even know what the word means."

"I know exactly what it means," said Carol Jeanne. "Just because you don't understand what *I* do doesn't meant that I don't understand *your* little quasi-science."

"Mother is not a psychotic. She has serious neuroses arising out of her upbringing and some traumatic—"

"Oh, is she your patient? Isn't it unethical for you to tell me your diagnosis of her?"

"She's not my patient, she's my mother!"

"And I'm your wife. Why not make the tiniest effort, maybe just one day out of the year, to actually see things from *my* point of view instead of always demanding that I understand *her,* that I be patient with *her.* She runs you like a puppet."

"I can see that this is not about Mother. This is about your resentment of my ability to maintain a warm relationship with—"

"If you dare to say one more word of this manipulative diagnosis of me," said Carol Jeanne, "you will be rooming with Stef by nightfall."

"Is that a threat?"

"I will not have you turn your psychological jargon into a weapon to be used to win an argument. What *I'm* seeing right now is a man who is so dominated by his mother that he is willing to throw away his marriage in order to protect her from the trauma of growing up and acting like an adult. So please do keep on shielding her from any chance of ever becoming a mature, productive, empathic human being, Red. I knew that was a facet of your life when I married you. But don't you ever dare to accuse me of being envious of the sickness that you call motherlove."

Red walked to the door of the kitchen. "I can't believe you created this scene in front of the children. Perhaps Mother is right, and you feel no decent concern for family. Or perhaps you are simply acting out the stress of your new assignment here at home, where you know that you are loved and will be forgiven." He turned to the children. "Girls, Mommy is upset and she needs a hug. Give a hug to Mommy."

It was the sickest thing I'd ever seen Red do. Of course Carol Jeanne could not refuse to hug Emmy and Lydia when they came to her with open arms. But it had to taste like poison in her mouth, to have her children's embraces come at Red's orders, acting out his condescending lie.

"I'm not upset at you, Lydia," said Carol Jeanne quietly. "Adults just get angry at each other sometimes."

"Don't you dare to exploit the children by trying to get them onto your side," said Red quietly.

Carol Jeanne was flabbergasted. "What do you—*I'm* not—*you're* the one who—"

"Come along, girls, let's let Mommy work out her feelings in privacy."

And Carol Jeanne had to sit there and watch as Red took Lydia and Emmy by the hands and led them out of the room. What could she do? She loved them too much to exploit them; she loved them so much she couldn't even stop Red from exploiting them.

I went to the kitchen computer, hit the escape key in order to clear away the drone message, and typed, "Like mother like son."

"I can't believe this happened," she said.

I typed: "It's been coming for years. Not your fault."

"Poor Stef," she said.

"Lucky Stef," I typed. "Poor you."

"Enough of that," she answered, rejecting my take on things. "Use the office computer to find out who sent that vicious message. *That,* at least, I can do something about."

It was easy enough to find out where the message came from. It came from "System." Which meant that the little bee animation had been sent with the authority of one of the system operators—the managers of the computer network on the Ark. For a moment I thought this meant that the message had been official in origin, that the government of the Ark was exerting pressure in an amazingly heavy-handed way. But then I settled on the more plausible explanation. Someone had learned how to break into the network operating system and make it *look* as though private messages were coming from the sysops.

So now the immediate problem wasn't tracing the message—that couldn't be done at the moment. The problem was figuring out how the sender had broken into the network mail program. Whoever did it must be able to break in with impunity—no one else guessing that he was doing it, or the sysops would already have taken steps. So what I had to do was find the same invisible way to enter.

Naturally, I started out using my own entry code and password. It gave me most of Carol Jeanne's authority to access information, which meant I could explore in areas that most citizens of the Ark could never reach. The problem was that by using my legal access, I was leaving trails all over the place. So I didn't want to do anything that I didn't want the sysops to know about.

Why did I feel that way? Why was I already worrying about being caught? If someone asked Carol Jeanne about it, she could simply say that someone had sent an anonymous message to her household computer and she asked her witness to search out who did it and how. Innocent enough, and perfectly within her rights.

Her witness. As I searched the network databases I remembered how she had stopped Red from seizing me or striking me or whatever it was he had in mind. Don't you dare touch my witness. It bothered me now, that she had spoken of me as an object, a possession. Her witness. Why *couldn't* she have said, Don't you dare touch Lovelock? Why did she still feel that the only fair protection of my safety was my status as a valuable piece of property, instead of speaking as if I had a *right* to be left alone? It was just one more sign that my relationship with Carol Jeanne was not and never had been what I thought it was. In the days of slavery in the American South, as black household slaves plaited their mistresses' hair there must have been conversation, perhaps even intimate confessions, the mistress playing out her thoughts in front of the listening maid. And perhaps the maids even fantasized that the mistress loved them, that they were friends. But then would come the awakening. The day when the family finances were in trouble, and money had to be raised, and they talked about selling this "friend." Or the day the maid did something wrong, or was suspected of doing something wrong, and in that instant the friend would become an enemy, an untrustworthy captive. How many "intimate friends" found themselves stripped and flogged? How many lay there bleeding on a filthy mat, suffering less from the wounds of the lash than from the realization that they were not and never had been anything but property?

I'm lucky to have found out now, I thought.

Instead of searching any further on the system, where I could be traced, I accessed local memory where the code supporting the network mail system resided, and began to read it. Since it was local volatile memory, the sysops couldn't know what I was looking at if they ever tried to trace me. And yet many secrets about how the mail system worked were there, for anyone who knew how to find them. Of course, in volatile memory it was the running program, not the source code, so it wasn't marked up with comments that helped human programmers figure out what each section of code was doing. But that was no barrier to me. I was an *enhanced* capuchin, and so I was able to remember the meaning of every computer instruction and follow the logic in my head. It was almost a mechanical task to snake through the code, following it to find the place where access was given.

In my mind it felt as though I were exploring a cave, in a mountain riddled with tunnels like a cheese. I would follow one branch tunnel until it looped back into the main tunnel; then I would follow another one to see where it led. Finally I ended up with a map of the entire mountain, and then I could begin to search for the tiny jewel that someone had hidden there. Along the way, though, there were surprises.

The first surprise was the discovery that this was a very old program. It dated from the era when the Ark project had first been launched on Earth. Apparently the people working on the Ark had become locked into one computer network system and had never changed it or even significantly updated it. This meant that encryption and security were primitive and that whoever had hacked the mail system hadn't had to be all that clever after all.

The second surprise wasn't a surprise at all, having found the first. The sysops were aware that their software leaked like a colander, and there was a secret project to install a new, high-level system with layers of encryption and security. Whoever had sent the bee message to our house would find it a lot harder when the new software came online. No—would find it impossible.

So should I report this to Carol Jeanne? The message is anonymous because it was hacked into the system, but it won't be a problem for long because within a week or so the new software will be up and running and the old hacks won't work. Very well, Lovelock, she would say. Good work. And she'd give me a treat.

Give me a treat. Give me a soul-destroying animal-tricking treat. Like one of Pavlov's dogs I was already salivating at the thought.

But I am not a dog. I don't have to do what I have been conditioned to do.

If Stef can wake up and find a man inside the shell that he had become, why couldn't I also find the man inside me? Not the *human* man, because I was better than human. But a man all the same, a male person, a citizen of the universe with natural rights and privileges like any other. If Stef could tell Mamie exactly what he thought of her and walk away, why couldn't I?

Because Stef could go live in bachelor quarters and still function on the Ark. Whereas I would be a runaway witness, an unheard-of anomaly, a failure of conditioning, and I would be hunted down and destroyed.

So I could not come out in the open as Stef had. I would have to live as Stef had lived for so long, hiding my real feelings as he had hidden his, so that up until the moment of his actual rebellion no one had guessed that he would ever find inside himself the power to act. When he did rebel everyone was astonished; but they were astonished only because they had never known him. No one had known him.

No one knows me.

No one knows who I am or what I can do. I'm like the hacker who sent that message. Anonymous. My disguise is perfect. I look like an animal. I can't talk with my voice. I'm small and weak-looking. They think I'm cute. And my conditioned devotion to Carol Jeanne is considered unassailable.

The terrible thing was that it *was* unassailable. Even as I thought these rebellious thoughts, I still felt that deep abiding love for Carol

Jeanne, that hunger to please her, that aching need to rush to her and tell her all that I had discovered in my searches through the system, so that she would know that I loved her and served her and she would give me a . . .

Give me a treat.

I found how the hacker had sent us the anonymous message. Sysops routinely sent system circulars, polling all the computers linked to the network and checking them for outgoing mail. It was possible to attach riders to the mail polls—the Ark government used this method to send news and notices. The system riders could also be addressed, not to any individual, but rather to groups or classes of individuals, so that notices could be sent to all the people working in the bakery, for instance, or to all the people living in Mayflower village. The hacker had simply attached a rider to the poll and had set it to be distributed to all households with members belonging to the gaiology division and counseling services who were also in Mayflower village and who had arrived within the last ten weeks. Thus the message, though technically still sent to a group, would show up only on our house computer.

But how had he attached his little animated message to the system circular? That, too, was easy enough. The ancient software had a back door. The sysops themselves signed on using their names and activating all the normal traces and record-keeping procedures. But the original programmers had built in a way to enter the system with even more authority than the sysop. It wasn't an intuitive entry—even in the old days, they were more sophisticated than to simply allow someone to type a generic name like "program" or "entry" and get in. What I found was that the network software installed in every linked computer scanned keystrokes when it was active, and while most of the branches from the keystroke scans led to obvious places in the program, one of them did not. It checked for an awkward combination of keystrokes that no one would accidentally enter: CONTROL-A [[<^ SHIFT-BACKSPACE. If someone pressed CONTROL-A and then followed it with the rest of those keypresses, he would find himself facing the same menu choices that the sysops saw, with all the powers that the sysops had—but without the software being "aware" that he was there at all, so no tracks would be left.

He? Who was this hypothetical he? *I* had this power now, no matter who else had it. I signed off as Carol Jeanne, then pressed CONTROL-A $[[<^$ SHIFT-BACKSPACE, and as far as the network was concerned, I was God, omnipresent, omnipotent, and invisible.

Now I could go look directly at the source code without arousing suspicion. As I suspected, the little routine that allowed the back door was completely undocumented. It didn't show up anywhere. The sysops probably didn't even know it was there, and the programmers who had created it for their own use while working on the program were no doubt all dead or at least retired. They probably didn't remember the back door themselves.

So how did the hacker who sent the bee message find it? Surely there was no one else on the Ark who could plunge into raw code and trace it in his own mind the way I had done. Surely no one had such mindless tenacity as to spend weeks of his life pressing random sequences of keys until he happened on this unlikely one.

There was a part of me that already wanted to stop searching. I had already found the jewel beyond price: I could go anywhere and do anything, I could read any message, I could examine any data, I could alter any part of the code, and no one would even know I had been there. And yet this powerful jewel would be snatched out of my hands in a matter of days or weeks, when the new software went online. Whatever I would do with this power I had to do immediately, and yet I had no idea what to do with it. When it eventually slipped out of my hands, *then* I would see its uses with all the clarity of regret and frustration and despair. I had to think, I had to concentrate on what my temporary omnipotence was good for.

Yet my assignment from Carol Jeanne was to find out who had sent the message. I now knew how the message had been sent, but not who had sent it. I had to bring her a report. I had to, I had to, it was a hunger gnawing in me, a hunger that only intensified as I contemplated telling her nothing, saying that it was a hack that I couldn't trace. Lying to Carol Jeanne? Unthinkable. I would have to tell her everything, especially the thing I wanted to conceal from her, this new power of mine. I *had* to tell her, I could hardly stand not to tell her, and the more firmly I decided that I would never tell, the more terrible the urgency to confess became.

It was like the proscription of sex. It was like my panic in freefall. I was out of control. They had stolen me from myself. I did not belong to me.

I leapt from the desk. I scampered to the door. Animal me, I thought, monkey me, scamper, leap, cavort while the hurdy-gurdy man turns the crank. Hold the cup as they toss in the money, and then give it to the human, give it all to the human.

I did not leave the room. I lay there trembling, going over the network code in my mind, mentally rewriting it to improve it here and there, coming up with encryption schemes with incredibly complex algorithms, doing anything I could to take my mind off the lie that I intended to tell Carol Jeanne.

And it worked. I calmed down. But I also surrendered, partly. I went back to the computer and began searching methodically for the hacker. If I brought her the specific result she asked for, I would not have to tell her the route I followed to find it out. I could keep it a secret, because I wouldn't have to lie.

In the end, it wasn't hard. I thought again about those original programmers. They were real live people, who lived in a less complicated age, a more trusting time. In the dawn of the computer age, hacking was a lark, and often the very people who wrote programs would get a great deal of pleasure out of hacking somebody else's. Also, there was an ideal then that information should be free, that everyone should be able to know everything. Wouldn't one of those programmers have shared this back door with somebody else, a hacker friend? Wouldn't this back door have been known, somewhere, by someone? Or maybe it was just a matter of age. The programmer got old. He wrote a memoir. It didn't occur to him that his software was still in use anywhere in the world. It had been so long ago.

I set one of the main network computers to work searching the library for the sequence $[[<^\wedge$. I was careful—I set it to use only ten percent of its processing time for the search, so that no one would notice a sudden degradation of computer performance that wasn't matched by a corresponding entry in the computer's automatic log. Even invisible men can leave footprints if they're not careful. But I was careful.

It didn't take long. It was a book on hacking written long ago, which included many anecdotes about particularly clever hacks. The author used the sequence CONTROL-A [[<^ SHIFT-BACKSPACE as a hypothetical example of a back door that would be relatively hard to come up with randomly. At no time did he imply that this particular sequence had ever been used.

But the author of the book had dedicated it to his dear friend Aaron Blessing, and it was a simple matter to verify that Aaron Blessing was one of the programmers who had created the networking software used on the Ark. Blessing must have told the author of the book, who then used the back door as a hypothetical example. It was an in-joke, just between the two of them.

Only three people had downloaded that book in the past year. Only one of them was from Mayflower village—the other two would almost certainly not have known or cared that Mamie and Stef were drones.

Peter Klarner. That nasty little sneak. I could just imagine him overhearing his mother, Dolores, complaining about the *drones* in Carol Jeanne's family and how awful it was and how somebody ought to do something only there was nothing that you could do or say because Carol Jeanne was so important. But Peter knew how to say something. He created his little animation and attached it as a rider to the system circular and sent it on its way.

How long ago had he found the back door? What had he done with it? Did he know that it was soon going to be useless? I found myself wishing I could talk to him—bragging, perhaps, because I had found out who he was. But also learning from him, sharing with him. As his equal. As another person who seemed powerless to others, but who had found a secret source of power that no one guessed.

Peter must have been reading the book, came across the hypothetical example, and just as a joke typed it into the household computer. And it worked. It must have seemed to him like a miracle. A cosmic joke. Like reaching puberty all of a sudden, without warning. Look what I can *do!*

He had the wit not to tell anyone. And yet he couldn't bear not to let somebody know. So he had sent that animation as much to demonstrate his power as to discomfit drones. What did *he* care whether Mamie or Stef had jobs or not? They were just the excuse for him to show off that he had access to the network that even the sysops didn't have.

Maybe he knew already—of *course* he knew—that the new software was coming online. So it didn't matter now if he let people know he was there. It would be kind of fun to strut a little, to show off, because in a week or two he wouldn't have the chance anymore.

Carol Jeanne had already gone to the office. When she gave me an assignment she didn't wait around for me to finish it—unlike Red, she didn't actually believe that every single breath she took should be watched by her witness. It was part of Carol Jeanne's fundamental humility. Her work was vital, so she accepted a witness in order to help preserve it. But her life was just a life, and she didn't mind if her witness, busy on some assigned task, happened not to record a conversation or two.

Of course I didn't knock on her door. I was her witness, wasn't I? I simply jumped up, palmed the I.D. panel, and the door slid open. How was I to know that she would be sitting on the edge of her desk, tears streaming down her face, with Neeraj sitting beside her, his right arm around her, his left hand gently stroking the tears from her cheeks?

Apparently the foolishness with the coconut had been forgiven. Apparently Carol Jeanne no longer thought of Neeraj as an obnoxious little man. I will never cease to be amazed at the ability of human females to overlook their first, negative, and frequently correct impressions of human males. In this case, though, Neeraj was definitely an improvement over her husband. I was not surprised that he had won this much trust from her so quickly.

When the door opened, of course, they looked up, startled, alarmed. But then she saw it was me. "Oh, Lovelock," she said. "Did you find out?"

If I had been a person, if she had thought of me as a friend, she would have explained what she was doing there with a man's arm around her. She would have said something about how her quarrel with Red had made her cry and how Neeraj was just comforting her. She would have been aware of the awkward appearances and done something to dispel the gossipy conclusion that another *human* would certainly reach.

But I was just a slave, and so nothing had to be explained to *me*. Instead, she explained *me* to *him*.

"That vicious little message I told you about, Neeraj. Lovelock must have found out who sent it."

Neeraj didn't take his arm from around her. But he winked at me and gave a little half-smile. I wasn't sure what he meant to convey by this. One male letting another know that this female was well in hand? Or perhaps one friend of Carol Jeanne's letting another friend know that she was all right? Either way, Neeraj was treating me as more of a person than Carol Jeanne ever did.

"Who was it, Lovelock?" she asked.

I clambered up to her computer. "Confidential," I typed.

"Oh," said Neeraj, "I understand." He finally unwound himself from her and stood. "My own guess, you know, is that your father-in-law sent it himself."

Carol Jeanne laughed and covered her mouth like a schoolgirl. "I didn't even—of course, how delicious! How right that would be!"

Totally wrong, of course. But in her eyes, apparently, Neeraj was very very clever.

I knew Carol Jeanne better than any other living soul. Better than she knew herself. So I knew right then, long before she understood it herself, that she was in love with Neeraj.

And why not? He was everything that Red was not. He was tender with her and cared about her and understood her work. He did not place his mother ahead of her. He did not make her feel like an inadequate mother as Red so often—and so deliberately—did. He was also vaguely exotic, which would add to the adolescent excitement of an affair. Carol Jeanne was already showing him emotions that until now she had shown only in front of me—or, in her own mind, had never shown to any *person* at all. Her private barriers were falling.

She's just like Stef, I realized. Here in a new world, where the old social role that she had grown used to on Earth could be challenged, could be changed, she was beginning to be restless under the burdens of life with Red. She was tired of the way Mamie used her, tired of the way Red criticized her. His little game this morning with the children must have sickened her—but it also frightened her, too, to realize that her children were so utterly under Red's control that he could flip a switch on their affection for her. If he could switch it on, as he had that morning, then he could switch it off. It meant he had power over her life, and that's one thing Carol Jeanne couldn't abide, letting someone else control her. She had stayed with Red all these years because she fancied that she was still freely choosing to be with him, despite all the problems with his mother. But now it seemed possible that he could take her children away from her if he wanted to. And so her role in the family was no longer secure. She was under his control.

How long had it taken her? A few hours, and she had another man's arm around her. Did Red think he could rule her? Think again, Red.

Humans are just as obvious and just as transparent as any of the other primates. It's all about sex and power, and power is all about sex—access to sex, control of sex. It's all about genes determined to reproduce themselves, and half of human behavior is nothing but those genes acting out their will to survive. How long before Neeraj would mate with Carol Jeanne? Days? Weeks? She would change mates and by doing so would bestow enormous prestige upon her new partner and deprive and punish her old one. She had the power, and Red would know it. This affair would not be secret for long. She would think it was an accident, but she would let something slip. She would find a way to flaunt this in front of Red. It was all explainable as basic primate behavior.

Behavior that I had been forbidden to engage in. She could do whatever she wanted to do with sex, but because I was needed as her slave, I was barred from ever, ever taking part in the great ballet of life. My genes were being murdered.

Neeraj left the room. I typed: "The hacker was Peter Klarner. Dolores's son. He probably thought he was doing his mother a favor, and she probably has no idea of what he did. If you want, I'll send him a message that will make sure he never does it again. I'm betting he only did it because he thought he could get away with it."

"Fine," she said. "Just so it stops. I don't want anyone to get in trouble over this. The last thing we need is to have the whole administration aware that Mamie's unwillingness to work is causing this level of resentment in Mayflower."

"Good," I said. "I'll send him the message right away."

"Use your clipboard, Lovelock, I need the big computer."

So I got out of her way as she sat down in front of the large screen and began calling up reports from the teams working on various aspects of ocean transformation and atmosphere maintenance.

My notebook was on a corner of her desk, but it was hooked into the network with a thin cable. She generally left it here these days, because she only used it for talking with me. Back on Earth she had taken it with her in her purse wherever she went, because she didn't always have access to other computers and didn't want to have our private conversations take place on other people's machines, anyway. But here on the Ark, she was either at home or at the office, and either way she had complete access to computers that she could use with privacy. The clipboard was now for me alone. If only I were strong enough to lift it and carry it along with me. I could slide it along the desk, but that was all.

Because she was engrossed with her work and couldn't see my clipboard's screen anyway, I felt free to access the back door to the network right there in the office with her. I wrote a simple message to Peter, created a new user named God, had that new identity send the message through regular mail, and then deleted God from the system and removed every trace that he had ever existed as a network identity. Peter would know, when he tried to trace the sender of the message, that it was somebody with as much power on the system as he had—and, I was fairly certain, with a good deal more knowledge of how to use that power than Peter would ever have.

Dear Diary,

Peter is such an idiot, he was really upset and crabby after school today and do you know why? It was just a message somebody sent him it didn't mean anything. "Keep your bees in the hive please" and they signed it God. I mean it was obviously just a joke and here he was working himself into a frenzy about it and saying "don't tell Mother" as if I was insane or something. I told him it was just one of his stupid friends at school and he said that shows how much *you* know and I said "No it shows how much *you* know."

I really hate sharing a room with him. I think we need a bigger house but the rules say children don't need separate rooms until puberty so I guess it's just wait for the tits or hope Peter's little weenie grows or he gets a beard or something. Nobody thinks that *children* might need privacy. Oh, no, it's only adults who get things like that. I can't even keep computer files secret from mother or my teachers which is why I have to keep all my thoughts on you, dear diary, and hide you in different places all the time. And it isn't easy you know. Finding hiding places on the Ark is like trying to hide a cow in a frying pan. But I will die before I let anybody read a word of you. I will *burn* you first. I hope you don't mind, dear diary. I promise that you won't feel a thing.

Now I'm getting silly so I better stop. Ta-ta for now.

CHAPTER EIGHT

Independence

After Stef drew the battle lines, there was nothing left to do but fight the war. But just as a skirmish couldn't be fought behind closed doors, Stef's battle for independence would also be waged in the open. As soon as Stef walked out the door, the breach became a matter for public speculation.

Normally Mamie would have been delighted to find herself in the public eye, but Stef had committed the unpardonable sin of being the one who did the abandoning rather than the other way around. People would talk about that.

As for the drone message that triggered the whole thing, any one of Mayflower's citizens could have put it on our household computer. Obviously someone already felt some hostility. How many someones, she couldn't guess. For all she knew, the whole town could be laughing at her behind her back.

Mamie was accustomed to being a gossip, although she would have used Red's euphemistic phrase: "other-centered individual." It was the role of gossipee that was new for her. Avoiding shame had been the great motivating force of her life, and the idea of people sneering at her behind her back was a greater torment for her than the loss of a husband who had never been, as far as I could see, much more than a fashion accessory. Imagining the lash of a thousand tongues, she sequestered herself inside the house for several days. She didn't even sleep for the first two nights, and because she roamed the house like a wraith I was denied my nightly excursion up the wall of the Ark. On the third day she got a prescription for sleeping pills; after that, I was able to resume my normal routine.

Her emergence came on Sunday, though she tormented the

household for days in her back-and-forth should-I-go-should-I-hide debate. Finally she decided that staying home from church would make other people think she had something to be ashamed of, whereas if she strutted to church as usual, head held high, people would admire her courage and might even assume that she'd given Stef the boot rather than him discarding her. So on Sunday, she dressed in her finest clothing and jewelry, as if it were a day of celebration. Mayflower's peacock had unfurled its plumage for all to see. I wrote a quick fashion critique and showed it to Carol Jeanne. She called me a bad boy but I could tell she loved it.

Mamie and Red took the girls and walked ahead of Carol Jeanne and me on the way to church, widening the psychological distance between us. Pink trotted behind Red and left a few well-placed farts in our path. I was disgusted, not by the bodily functions, but by her egregious partisanship when her master was so clearly in the wrong. True, Pink's loyalty had been programmed into her; but I had also been programmed to love only Carol Jeanne, and that hadn't stopped me from seeing the truth about her. Having been enlightened, I was naively impatient with others of my kind who were still deluded. I felt that Pink and I should have been allies; instead we were strangers to one another. She was a sentient being; how could she be so content in her servitude? I could only conclude that pigs were innately inferior to primates, so that even when enhanced they remained a lesser order of being.

I watched her little piggy butt jiggle as she trotted complacently after Red, and I was disgusted by her obsequiousness. It never occurred to me then that my own scampering, my begging for treats, my infernal *cuteness* telegraphed the same contentment to others that I found so distasteful in her. I knew by then that when I did those things, I was merely pretending to be a happy slave. It did not occur to me that perhaps *all* happy slaves are pretending, some perhaps doing it so well that they deceive even themselves.

Mamie preceded the rest of us into the chapel, leading the procession with her adoring family in her wake. She pushed herself into a partially occupied pew instead of an empty one, so that once she had spread herself out on the bench with her dear boy at her side and her loving grandchildren vying for her lap, there was no room for Carol Jeanne and me. For the benefit of those who watched, Mamie raised her hands in dismay as though it were all an oversight. She clucked for Carol Jeanne to sit in the row behind them, and Carol Jeanne was too surprised to do anything else. It was a nasty thing to do. Even in her time of trouble, Mamie could find time to vent her malice. Perhaps she was thinking that if she couldn't have a husband beside her, nobody should. Or perhaps she thought that if Carol Jeanne and Red were together, Mamie would look like the lonely extra person. Even though it was Mamie who had lost her husband, she apparently felt it more appropriate for Carol Jeanne to look the part of the single woman.

Finally, though, I realized that Mamie was fighting for survival in the little community of Mayflower, and her analysis of what would help her achieve that goal was excellent. Carol Jeanne was famous, but it was Red who was well liked and personally admired by the people of Mayflower. On the Ark as a whole, Carol Jeanne was a far greater asset than Red; in Mayflower, the situation was reversed. Mamie was determined that people picture her in Red's company.

I understood this, but of course Carol Jeanne was oblivious. She was annoyed at having been shunted off, but she had no idea of what it really meant. And even if I had explained, it was quite likely that she would have shrugged. What did she care, then, how the meaningless little community of Mayflower felt about her? Unlike Red, Carol Jeanne hadn't grasped the fact that life in the Ark was a significant change from life in America. There, your professional community was your neighborhood, and you hardly cared where your house was. In the Ark, the professional community was far smaller and the physical neighborhood mattered far more. It had been planned this way, so that during the hard early years of colonization, people would be able to work together smoothly in creating many small, agriculturally self-sufficient communities. On the new planet, there would be no cheap, fast transportation to link the towns. If you didn't have friends in your own community, you wouldn't have friends at all.

Carol Jeanne, if asked, probably would have said that she didn't *need* friends, that her work was her life. But it would have been a lie. Even the most profound introverts need somebody. What else would explain her bizarre friendship with Neeraj? Carol Jeanne was desperate for a friend—but only on her own terms, which meant that she could only be close with someone who understood and valued her work.

That could have been me, and if it had been, I would be writing a very different account, if I were writing one at all. But Carol Jeanne, who had once seemed to be the beginning and the end of the world to me, was clearly not the sort of person who can perceive hidden value in others. In her own way, she was as much of a user as Mamie. She was merely less conscious of what she was doing as she ignored the love of her best, most loyal friends and bestowed what love she offered on the undeserving.

Maybe that's the only kind of human being there is. Certainly the people at church valued Red even though he was a parasite. Why? Because Red went through the motions of assuring others that he valued them and their community and its stupid little rituals and rules. Men nodded and women waved at him from across the church, and although there may have been one or two knowing glances, Mamie could easily fool herself into thinking that the affection Red had won belonged as much to her.

Carol Jeanne, not Mamie, was the pariah. Nobody waved or even smiled at her. They snubbed her, just as she had snubbed them from the beginning. She and I were alone.

For most of my life, being alone with Carol Jeanne had been my fondest dream. But she had made it plain that I was no more to her than a sentient toaster, and I was bitterly aware that when she was with me, she thought of herself as being utterly alone. While the prelude music was being played I groomed her hair to distract her attention from the Mayflowerites who preferred her husband to herself, but I did this more out of habit than affection. She detected no difference. Why should she? The toaster was popping out toast just as it had been programmed to do.

Once the services began, I allowed myself to relax. I have never had much use for human religions—I knew who *my* maker was, and it was not an omniscient being. Lately I'd been discovering that my maker might not have been omnipotent, either. But there was no religion in it.

Nevertheless, I enjoyed the weekly Presbyterian services as much as Carol Jeanne loathed them. She needed the solemn rituals of mass, but I preferred the greater casualness of Protestant worship. Would old Mrs. Burke drop her hymnal on the organ keyboard during prayers? Would Mr. Watters snore through the sermon again? These were variables that were sorely lacking in the Catholic religion.

The music director was a treat to watch. She was a large woman, not as tightly built as Penelope or Mamie, and her fat billowed underneath her clothes. She favored pastel linen suits that were more transparent than she realized, and the torso that peeked through the fabric resembled the face of a surprised man. When she waved her arms to lead the music, the eyes rolled around and scrutinized the congregation. Apparently no one else had thought to inform her of the need to change her wardrobe; or perhaps they had, and she was a closet exhibitionist.

What I liked best about the service was the spying—no, data-gathering—I got to do when the plate was passed. Money wasn't a big commodity on the Ark, so instead of putting coins in the plate, churchgoers dropped promises there instead. There were pads of paper and blunt-tipped writing implements behind every pew, and while the offertory was sung people wrote their offerings down. The idea was to volunteer service to the church or the community, or to make a promise of some kind to God.

Whenever the plate was passed on Sunday, I took advantage of my monkeyhood and my rights as a witness, and moved around, ostensibly stretching one last time before the sermon. Nobody seemed conscious of how good my eyesight was, and therefore how far away I could be and still read what people wrote. Usually the offerings were as pedestrian as the people who made them. A woman would promise not to speak sharply to her husband, or a man would vow to spend more time with his children. These offerings held little interest for me except that they confirmed the dullness of the offerers' lives.

Sometimes, however, my observations yielded more interesting results. I once saw a man write an anonymous note promising God to give up his mistress. He was a little gnome of a human, and the thought that he had two women on a string was both surprising and appealing. Another man vowed to do a better job pleasing his wife sexually, even though, as he added nastily, she made no effort to please *him*. Thus was an intimate complaint cleverly disguised as a loving promise. I stored these nuggets away as part of my ongoing effort to understand human behavior. Once I had told myself—and believed—that I studied humans in order to be better able to serve Carol Jeanne. By then, however, I knew better. I studied them to try to understand what it meant to be a person. If Carol Jeanne had ever asked me what kinds of things people wrote in their offerings, I would have told her—my conditioning was too strong for me to do otherwise. But she was not other-centered enough to ask. And I was not so stupid as to volunteer what I knew; if she had known how much I learned about Mayflower from spying on their offerings, she probably would have told me to stop.

Some offerings were signed and some were not. Promises made to God were always anonymous because they were nobody's business but the worshipper's and his maker's. But community commitments were signed with the name of the person making the offering. When a member of the congregation vowed to weed the nasturtium patch in front of the chapel, the minister needed to know who it was who had signed up.

Mamie's favorite offering was to invite Pastor Barton's family to dinner on Freeday—a safe proposition to make because there were five hundred eager villagers and only one minister. On almost every occasion Mamie made this particular offer, Pastor Barton called with the sad news that his time was already taken by another member of the congregation. Thus Mamie got credit for asking without having to take the trouble of fulfilling the offer.

Carol Jeanne's notes almost invariably said nothing. She merely scribbled on the paper, shielding her meaningless doodles from prying eyes before folding the slip neatly in quarters as ritual demanded and dropping it into the plate. She was not the only one to do this; few had the cheek to openly write nothing. Today, though, she sighed as she reached for her pad of paper, a sure sign to me that she was going to write something real. I craned my neck to read the words.

"I miss You," she wrote, and the capitalization told me, to my surprise, who it was she missed. Perhaps sitting there alone on the bench had reminded her that along with Earth, she had also abandoned the God of her youth. As much as I loved Carol Jeanne, I had

long been aware that at an unconscious level she was deeply super-
stitious, despite her achievements as a scientist. Naturally she was
uncomfortable attending Presbyterian services instead of the Catholic ones of her childhood. But this was hardly the true cause of her
unhappiness in everyday life. It never would have occurred to her
that if she wanted to know the source of her unhappiness, she
should look, not to God, but to herself, for having made a bad marriage and not having had the wisdom to end it before leaving on
this voyage.

Unlike the others, of course, Carol Jeanne knew *exactly* how well
I could see, and when she noticed me looking at her note, she
shielded it from my eyes. That stung. I was her witness, after all; I
was *supposed* to look. But I feigned indifference by jumping off her
shoulder and landing on the back of Red's pew. I loped to the end
of the pew and jumped to the one in front, and then the one in front
of that. Few people even noticed me anymore, because I always
gamboled this way when the organ played. Those who had complained at first that it was disrespectful to have "pets" playing
around in church had long since become resigned to the fact that
the witness laws took precedence over decorum in the sanctuary.
And some even looked my way and smiled. Even the toaster knew
how to make himself more likable than Carol Jeanne.

One person I knew I had to check out was Peter, the kid who
put the bee animation on our household computer. He and his sister
Diana were sitting with Dolores, their mother, near Penelope. It was
tricky getting near them, since both Penelope and Dolores had taken
an active dislike to me. But the kids liked me well enough, and Peter
would have no way of knowing that I had sussed his anonymous
message. To get there I scooted along under the pews until I got
behind theirs, then scrambled up the back of the pew by getting a
grip on the hymnal holder. I ended up directly between Peter and
Diana and held very still, so Dolores and Penelope wouldn't notice
me. This was easy enough, since, like Mamie, they were spending
all their effort trying to look pious and cheerful.

Peter and Diana, for their part, didn't betray by so much as a
twitch that they knew I was there. Until Diana wrote on her paper
"Hi Lovelock." Peter, however, merely shielded his—but badly, so I
could read it anyway. "Mom never notices anything good I do so

stuff it I won't do her any more favors. Penelope says that thing I did caused a divorce but I don't care. Marriage is a fake anyway." Hostile kid.

Diana was trying to be sweet—but there was rage underneath her message, too. "I solemnly vow to write to daddy once a week even tho he doesn't ever write back even tho he promised. I will not think bad thoughts about Certain Person for making us leave daddy." Children were young enough to tell the truth without realizing how much they were giving away.

Adding today's clues to what I'd learned from Peter and Diana in the past, it wasn't hard to piece together the family situation. Their mother was wanted on the Ark; their father would have been a supernumerary like Red. At the last minute he decides not to go, but Dolores insists on going anyway and takes the kids, even though she's not that loving a mother. She took them because that's what mothers were supposed to do. Not that the children minded going, not at first. It was a neat space voyage, as far as they knew, not realizing how permanent or painful the separation from their father would be. Now they felt guilty for wanting to go, and it made their anger against their mother and father burn even hotter.

Her message finished, Diana reached up to pet me. The movement drew her mother's eye, of course—Dolores's alertness to her image of piety included her children's behavior in church. So I slipped down off the back of the pew and dangled from the hymnal holder.

The person sitting at the end of this pew was Nancy, the horse-faced girl who had taken Pink home from Odie Lee's funeral. I had seen her across the common on Freedays and Workdays, and she always came to church. Otherwise, our paths hadn't crossed much. Up to now, with two grandparents in the house, Carol Jeanne had seen no need for her babysitting services. But it occurred to me that with only Mamie left, Carol Jeanne would probably need to get a good babysitter now and then, and it would be helpful if I had some idea of the kind of person this Nancy was. Besides, I had just been reading kids' offerings and extrapolating from them about their family life. I was in the mode, so why not keep going?

I had been aware of her before, as I was aware of everyone in Mayflower. She always stood as though she were trying to disappear inside herself, and today, in church, she sat hunched so far toward the edge of the pew that anyone who walked carelessly down the aisle could knock her right off the bench. She leaned over a piece of paper as she wrote her weekly offering, hiding her words from the adults sitting next to her by using her long hair as a screen.

She was one of the believers—the people who wrote at great length, pouring their hearts out. I always thought of them as secret Catholics. They needed the anonymity of a confessional, but the offertory was as close as they could get. She was shielding her paper so thoroughly that it took some real maneuvering to get a good angle. I ended up hanging from one of the arching pipes that held up ceiling light fixtures inside the balloon-structure of the meeting-house. Even then it took some real effort to see what she wrote without making it obvious to everyone in the room what I was doing.

> I promise I won't hate my father or hope he goes to hell or Mom because she won't believe me or my teachers because they talk to my parents and make it worse. Please forgive me for hating them before and don't let me get pregnant unless it's your will for me to have a holy child. Amen.

A holy child? It was sweet and sad, the daydream world she must have created for herself, to allow her to survive in what was obviously an incestuous and abusive family. The mother's not believing her was a normal response, I knew, but apparently she had told her teachers and they had gone straight to the parents. What kind of idiots were they? Surely there was a prescribed response to a child's accusation of parental abuse, and surely it didn't include talking to the parents without protecting the child.

If she had really made such an accusation. What if she had merely told them about her fears of having a "holy child" by the will of God? Or some other half-formed daydream? They might not have understood what she was telling them. Still, I would take a look in her records.

As to having Nancy babysit Emmy and Lydia, that might be a problem. Abused children were often abusers when they got responsibility. But then, sometimes they were especially tender and nurturing. Both responses were part of the literature. And unless the issue of babysitting came up, it was none of my business. The humans were supposed to take care of this sort of thing. As usual, they were screwing up, but if I tried to fix every case I saw where humans were hurting each other, I'd have no time left for witnessing. I had my priorities—most of them forced on me by my conditioning.

Yet I knew I would still look up Nancy's records. Was I a person, or not? The equal of the humans, or not? Civilized, or not? And if I was a civilized male person, should I not feel and respond to the same urge toward protection of the female and the child that civilized human males felt? Of course I did not think all this through at the time. I'm not sure I always remember exactly how much I understood or thought about at the time. I only know what I did, and what I think I remember that I felt and thought. It's not always the most reliable source of information, but it's the only one I have, and even if my memory is selective or ascribes greater wisdom and self-understanding to me than I had at any particular time, at least I'm not *consciously* trying to make myself look good. When I remember myself doing something stupid or slimy, I write it down along with everything else. Or so I say. You, reading this—if anyone ever reads this—what can you know of me except what I tell you? What will you do, check the computer to verify what I say? That's a laugh.

When she finished writing her pathetic little offering to an apparently illiterate God, Nancy folded the slip of paper in half and in half again. She waited for the plate to come around, and then she pushed her offering to the bottom of the dish, away from prying eyes.

I found myself wishing that I hadn't looked. Even though I tried to be hardnosed about it, in fact this was the first time I had realized that human children could be slaves just as I was, forced into living a life that was unlivable. Despite myself, I was momentarily overwhelmed with compassion, with anger, with revulsion. I identified with her, not because she was a human, but because she was a victim of humans. Maybe Nancy didn't have a plug in the back of her neck, but the result was the same. Her father could do anything he wanted to her, and her only recourse was to ask for forgiveness because she hated him so much.

When the collection bowl had moved on, I dropped down to the back of Nancy's pew and patted her on the shoulder. She almost jumped through the balloon roof of the chapel. Then, seeing it was just the harmless monkey, she reached up and patted my hand, turning red in embarrassment at having been startled that way. I had no way of telling her I was sorry for startling her, and sorry she was a slave like me, except to give her my sad face and pat her again. She must have got some part of the message because she relaxed back into her hunching posture and let me sit on her shoulder and groom her hair for a few moments. Then her father noticed me. He began trying to get his wife's attention so she could shoo me away. For Nancy's sake I did nothing to cause her more trouble than she already had; I scampered away, playing the clown, and got back to Carol Jeanne just as the offertory was ending.

As I jumped across his pew, I noticed that Red had not put his own offering in the collection plate. Instead he was wadding up his slip of paper and putting it in the pocket of his pants as I passed by. I made a mental note to retrieve that slip of paper, if I could do it without Pink's knowledge. I wanted to see what it was that Red had written and then had been unwilling to give.

The sermon was long and as useless as usual. Basically I thought of sermons as group therapy by an incompetent therapist who subscribed to a psychological theory invented by cows. I spent the time thinking about children and human families. Peter and Diana and Nancy had all had their lives screwed up by their parents. Burdens had been laid on them that they would carry for the rest of their lives. By comparison, Emmy and Lydia had normal, stable lives. I might think Red was an ass, but he was involved with his children and he didn't beat them or have sex with them. Maybe that wasn't cause for extraordinary praise but it was something, wasn't it? And Carol Jeanne was no easy spouse to deal with, but he stayed with her, and she stayed with him even though he wasn't close to being her intellectual equal and his mother was the queen of hell. Emmy and Lydia were brats, but they'd grow out of most of that, and their parents had given them a stable foundation. Even Mamie, in her smarmy, self-righteous way, had helped surround the children with love and security—*they* had no way of knowing that she only did it in order to maintain her image or get control over other people or make Carol Jeanne look like a bad mother. Compared to some other families, Carol Jeanne's little household was downright healthy.

But then, even if Red had had a proclivity toward pedophilia or child torture, he couldn't very well have indulged it, not with Pink dogging his steps. Nor could Carol Jeanne express her impatience or anger at her children or her husband all that readily with little old me on her shoulder. For obvious reasons I had never seen how they would behave without a witness present. Perhaps all families would be healthier if they had an enhanced animal as a slave to watch and record their every word and deed.

It was then that it occurred to me that Carol Jeanne had been sending me away regularly at work, declaring that what she was doing was just routine and giving me assignments that didn't take me a fraction of the time I pretended to spend doing them. I had been resentful that she didn't seem to want me near her as much, but grateful as well, since it gave me time to explore the computer system and work on my own projects. What never crossed my mind was the fact that maybe *she* was doing something that she didn't want her witness to see.

In a way, that was flattering. Carol Jeanne knew that I would never—*could* never—disclose anything I saw her do without her consent. So if she was hiding something from me, it meant that she cared what *I* thought. I found myself, in the midst of a sermon on love and forgiveness of our neighbor's shortcomings, feeling something like love and forgiveness toward Carol Jeanne, toward Red, toward their miserable bratty little daughters, and even, though I find it hard to write these words, toward Mamie. No wonder Marx called religion the opiate of the people. I was drugged to the gills that day.

At last church ended. We escaped the hordes of Mayflowerites and walked home in clumps. Although most of the family lingered to greet Red's adoring fans, Carol Jeanne strode ahead of the others with me on her shoulder as if escaping the Protestant contagion she had been forced to endure. I perched on her shoulder, though, and watched the progress of the rest of the family behind us. Sure enough, Red stopped at a trashcan on the common and dropped something from his right pants pocket there.

Garbage wouldn't be collected on a Sunday; I had the rest of the day to retrieve the promise that Red had made to God and then retracted. I might have been filled with charity toward all men, but I was still a sneaky little spy. You can't fight your own nature.

Dinner was a silent affair, interrupted only by the prattle of the children. Carol Jeanne cooked spaghetti and meatballs as she frequently did after church, claiming it was an easy meal to cook. Mamie turned up her nose at the plebeian fare. Italian food was beneath Mamie's station in life, which, I suspected, was one reason Carol Jeanne served it so often. But Mamie had no desire to help cook the family meals, and years ago Red had responded to her hints about hiring "some kitchen help" with a firm *no* that even Mamie understood was final. So Mamie heaped up the pasta on her plate and, while making a show of distaste, ate an ample share.

Visitors arrived as the meal ended. Mamie sprang up to hide the evidence of our Catholic menu, removing plates and mopping spaghetti sauce from the children's faces as Carol Jeanne answered the knock. Penelope filled the doorway, her face plastered in smiles, with Dolores standing solemnly behind her.

"It's just us," said Penelope brightly. "You've been here nearly two months now, and we have to make one official visit every other month."

"*Get* to make," Dolores prompted.

"Of course. That's what I said."

Carol Jeanne frowned. "Penelope, you've been in this house a dozen times since we moved in."

"Not with Dolores. Those were mayoral visits, and *friendly* visits."

So apparently this was a hostile visit? I had no doubt.

"What she *means*," said Dolores, "is that she and I are your family's *fellows*."

Ah—another word from the famous unread prospectus. Fellows were village visitors, and every family on the Ark got assigned a pair of them. Fellows supposedly looked after the needs and wants of each member of their chosen families, but I was confident that the real purpose was simply to make sure that nobody was able to be cut off socially from their village. *Someone* would come to their house at least six times a year.

The task of making the fellows assignments was just about the only official function of a village's mayor; it was no coincidence that Penelope picked its most exalted citizens for her own route.

"We need to visit you at least bimonthly, just to see how you're doing," Penelope explained. "A visit doesn't count unless Dolores and I are together. You're assigned to both of us."

Dolores stretched the bark of her face into a smile. I thought about the husband she had left on Earth, and wondered if he had retained any capacity for pleasure after years of marriage to this stolid tree of a woman. I hoped he was living it up.

"Aren't you going to invite us in?" Penelope wedged her foot between the door and its jamb so Carol Jeanne couldn't shut her out without causing bodily injury.

"Sure we are." Red's booming voice startled me, and the women as well. "We're always glad for company. Open the door and step aside, Sweetheart, so our visitors can come inside."

The family gathered in the living room, unsure of what constituted an official fellows visit. Mamie poured coffee for each of the adults, making a show of telling Carol Jeanne she had served the coffee just the way Carol Jeanne liked it, even though Carol Jeanne and I both knew that she didn't even drink coffee except when she was working late and needed the caffeine. Just one more effort to make it seem as though the whole household was centered around catering to Carol Jeanne's every wish.

Apparently an official visit consisted of gossip. Penelope's fanny hadn't even warmed the sofa cushion before she told the family that Cyrus Morris was dating already. Odie Lee was barely cold in her grave (never mind that she'd been recycled), and Cyrus had already been seen three times with his executive assistant at work, a woman noted more for her feminine pulchritude than her professional accomplishments.

Carol Jeanne's eyes glazed over and Red wore his professional nice-guy face, while Mamie, who really loved this stuff, tsk-tsked at the appropriate places, shaking her head in mournful delight. Penelope blessed her with a beatific smile before continuing her litany of rumors.

George Bowman, who was only familiar to me as a name on Mayflower's roster, was having some trouble with alcohol. Another stranger, Etta Jenks, appeared to be sleeping with the itinerant handyman who served Mayflower and a half-dozen other villages. Dolores was certain of this. As Etta's next-door neighbor, she had seen Franklin Jaymes go inside the house twice without his tool kit. And Liz and Warren Fisher were arguing again; their neighbors could barely sleep at night.

At this, Carol Jeanne could stand no more. "Why are you telling us all this?" she asked. "Liz is my friend, and we don't even know the other people."

Dolores didn't miss a beat. "If you don't know what others are struggling with, how can you *pray* for them? You do want to *help*, don't you?"

"*I* want to help," Mamie said fervently.

"We *all* want to help," said Red, but he wasn't speaking for Carol Jeanne.

"But isn't there something *else* we do?" asked Mamie. "I want to be a *friend* to these people. I want to be a part of this village."

Here was the perfect opening for Penelope to bring up Mamie's refusal to work. As the mayor of Mayflower, surely she knew about the villagers' dissatisfaction. Dolores must have expressed her contempt for drones to Penelope, since she had certainly spoken of it to her children. Penelope must have realized the best way Mamie could blend in with the Mayflowerites would be to get a job like everyone else. But Penelope had other fish to fry.

"Well . . . I *do* have a suggestion."

Mamie beamed.

"The town desperately needs a new set of fellows. Odie Lee's death left a big hole among the prayer partners, and we need someone extra special to take her route. As the mayor, I was hoping you and Carol Jeanne could take over her circuit."

Mamie's "Oh, yes!" was overlapped by Carol Jeanne's equally fervent, "We couldn't possibly. My work takes far too much time for me to accept an assignment like that."

Red shot Carol Jeanne a look of disgust. Mamie's lip quivered, and I thought she might burst into tears. Even little Emmy looked away diplomatically, but Penelope and Dolores only stared. Penelope apparently wasn't used to having people tell her no.

"Well, of course you'll have to think about it," Penelope said. "We'll get back to you in the next couple of days."

Pointedly, Dolores added, "*Everybody* takes a fellows assignment." If that were true, of course, then everybody would be visiting just one other household, and I knew that wasn't the case. But Carol Jeanne didn't bother to argue.

"I don't need to think about it. My responsibilities to the Ark as a whole won't allow my being distracted by local matters. I understand and respect the purpose of the fellows program, but I was told already that administrators at my level are exempted."

"If they want to be," said Red quietly.

Carol Jeanne stiffened at his disloyalty.

Penelope looked wounded. "Don't you have time for our little village?"

"I'm afraid I don't right now. Why don't you find another companion for Mamie? I'm sure *she'd* enjoy being a fellow, since she's a little lonely without anything else to do."

I almost cheered—it was the first time I could remember Carol Jeanne actually being catty. "A little lonely" indeed. What a deft reminder that Mamie hadn't been able to hold on to her mate, and that she was bored because she flatly refused to work.

Mamie glared, until she remembered herself and changed to an expression of patient suffering. Dolores smirked. Penelope's eyes rounded. Finally Mamie ended the silence by saying, in her sweetest, meekest voice, "I'd be glad to serve as a fellow even *without* a companion, just so I can help the wonderful people of Mayflower."

Mamie might have been a drone as far as employment was concerned, but now that she understood that fellowing meant pious gossip, she would be the queen of community service. She would fellow every family in the village if she were called to do so, loudly moaning about her heavy burden even as she relished the task and assiduously spread every scandal she heard or guessed or invented. If Odie Lee were still alive, Mamie could out-Odie her in glorious martyrdom. And it only sweetened the prize that Mamie would make Carol Jeanne look bad in comparison every time she made her rounds.

"You can be sure we'll find a companion for you, since *you're* so willing to serve," said Penelope.

We endured the rest of the visit. Mamie, smug as a cat, vowed to pray for Mayflower's sinners, and once again Dolores stretched her lips into a grim smile. Even with her husband gone, there was clearly a chance for Mamie to penetrate the inner social circle of Mayflower. Carol Jeanne's chances were dimming moment by moment. By the time Mamie became a brahmin, Carol Jeanne would be untouchable.

It was only after Penelope was on her way that I realized she hadn't broached the subject of drones, even though she would have been aware of the official complaint Red had filed immediately after the incident. Penelope should have commiserated, at least. Her silence told me that despite what she had said to Peter about causing Mamie's divorce, she was secretly glad that he had sent the message with the animated bees.

The door had barely shut behind Penelope before Red and Mamie started in on Carol Jeanne.

"Are you deliberately *trying* to sabotage us here in Mayflower?" he asked.

Mamie chimed in. "If you've ruined my chances to be a prayer partner I'll never forgive you. I'm bored *stiff* on this spaceship, and *finally* I had a chance for something to do."

Carol Jeanne chose to answer Mamie rather than Red. "You could get a job." Her voice was quiet, yet it reverberated in the silence that followed.

A tear came to Mamie's eyes. "So you're the one who goaded Stef about working," she said. "You're the one who made him feel that he needed a job more than he needed a loving home."

Maybe Carol Jeanne would have said something nasty about Stef's lack of a loving home, but Red didn't give her a chance. "The *hell* with the job!" he thundered. "Nobody's worried about the job except you, Carol Jeanne. I wouldn't be surprised if you had Lovelock put that damned bee animation on the computer!"

Carol Jeanne could have answered him—she knew as well as I

did who the source of the animation was. But she was so near tears
that she couldn't speak without crying. And rather than shame herself by showing such weakness in front of her husband and mother-
in-law, she simply left the room.

I had no doubt that Mamie would now spread the rumor that
Carol Jeanne was the one who had broken up her marriage by her
nasty insistence—including a vicious animation on the computer—
that Stef had to get a job in order to be a real man. Mamie, the
classic castrating female, was going to give Carol Jeanne the reputation that Mamie herself deserved.

We went to Carol Jeanne's office, which wasn't a public meeting
place the way her bedroom seemed to be. I was glad of that, since
it gave me a computer to use as my voice. Carol Jeanne sank into
her chair and leaned her elbows on the counter. I slid the keyboard
out to where I could use it. Her shoulders were heaving, so I knew
she was crying though she made no sound. I was going to write her
a message. I can't remember now what it was I was going to say.
Perhaps I was going to comfort her. Or reassure her that she was
within her rights, so screw Penelope and Mayflower too. Or perhaps
I had thought of some subtle inoffensive way to tell her that her
neglect of the village was going to hurt her in the long run. This
much I'm sure of: I still felt a great deal of love and responsibility
toward Carol Jeanne, and so my message was going to be an asser-
tion that I was on her side.

Whatever it was going to be, I didn't get to write it. No sooner
had I slid the keyboard to where I could reach it than Carol Jeanne
reached out and slid it back under her own hands. There were tears
still streaming down her face as she logged on, entered the mail
program, and composed a note to Neeraj.

"I've got to see you. Please." She sent it, then immediately had
second thoughts and tried to cancel it. But the message had been
sent. She got up from the chair and paced to the window. Then she
sat down again and composed another message to Neeraj, saying,
"Never mind. Everything's fine."

I, of course, was now certain that I knew exactly what had been
going on when she sent me away from the office during the day.
Neeraj was more than the perfect assistant. And the charm that he

had used on me apparently worked just as well on Carol Jeanne. She had a friend, and it wasn't me.

Two friends, apparently. Because now she composed a message to Liz. "Can we talk? Do you have time today? I hope so, because I'm going to take a walk now and I think I'm going to end up at the children's park and I hope you'll come join me. I know you can see the park from your window so if I'm still there, please come."

She sent the message, then stood up and wiped her eyes on her sleeve. "Do I look like I've been crying?" she asked me.

Her eyes were red and puffy and her hair was a mess. I nodded largely.

"Well, that's just too damn bad," said Carol Jeanne, and she stalked out of the room. I followed. I wasn't going to miss this little meeting for the world—if Liz got the message and came.

Carol Jeanne didn't run into anybody on the way out of the house. Mamie was apparently in her room, and I dodged into the kitchen to see Red typing at the household computer while the girls played on the floor. He, too, was composing a message to somebody. Apparently they both had friends they turned to in their time of need.

On the way to the children's playground, we passed on the other side of the church. I parted with Carol Jeanne long enough to run to the garbage can where Red had dropped his aborted offering. Unfortunately, the Sunday school had apparently given chocolate treats wrapped in wax paper to the children, so the can was full of sticky smeary paper that I had to plow through to get to the bottom. But I'm a monkey, right? I play with my own feces. What do I care about getting filthy in service of my insatiable curiosity?

His message, crumpled as it was, was easy to read. "I will be faithful to my wife." Well, well, well. That was fascinating, wasn't it? I recrumpled the message, dropped it back into the can, and scurried back to Carol Jeanne as fast as my little legs could carry me. I must have looked cute to her as she saw me scampering along the path to where she sat on one of the swings in the playground. All the while, though, I was trying to decide whether Red's offering meant that he was merely contemplating adultery or had already begun an affair and was trying to stop. I also was wondering whether the fact that he discarded the message meant that he had decided *not* to give up on adultery, or had merely decided not to mention it in the offering, which was read by a minister who may or may not have been the soul of discretion. Who was it that Red was writing to when I left the house? Such fascinating mysteries these humans provided for me.

Carol Jeanne and Neeraj. Red and . . . somebody. Perhaps they, too, were going to lead their children into the wonderful world of marital collapse and family instability. It couldn't happen to a nicer pair of children. The sexual behavior of us lesser primates wasn't looking so bad. Sure, we male monkeys masturbated our brains out in public—if we weren't programmed not to. Sure, male chimpanzees kidnapped ripe females if they could and raped them to exhaustion in some secluded little rendezvous. Sure, male baboons made friends with babies in order to weasel their way into acceptance in the troop. But by and large they provided a healthy environment for their offspring. Humans acted more like male lions, who killed the younglings when they defeated an old male and took over his harem. Hang the children, they're in the way of what *I* want. If I ever had a mate and children, I vowed right then, I would be more loyal to them than this.

We had only been there a few minutes when Liz came strolling along and took a seat on the next swing. "So what's up?" she asked.

Carol Jeanne began, not with her problems with Red and Mamie, but with Penelope's and Dolores's gossipy visit. Liz didn't get upset about it.

"Oh, well," she said. "I hoped when Odie Lee died, this sort of thing would die with her, but her influence lives on."

"Odie Lee hardly invented vicious gossip," said Carol Jeanne.

"No, she simply invented the idea of claiming that you were spreading gossip so people could help the poor sufferers, or at least pray for them. She turned backbiting into a holy sacrament. If you do it in the name of Christ, how can anyone complain? Aren't we lucky to have Peloponnesia and Dolores carrying her cross?"

Liz's ironic tone was contagious. "Liz, it's their duty," said Carol Jeanne, with just the right amount of mock piety in her voice. "They're prayer partners." Then she added something that hinted of her real source of pain. "And of course my dear mother-in-law wants to be one of the crew."

Liz sailed right by that little hint without picking it up. "You ought to know, though, that every word that Penelope and Dolores told you is true, more or less. Cyrus *is* dating, although his executive assistant has more substance to her than Penelope indicated. I haven't heard anything about Etta and Franklin, but George Bowman does have a drinking problem; I know that personally because he tried to get Warren to give him his liquor allotment this month."

It was Carol Jeanne who made the personal connections. "What about what they said about you and Warren?"

Liz grimaced. "Right on target, but it's hardly a secret. You've seen Warren and me together—if not in person, I know Lovelock kept pretty close tabs on us during the funeral and you probably got the playback."

I bowed in deference to Liz's perceptiveness. Carol Jeanne shrugged. "I don't see everything that Lovelock records."

"Well, let's just say that if I ever have another child that looks like Warren, it will be by divine intervention. Warren hasn't touched me since we left Earth, and that's made me just a little edgy. Did I say edgy? I have so many hormones flowing through my veins that you could make an herbicide out of my blood. And the worst thing is that I can't figure out why he stopped loving me. *I* haven't changed."

"Maybe the Ark is a tough adjustment for some people," said Carol Jeanne.

"Yes, well, it hasn't made him impotent. He still gets erections in his sleep."

Carol Jeanne blushed a little.

"Oh, don't you talk about things like that? I thought being married to a therapist you were completely frank about other people's sexual behavior."

"We don't . . . bring our work home," said Carol Jeanne.

"Of course not," said Liz. "I mean, I wouldn't have gone to Red for therapy if I thought he was going to chat about it around the supper table. Not that it would bother me if *you* knew my problems—I'm telling you myself, aren't I?—but somehow I suspected that Mamie wasn't exactly a reliable confidante."

"You can trust Red," said Carol Jeanne. "He never betrays a confidence."

"I assumed he didn't. But that means you don't know anything about his work, doesn't it?"

"I know as little about his as he does about mine," said Carol Jeanne.

"The difference is that *your* work gets written about and talked about, but even the people he helps aren't likely to broadcast his achievements," said Liz. "You should know—he's a wonderful therapist."

Carol Jeanne chuckled dryly.

"Oh, don't you think so?"

"No, no, I'm sure you're right," she said. "It's just ironic. You see, Red and I just had a big fight and that was what I really wanted to talk to you about. Only I can't very well do that because that might undercut him as your therapist."

It was Liz's turn to laugh. "Oh, I don't think that just because somebody is a wonderful therapist it means that he's necessarily a perfect husband. After all, I can tell you all about how to be a perfect mother, but I'm not one myself. Don't worry, you can talk to me and it won't change my ability to benefit from my sessions with Red."

"No, it's all right," said Carol Jeanne. "Really, you've already helped me. I guess I had forgotten that I'm not the only one who has already plunged into my work here on the Ark. Red's work is just as important as mine, in terms of making the eventual colony a success. I never really doubted that it was, of course. I was just forgetting that he's under a lot of stress, too."

"It *is* ironic, though, isn't it," said Liz. "Helping other people cope with *their* stresses puts *him* under so much stress that he's not getting along with his own wife. Who theraps the therapists?"

They both laughed. But I knew what Liz didn't know—that Carol Jeanne's laugh was bitter and she was not really amused.

"So," said Liz. "What was the fight about?"

"Nothing. Everything." Then Carol Jeanne told all about Penelope calling her to be a fellow with Mamie, and how Carol Jeanne refused, and how that led to a fight with Red.

"Well," said Liz, "the truth is that while you *can* exempt yourself from fellowing, it's really a very good way to get to know people and be part of the community."

"I know that," said Carol Jeanne. "What I couldn't very well say in front of everybody was that I'd be perfectly happy to fellow— well, no, that's a lie, but I would have been willing to do it. What I could never bear to do is be partnered with Mamie."

"Mother-in-law problems?"

"If Mamie were a *total stranger* I would loathe her," said Carol Jeanne. "There, I've said it to somebody at last."

She had said it to me several times.

"And you have to live with her."

"Why couldn't she and Stef have stayed on Earth? It's one of the things I was looking forward to about the voyage—that at last Red and I could find out who we were out from under his mother's monolithic shadow. And then, when it was too late for me to back out— no, when I didn't *want* to back out because I was already involved and excited about shaping the ecosphere of a new planet—Mamie announced that she and Stef were coming, too. I know Stef didn't want to. I know Red didn't want them to come, either, or at least that's what he said to me. But he never, never, never could say no to his mother."

"He married *you*, didn't he?" asked Liz gently.

"Mamie didn't say no to that."

"You think not?" said Liz. "I'm betting that she did. I'm betting that Red had to fight tooth and nail to get her even to come to the wedding."

"Well, they kept it a secret from me if that's what happened," said Carol Jeanne. "As far as I could tell, Mamie spent months making sure that everybody in New England knew her little boy was marrying this famous scientist. It was deeply embarrassing how she kept throwing my credentials at everyone we met. I begged Red to get her to stop, but as far as I could tell he never even broached the subject with her. She still drops my name every chance she gets—even as she does her level best to undermine me with all our friends."

Liz looked doubtful at this. Now why, I wondered, would she doubt what Carol Jeanne was saying? It was nothing but the simple truth—Mamie was the person most impressed with Carol Jeanne's fame, and she namedropped with excruciating consistency. The only person who was blind to this was Red himself. And, apparently, Liz. She probably hadn't had enough chances to see Mamie in action.

"Well," said Liz, "you can't change his mother. But you *can* do something to keep from having your social position in Mayflower completely undermined."

"Take the fellow thing?" said Carol Jeanne. "I can't do it, really, Liz. To have to tag along with Mamie—"

"No, no—most people aren't fellows. There are other community service jobs. Red is so outgoing, so involved with the community, and I bet it would bring you closer if you were involved, too. Why don't you go to Pennyloaf and ask her for some community service position that you and Red could do together? She'll have to say yes."

Carol Jeanne sighed. "I really *don't* have time for things like that. Or, no, well, I have *time*. I'm just not good at concentrating on two different jobs at the same time. Red can do that. I can't. My work as a gaiologist consumes all my attention."

"Well, don't you let *that* worry you," said Liz. "Most of us don't pay the slightest attention to our community service jobs." She grinned. "If we did, do you think we'd put up with Pennydope being in charge of them?"

"You're right, Liz, I'm glad I talked to you. I'm glad you checked your mail and came out here."

"Mail?" said Liz.

"I wrote you a message asking you to come."

"Really? I just saw you from my window and I thought you looked like you needed to talk! You *asked* me to come? Well, I'm flattered. I'm glad you feel that way about me."

Liar liar liar, I thought. She got that message. Why would she lie?

Carol Jeanne and Liz hugged each other and said good-bye while I went behind a tree and peed against the trunk. Something was wrong here. Liz was giving Carol Jeanne good advice, yes, but she was lying and now that I thought about it, she had been on edge through the whole conversation. Something was wrong, and I wanted to find out what. I would begin by making sure that Liz had received that message from Carol Jeanne. Let's get home, Carol Jeanne, I said silently.

Instead we went to Penelope's house. No one was there. So we went to Dolores's house, and sure enough, Penelope was inside. It was Peter who opened the door, however, and he looked so nakedly aghast at seeing Carol Jeanne there that apparently she couldn't resist teasing him a little. "You must be Peter," she said. "Lovelock tells me that you're quite the little computer wizard."

"Not really," he said wanly.

On Carol Jeanne's shoulder, I grinned at him and then wiggled my butt tauntingly. He looked at me and I winked. That relaxed him a little. Apparently he thought of me as a kind of friend, and he trusted my reassurance. Not that I knew Carol Jeanne wouldn't mention Peter's computer malfeasance. It's just that I knew she didn't care enough about the bee animation to bother bringing it up. She had other problems on her mind now.

At Carol Jeanne's request, Penelope stepped outside and talked with her on the walk in front of Dolores's house.

"I'm afraid I gave you the wrong impression earlier," Carol Jeanne said. "I *do* want to do community service in Mayflower. I'd just rather take a job that's a little more . . . behind the scenes. I'm not good at small talk or making people feel at ease, the way fellows have to do. You're good at that, and I'm sure Mamie is, too, but I'm not."

Penelope preened. I was a bit surprised. Apparently Carol Jeanne knew how to suck up to people just fine. It wasn't that she lacked the skill, it was that she hadn't ever found anybody she thought it was worth sucking up to. And even now, she was only doing it to try to get closer to Red.

"Well, we do have other openings. We need a babysitter during church services, and we need an operator to post Workday assignments. But those are hardly the sort of thing a person of your stature should be doing."

"Not at all."

Not at all? I tried to picture Carol Jeanne tending little children during church services. What had Liz's comments *done* to my master?

"I want to do my part in the community," said Carol Jeanne. "If a job needs doing. . . "

"I'm thinking," said Penelope.

"Of course," said Carol Jeanne, apparently just remembering the rest of Liz's advice, "it would be nice if it were something Red and I could do together."

"That's it, then," said Penelope. "Social director."

"What?"

"We always call a couple as social directors. It's not really that time-consuming. And it's behind the scenes—you just make assignments for people to bring refreshments and do cleanup after our monthly get-togethers. Maybe come up with some games. I was wishing I could call Red to do that, but until you spoke to me today I never dreamed you'd be willing, and I couldn't very well call somebody *else's* wife to serve with him!" Penelope laughed hugely at her own jest. Or was it a jest? I remembered Red's offering note, and wondered if Penelope was already aware of rumors that she hadn't bothered to share in Red's own house.

"Of course I'll have to talk to Red," said Carol Jeanne. "But I'm sure he'll say yes."

I wanted to laugh out loud. Carol Jeanne as social director? You might as well ask a Muslim to run a pig farm. In no time at all, she would be dumping all the duties on Red, who would do them splendidly but resent her all the more for not helping him. Carol Jeanne, why don't you ever ask *my* advice before you do something as self-defeating as this?

Carol Jeanne made her good-byes to Penelope and our esteemed mayor swung her bosom around and toted it back into Dolores's house. As I rode Carol Jeanne's shoulder down the walk, I tried to imagine her stomping away at a square dance with Red. Even Pink would make a better partner as social director. My guess was that what this was really about was Carol Jeanne's guilt at her feelings toward Neeraj. She had to make things right between her and Red precisely because she was falling in love with somebody else. There was no accounting for what humans would do just because they felt guilty. I was glad that capuchins were spared such vain and unproductive emotions.

* * *

Thanks to the things I learned while tracking Peter's little bee animation, it was no trouble at all to discover that Liz had indeed opened the message from Carol Jeanne within moments after she received it. That had to mean she was already on the computer at the time and so heard the tone that signaled the arrival of mail. What was she doing? Why, she was reading another message which she had opened only moments before. A message from Red.

I scanned her whole correspondence record for the day and discovered that Red had already sent Liz one message early in the morning before church, and then two messages right after his quarrel with Carol Jeanne. Liz had answered all of them almost as soon as they were sent. But then came Carol Jeanne's message.

Red would have erased all his messages—he knows the computers in the house can't keep secrets from Pink or me. But Liz had erased nothing. I read the whole correspondence. Red's and Liz's morning messages were damning evidence—along the lines of, Oh my darling how I wish I could have awoken in your sweet arms and it drives me mad to remember how it feels to have your breasts/manhood pressed against my chest/loins. The after-the-quarrel messages were much more therapeutic, but no less disloyal, with Red pouring out his frustration with his cold, unloving wife who can't see anything more important in life than her own work and she cares nothing at all for the life that her family has to live in Mayflower and if I had known how passionless my life would be I would have chosen a different woman to be the mother of my children but in those days she was a different person and she had time for love and caring but those days are gone. Liz, for her part, was all You poor dear and I understand.

Then came the panicked message—Red, darling, she just sent *me* a message. She wants to talk to *me* what will I *do?*

And the answer: Talk to her of course. Try to help her understand that she needs to put her family first. That she needs to take some role in the life of the village. Heck, I'll even do the *work* if she'll just take some kind of position so the embarrassment will end.

I could hardly believe this. If Red had said anything half this strong to his mother about *her* need to take a job, his father might still be living at home. But apparently he only had such wisdom and good advice for his wife.

I wanted to kill Liz. I wanted to kill Red. I wanted to rush to Carol Jeanne and lay before her the evidence of their perfidy.

And then I thought: Will that make Carol Jeanne happy? Will it make her more effective in her work?

But she would want to know. Carol Jeanne was not the kind of woman who would want to be deceived.

I knew this, and yet I still felt this driving impulse: Will this make her more effective in her work?

This situation had never come up before. Until now, Carol Jeanne's interests always coincided with the promotion of her career. But at this moment, what Carol Jeanne would want—to know the truth about her husband and her "friend"—would tear her apart, which would doubtless make her completely useless at work for days, perhaps weeks.

And at this moment, what was my deep, inmost conditioning telling me to do? To give preference to *what was good for her work*.

Giving her a witness had been valuable, yes. But I was not programmed to be her friend. I was programmed to help keep her productive. I was an agent of the authorities. I was a Trojan horse and never suspected it.

And here I thought I was *her* slave. Turns out that we're all slaves to somebody, aren't we, Carol Jeanne?

Well, she had consented to it, hadn't she? Whatever they did to me, she had gone along with it from the start. I was just a machine to her. So if my programming told me not to tell her the truth, why not just go along? What did I really owe to her? Had she ever been my friend?

A part of me answered, Carol Jeanne *needs* a friend right now, since the one she has, Liz, is betraying her.

But was that the part of me that was making the decisions?

I went to see Stef.

Carol Jeanne was taking a nap, and I was free. I went out the bathroom window and dropped down into the tube and rode to the residential area where Stef had his new bachelor's quarters. He let me in, immediately hiding his surprise at seeing me.

"Couldn't Carol Jeanne come herself?" he asked.

Of course I couldn't answer until I had access to his computer, which wasn't even connected. Why should it be? Stef wasn't tied to the intellectual life of the Ark the way Carol Jeanne was. Computer programs weren't an important part of his world. He was of another time.

As Stef hooked up his computer, I inspected his quarters. He and the few other singles had been housed in makeshift apartments in the area that would house everyone on the Ark during changeover and launch. When the Ark had been designed, its creators had envisioned men and women boarding it two by two, like giraffes. No one had ever thought that a giraffe might rebel against its mate and elect to go forward as a single entity. It was only when the strain of Ark life started causing marriages to shatter that the singles' quarters had been erected. Large common rooms were partitioned into tiny studio apartments that were barely worthy of being called home. The apartment was cramped almost as if by design. Perhaps the humans who created the singles' quarters hoped that the closed environment would inspire their occupants to sally forth, finding new mates and once again moving into the larger Ark community.

But Stef's room didn't look like temporary housing. I could easily imagine that he intended to remain hidden away in this small bunker for the rest of his life. Looking around his spare room I saw homely touches. Books were left lying open, some of them even dogeared. Mamie would never have permitted such sloppiness—everything had to be put away, or at least everything of Stef's. His shoes had been kicked off into a corner of the room and he was in his stocking feet—another unthinkable act. He was free at last. But such a tiny freedom it was, such pathetic little acts of rebellion he now allowed himself.

Except they weren't acts of rebellion, were they? They were simply natural human actions without any reference to Mamie at all. His servitude was over. When he kicked off his shoes, it wasn't to rebel against her. It was because he didn't want his shoes on and there was no particular reason to put them neatly away. Someday I would be free like that.

When his computer was running, I hopped up and logged in, then pulled up a memo screen and wrote to him.

"Carol Jeanne doesn't know I'm here."

He looked surprised. "I thought you were . . . tied to her."

"She's having trouble at home. Mamie and Red."

He hooted. "Poor Carol Jeanne. Well, I set the example, if she has the courage to follow it."

"Is your solution the best for everyone?" I wrote.

"No, of course not," he said. He looked annoyed. "What does any of this have to do with me? I'm divorcing Mamie—she'll get the official notice of it tomorrow. I rather imagine she'll get custody of Red, so I'm not really Carol Jeanne's father-in-law anymore. If I ever was."

"You're still Emmy's and Lydia's grandfather," I wrote.

"Oh, I'm *sure* they'll grow up with a great deal of love and understanding for *me*. Mamie will see to *that*."

"Do you only love the people who love you back?" I wrote.

"Did they program you to be a self-righteous asshole?" he asked me.

"No, I'm a volunteer," I wrote.

He laughed and sat down on the edge of his bed. He could still see the screen. "All right, yes, I still love my grandkids even if they *do* remind me too much of their grandmother. And I love my son, even if he lets Mamie run him around on the end of a stick. He had my example to follow, didn't he? So what are you here for, Lovelock? What's the game?"

"Red is having an affair."

Stef took that in silence for a while. Then he said, "The little shit."

"I can't tell Carol Jeanne," I wrote.

"Oh, and I'm supposed to? No thanks, Lovelock."

"She needs to know that she can't trust the woman she thinks is her best friend. Liz. Do you remember her?"

"Yes, I think so."

"All you need to do is raise the suspicion in Carol Jeanne's mind.

So she won't open her heart to this woman anymore. Can't you do that much?"

"Why did you think of *me*?" asked Stef. "What did I ever do to make you think I could do something subtle and clever with a woman?"

"Who else but you?" I wrote.

He thought about that. "I'll try. If you can get her to come to me, or send me a message, or something."

"I can't," I wrote.

"Well shit then," he said. He thought some more. "OK, I'll send her a message. Telling her about the divorce so she can prepare the children. How's that? And in the message I'll drop some hint about Red and how she should tend to her own backyard, too."

I wrote: "Mention that Red is sometimes tempted to get involved with some of his love-starved, emotionally needy patients. Liz fits the description."

"Red never talks to me about things like that."

"She won't know that," I wrote. "Do it, so she has a shot at keeping her marriage together. For your grandchildren's sake."

"You manipulative little son-of-a-monkey."

"No, I'm a son-of-a-test-tube."

"Yeah, I'll do it."

I logged off and watched him as he wrote his message. It was good, it was clear, it would do the job. "OK?" he asked me.

I nodded. Then, on impulse, I jumped up onto the desk in front of him and held out my hand. With only the slightest hesitation, he took it and shook hands with me. Like a man.

Carol Jeanne must have awoken and received the message before I got back, because she already had a haunted look on her face and she was surly with me. Yet the message had the effect I wanted. She had made the connection between Stef's remarks about love-starved, emotionally needy patients and Liz. She was worried now about keeping her marriage together, not just smoothing over a quarrel about involvement in the life of Mayflower.

I had to know how things were going to work out, didn't I? So I hid in their bedroom, under the bed.

Sure enough, Carol Jeanne broke the silence between them. It was abject. I was humiliated for her. She apologized to him as if everything were her fault. She told him that she was sorry she had been so caught up in her work that she hadn't given him the love and affection he needed. She told him that she realized now how important the life of Mayflower was for him, and that she had asked Penelope for a position they could do together. And then she blew me away.

"Red," she said, "the colony is going to need more children, and we've made some rather splendid ones together, haven't we?"

That was a matter for some debate, I thought.

"Red, it's the right time of the month for me. Let's make another baby."

They went through the rigmarole of foreplay and all of that, but I didn't care. I was just lying there under the bed, thinking, She's going to try to bring another child into the world just so she can hold on to her husband. What a miserable, stupid thing to do. What if it doesn't work? What do you do with the kid then? And yet I knew that from time immemorial, people—even people reputed to be intelligent—had been doing exactly the same thing, over and over.

What really galled me was not any concern about the kid they might make together, I'll tell you that right now. What stuck in my craw was that when she was worried and upset she could get laid— and Red was good at relaxing her, I'll give him *that*. But I couldn't. Carol Jeanne was trying to fix her marriage by doing the very thing that I was most deeply prohibited from doing. It really pissed me off.

I wanted nothing more, in that moment, than to be able to have sex. Not because I was feeling any lust, or had an estrous female to mount, or anything rational like that. I wanted sex specifically because I had been forbidden to do it.

I grabbed myself as I had done that terrible night and started to arouse myself, and of course at once I was swept by as much pain as if—no, more agony than if Carol Jeanne had used the painword on me. It was all I could do to keep from crying out.

Why not cry out? That would stop Carol Jeanne and Red in their tracks, wouldn't it, to find out I was under the bed! But no, I mustn't do anything to interfere with *their* pleasure, must I. I had to let them get it on because my whole purpose in life was to keep Carol Jeanne happy . . . happy and *productive*. I guess making a baby would be included in *that* idea, wouldn't it.

Then, in one glorious moment of enlightenment, I realized how I might be able to overcome my conditioning against sexual pleasure. Arousing myself caused pain, but thinking about giving happiness or pleasure or contentment to Carol Jeanne had been programmed to be my greatest source of joy. If I thought of pleasing Carol Jeanne while I masturbated, I might be able to use one aspect of my programming to defeat another.

Taking a deep breath for courage, I thought, not of mating with a fellow capuchin, but of what was going on between the humans on the bed above me. I imagined that I was giving pleasure to the human I had been programmed to love, and therefore *did* love. I reached down to touch my erection, and yes, pain did sweep over me like a wave, but it wasn't as terrible as it had been before. I could bear it, and besides, there in the background, in the shadows of the pain, there was also sexual pleasure. For the first time in my life, I caught a glimmer of what that might feel like.

I not only didn't lose consciousness, I also maintained my sexual arousal. Maintained it, increased it, by picturing them on the bed above me, picturing myself jammed into Carol Jeanne and filling her with myself, my seed, my hunger, my will to dominate, my desire to please her. At last my generative organ leapt in my hand even as I doubled over in agony.

I lay there, panting. On the bed above me, the bouncing grew still; they, too, rested, breathing heavily.

I will have to clean up this spot on the floor, I told myself.

But then, after this slave thought, another idea came to me, swept over me. I am a free man now.

CHAPTER NINE

Subterfuge

I must have made the decision unconsciously long before that night when I lay under Carol Jeanne's bed and listened to her and Red trying to make a baby. Because when they were both breathing slowly and heavily in sleep and I slipped out from under the bed, there were things I didn't have to look up on the network. I didn't have to look up whether there would be time enough for one of the capuchin embryos to gestate before launch, because I already knew. I didn't have to look up where the gestation chambers were, nor did I have to check to see whether they were being guarded or checked in any way. I had already looked up all this information. Accidentally stumbled across it, actually, on the way to looking up other things. But I remembered it. Why did I remember it? Because I must have known that somewhere along the line, I would overcome the inhibitions on sexual pleasure they had forced on me, and I would be able to mate.

Yet perhaps I didn't know anything of the sort. Perhaps I simply desired it so much that I had to find out those things even though I never believed, at any level, that I would win my freedom from even one of the shackles they had placed upon me. Revolutions begin, not with foreknowledge of victory, but with such deep and powerful desire that the question of success is not a part of the equation. The attempt will be made, no matter the odds, no matter the utter lack of rational hope.

I still had two problems to solve before I hatched me a monkey. The first was easy enough—to alter the embryo inventory to show that one more of the capuchin embryos had been among the transfer wastage than the current records showed. I couldn't just change it on the current records, of course. I had to break in to the secure backups, which required writing a little bit of temporary piggyback code on the backup software that would make the backups agree with my inventory without reporting the discrepancy. Not hard.

The harder one was this: The new network software should have been online the week before, and I couldn't count on it being delayed much longer. When it came on, my access to the system would probably be severely limited. With the old network, thanks to what I had learned while tracking Peter's little message, I had learned how to navigate pretty easily. But if I was going to be able to maintain secrecy, I had to have as much power in the new software as I had in the old. And it was deeply unlikely that the new network operating system would have convenient back doors left in by careless programmers. Those days were long gone.

The thought did occur to me once that maybe I didn't need to conceal what I was doing. Maybe I could just tell Carol Jeanne that I had overcome my programming and I could probably hump some nice little piece of tail (why do *humans* use that expression?) if she would just do me the favor of thawing out a little capuchin bimbette for me.

Naturally, Carol Jeanne, being a loyal friend with such deep respect for my rights as a person, would go straight to the security people and tell them that her witness's programming had failed and dear little Lovelock would need to be destroyed. The toaster is broken, and I'll need a new toaster. . . . Oh, too bad, there *aren't* any more toasters? Well, I'll just make do without. *This* one just isn't safe anymore. Maybe you can cannibalize it for parts.

No, I'd keep it a secret, thanks.

I needed every spare minute to explore the new software, devise my control system, program it, and install it undetected by the sysops. Yet, officially, witnesses didn't have free time. I was supposed to be with Carol Jeanne every waking moment of her life, because humans have the idea that every last thought or action of a famous human is cause for admiration and speculation, of great import and interest to the teeming masses.

Fortunately, Carol Jeanne was well aware that humans would be venerating my biographical dumps on her for generations, and she was ill at ease with the idea of college students studying her bathroom habits or her procreative efforts or her extramarital flirtations. Just as in other systems of slavery, there were times when this master didn't want her servant around, and the servant could *pretend* that these moments of disregard were "freedom." Thus I had free time.

Lots of it. Carol Jeanne's little experiment in babymaking didn't change the fact that Red was being an unbearable mama's boy, and Stef's message had done its job—Carol Jeanne wasn't accusing anybody, but she was avoiding Liz. Neeraj, however, was still there, still charming, still genuinely appreciative of Carol Jeanne as a scientist, as an administrator, and as a woman. I don't think Carol Jeanne and Neeraj were making the beast with two backs yet, but they were enjoying some heart-to-heart conversations and extended work sessions, and more and more both I and the cockatoo were not needed to witness such "boring" and "routine" work when we could be doing "vital" assignments in filing and research.

The research I spent my time on was the region of the network where the new software was being designed, and it was not easy to breach. The sysops might not know the back door that Peter and I had found, but they certainly knew the old system leaked, and so the work on the new system was taking place off network. All the computers working on its design were disconnected from the rest of the computers in the Ark. For a day I despaired.

But human beings aren't perfect, right? They even take pride in this. "I'm only human." They say that a lot, especially when they screw up and want to be congratulated for it. So I found ways. A lot of these programmers took work home. They had to handcarry tiny little disks, and they were all very conscientious about erasing their work when they signed off. But it wasn't hard to install little routines on their home computers—which *were* tied to the old network—that would make clandestine copies of everything that they erased. This close to the end of the project, many of them were debugging high-level interoperativity problems, which meant they had to install much of the finished software in order to test any part of it—and all parts were being tested. In three days I had assembled, in bits and pieces, a library consisting of, as near as I could tell, the entire network system.

How to get into it? How to hide? I could install a back door, of course, but it would be hard to make it unfindable. I had found the back door to the old software just by checking the routines that read keystrokes. If anyone started getting suspicious of me, that kind of back door would be easy to find.

I studied the plan of it, how the software worked, how it kept unauthorized users out, how it checked its own integrity. File sizes and parity checks were continuous; I couldn't alter the code. Once it was running, I couldn't access the underlying systems without leaving tracks.

So what I finally did was this: I wrote a little program that lived in volatile memory all over the existing network. It functioned only during hardware interrupts, and it hid its memory use and storage in unused disk space without telling the operating system it was there. If it was about to be overwritten in one place, it moved itself to another. It evaded all the software they used to check system activity. And when they made the benchmarks against which they would measure future system performance, my little program would already be there, so that from then on, "normal operation" would include whatever processor cycles it stole.

Besides hiding, what does my little sleeper program do? Why, nothing that anyone would notice. It replicates itself at every opportunity so it can't be erased. And it checks keyboards for my own little entry code. Which I'm not going to write here because I don't know for sure that this file can't be found.

When it detects my entry code, my sleeper does something very simple. It allows me to replace sections of the operating system with my own altered versions. I can make new ones at any time, on any computer, and slip them into place. As long as I program well and don't crash the system, I can replace any section of code that I want, and while I'm using it my little sleeper program will protect it from all error checking. Then, when I've done what I needed to do, my sleeper puts back the original network code and my special version goes back into hiding in secret unfindable places on disks scattered throughout the Ark.

Unfindable? Well, actually, nothing is unfindable. But it's very hard to find, and my sleeper watches to see whether someone seems to be looking for it. If they are, my sleeper destroys all copies of my programs hiding on that particular disk. It won't matter—there's always another copy somewhere. And if by some miserable stroke of ill fortune they manage to find and destroy every copy of all my programs on disk, my sleeper will still be there, ready to let me in to write new ones. Because they can't ever, ever get rid of my sleeper. Not unless they shut down every computer on the Ark. And if they did that, the Ark's life support systems would cease and everyone would die before the computers could get back online.

I thought my solution was simple and elegant. It would work. Until the new network was put online, I would use the same back door that Peter was using. After that, I would be the only one with special access.

It took me five days. I'm really very good at this. After all, I've been enhanced.

Here I am, Diary,
It's late and if mother sees the light she'll hit the roof, just like she did on earth when we had to pay for electricity. Peter calls Mother a picklemouth and that's tacky but she never smiles and she never wants us to have fun. She was really a picklemouth today, because I got a letter from Dad and it didn't mention her and I was glad to get it anyway. It's not my fault he didn't mention her name, since *she* left *him*, or at least she didn't stay behind when he decided to stay on earth. I wish he was here because we'll be flying off soon and he'll be dead and we'll never hear from him again. Then I'll be half an orphan for real, instead of half an orphan because Mother is here with us and Dad is by himself on earth.

Everyone else on the Ark has two parents, except Emmy and Lydia who get to live with the monkey. They have two parents *and* they used to have two grandparents only the grandfather ran away and the grandmother can't tend the kids alone which is fine with me. Peter and I went there tonight to babysit because there was a square dance for all the grownups and Nancy is actually considered a grownup for square dancing purposes so she got to go so there was nobody to babysit but me. Peter was a human fart all night long, playing on the computer instead of helping me the way he should have after begging so long for me to let him go with me. But the little kids were really cute. Lydia plays just like a little mother and Emmy blinks her eyes and smiles just like a babydoll only that makes her sound like she's stupid and she's not, she can line up most of the alphabet blocks in the right order which isn't bad for a kid that small. Of course, the monkey is even smaller and he's *mega*smart but what do you expect, they put a robot inside him or something like that. I wish the monkey had been there because I wanted to talk with him but he was off at the square dance being a witness to all those old gomers having a "good" time. I wonder if he watched Mother and if she had a good time or if she's a picklemouth around her friends just like she is at home.

Peter says the monkey is a sneak and a spy, and I said how do you know that unless you're a sneak and a spy, too? To which he didn't have an answer because he is Peter, The Human Fart Who Reads Other People's Diary Entries Over Their Shoulder Drop Dead Yourself Flatulent Emanation Of The Universe!!!!

When I'm old will I think square dancing is fun, too? Or will that just be one of the things I pretend to like because I have to do it and I don't want any of the other grownups to know that I hate doing it? Dr. Cocciolone (as Mother says I must refer to her at all times lest people think I was raised by baboons) is like that about square dancing I think. She did not seem to be looking forward to it when she left and she did not look like she had a good time when she got home. She was just pretending for her husband only I think he wasn't exactly fooled, he knew it was something she only did because she had to.

Most of the things grownups do fall into that category in my opinion. I think if you left grownups to do what they really actually wanted most in all the world to do, every single one of them would lie down and take a nap for the rest of their life. I know this because that's what every grownup does as soon as they're alone. Even if they claim they're going to read or watch a vid they always end up taking a nap. I hope I'm never so old that taking a nap is the most fun thing to do. I mean, how is that different from being dead, except for the air conditioning?

The gestation chambers are completely sealed off until we get to our destination. Then they'll go like gangbusters for a few years

until the new environment is stabilized, after which they'll be useless again. Everything depends on them, since this is where Earth
species of edible, employable, or ecologically necessary animals will
be revived from eggs and frozen embryos. There has to be a lot of
space because literally thousands of animals will be needed at once.

I only needed one. And after all my planning, it was really pretty
easy. I removed the single female capuchin monkey embryo from
one of the icehouses, took it to the most remote gestation chamber,
and got it started.

Of course there was more to it than that. There was the computer work: altering the inventory lists, making sure the backup
software didn't catch the discrepancy, and then rewriting the gestation chamber monitor software so that it didn't report on the one
operating chamber and yet still allowed it to run. That was the most
complicated part of the task, but once my alterations were in and
running, there was nothing more to it. Then it was a bit harrowing,
moving through the air circulation system and crawl spaces, finding
the right icehouse—one of forty square tubes, three meters on a
side, which were always kept at −40°C—and then climbing down
when nobody was looking to get the embryo. It was intense.

I found myself making mental speeches to that little chunk of
ice in a tube as I carried it through the crawlspaces to the gestation
chamber I had chosen. Come on, babe, stay cool, stay cool. We got
a date in a few months. Got to get you prettied up for the prom. Got
to raise you from a pup till you're a full-fledged bitch. Oh, if only I
had a voice, how clever I would have sounded, chattering away in
my nervousness.

But I got to the gestation chamber without mishap and put her
smoothly into the incubator I had rewired and reprogrammed. The
robot machinery was ready to extract and thaw the embryo, then
provide it with nutrients and the proper environment until it was
mature enough to pop the bun out of the oven. All untouched by
human hands. Or even mine. I closed the door, sealed it, and then
told the computer to start. I got one minute of feedback from the
computer, telling me that everything was working perfectly. Then,
as my program was designed to do, the computer seemed to shut
down. There was no visible outward sign that this one was any different from the hundreds of idle incubators. Only if you went

around randomly trying to open doors would you find out that *this* door wouldn't open. In the meantime, if someone tried to open the door I would be notified wherever I was on the network, and I would have to come up with some kind of plan to deal with it. But I wasn't worried. My protection was that nobody had any reason at all to enter the gestation chambers. They weren't even cleaned, since the atmosphere there was so perfectly controlled that there wasn't any dust.

Just whatever monkey hair I shed while putting my baby in the box. Baby, baby, baby, baby, I need your lovin'. Baby I'm-a want you. Come to papa come to papa come to papa do. There had to be something vaguely pathological about that long phase of American pop music in which lovers spoke to each other as if one were a parent wanting to have sex with his or her little child. Sick as it was, with its implications of pederasty and incest, such song lyrics described my situation almost perfectly.

My baby, my girl, my date, my bride, my wife, my chattel, my property, my dumb little monkey bitch, my hope, my only hope, the mother of my offspring—she was in the pot, nine days old, and there was nothing for me to do but pretend to be a normal witness and trust to the machinery to bring my future to pass.

Delays," said Neeraj. "They're having some unnamed trouble with the new network and they won't even authorize final preparations for launch until they're resolved."

Of course I perked up at *that*. Was it possible that the unnamed trouble was my sleeper program? No, not likely.

"Delays are good," said Carol Jeanne. "When we launch, our deadline becomes firm. We have to hit the ground running, and we don't even know what the ground is going to be. So I don't mind having time to come up with alternate strategies."

"Delays are good for gaiology," said Neeraj. "But as for my own self, my biological clock is ticking."

Carol Jeanne laughed. "Men don't have biological clocks."

"Yes we do," said Neeraj. "It requires us to fall in love with fertile women."

Carol Jeanne fell silent. I knew what this was. This was a continuation of a conversation they had had in my absence.

"Well, there's no shortage of fertile women," said Carol Jeanne.

"But the discriminating male chooses the best available genes."

"He also chooses the most nurturing female to raise the babies." Obviously she had warned him that she wasn't the most conscientious of mothers.

"Or perhaps he doesn't give a damn about his biological clock and has simply fallen in love, mindlessly, hopelessly, with a woman that his parents would never, never have chosen for him, and who would never have chosen him for herself, either."

"Not now, Neeraj."

Oh, this was so stupid, her trying to keep this a secret. Did she think that I didn't know?

So I popped up onto her desk and typed on her computer, "Eyewhay otnay ooze-yay ig-pay atin-Lay?"

She laughed. I liked that sound. It still filled me with pleasure, even then, when I had begun my rebellion in earnest. Such is the power of programmed love.

"Lovelock is telling us that he's already guessed that there is an emotional connection between us," Carol Jeanne said.

"I told you that all the subterfuge was unnecessary," said Neeraj.

"I wasn't worried about the fact that *he* would guess. I don't keep secrets from Lovelock. It's just that when I die . . . if this didn't come to anything, Neeraj, I didn't want it to be on the record."

"Well now it is," said Neeraj. "And the people who study our lives won't be stupid, either, you know. They'll figure out why there are gaps. So let's just put it on the record. I want you, tall wop woman, in my life, in my house, in my bed. Whereas you want to be friends, because after all, you have a responsibility to your children, though in fact you don't spend much time with them and your husband is by far the more nurturing parent. Plus you confess to a weird, perverted desire to miscegenate; a dark Dravidian whose name ends in *J*, mating with a Sicilian-American Princess whose name ends in a vowel."

"That makes me a SAP," said Carol Jeanne cheerfully.

"And what does it make *me?*" asked Neeraj. He turned to me.

"Lovelock, sometimes I envy you. You get to jump on her shoulder and pluck imaginary lice from her hair whenever you want. You can climb right up her chest, putting hands and feet in territories where I have neither passport nor visa to enter."

"Don't talk dirty to my witness, Neeraj," said Carol Jeanne testily. "For heaven's sake, just because we're not trying to hide it from his view anymore doesn't mean you have to make us look like horny teenagers."

"Why not?" said Neeraj. "I *am* a horny teenager. I want to get you naked and bounce around on a bed with you. But I'd settle for long embraces and heartfelt conversations far into the night."

Carol Jeanne was clearly miserable. Neeraj was teasing, yes, but this was obviously a crucial time in their relationship. He was pushing for an answer. That was why he had hinted so broadly about their relationship in front of me, until I made it clear that it was now in the open. He wanted things to change.

And so did Carol Jeanne. "Do you enjoy tormenting me? I haven't had an exciting moment, not even really a loving moment, in years. I should have backed out as soon as I met his family. I should have known that he would always be another woman's property. But it was a chance for a . . . a complete life. How could I have guessed that I would meet *you?*"

"I surprise everybody," said Neeraj. "I go through life having to see people with startled faces."

"I've told you, Neeraj. If I were no longer married, then I would turn to you. But I'm not going to sabotage my marriage in order to have you. If I betrayed my husband for you, then you would spend the rest of our lives wondering whether I was betraying you for somebody else."

"So what was that hint from Stef about other women in Red's life?"

"It wasn't explicitly an accusation," she said. "And even if he is having an affair, it doesn't necessarily mean that the marriage is over. The children need a stable home."

"I don't get this double standard," said Neeraj. "If *he* has an affair, that's OK, the marriage can still be saved. But *you* can't have an affair because it would wreck your marriage."

"It would," said Carol Jeanne. "Because I can't lie. He'd know.

And he would never forgive me. It would be the end of the marriage."

"Whereas if *he* is having an affair . . . "

"It doesn't matter, Neeraj. Because I'm not the kind of woman who has affairs."

"That is such pure, highminded-sounding bullshit, my love, my darling, thou object of my erotic imaginations. You are precisely the kind of woman who has affairs—you are miserable with your unloving, disloyal, self-serving, manipulative son-of-a-bitch of a husband, and you are in love with a caring, sensitive, short dark Indian guy who does a great Gandhi imitation."

"I won't be the one who breaks up my marriage. And you wouldn't be happy with an affair, anyway. You want a marriage, too. Find somebody else, Neeraj."

"Personally," said Neeraj, "I think Red is a homosexual who only married you because that's what his mother expected. I think Stef is a homosexual too, who stayed with his loveless marriage because it absolutely fit his definition of what marriage was in the first place."

"That's why you're a gaiologist, Neeraj, instead of a shrink," said Carol Jeanne.

"Red's affair right now is probably with a woman, but when his marriage with you finally breaks up—something that he has been longing for from the start, I might add—he will then break *all* restraints and finally have the longed-for relationship of his life—with a man. A very *butch* man, too, I'll bet."

"Damn you," said Carol Jeanne. "This isn't funny, not in front of Lovelock, Neeraj."

I typed again. "I think it's hilarious."

I also wondered if there might not be some truth behind it. Neeraj had met Red at several department functions. And Neeraj was good at seeing into people. Which is one reason why his passion for Carol Jeanne must have been gratifying to her. He saw through her facade of cool competence and found the woman that Red had never seen. The trouble is, that hot-blooded, passionate, loving woman was not the woman who was in charge of Carol Jeanne's life. She was still making decisions on the basis of what she thought was right, rather than what she knew she needed.

I rather admired her for that—and I don't think that was because of my programming. I liked the fact that she was the sort of person who would suffer great personal loss in order to help keep her children's home and family intact. All the more so because I liked Neeraj. I thought he really would make her happy. And she was turning him away.

"Lovelock thinks you're a hoot," said Carol Jeanne. "Perhaps he wants you to swap witnesses with me."

Neeraj laughed. "Everyone knows that the capuchins are the cream of the cream. You need Lovelock like you need air, and you know it."

What did he mean? She needed me? For what, the esteem of having a capuchin? Cream of the cream . . .

"He's almost a friend," said Carol Jeanne, stroking my fur.

Neeraj smiled sourly. "Like I'm almost a lover?"

Neeraj understood how a single word could hurt. He even identified with me, for that moment, perched on the verge of something that promised to be glorious, and yet always held back, tethered, unable to leap and fly. Almost a friend. Almost a person. Almost alive. Almost real. But still not.

Well, Carol Jeanne, my dear almost-friend, I've got a bun in the oven my own self. I don't need you and I don't need Neeraj. I don't need *humans*. I'll take what I want from your decadent culture and your self-centered arrogant lives, and then I'll spit in your faces while my children and I create something new and fine. *We*, at least, will always know that there are other intelligent, valuable species in the world besides ourselves. *We* won't think that just because we have cleverly defined every other species as "animals" it gives us the right to destroy them, hurt them, ignore them, disdain them.

I'm ranting. Why shouldn't I? I wanted to rant at the time, but I couldn't. I simply moved out from under her hand and perched on the edge of her desk, looking off into space. She didn't even notice I was pissed off, as far as I could tell.

But Neeraj knew. He knew things about people. And he treated me more like a person than any other human. Had he analyzed me the way he analyzed Red? Lovelock is actually a horny little monkey, Carol Jeanne, and my guess is that his own biological clock has induced him to overcome his antisexual programming and steal a female capuchin embryo so he can develop it into a mate. What *else* would you expect from an enhanced capuchin who is being consumed by resentment and a vicious love-hate relationship with his owner?

No. Neeraj can't see that in me. My face has no expressions *he* knows how to read. He has never lived a day of my life. He keeps a witness himself—if he truly understood me or any other witness, he couldn't do that. He knows nothing about me. None of them do. None of them ever will.

But I know all about *them.* And I not only have more compassion for human beings than they have for me, but also I have more compassion for them than they have for each other. That's why, knowing what was happening to the girl Nancy, I couldn't just sit back and do nothing.

Ever since I read her offering that Sunday, I had been trying to think of what I could do to help her. I toyed with sending anonymous computer messages to her father, so he'd know that somebody was on to him. But that ran the double risk of exposing what I was capable of doing with computers and also of causing the father to treat Nancy even worse, since he would assume that she had told somebody. No, I needed to do something that would quickly, simply, efficiently get her out of the man's house and make sure he was eliminated as a threat to her and any other child.

I researched the applicable laws, and found that the legal code on the Ark was entirely oriented toward protecting the child. A parent convicted of either child abuse or incest would be expelled from the colony if the offense took place before launch. After launch, however, when the ties with Earth were severed, the penalties became much more draconian. This wasn't in the prospectus, but it made a brutal kind of sense. There were some offenses that simply couldn't be tolerated in the community, and since there was no way to handle imprisonment or exile, a person convicted of deliberately violating the safety of children would have a choice. He could allow the surgeons on the Ark to perform an operation on the limbic node to cause all libido and aggression functions to cause him excruciating pain. Or he could choose to be put to death.

The operation sounded vaguely familiar, even in the dry legal language of the penal code of the Ark. And when I researched it a little further, I discovered that the operation used as optional punishment for extreme crimes of aggression was one that had first been perfected in the witness program.

The worst penalty that the law allowed on the Ark was to do to a human being what had been done to me. That limbic node operation had installed a little device that Carol Jeanne could trigger with the painword, or I could trigger myself just by thinking of making love to a female. And it was done to me, not because I had committed a crime and deserved it, not because I was a defective creature who harmed its own young, but because I was to be "enhanced" and therefore needed to be kept under control.

I knew a secret, though. I knew that the limbic operation was not foolproof.

So I had to expose Nancy's father now, right away, when he could still be sent away from the Ark. Back to Earth. While Nancy and her mother stayed here.

Yet I didn't want to accuse him myself. If people realized I was spying on them during the offering, they would start resenting me, fearing me. I had to remain invisible to them. An amusing little monkey. Worse yet, it would reflect badly on Carol Jeanne, since they would assume my spying was on her behalf. Nor was an anonymous accusation by computer a viable option; since it was not evidence and wouldn't be enough to get Nancy away from her father, it would only make things worse for her.

I toyed with the idea of telling Carol Jeanne, flat out, what I had read on Nancy's offering, and simply letting her handle it. But that would have to be my last resort. No one would believe she had read the offering herself, so however she managed to handle things she'd end up revealing my role as a spy and it would harm both her and me.

But there was someone who could make the accusation without linking it to me at all.

God is back on the network again. He sent me another message. Only this time it wasn't snotty. I don't know what to do. I didn't even know stuff like this happened. Why doesn't Nancy just tell?

Her own father. Fathers don't do things like that. They might decide to stay on Earth and let your mother take you to some other planet without them, but they don't touch you. That's grosser than gross.

I picture Dad doing something like that to Diana and it makes me want to kill him. Only I know Dad never would. I want to kill Nancy's father.

The monkey's right, though. He may have found out by spying on the offerings (I knew the little bastard was spying!) but he can't very well use that as evidence because the offerings are sealed and can't be opened in court even if the minister hasn't destroyed them which is what he's supposed to do.

So I'm going to tell Diana and maybe she can help figure out a way to get Nancy to tell us herself. Then we can go to the police and "God," bless his tiny hairy butt, won't have to get involved.

Peter showed me a note from "God." I cried all night. Poor Nancy. I don't know how we're going to get her to tell us. You just don't walk up to somebody and say, I understand your dad commits incest and wondered if maybe you were the victim, and if so would you like to tell us so we can get you taken away from him? But I'll think of something or maybe Peter will.

I was going to say something snotty about how Peter never could think of something useful, but when I wrote it down it felt so stupid. Teasing Peter and talking about how dumb or awful he is or whatever, it feels so childish to act that way when something really serious is going on. All that stuff about fighting with Peter—he never hurts me, really. He teases, but he never hurts me. Not everybody feels as safe with their family as I do. And I guess that makes Peter not a bad brother after all.

CHAPTER TEN

CAGES

Justice moves swiftly on the Ark, something that I need to remember. It took only one day after my message to Peter for Nancy's family to feel the hand of the law. Peter told Diana, of course, and Diana went to Nancy and hinted sympathetically until Nancy spilled it all to her. I wish I'd seen it—I knew Diana was smart, but smart doesn't always mean you can get other people to do things.

Once Diana had heard about the abuse and incest from Nancy herself, she went straight to Red and told him all about it—without a clue of the message that had appeared on Peter's computer. I know how perfectly she handled that conversation with Red because I downloaded it from Pink. Pink doesn't mean to be my spy in Red's private meetings. It's in the nature of pigs to be exploited.

I'll give Red credit. He may be his mother's emotional stepan-fetchit but when it came to a problem outside his own family, he acted with absolute fairness and swiftness. By the book. He first checked with the school counselors and learned that Nancy's aberrant behavior had been noted with "possible abuse" marked in the file. The counselors had tried to draw her out, but the rules on soliciting testimony against parents were strict, and Nancy had not said to them anything clear enough to use.

Coupled with Diana's testimony, though, their observations provided ample corroboration to move ahead with the investigation. So the next morning at school, Red came and, with the counselor who had tried hardest to get through to Nancy, he confronted her with what he knew. He didn't mention Diana's name, but of course Nancy knew at once. Pink was there, so once again I got the scene.

"Diana wasn't supposed to tell," said Nancy dully.

"Everyone is supposed to tell about things like this," said Red. "That's the only way it will ever stop, is if people tell. What we need now is for *you* to tell."

"I'll never tell on my father."

"Do you know what, Nancy? If you simply say to us that what I have been told is true, we will immediately remove you from your father's house and take him into custody. He won't be able to punish you ever again. He'll be sent away from the Ark, and you'll have the choice of going back to Earth separately or staying here with your mother."

"Mother won't stay here without him," she said. "She only left Earth because he made her."

"Did *you* want to come?" asked Red.

Nancy nodded.

"If your mother decides to go back to Earth with your father, you can still stay. You're old enough to make that choice. And we'll all be proud of you for having the courage to tell the truth and put an end to his abuse of you."

Nancy looked sidelong at Red. "It's true, all right," she said in a little voice.

As I watched this replay from Pink's visual and auditory memory, it occurred to me that if she was old enough to choose to stay alone on the Ark, she was old enough to have walked out of her father's house and put a stop to the incest herself. But of course, the incest and the physical punishment had been going on for long enough that it was doubtful Nancy had much will of her own. How long would it take her to recover once she was removed from her father's house? Slavery changes a person, and it isn't that easy to decide to be free, even when it's within your power.

In fact, as I think about it, it occurs to me that Red's key phrase was "we'll all be proud of you." What Red implicitly promised was the fatherly approval that her own father never gave her, fatherly approval that she yearned for so deeply that, in the hope of someday attaining it, she would endure all the terrible things he did to her.

But I'm digressing. In fact, I think I'm really analyzing myself. I, poor fatherless creature that I am, also have that primate hunger for approval from a powerful male figure. Who is *my* father? Not

Red. I am not as desperate or ignorant as Nancy, to seize on Red as my father figure.

Within an hour, Nancy's father was in custody, being interrogated in the presence of a lawyer—and Red, Nancy's new advocate and protector. He admitted everything, weeping as he alternately accused Nancy of seducing him and begged for them to punish him for being so terrible to her. It was sad and sickening to watch.

Sadder still, though, was his wife's firm denial that any such thing had ever happened. "Sometimes he has to punish her, of course, because she's a sullen, rebellious girl," said the mother. "But those other charges are just a vicious little girl's way of trying to get out from under the strict rules of a righteous family."

The next transport back to Earth came in two weeks. Nancy's father and mother were on it.

In the meantime, though, Nancy came to live, temporarily, with us. She got the couch where Stef had slept for his first weeks in Mayflower. It was soon obvious to anyone who cared enough to pay attention that she had fixated on Red as her savior—and on Diana as her enemy. Odd, isn't it? To Nancy, Red was the one who had rescued her from her father's cruelty and his constant demand for sexual release, while Diana was the one who had betrayed Nancy's confidence, causing her to lose the love of her parents. Never mind that both results were inseparable—Nancy, disturbed as she was, was quite capable of separating them. She refused to stay in the house if Diana came over, which made it tricky to have Diana babysit for us.

The first time the subject came up, Nancy insisted that we didn't need any other babysitters, because she could babysit perfectly well herself. I had already warned Carol Jeanne that Nancy was seriously unstable and should *not* be left alone with Emmy and Lydia. Victims of abuse often become abusers, I reminded her. But in the event, my warnings weren't needed. Red himself laid it down as law. "Nancy," he said, "you still need to rest and recover from all that's happened to you. Tending little children is far too much stress for you. It will be years before I can consider allowing you to babysit anyone."

From him, Nancy took it without argument. But later that evening, as she sat alone watching a video while Carol Jeanne and Red were putting the children to bed, I watched and listened from the hallway.

"She just wanted to take away all my babysitting jobs," Nancy murmured. "That's why she did it, the little tattling bitch."

The meaning was obvious enough to me. Just as Nancy's father had blamed everything he did on her—calling her a bitch in the bargain—Nancy was blaming everything on Diana, and using the same name. You didn't have to be a shrink like Red to understand it.

What was frustrating was that Nancy wasn't stupid. She was almost bright, for an unenhanced human, and yet she couldn't see how absurd her own reasoning was. Babysitting had been the happiest part of her life, since it got her out of her father's house and into other homes where some kind of peace and normality prevailed. Now that Red had decreed that she could not babysit, Nancy "knew" that this had been Diana's motive all along. Nasty little child, taking her babysitting away from her . . .

Whenever I was home, I watched Nancy as much as possible. She never spoke her paranoid imaginings aloud again. All she did, at least when I was looking, was gaze at the video screen or watch Emmy and Lydia playing or just sit there, staring out the window of the house at the distant villages rising up the curving floor of the Ark into the sky. Her eyes were usually dead, but sometimes I saw them fill with tears or narrow with rage.

She said little, fitting smoothly into the routine of the household, even allowing herself to become something of a servant for Mamie. "Oh, Nancy, dear, could you fetch me that book I was reading?" "Oh, Nancy, sweetheart, be a dear and bring me a glass of water from the kitchen? Just one little bit of ice, that's all, if it gets too cold it just *burns* right down my throat, you *know* how it is when you get old, Nancy, you should get down on your knees and thank the Lord for your youth and bright spirits."

Which showed just how much Mamie noticed anything, since Nancy's spirits were about as bright as a rat's rectum. But Nancy, having been raised in utter servitude to another's will, responded as if Mamie were doing her a favor by giving her things to do. After all, she always asked nicely, which her father had never done. And

her requests gave the girl a sense of purpose, which was sorely missing now that her father was gone.

Sometimes, when her eyes were tight with rage and hate, she
would notice me, and try to wither me with her glare. The first few
times I looked away, but then I became resentful—why should *I*
hide from her? In the first place, she had no idea of my role in her
liberation. And in the second place, I cared not at all whether she
hated me or not. What could *she* do to *me*? So I smiled at her and
cavorted cheerfully whenever she glared at me. I'm really good at
clowning. Everybody laughs. But she never did.

It was during this time that two agents from the "physical fitness
department" showed up at Carol Jeanne's office. Two women, with
that wiry muscularity that made even marginally feminine clothing
fit them like a bad disguise. Looking at how lean they were, I estimated that neither of them had menstruated in years. I imagined
skin with veins standing out like gopher trails. Breasts like tennis
balls stapled onto otherwise masculine chests. Either of them could
have crushed my skull in one hand.

"We've come to talk to you about computer security violations,"
said the taller one, whose name turned out to be Mendoza.

Naturally, I had one terrible moment in which I thought all my
clever computer penetrations had been discovered and I was now
going to be destroyed. Instinctively I leapt for the highest point in
the room. Fortunately, Mendoza and Van Pell had no idea that what
they were seeing was the way a capuchin acts out guilty fear. Carol
Jeanne might have realized what my action meant, but she had
stopped paying attention to me years ago.

"Specifically," said Mendoza, "that unidentifiable message that
your family received a while back."

"We knew that our network was permeable," said Van Pell, "and
so when you arrived we installed some monitoring devices to make
sure we were alerted if someone broke into your system. You deal
with a lot of sensitive information, Dr. Cocciolone."

"Well, then," Carol Jeanne said. "You probably know more than
I do."

"Actually not," said Van Pell. "You see, someone neutralized our monitors. They were still in place, but it turns out that they've been sending us garbage."

"Oh," said Carol Jeanne. "Are you sure they weren't defective?"

"What we're sure of," said Mendoza, "is that they were rewired."

I toyed with the idea of denying having done anything. Let them think some clever spy was at work.

"Oh, is that all?" said Carol Jeanne. "I'm sure Lovelock did that."

So much for that idea.

"Lovelock?" asked Mendoza.

These goons were supposed to be the hotshot security force on the Ark, and they didn't even know the name of Dr. Cocciolone's witness? Hey, working out till you have less than two percent body fat doesn't make you efficient, it just makes you stringy.

"My witness," said Carol Jeanne. "Lovelock always checks out the security of my data. He undoubtedly found your devices and assumed they were some kind of attempt to spy. He's really very good with computers."

Why shouldn't I be? I've got a jack in the back of my head.

Mendoza and Van Pell looked at me with expressionless faces. I assumed they were sizing me up. Good with computers, eh?

"Your monkey's interference made it impossible for us to detect the source of that particular system penetration," said Van Pell.

Carol Jeanne laughed in their faces. "My witness was merely doing your job—protecting the security of my data. And, I might add, he did it better than you."

Thanks, Carol Jeanne. Let's make these goons really like me. Someday my life may depend on how cute and lovable they think I am.

"Next time you want to install some device in my computer," said Carol Jeanne, "tell me about it so that Lovelock knows to leave it in place. And even then, I suspect he'd still jimmy your devices, because he won't trust you to maintain security as well as he does."

"If he's so good," said Mendoza, "then he no doubt knows how the network was penetrated in order to send you that anonymous message."

"Lovelock?" asked Carol Jeanne.

I sprang to her computer. Mendoza and Van Pell, still standing at attention like Marine drill sergeants, oriented themselves so they could see what I typed. I acted confident, but in fact I was dying inside. My sleeper programs would only kick in and work for me when the new network went online. So if I showed them Peter's and my back door into the old network, they'd close it down and cut off my special access. That wouldn't be an absolute disaster, because I could write another access for myself. However, any new back door I created now, for the old software, increased my chances of getting caught before the new network even came online.

Still, I knew that it was better to tell them about the back door so they wouldn't keep searching for it. A really effective search *might* turn up my sleeper instead of the back door, and that would be by far the greater disaster. So I would give them the back door and they would stop searching.

"I discovered the means of entry within hours after the message was sent," I wrote. "I did an analysis of all network routines reading keyboard input and found one that responded to this password." I typed the backdoor password. "It gives master access, even more powerful than the sysops. The original programmers must have left this in."

They looked at each other with faces that might have registered astonishment if they had been capable of showing any expression more complicated than solemn narcissism.

"How did you break into the system in order to read the keyboard interpretation routines?" asked Van Pell.

I ostentatiously looked at the ceiling for a moment, to show them that I thought of this as obvious, easy, baby stuff. When I had demonstrated the technique, they both stood in silence for a long time. "You know," said Van Pell, "I'm going to be glad when we get rid of that shitty old software."

"When *is* the new network going online?" asked Carol Jeanne. "It would really help our work to be able to access all of the databases without having to change systems."

"Soon," said Van Pell.

"Sooner, in fact, now that we know that these most recent breaches of computer security come from problems that won't be present in the new software." Mendoza gave me a formidable glare. "In the meantime, don't let your monkey prowl in the system. He could do all kinds of damage without realizing it."

Every instinct demanded that I defecate into my hand and throw the pellet at her. But I restrained myself. Don't ever let it be said that monkeys can't be civilized. Besides, it would only make Mendoza all the more certain that she was right about me. Let her go on thinking that I was just an animal that somehow could access delicate computer equipment. It was my best protection, to have the security people think of me as a cleverly trained pet.

I had also managed to keep Peter's knowledge of the back door a secret. But since they would immediately set up traps now that they were aware of the back door, I would have to send Peter an anonymous message right away, warning him that the back door had been discovered and was now a trap. Plenty of time—it would take them hours to set up new routines.

Even as my thoughts were racing, Carol Jeanne was answering them—rather testily. "My witness was not prowling in the system. Lovelock merely investigated two breaches of security and dealt with them."

"Our monitoring devices were not a *breach* of security. They *were* security."

"When someone puts a monitoring device on my computer without asking my permission, ladies, that *is* a breach of security. Don't ever do it again."

They glared at her. It was a delicious confrontation—the hard-bodied law enforcement officers trying to face down a soft-bodied scientist. When they finally wilted beneath Carol Jeanne's benign gaze, it only showed that the kind of will that builds strong bodies twelve ways isn't a match for the kind of will that conceives of entire biospheres and brings them to life.

When they had left the room, Carol Jeanne laughed and reached for me. I jumped onto her soft chest and felt her fingers stroking me, and for a few moments I was insanely happy. Good slave. Attaboy. Good, good slave.

I checked the incubator as often as I could; after the first month, I did it every day. I knew that the real trial of my life would come when the baby emerged. Primate babies are born stupid and needy. They can't do anything for themselves. They need nurturing. I read everything I could find about the care and feeding of capuchin monkeys, learning everything that the humans meant to do to raise them properly so they could eventually fend for themselves in the wild on our new world. I carried the parts of a cage up the wall of the Ark to a recessed, secure hiding place and assembled them there, so that the baby wouldn't fall out when I had to leave her. I stole a hugger— a soft, yielding monkey-fur doll designed for hatched-out monkey embryos to cling to in order to satisfy their need for physical warmth and affection. Monkey fur . . . I'm *sure* the monkey they got it from died naturally.

Monkey chow was trickier. The supply was limited—only enough was being produced on the Ark to feed *me*. At first it wouldn't matter, because I would be feeding the baby a non-milk-based formula through a baby bottle, both common as dirt and easy to steal. In a few weeks or months, though, to give her a well-balanced diet I would have to steal from myself. Which meant that to eat adequately, I would have to get a good supply of fruits, flowers, and vegetables. Or else start eating leaves, which meant getting the runs in a big way. We capuchins are built so that during lean times, when there's nothing to eat but greens, our digestive systems kick into overdrive and process the roughage in a matter of three or four hours, so we can eat more and thus—maybe—get enough nutrients to stay alive till some fruit or other comes into season. What this translates to is, no more hard little pellets of poop. I would leave streaks of diarrhea everywhere I set my butt, and Carol Jeanne would take me to a veterinarian and he might well realize that I wasn't eating my monkey chow.

In other words, I was really planning ahead. I knew how everything should go, I knew all the dangers, and I was set.

Dearest beloved diary,

Nothing ever works out right. Peter and I get Nancy out of her terrible family and now she's not only not speaking to me, she's actually being nasty. Zoni told me at school today that Nancy is saying that I'm jealous of her and I'm always trying to get anything of hers that I can steal or copy or whatever. It's the stupidest thing ever said by any human who is not Peter. Why would she say things like that? Zoni says she's also been telling people that they better not let me know any of their secrets because I tell secrets all the time just to get people in trouble. This is NOT TRUE and I almost told Zoni that the only secret I ever told was that Nancy's father was being bad to her, but then I realized that even saying that would be telling a secret and it would make what Nancy was saying true. Which means that really I can't defend myself, because what do I do, go around telling people lists of all the secrets that I have kept? Anyway my true friends will still be my friends anyway, and who needs the other ones anyway?

So there I am putting up with really nasty gossip at school, and do you think Mother has time to listen to my woes? No, of course not, darlingest of diaries, you are the only one who listens to me. Mother is too busy floating around the house acting all feminine and lovely because of this short little Indian guy who's dating her. I mean, I'm glad Mom is happy and all that, and maybe it's good for her career because Neeraj is a big high muckymuck in the biology division which makes him a great contact for Mom. But I don't think she's thinking "career" when she gets so silly and moony-eyed. Peter says that Neeraj is just the first man who's treated Mother like a woman since we got here and she's horny as an upstream salmon, but I think that's disgusting. Women aren't like men, they don't ruin their whole lives over some man. Neeraj is short and ugly, and I don't think that makes me a bigot, he's not an American, that's all. I mean, why do we have these stupid villages anyway if you're just going to go off and marry somebody from another continent? What will we do if they get married, move to Ganges? Will we have to stop eating meat? Will I have to start putting a stupid dot on my forehead? Peter says that if Mom would just sleep with the guy and get it over with, we'd get rid of him sooner, but Mom's not that kind of woman. And I don't think he's that kind of man. I think they're going to get married and Peter thinks so too which is really scary because it's not like anybody's asking us for our vote, and we're the ones who are going to get our lives screwed up without any of the compensating benefits.

I don't want a father because I already have one, thanks. If

Mother marries him I'm going to run away and hide in the air conditioning and freeze to death and they'll find my desiccated, freeze-dried body in a duct somewhere and that will be fine with them because as Peter points out Mother is still fertile and she'll probably want to have a bunch of new cute dark brown babies that can grow up to worship cows.

When a new lion takes over an old lion's family, he kills all the cubs so the females will all come into heat and have his babies. Peter says that if we didn't hate Neeraj so much we'd probably like him. But I think that's horse pucky.

I found out about Neeraj and Dolores the easy way—I saw them together. I was on one of my clandestine journeys to the gestation chambers when I saw them under a tree in the dim light of evening. They were sitting there talking, that's all, but they were holding hands and it didn't take a Ph.D. in psychology to recognize that Dolores was flat-out in love with Neeraj.

My first thought was: It sure didn't take him long to find a substitute when Carol Jeanne made it clear she wasn't going to be available for marriage.

My second thought was: Dolores is in Mayflower. Neeraj couldn't have picked a mate under circumstances more likely to make Carol Jeanne writhe. Because I happened to believe that Carol Jeanne was still besotted with Neeraj, even as she tried to make her marriage with Red work.

My third thought was: Dolores is Peter and Diana's mother. Neeraj is the one adult human I've known on the Ark who seems to think of me as something like a person. Maybe there's some benefit for me in getting Neeraj into the same house with Peter and Diana.

I wasn't sure—I'm still not sure—what my motive was in going to Neeraj the next day. Was I trying to protect Carol Jeanne? Or project myself into Neeraj's new relationship? Both, probably.

He seemed delighted to see me. Actually, he seems delighted to see everybody, but that means that at least he thinks of me as *somebody*. I got straight to the point, typing on his computer that I wondered when he was going to talk to Carol Jeanne about his relationship with Dolores, and that I had been waiting for some time so he could tell her himself but that if he didn't do it soon, I would. "You're getting more careless," I wrote. "You were observed last night, and word is getting around."

"You're right," he said. "I'm such a coward. And besides, I didn't know until last night that—Dolores is going to be my wife. We worked it out. I'm joining Mayflower village and living with her."

"How kind of you," I wrote. "That will make it easier for Carol Jeanne, I'm sure."

"Carol Jeanne is not part of this equation, Lovelock," said Neeraj. "She made her decision. And now Dolores and I have to make our decisions without reference to anyone else. Except her children. Dolores would gladly have come to Ganges with me, but her daughter is obviously terrified of our relationship disrupting her life, and so Dolores and I decided that remaining in Mayflower was best for *them*. It's unfortunate that Dolores is in the same village as Carol Jeanne, but that's not how I met her or fell in love with her."

"I know," I wrote. "You only prowl at work."

For a moment he looked angry. Then he calmed himself. "Lovelock, is your snideness because of your programmed loyalty to your mistress? Are you only angry at me because you perceive this as harming Carol Jeanne? Or do you think that I've really done something wrong?"

The reference to my programming was a pointed insult, if I looked at it one way. But if I looked at it another way, it meant that Neeraj actually understood the basis of much of my behavior. And, take it how you will, he *was* asking me my opinion of his behavior. As if it actually mattered to him what I thought.

And I had to admit that there was nothing intrinsically wrong with his mating with Dolores. "I know the kids," I wrote. "They're very smart."

"Yes," said Neeraj. "They talk about you a lot. To them, Carol Jeanne is the woman that Lovelock lives with."

Talk about me a lot? I didn't dare ask, but I worried. How discreet were they? Had they mentioned our joint computer escapade?

"They're good children," said Neeraj, "and even though they don't realize it, they're desperately in need of their father. I can't replace him, but I can still provide the approval and sense of orderliness that children need from some male figure in their lives."

Nancy had chosen Red as her father figure, but he was not and never would be part of her family. If Neeraj married Dolores, however, he *would* be part of Peter and Diana's lives, and I had seen how effectively Neeraj worked on people. They would fall in love with him soon enough. And he would be loyal to them. He would *be there*. Something that Red couldn't really do for Nancy. Peter and Diana had no idea how lucky they were.

"When we're married," said Neeraj, "I don't imagine I'll have much contact with Carol Jeanne except professionally. However, I hope you know that you will be welcome in our home always. The children would welcome you. And so would I. I know that your duties keep you with Carol Jeanne most of the time. And I'm not being altruistic. If the children perceive me as your friend, it will make me more attractive to them. But I hope you realize that insofar as it is possible, I really *am* your friend."

The words struck deep in my heart. No human had ever said such a thing to me. It was like being thirsty to the bottom of my soul, and suddenly, unexpectedly, somebody had given me a drink. His offer of friendship spread through me like a warm fluid, watering places that had always, always been dry.

I wanted to embrace him. I wanted to speak to him of what these words meant to me. Instead, I had to type my answer on a screen. "And I am your friend, as far as my programming allows." It was a brittle, self-pitying thing for me to write, and I regretted it even as I typed it, yet I could not escape from my sense of my own powerlessness long enough even to accept wholeheartedly this good man's offer of friendship.

Yet he seemed to understand. He reached out and touched my back, not stroking my fur the way people do when they think of me as a pet, but rather letting his fingernails dig into the fur enough to lightly scratch my skin under the fur. Grooming me. He knew what would feel good, and he gave that to me.

He gave that to everyone. Why else had Carol Jeanne and Dolores both fallen in love with him? He had an instinct for needy people, for what would satisfy them, and he gave it freely.

And yet I still couldn't answer in the same generous spirit that he offered. "Why don't you have a family already?" I wrote.

He laughed gently. "Lovelock, haven't you done a dossier search on me?"

Of course I had, but it didn't say anything beyond the fact that he had been married once for barely a year, and there were no children. Since the marriage coincided with his application to enter the Ark, I had assumed it was a marriage of convenience. Not the great love of his life.

"I did not marry at the usual age, Lovelock, because I'm an untouchable. The caste that used to handle sewage and garbage in ancient India. The caste system has been legally dead for more than a century, but it still lives on in the prejudices of the people. Before I came to the Ark, I moved among the most educated intellectuals of India, and at the university there was never a hint that my caste was even noticed. But the families that can afford higher education for their children—especially their women—are of the upper castes. *Working* with me was fine, but their families would never have accepted me as a son-in-law. I fell in love several times as a young man, but I saw very quickly that to marry me would mean my wife giving up her relationship with her family. That's not what I wanted for my children, to live in a fragmented family. Two of the women broke up with me, and I broke things off with the third, all for the same reason. And for the same reason, I'm not sorry to leave Ganges village. There's no future there for me or any children I might have."

I understood now why he could look at my situation with such compassion. Untouchability was no longer the same kind of hopeless serfdom that it had once been, but it still gave Neeraj a taste of isolation and undeserved inferiority. He knew what my life might be like. He was at least able to imagine it.

Not that untouchability explained everything about Neeraj. Plenty of people in his situation would have been angry and bitter. Many would have reacted by *insisting* on marrying a Brahmin, just to prove that they were just as good as anybody else. No, Neeraj's compassion and sensitivity arose from himself. Untouchability had perhaps served as his teacher, but it was not the source of his character.

He smiled grimly. "I did marry, eventually. She was terminally

ill and didn't want to die alone. I needed a wife in order to be allowed to come on the Ark. It was a fair bargain, and we were very
good friends until she died. I even loved her, but I was also aware
of why she could bear to marry an untouchable—she knew she'd
never have to face her family again." He looked wistfully away from
me. "And her condition prevented her from having children."

The hardest thing for him, apparently, was that he had not been
able to reproduce. Surely he could understand my need to have
children. For a moment I was tempted to tell him my plan, to ask
for his help, so I wouldn't have to bear the burden entirely alone.
But then I came to my senses. He might be kind, perceptive, fair-
minded—but he was still a human, and I was not. I could not en-
trust the precarious future of my species to him.

Now, though, I could answer him without harshness. "I'm an
untouchable, too," I typed. This was as close as I could come to
telling him my yearnings. "Yet you have touched me," I added.

In answer, he groomed my fur again.

Later that day, he came to Carol Jeanne's office and told her. He
was gracious enough to treat it as happy information that he wanted
to tell her himself, and not as some serious news that he had to
"break" to her. "We're not doing a big wedding thing," said Neeraj.
"We're both too old for that. But I imagine rumors will start flying
in Mayflower even before we make it legal and I move in to Dolores's
house. So I wanted you to hear the good news from me." It was his
way of explaining that she wouldn't have to put up with his wedding
as a social event in Mayflower, but that he *would* be living there.

"Congratulations," she said cheerfully. "You need to be married,
Neeraj, and I think you'll be good for those children. They're so
bright, and so lonely."

His eyes lingered on her for a moment too long. Some remnant
of his love for her? I thought not. No, his silent gaze was a substitute
for saying the obvious: That Carol Jeanne, too, was so bright, and
so lonely. That he would have been good for her, too, if only she
had chosen to accept him.

But by marrying him, Dolores was providing her children with
a substitute for a father who was already gone. Carol Jeanne would
have had to take her children away from a father who was still very
much present. There was no analogy. Both Dolores and Carol

Jeanne might have been in love, but they also acted for the benefit of their children, as best they understood it.

Carol Jeanne knew all of that. But a few minutes after Neeraj left, she asked me to lock the door. I did. Before I could even turn around, she was crying into her folded arms, leaning across her desk. I sat on her arm and groomed her hair, but I don't think I was much comfort to her.

My betrothed emerged from the incubator with an attitude. Specifically, an attitude of unrelenting hostility.

I was ready to let the primate cuteness response take over. A tiny-fingered, big-headed, fuzzy, wide-eyed youngling with jug ears and a button nose—I felt a surge of positive emotions as the endorphins in my brain rewarded me for being kind and nurturing toward the cute little tyke.

But my baby capuchin had a chip on her shoulder from the start. It was as if she knew that she was not just illegitimate but illegal, and resented the disadvantages this would cause her. I knew, of course, that such thoughts were really a projection of my worries and fears and feelings of guilt. But she really did seem annoyed at everything I did and didn't do.

I wasn't ignorant. I had read the books. But I'm not a female, and so I don't have a lot of instinct on my side. Primate males are predisposed to protect and play and even, proudly, to provide. But feeding, cuddling—we can do it, but it isn't with the same inborn ease that females usually bring to it. Plus we don't have the same urgency to feed the infant that comes from the pressure of milk in the breast, and there's no pleasure response from suckling. At best I was going to be a substitute for the real thing.

But at least I knew what was needed. And everything worked according to plan. I went through the process of separating her from the umbilicals by the book, and everything went smoothly—as it should have, since, next to life support during the voyage, the gestation chambers were the most vital system on Ark. When I got her out of the fluids, I bathed her and dried her. Of course she cried and fussed in protest, but soon I had her clinging to my fur, which she took to naturally, and I tried to ignore the immediate crawling search for a nipple. Time enough for that at the nest I had made, where formula and water were stockpiled.

It was night, and I made sure to follow the patterns that I had established for my freefall practice. Since I had been smuggling objects up the wall for weeks, it was even easier to carry her, since she clung to me.

I had rigged a room in an area where an array of pipes and electrical conduits crossed over and under each other. Some of the pipes stood almost a foot away from the surface of the wall here, and it had been simple to build a secure structure behind them. It wasn't as good as human daycare and *way* worse than a careful mother, but I wouldn't have to worry about the kid falling out and landing wherever the low gee environment allowed her to land. And since the basis of the structure was a heavy-gauge wire box designed for locking dangerous switches or breakers that still had to remain visible, I could see in and she could see out. She would get brightening and darkening that would help establish the rhythms of the day for her. She would get a sense of space. And it was still low enough on the wall that she was getting more than half the gravity effect that we got down near the surface.

The trouble was that we didn't even get a full gee at the surface, either, and that meant she felt as though she were in orbit from the start. As I climbed to the cage, her grip on my fur got tighter and more frantic. Then, inside the cage, when I pried her off of me and tried to get her to cling to the hugger, she didn't take it well. She cried and, to my shock, *let go*. She dropped, rather slowly, to the bottom of the nest, and her arms kept jerking around. This is a maladaptive response, I thought. Until I realized that what I was seeing was the startle reflex, over and over and over again. It was hard to distinguish it from a seizure.

I held her again. Now her clinging was even more desperate, and she no longer rooted for a breast. She just hung on, her heart racing.

What could I do? I had already established the nest at the lowest elevation on the wall where it could remain completely hidden. She would *have* to adapt.

I had already mixed the infant formula and soon managed to get the nipple into her mouth. Her sucking was not strong and in her fear she kept forgetting to suck on it. It took an hour before she got even the tiny amount that the book said she should be expected to get so soon after birth.

It was a good thing she wasn't nursing from me. The hormones of fear and anxiety would have been at intoxicating levels in my milk, if my body had known how to make any. Things had gone so smoothly, too. I just hadn't counted on the fact that my betrothed might not take to high elevations. She just wasn't acting as I needed her to act.

And what did I expect? Even if she had been an enhanced capuchin like me, she was still an *infant*. Primates have such big skulls, to hold all those brains, that they have to be born earlier in the brain's development than lesser animals, so the head can still get through the birth canal without killing the mother. That means that they're stupider at birth than, say, baby horses, even though they have more mental potential in the long run. An adult monkey, even unenhanced, is quite adaptable to different environments, as long as there's a recognizable food supply. But she was no adult. Under the stress of low gravity, she needed a parent for constant comfort.

Well, that's what she got. For about twelve hours. Dangerous as it was to disappear for so long, I stayed with her until she slept, and then when she woke she ate a little better than before. Finally she was calm enough that I could put her on the hugger and she would cling to it instead of going into that startle reflex reaction and dropping to the floor of the nest. I could leave.

Not that she liked it. I could hear her mewling cries half the way down the wall. The flip side of that cuteness response is that the sound of an infant crying is the most unbearable sound a primate can hear. The anxiety level is amazing. You feel like you have to *do* something. That's why humans hate the sound of a crying baby on an airplane. It causes fantastic levels of anxiety at an already-anxious time, and there's nothing they can *do*. Well, that's the sound I heard, and believe me, all I really wanted to do was climb back up and hold the baby so she'd be quiet.

But if she and I were to survive at all—and, with us, any hope of a tribe of free enhanced capuchins—then I had to keep us from being discovered. And that meant getting down the wall and back into more normal patterns of life. She would have to live with less frequent feedings than she needed sometimes. She would have to live with low gravity. And I would have to leave her crying sometimes. Maybe often. Maybe every time.

Perhaps Carol Jeanne would have noticed my frequent long absences, except that her own life suddenly became overwhelmingly confused. It began the third day of my betrothed's life. I had been monitoring Pink's memory regularly, mostly to get information about Nancy and to make sure Red and Carol Jeanne weren't discussing any strange behavior on my part when I wasn't there. But on that day I noticed that there were a lot of long gaps in Pink's data. A lot of times when Pink wasn't with Red.

This was disturbing. It suggested that Red was afraid that I was doing exactly what I was doing—monitoring Pink. Who else could? And he was doing something he didn't want me to know about.

No, strike that. He was doing something he didn't want Carol Jeanne to know about. Red didn't think of me as a person; he never had. He was afraid that if Pink was witness to whatever he was doing during these two- and three-hour blocks of time, Carol Jeanne would get wind of it.

So I followed him. I was going to visit the baby for another frustrating feeding in which she would sullenly refuse to eat enough until I coaxed and coerced the right amount down her throat. Needless to say, it was emotionally painful enough that I didn't mind delaying a bit to find out where Red was going without Pink.

I had assumed that he was carrying on an affair, and I was pretty sure that it was with Liz. But to my surprise, Red headed for his father's apartment in the singles' quarters. It had to be his father he was going to see—there were only a couple of dozen single adults on the Ark, and Red didn't know any of them except for Stef. Could it be that Red was simply making time for a closer relationship with his father? Could he actually be less dominated by his mother than I had thought?

But when he got there and knocked on the door, it wasn't Stef who opened it. Of course it wasn't. Stef was at work. Red was simply using his apartment for his clandestine meetings with his lover. It *was* an affair. And, when naked arms reached out to embrace him and pull him into the apartment, I also heard a voice uttering sweet nothings with surprising enthusiasm. The enthusiasm I couldn't comprehend, but the voice I knew well enough. It was Liz.

Just as I had expected, after all.

The only surprise was when I went back down the corridor and turned a corner and ran into Neeraj.

He reached down for me and brought me up to his shoulder, where we could converse quietly. Well, where *he* could converse.

"So Stef is playing at Pander," he said. "Dolores was sure Liz was having an affair with Red, but I told her that was just malicious gossip. I have to hand it to Mayflower village. Their gossips may be spiteful and voyeuristic, but they're also fairly accurate."

I nodded. That had been my observation as well.

"So now what, Lovelock? Do we tell Carol Jeanne, or let her go on thinking that Red actually wants their marriage to succeed?"

I shrugged elaborately, then cocked my head and looked at him sideways. Being Neeraj, he understood the gesture.

"Ah, there it is. What is *my* motive? Do I want to disrupt Carol Jeanne's marriage so that I can perhaps marry her after all? The answer is no, Lovelock. My commitment to Dolores is final. Partly because I do love her. And partly because I am not a man like Red— even if I change my mind later, even if I fall in love with another woman, I will keep my word to Dolores. Carol Jeanne knows that, too. Even if in her anger she thinks I am being vengeful or trying to get her away from Red, she will soon realize that is not in my nature."

I shrugged. He was giving Carol Jeanne credit for more reasonableness than I thought she would manage. I was quite sure that whoever told her about Red's affair would become loathsome to her for a long time to come.

I pointed at Neeraj.

"Yes, of course, it would be better if the news came from me," said Neeraj. "I won't have to face her every day afterward for the rest of my life. Well, actually, I will, won't I, given our two careers. But she won't have absolute power over me, and if she cuts me off emotionally, I have other resources. So it's me, I agree with you."

I nodded vigorously.

"But now the hardest question comes. Should I tell her at all? I've been puzzling that one out for days. Dolores says definitely not, never, because it will only cause pain. But I say that the very fact that the Mayflower gossip mill has the story suggests that *someone* is going to tell. So, will it be a villager who already resents Carol Jeanne because of her fame and her reputation for aloofness? Or will it be a friend?"

I shrugged.

"So. You don't want to commit yourself, eh? I gave you credit for more courage than that, Lovelock. You know her better than anyone. Would she rather know the painful truth? Or would she rather live the blissful lie?"

I knew what Carol Jeanne would *say*, if asked that question. I'm a scientist, she would say. I want the truth, no matter how hard it is to hear it. But I also knew that she was more fragile than anyone expected. Her outer toughness was a protective device. She would not cope well with betrayal.

For me, though, the clincher was the fact that she would find out eventually anyway, and the longer it went on before she found out, the more deeply betrayed she would feel—not just by Red, but by all who knew and didn't tell her.

I nodded. And then, to make the message clear, I reached up and parted his lips.

"So I should open my mouth, is that what you're saying?"

I patted his cheek and nodded.

"Thank you, Lovelock. I will play the bad guy. Just make sure you're there for her as she deals with the pain of this. You've been off gallivanting around lately   Carol Jeanne knows you've been going through a hard adjustment to the Ark, and she hasn't minded your not being with her as constantly as before. But this time you need to sacrifice a little and *be* with her. Not as her witness, but as her friend."

I nodded my agreement and then held out my hand. He took it between his fingers and we shook on it. A promise. A deal.

I was lying, of course. Because I knew what Neeraj could not understand: that Carol Jeanne was my master, not my friend. I would pretend to love and comfort her, but in fact I would be with her no more than necessary. In the disruption of her marriage I saw the potential for chaos, and in that chaos I could do a better job of nurturing my betrothed. *She* was the one going through a hard time. *She* was the one who needed me. Not Carol Jeanne.

Neeraj told Carol Jeanne within the hour, while I was struggling once again to get my baby to eat. By the time I got back home, the scene was already under way. Carol Jeanne was watching in icy silence as Red packed up to move out of the house. Mamie was crying bitterly and insisting that it was all a misunderstanding. The children were over at Dolores's house. Nancy was watching malevolently from a corner—her hatred directed at Carol Jeanne, I noticed, and not at Red. No doubt her sick little mind saw this situation as Carol Jeanne cruelly throwing out sweet, wonderful, wise Red, and all because he had been forced by Carol Jeanne's cold, unloving nature to seek comfort in another woman's arms.

"This is nothing to break up a family over," Mamie was saying. "It's just idle gossip, Carol Jeanne, Red would never be unfaithful to you."

Carol Jeanne didn't so much as glance at her.

"You have no heart," said Mamie. "You are made of ice and steel. God did not make a woman when he made you."

Carol Jeanne might seem unemotional to Mamie, but I knew that her silence represented barely concealed emotion. Carol Jeanne dared not speak to Mamie, or she would break down in abject weeping, and to Carol Jeanne that would merely compound her humiliation.

Finally Mamie's denials began to give way to some connection with reality. "Where will we live, Red? How much of my furniture can we take with us?"

Red looked up from his packing, surprised. "Not *we*, Mother," he said. "I'm going to the singles' quarters."

"You're not moving in with Liz?" asked Carol Jeanne quietly.

"Liz isn't about to break up her marriage over this," said Red coldly.

Mamie was oblivious to anything but her own predicament. "You're going to leave me here alone?"

"I'll be here every day while Carol Jeanne is at work, to look in on the children," said Red. "But yes, I'm leaving you here."

"With your furniture," said Carol Jeanne quietly. It was as close to a nasty retort as she could allow herself.

"But that's silly," said Mamie. "I'm *your* mother, not *hers*. Why should I stay here?"

"To take care of the children, Mother," said Red.

"I can take care of them," said Nancy, from her corner.

"Your counselors and I agree that you cannot handle the stress of child care," said Red. "In fact, you shouldn't be trying to handle the stress of this little scene, either. I wish this had happened while you were at school. We'll have to find another home for you."

I knew what Nancy was thinking—that she would be glad to set up housekeeping with Red. In your dreams, Nancy.

"I have the best plan," said Mamie, abruptly putting on her happy little good-idea voice. "Since I'm your mother, and my furniture fills this house, and I'm needed to tend the children, then *you* should stay here, Red, and Carol Jeanne should go to the singles' quarters."

That was the straw that broke the camel's back. Carol Jeanne turned to her, fire leaping from her eyes even as tears welled over and spilled down her cheeks. "I'm not the one who broke my marriage vows, Mamie. I'm not the one who went screwing around with my spouse's best friend. So I'm certainly not the one who's going to move out and leave my children. However, you are free to take *my* furniture out of here. I never wanted you to bring it and it clutters up the house."

Carol Jeanne shouldn't have tried direct argument with Mamie. When it came to snideness, she was out of her league, taking on the queen bitch. "Apparently your petty vindictiveness is so wide-ranging, Carol Jeanne, that it extends to inanimate furniture. Red, dear, be sure to leave your toothbrush so Carol Jeanne can pull the bristles out one by one."

Red was through packing his clothing and personal effects into two duffels. He carried them to the front door, speaking as he went. "Carol Jeanne will never let me keep the children, Mother. Not that she particularly wants to be a mother—that has never been either her interest or her talent. She simply couldn't bear the public embarrassment of letting me have them, even though I've been their primary caretaker all along." Thus he proved that even family therapists were not above using the truth as a weapon.

It was now, with his bags at the door, that Mamie pulled out all the stops. No more illusion of rationality: She wept, she pleaded, she hung on him and tugged at his clothing, accusing him of conspiring with Stef to destroy her, of leaving her to languish among people who hated her. Having seen Red cave in to her emotional theatrics time and time again, I kept expecting him to give in, to take her with him into a new household, to do *something* to mollify her. But instead, for the first time since I had known him, he was absolutely stolid. He allowed her to vent her emotions—he *was* a therapist, after all—but not by even a twitch of his face did he show that her pleas were having any effect on him.

It dawned on me that it wasn't Carol Jeanne that Red was leaving, or not *just* Carol Jeanne. He had no desire whatsoever to take his mother with him.

My whole concept of Red changed in that moment. His kowtowing to his mother over the years was not because he was really devoted to her. Rather it was a survival strategy he must have developed during his childhood: Giving in to Mother meant peace and quiet at home. Giving in with enthusiasm made her so happy that she would allow him a little freedom now and then. It also allowed him to win the competition with his father for power in the house. All the while, however, his inmost self resented her control. He longed to be free, but couldn't find any way to achieve that. Even marriage hadn't helped. But now, by breaking up with Carol Jeanne, he had found a way to get free of *all* the women in his life, all the responsibilities, all the emotional demands. I suspected he even wanted to get away from the children. Now he could visit them when *he* wanted to, and then walk away. And he wasn't walking into a new set of responsibilities, either. Liz had no intention of breaking up her marriage? I would bet that Red had persuaded her not to do it.

I wouldn't be at all surprised if Red broke off his affair with Liz right away. It wasn't Liz that he loved. It was the idea of breaking up his oppressive home life. Now that the affair had served its unconscious purpose, he would lose interest quickly.

Admittedly, I didn't understand all this as I watched Red cast off Mamie's emotional grappling hooks. All I really knew at that moment was that Red had far more strength than I had ever thought, and that he was loving it as his mother exhausted herself trying to win his compliance.

I also knew that if he had shown even a fraction of this strength with his mother a year ago, he could have left her and Stef on Earth and perhaps worked out a decent marriage with Carol Jeanne. Maybe he had never wanted the marriage to work out. Maybe he didn't want to be married at all. Maybe that's why, in marrying, he had chosen a woman who was unable to be as emotionally giving as he needed. Maybe he unconsciously chose to marry a woman he could walk away from when the time at last came.

In the meantime, Mamie was spewing forth the evidence of her victimization. "This is the bondage of women! Always forced to comply with the will of the *men* in their lives. Telling me where I have to live, forcing me to stay where I'm hated. Women have no choices in this world!" This from the woman who had ruled her home with an iron fist for decades.

It took half an hour, there at the door, for Mamie to wind down and fall silent. She was in the most dramatic possible position, sprawled on the floor, clinging to his legs, sobbing quietly. Red picked up the duffels and stepped over his mother's supine body as if she were a pile of books or a rolled-up rug. "I'll see you tomorrow, Mother, when I come to see the children. Have a nice night." To Carol Jeanne he offered no good-bye at all. He just opened the door with the soft whoosh of air that always came, held it open while Pink trotted out, and then he was gone.

The door closed with a soft popping of air pressure. The silence was perfect, except for Mamie's soft sobs and whimpers. Carol Jeanne looked at the door for a few moments, then went to her bedroom. Before I followed her, I looked at Nancy and saw that her cheeks were streaked with tears. Despite Mamie's hysterics, I suspected that it was Nancy, of all the women in the house, who would miss Red the most.

Carol Jeanne hadn't gone to her bedroom as I expected. Instead she was in the office, sitting before the computer. I came in and perched beside the monitor. She looked surprisingly calm. She looked at me and gave me a grim little smile. "He'll never breathe a word of it, I'm sure, and neither will I," she said, "but I can tell *you*, Lovelock. I didn't tell him to leave. I didn't even ask him to leave. In fact, I asked him to stay." She gave a harsh little laugh that had one good solid sob in it. "The story will go through Mayflower village that I threw him out of the house, cold unfeeling bitch that I am— Mamie will see to it that that's the story that's put around. But the truth is, he wanted to go. He wanted to go."

So she had seen it, too. Red was a complicated fellow after all.

Carol Jeanne sat there for a long time, saying nothing. Finally I realized that she was really working on the reports and analyses she was calling up on her computer, not just pretending to work. This was the solace she wanted right now. Still, I stayed with her, even though I wanted to go see my betrothed. I sat on her shoulder, grooming her, stroking her neck, and she must not have minded, because she didn't send me away. For a while, physically close to her like that, I could almost pretend that I was her friend, and not her servant.

Later, after she had cleared the most important work, Carol Jeanne logged off and leaned back in her chair. "Lovelock, I want you to be present during all of Red's visits to the house when I'm at work." Then she got up and went to the bathroom.

She didn't explain her reasons. I knew what they were anyway. She needed me to make sure Red didn't turn the children against her behind her back.

To me, though, it meant that I would have a lot of chances to slip away and visit my own baby.

My betrothed. My beloved-to-be. Someday the mother of my children. That was the day that I finally decided on a name for her. Given what had just happened between Red and Carol Jeanne and between Carol Jeanne and Liz and between me and everybody else, the name was definitely ironic, but also intensely appropriate, I felt. Because the one thing I would never do, I was sure, was betray *my* mate as Red had betrayed his.

I named her Faith.

CHAPTER ELEVEN

DISCOVERIES

Faith was not thriving, and I didn't know what I could do about it. When I came to feed her, she was listless; the panic and desperation had now given way to a kind of resignation that frightened me. She ate little. She clung to the hugger and to me, but there seemed little comfort in it, for either one of us.

But what could I do about it? The cause could be the discomfort of the lower gravity so far up the wall, but could I move her down into the areas where humans were far more likely to go? Or it could be the loneliness and lack of physical comforting, but how could I spend a moment more with her than I did? Or it could be some disease, but I couldn't very well take her to the veterinarians on the Ark, could I? They weren't in business right now anyway, except for the ones who were on call for sick or injured witnesses. I couldn't very well show up with a sick baby capuchin. It was my life on the line, not just Faith's.

So I kept on, doing my best to get away and spend time with her, and there were times, as she made feeble attempts to groom me or to play, that I felt a bit of hope that, hard as her infancy might be, she would prove resilient, would recover the natural ebulliency of young primates, and would eventually become, not my ward, but my mate.

Mate. Not wife. For she would always be a capuchin, unenhanced and therefore incapable of true communication with me. As for our children, they would prove whether this work was worthwhile. If they inherited even a portion of my enhancements, there was hope for us to survive as an independent sentient species on the new world. If I could keep us alive on the Ark till then. If I could find a way to get us to the surface of the planet.

Was Faith's despair contagious?

One afternoon I came to Carol Jeanne's office to find Neeraj and several other top scientists just arriving. They quickly gathered around Carol Jeanne's computer, where she was explaining something.

"The databases are still separate, and require a separate log-in," she was saying. "Your old log-in will work until six o'clock tonight, so get in and change your passwords to fit the new protocol. If you miss, it will be a lot of bureaucratic rigmarole to get you access to the secure databases, and you'll have to give a written explanation of why you didn't sign in to change your log-in. Remember that you will now have two passwords, a primary and a secondary. The secondary is used for encryption and you'll be asked for it at random intervals. You're also required to change both passwords at least every ten days, which means a lot of trouble memorizing them, I know, but it's worth it to have the convenience of having all the databases accessible from the main network. Any questions?"

I had a few, but I suspected it wouldn't be wise for me to mention them. Secure databases? I thought all the databases were secure. But apparently there was an important secret database that all of these people knew about, but which Carol Jeanne had kept secret from me.

Secret! From me!

"And just in case any of you are wondering," said Carol Jeanne, "we take security so seriously that I have never allowed my witness to see my passwords to the secure databases. In fact, I've never allowed him to watch me log in, and I know Neeraj has been equally discreet. That way nobody can get the information from our witnesses' electronic memory. Do likewise. Never log on in front of another person, even someone who has full access to the secure database. In other words, never log on even in front of me. You never know when someone might have their log-on taken away from them, and you certainly don't want them to be able to get into the system using yours." She looked around at them. "Any questions?"

"We can just use our regular computers now?" asked one man, dubiously.

"We won't be maintaining two separate systems anymore. The locked rooms will now be open, just like any others. We'll be moving people into those spaces so our offices won't have to be so cramped. That'll make it worth the pain of changing passwords all the time. Any other questions?"

"Just one," asked a woman. "Does this mean we can launch now?"

"The announcement will be made officially in the villages to-night," said Carol Jeanne, "but the rumor's going to fly much faster than that. Launch is set for two weeks from today, at noon. Which means that we must be moved into our launch compartments by midnight the night before, and all work in all departments except crew and life support will cease as of noon the day before launch. So anything you need from Earth, get it now. And I mean *now*. They're going to be swamped by last-minute requests from every-body. We're supposed to have been ready to leave at a moment's notice, but I have a feeling everybody here is going to think of at least one massive report or database or record that you just can't live without." If Carol Jeanne had smiled during that last remark, it might have been taken in good humor. But she didn't smile, and so it sounded like she was accusing them of being nervous fools. I could see a few of them clenching their jaws or looking away. Poor Carol Jeanne. I knew she meant nothing by that remark, that in fact it was a kind of joke about human nature, but no one else had a clue.

Except Neeraj. He chuckled in response to what she said. But Carol Jeanne didn't want to hear his warm laughter. With her family collapsing around her ears, she didn't need to be reminded that she *might* have had him in her life, if she had been just a bit less correct in her behavior. It was her turn to clench her jaw and turn away. "All right, that's it," she said. "I urge you to go to your terminals and *immediately* change your log-ins on the secure database. Otherwise you'll get busy and forget."

Again, some of them seemed to take it as an affront. What does she think we are, idiots?

Well, yes, actually. Brilliant, but idiots. It's not as if she didn't have plenty of evidence of absentmindedness from every one of them.

But not from me. She knew I paid attention. She knew I noticed things, that I remembered them, that I followed through. And during all our time on the Ark till now, she had managed to conceal from me the very existence of the secure databases. Now, of course, all those assignments she had given me while she left the office to "check up on things" made sense. The work I did had been real enough, but it was also a way to keep me occupied while she went to a locked room and used a computer on a different network.

Well, Carol Jeanne, you sweet trusting thing, you, I won't be *needing* your password anymore, if my sleeper did its job.

I was dying to get off by myself to check out the new network, but it was two hours before I could slip away from Carol Jeanne. In fact, I engineered my departure by typing her a note on the clipboard computer she had set up for me on top of the filing cabinets, and sending it to her via the network.

carol jeanne, have YOU changed your log-in?

I knew her very well. She read the message the moment it popped up on her screen, and she blushed. "I ought to follow my own advice more often," she said. "Lovelock, I'm not allowed to do this in front of anybody, not even you. Would you mind leaving the room?"

Mind? Would I *mind*?

I typed my answer. "Why don't I go home and look in on the girls?"

"Excellent idea, Lovelock."

Ten minutes later, having ascertained that it was naptime for the children and that Mamie was entertaining Penelope with tales of her suffering as a babysitter for her ungrateful coldhearted husband-castrating daughter-in-law, I was alone with Carol Jeanne's computer.

Before I tried my sleeper program, I opened up Carol Jeanne's computer and checked it for new electronic snooping devices. The old one was there, with my bypass maneuvers still in place. I almost took that as a sign that the security people had given up, but then I remembered Van Pell and Mendoza's expressions of blank determination, and so I also opened up the monitor and the keyboard and the mouse and the printer, and sure enough, they had installed devices in all of them, so that they would get a complete record of every keystroke typed and every character displayed on the screen or printed out. I didn't try to finesse these as I had the first snooping device. I just removed them, broke off all the breakable parts, and laid them on a white sheet of paper on Carol Jeanne's desk. Let her fight it out with Mendoza and Van Pell.

With the snoops gone, I typed my access and, sure enough, my sleeper came up. I wasted no time. I went straight to the password system and found out Carol Jeanne's primary and secondary passwords. While I was at it, I also got Neeraj's and the special passkey codes that Van Pell and Mendoza had. It wasn't easy to get them, of course—they didn't just keep a file somewhere listing them all. They were encrypted, but I had complete control over the system, and so I got it to do what even Van Pell and Mendoza couldn't have done—decrypt the passwords without my knowing either of them. My sleeper worked perfectly. The system was my slave, and I felt exultant and powerful. It was an unaccustomed feeling, and I liked it. But it didn't last long.

Because, having once armed myself with their passwords, I began looking into secret places that I had never been able to see before. Van Pell and Mendoza had a very large file on me—much larger than their file on Carol Jeanne. My previous impression was wrong. They didn't think I was a harmless monkey, doing only what Carol Jeanne told me. Their reports and memos made it clear that they thought Carol Jeanne had lost control of me, and they had already filed several recommendations that I be destroyed, if it could be done in a way that wouldn't arouse suspicion.

"Should be easy enough," said Van Pell's latest memo. "He's off by himself a lot. He could 'fall' from the wall. Not good to have anybody with his computer ability at large, especially since he is clearly pursuing his own program."

And here I thought I already knew what fear felt like.

When I was calm enough to think straight, I realized there were a couple of nice things. They might be deciding whether or not to kill me, but at least they called me "he" and used the term "anybody" in reference to me. And they had no clue about Faith. They didn't know I had been stealing materials to build Faith's nest. I realized then that they were merely observing me from a distance, and only now and then—enough to know that I was away from Carol Jeanne a lot; and as for their knowing my computer abilities, I had blithely demonstrated them myself.

The answer was obvious. Stick to Carol Jeanne like glue. They'd never dare to kill me in her presence.

Trouble was, I couldn't do that if Faith was to have any hope of thriving.

I had been at it for a couple of hours, and it was time to check in on Faith and then get back to Carol Jeanne. My dilemma was now worse than ever. And the worst thing of all was that with the launch coming up, the nest would have to move. The obvious reason was that when we launched, the rotation of the Ark would cease, and instead acceleration would provide our artificial gravity. At that point, the "wall" where I had built the nest would become the floor. All the soil would fall from where it now was down onto the floor, completely burying all the pipes and ducts and wiring.

But we had to move much sooner than two weeks from now. Because the maintenance people would naturally inspect every inch of every pipe and conduit on the wall. It would probably take them a couple of days to get started—I had already researched their routines and they could do a full inspection of the wall in six days. That meant they wouldn't need to rush into it tonight. But the most I could be sure of was a day in which to move the nest.

This was the time I had dreaded all along. The human population of the Ark would be crowded, four to a room, into the tiny cubicles that now provided the singles' quarters. Nobody would be out in the villages. All the substantial trees and bushes would have their roots balled and be moved from the surface down into warehouse space that was currently empty. In other words, the entire Ark would be a maelstrom of activity, and there would hardly be a cubic centimeter that someone wouldn't see, let alone inspect carefully, during the next two weeks.

Somewhere in all this I had to hide Faith.

Worse, I had to do it knowing that Mendoza or Van Pell or another of their hypertrophied clan might be looking for a chance to off me in some accidental-looking way. Oh, we're so sorry, Dr. Cocciolone. Your witness seems to have been crushed to death under a giant rootball. Your witness seems to have been electrocuted by current running through a wire that hadn't had any current in it before. Your witness seemed to be carrying a large metal box down the wall, and he fell. We're so sorry for the inconvenience. Perhaps your next witness will be a more docile animal. A pig, for instance. Or perhaps a guppy. You carry it around in a plastic cup like a urine sample. It never goes off on its own, dismantling security devices.

Not that they could come up with a new enhanced animal for Carol Jeanne. Perhaps when I was dead they'd co-opt Pink. After all, it would be ludicrous for Red to have a witness when Carol Jeanne didn't.

What a morbid line of thought. But death seemed like a real possibility to me as I went up the wall to Faith's nest. She didn't even look at me as I came in, and for the first time I realized that her hair was falling out. There were a couple of little hairless patches. She was famine-thin, too. But if somehow I got her unnoticed off the wall and down into the underground, perhaps the higher gravity would help her. She could still recover.

Of course, there would be that long weightless day or two as they stopped the spin of the Ark and began the acceleration. How would she respond to *that?* I would have her strapped down, but I wouldn't be able to visit her—they'd have *me* strapped down somewhere, too. I had always known that when the launch came, she'd be left with nothing but water for the launch itself, but I had always thought that she would be strong and healthy then. And older. I thought it would take longer before the launch and she'd be old enough to deal with it better. Now instead of the launch being a single trauma in an otherwise-happy infancy, it might well be the final straw. I imagined her in the terror of dark weightlessness. Sensory deprivation. Hungry, with only a nipple of water to suck on.

She looked at me with listless eyes and showed no interest in the food I offered. I put it in her mouth and massaged her cheeks and finally pinched her shoulders until she began to suck. Only once did her eyes actually make contact with mine. Was it my guilty imagination that read seething resentment in her face? She couldn't speak, probably couldn't even think. But if she could, what would she say to me? What sort of selfish plan did you have, Papa, that you brought me out of my fetal hibernation in order to live in this unbearable fear and loneliness?

Monkeys died of loneliness. I knew that. A primate infant that lost its mother could sometimes thrive with a parent substitute— but it was rare. They usually died. Why had I thought that with a hugger and a few visits a day I could do better with Faith? I might be an enhanced capuchin, but that didn't mean that the laws of nature would bend to my plans. Faith was going to die. My plan was going to fail.

I smiled at her, caressed her, groomed her. She seemed to respond a little. Her tiny fingers gripped my fur. Not strongly, but enough to give me hope.

And more than hope. I realized as I held her that in all my skulking about, all my fears for her, all my hurried, hidden visits, I had come to feel something for her. Love. Not love like a man for his mate, but love like a father for his daughter. I didn't just fear her death because it would mean the failure of my plans. I feared her death because I cared for her.

A voice in the back of my mind whispered, She's just an animal. A pet is the most she could be to you. She hasn't the intelligence to be any more than that.

But that was the voice of reason. It could not overwhelm the insistent wordless voice of my own instincts, which made me feel an overwhelming desire to protect and provide for my young. Not the maternal instinct, but the paternal one. The need to guard all who were within my territory. The need to see that no harm came to them. The desire to see them thrive.

Faith wasn't just a plan anymore. She was alive, and she was mine. Somehow I would get her off the wall and into a new nest. I would track where the maintenance people had already inspected and move her into an area where they had already checked everything. I had computer access, after all. I would know what I needed to do to keep her safe. We would come through this. She would live.

When I got back to Carol Jeanne's office, she was gone. That surprised me. It wasn't even six P.M. yet, and Carol Jeanne almost always worked a little late. Perhaps, though, with Red gone she felt more urgency about getting home.

She wasn't home, either. But Penelope was still there, and now it wasn't just talk—she had her arm around Mamie's shoulder, and Mamie was actually crying. What was going on? Mamie would never show such indecorous emotions in front of a woman she wanted to impress.

The girls were awake in the kitchen, and Nancy, looking triumphant, was feeding them their dinner. She looked at me and sneered. "You can tell Carol Jeanne that it's *not* too stressful for me to take care of the girls."

I hopped up in front of the kitchen computer and typed, "Where's Carol Jeanne?"

"Some witness *you* are," said Nancy.

I pointed to the screen again, insisting on an answer.

"If you must know, someone whose name I can't mention in front of impressionable young ears has had a stroke, and Carol Jeanne is at the hospital."

Now I registered what Mamie was saying, over and over again, in the front room. "I drove him away, I forced him out of the house, if only I had let him do some stupid job he could have been here with me in the last weeks of his life. . . "

"Now, now," Penelope was saying, "it was probably his work that caused the stroke, you were only trying to save his life by keeping him home."

Stef. A stroke.

The list of hospital patients and their room assignments was easily accessible using my legitimate password. I found out where Stef was staying and left at once.

He looked awful. He was tubed up to the gills, including a urinary drip. Carol Jeanne and Red were across the bed from each other, and it was obvious from where each was standing that Carol Jeanne had gotten there first—she had the chair and had been reading a book, while Red still had flowers in his hand. Flowers. What did he think was going on here? He had stopped for flowers.

Pink was lying on the floor in a corner, taking in the scene. I resisted the impulse to jack in and get a memory dump. It wouldn't be good to let Red see how easily I ripped off his witness's memory.

To my surprise, Stef was awake. And he was talking. His speech was slurred, and I could see that one side of his face sagged, but he had not been paralyzed. Comparatively speaking, it was a mild stroke.

"Think of it as flu," he said. "Nothing major. Some people die of it, but I won't."

"A stroke isn't the flu, Dad," said Red. "And I think you should let Mother come and visit you. She wants to see you, and your forbidding her to visit is really hurting her."

"Shedding big crocodile tears, is she?" asked Stef. "Tell her to screw herself." The word *screw* was a challenge for him to say, with his semiresponsive lips and tongue.

"Maybe you shouldn't upset him by being Mamie's advocate right now," said Carol Jeanne quietly.

I couldn't see Red's face from where I was, but I imagined that his silence was accompanied by a savage glare.

"I hear you gave her the boot yourself, Red," said Stef slowly.

"I couldn't take her with me into singles' quarters."

"Bullshit," said Stef. "Didn't want her."

Red said nothing. I imagined another glare.

"If you'd done it long ago, maybe your marriage wouldn't be in trouble."

"It wasn't Mamie who made our marriage fail," said Red coldly. "Our marriage could never have worked. I should never have married at all. It's not Carol Jeanne's fault that she's an emotional iceberg."

"Is this really the scene you want to play here, now?" asked Carol Jeanne quietly.

Red ignored her and kept talking to his father. "Even if Carol Jeanne had been warm and loving, it wouldn't have made any difference. I'm not a bad father, but I could never be happy as a husband, it's that simple. So if you don't blame Mother, I won't blame Carol Jeanne. How's that for fair, Dad?"

"I can blame Mamie if I want to," mumbled Stef, but there was humor in his eyes.

"Blame her for the failure of your own marriage," said Red, "but not for the failure of mine. That one's my fault, pure and simple."

It was Stef's left side that he still had good control over, and so it was with his left hand that he clutched at his son until Red reached out and took his hand and held it. "I wanted," said Stef, "to see you happy before I died."

"You aren't going to die from this, Father."

"I'm not?" said Stef. "Too bad."

"And I'm not unhappy, Father. I feel guilt-ridden about the way I caused it, but the breakup of my marriage was inevitable. Carol Jeanne doesn't see it that way, but I hardly expect her to. It will hurt the children, but we'll do our best to help them get through it. You can rest assured that your descendants will not be in dire agony."

"You know what pisses me off?" asked Stef. "That Mamie will get to plan my funeral."

"No she won't," said Carol Jeanne.

"I don't want her to speak at my funeral," said Stef. "You're my witnesses."

"You're not going to die, Father," said Red.

"Promise me," said Stef.

"Father, do you really want to reach out from the grave and hurt Mother one more time?"

"Don't want the old bitch gloating over my corpse."

"I promise," said Carol Jeanne. "And I'll see to it that we get it legally put into your will today."

"And none of that crap with dandelion puffballs," said Stef.

"We won't allow them to 'spread the word,' " said Carol Jeanne.

Red snorted in disgust. "That's good, Dad. You and Carol Jeanne go ahead and thumb your noses at a bunch of good, well-meaning people. If either of you would make the slightest effort, they could be your friends."

Stef raised one eyebrow. He had never been able to raise just one eyebrow before. Amazing the new skills a stroke can give you. "Penelope?" Stef said. "Friends with a cow?" And he laughed, his body shaking under the sheet.

Red gave up in disgust. "I'll be back to see you later tonight."

"Good," said Stef. "Sorry I'm being bad."

"You *are* being bad, but I suppose between the stroke and the drugs you can act however you want and I won't hold it against you," said Red. He bent down and kissed his father's forehead. "See you later tonight." Then he left.

"Prissy little asshole," mumbled Stef when Red was gone.

Carol Jeanne giggled. It was a rare sound, and to me it meant that, with Red gone, she felt truly comfortable. As if Stef were her true family. And then she went ahead and said it, taking the old man's hand in hers. "I'll miss you if you die, Dad. I want to keep calling you that, you know. Even when the divorce is done."

"You always called me Stef."

"Only because I couldn't bring myself to call Mamie 'Mother.'"

"Good point," said Stef.

"Do me a favor and get better from this," said Carol Jeanne.

"Just for you," said Stef.

"Now you can go back to sleep," said Carol Jeanne. "I brought a book."

"Don't the girls need you?" asked Stef. "Don't leave them to Mamie."

"Mamie will be fine with them. It's just for tonight."

I thought it would be a good idea to tell her what was really happening. I jumped up onto the bed. Stef gasped in surprise. He must not have seen me come in. "Hi, Lovelock," he said.

I pointed to Carol Jeanne to get her attention, and then began to spell out words on the bedsheet. "Not Mamie," I wrote. "Nancy."

"Oh damn," said Carol Jeanne. "I should have thought of that. I've got to get that girl out of the house. It was fine for Red to bring her there when he was in residence, but he'll have to find another foster home for her. I can't have her tending the kids."

"Who?" asked Stef.

"A girl who was being abused," said Carol Jeanne. "She's only marginally sane at the moment, and I'm not surprised that Mamie left her alone with the girls, but I've got to go put a stop to it at once. Can I get you anything before I go, Stef?"

"Nope," he said.

She kissed his lips and left. She didn't tell me to come along, and I might have stayed with Stef a bit longer, except that he immediately closed his eyes. He wanted to sleep, I thought. And it's not as if I could converse with him even if I stayed. So I followed Carol Jeanne out into the corridor, then scrambled up her body and rode her shoulder home.

When we got there, Red was already there, and Nancy, sullen and tear-streaked, was packing a bag. Red explained at once. "As mayor, Penelope has agreed that Nancy should stay with her for a while during this time when Dad's in the hospital. I've arranged for Dolores to help Mamie take care of the girls during the day, and her children will come over and do their homework here at night. That will give you plenty of help with the girls. Diana in particular really loves them and she's good with them."

I caught Nancy's face as he said this. It would be a good idea, I thought, to warn Diana never to let herself get caught alone with Nancy.

Mamie was stretched out on her bed, a damp washcloth over her eyes. As soon as Carol Jeanne came into her room to check on her, Mamie began weeping. "He was a wonderful husband, and I drove him out of the house."

Instead of reassuring her by denying the obvious truth of that statement, Carol Jeanne only answered, "Is there something I can bring you?"

"Bring me my husband!" wailed Mamie.

Carol Jeanne refrained from laughing, which I thought took some real strength of character. "He seems to be in fair condition and good spirits," said Carol Jeanne. "But he's quite adamant that he doesn't want you to visit him, and his doctor agrees. It would cause stress, and that's the one thing he can't have. I'm sure that in your great love for him you'll be glad to comply."

The irony in this last remark was not lost on Mamie. Her crying stopped and her voice sounded wooden when she answered. "I see that I am surrounded by hatred," she said. "And I deserve it all, I'm sure. Just leave me alone. I don't need anything. Certainly not dinner. Do *not* bring me a tray."

"Whatever," said Carol Jeanne, who, I was sure, would never have thought of giving Mamie a meal in her room. After all, it wasn't Mamie who'd had the stroke. Though I noticed that it was Mamie getting the sympathetic visits and help from the women of Mayflower. She could turn anything to her advantage. Stef's stroke was really working out well for her, in terms of helping her make friends with the women of the village.

The new network really sucks. I can't get anything except a normal children's access and that means I can't do dick. I tried accessing some of the remote databases and on the third try I got this jerk from System Security asking me why I was trying to access that database, and if I needed to get information like that for a school assignment I should ask my teacher to get the information I needed. What a crock! It's like children are slaves who have to be manacled the whole time they're on the computer. I can't get in and do *anything*.

And the worst part is that I have to go with Diana over to the Monkey House as she calls it so she can play house with Emmy and Lydia. At least the monkey can't get into the system either, so that's something. And it was decent of him to warn me when they found out about the back door. If they'd caught me doing that, they probably wouldn't even let me have the pathetic access I've got now. At least I can still play Colony, and it doesn't take special access to the network to beat the snot out of Belos and Conceição.

It occurs to me that maybe the monkey *does* have special access. I'll have to keep my eyes open and see how he uses the network. If he keeps going off by himself to use it, that'll clinch it—if he only has the same kind of access I have, or even a normal adult's access, he won't have to hide it from anybody. He thinks he's so smart, but an enhanced capuchin is no match for a smart human.

And how smart are *you*, Peter? Why, I think the technical measurement is "pretty damn." We'll see if I'm a match for a monkey.

It was midnight before I could get back onto the network using my sleeper. Peter was watching me too closely all night for me to even think of going near the computer. Apparently he's frustrated at having his back door removed and he's hoping I'll show him a way in. Fat chance, little boy.

I didn't know what to look for, really. Mostly I just wanted to find out what it was that had been kept from me for all these months. First I browsed through the secret files of the security department and found out a few things. For instance, Carol Jeanne is important enough that they watch out for her "well-being," which is why they were watching me in the first place, before they knew I had any particular computer skills. They were also watching Red. And I discovered that in their view, his liaison with Liz was deliberately flagrant. He wanted to be discovered. Well, that was old news. The surprise was that his whole affair with Liz was just a cover. Turns out the old boy was also doing therapy with Liz's husband. Only the security people didn't think it was therapy. They think Red has been a closet homosexual for a long, long time, and so has Liz's husband, Warren. They have both Red and Warren on their list of sexually noncompliant citizens who slipped past the original psychological screening.

The notation with Red suggests that he might not have realized he was homosexual until he had Liz's husband in therapy, at which time he might have recognized his own feelings in some of the things Warren talked about. Warren himself had simply lied his way onto the Ark. The security people didn't seem too excited about it, though—they weren't going to do anything, even though the Ark had been clearly limited to heterosexuals in order to maximize the breeding potential of the human population on the new world. After all, both Red and Warren had fathered children, and might well do so again. So whatever they did for pleasure was not going to cause problems as long as they were discreet. It was nice to know that they weren't planning to give *Red* a little accident, the way they wanted to do with me. But then, Red is human, and I'm just an animal. Only one step up from a handbag.

It wasn't even hard to decide not to tell Carol Jeanne. There was no telling how she would react to Red's affair really being with Warren instead of Liz. It might be a relief—it wasn't her failures that broke up their marriage, but rather his deep-seated sexual proclivities. Or it might be an even worse blow. Who could guess? It didn't matter. Red had been careful to do none of this in front of Pink, so I could never have found it out from jacking in to his witness. There was no way I could know about his homosexual activities except from security files that I couldn't possibly have legal access to.

When I had exhausted the possibilities of gossip, I began to look into the secure database that the gaiologists had all been using. The first thing I discovered was that it included a complete inventory of all the living material on the Ark. I could not believe that this had been a secret from me. When I so cleverly altered the open inventory to conceal the number of capuchin embryos, it never crossed my mind that a duplicate inventory existed on another network. I quickly searched for the capuchin embryos in order to make this inventory match the one I had altered to hide the fact that Faith had been brought out.

What I found was that a search on the word *capuchin* brought up two locations, not one. The first was the inventory I was looking for, and it was only a matter of moments to reconcile the two data-bases.

The second *capuchin* entry was the shocker. It led me into a database region that had no counterpart in the open inventory. The key word was *enhanced*. A dozen different species of genetically en-hanced animals, including more embryos of enhanced capuchins than of the normal capuchins in the open inventory.

There were more like me. I could be replaced.

No, no, that's not what matters, I realized. Not that I can be replaced, but that *they brought more like me.*

There were notations all over the enhanced section. Detailed instructions about how to perform the surgical operations that would hook up our i/o jacks. About inserting the discipline modules that would release endorphins as a reward and stimulate pain cen-ters in the brain as a punishment. About how to train each enhanced species to be reliable witnesses.

And no section was bigger than the one on enhanced capuchins. I was pleased to learn that we were the smartest and most useful of all witnesses, by miles—but there were clear warnings about how unstable we tended to be and how to watch for signs that an en-hanced capuchin was "out of control" and was therefore "an appro-priate candidate to be destroyed." Now the words about me in the security department's files made sense. It wasn't just that the body-builders were eager to kill monkeys. It was *policy*. It was in the instruction manual that came with the enhanced model capuchin.

I certainly fit the list of warning signs. I was definitely out of control. I was pleased to see that successful masturbation was one of the most important signs. "If the capuchin is able to override the disciplinary response to sexual stimulation, it must be destroyed at once, whether there are potential breeding partners available or not."

Apparently I wasn't the first to try what I was trying. I imagined some predecessor back on Earth, struggling as I was struggling, and then getting caught. They probably killed him in a humane manner—a needle in the neck? Or did they take more relish in it? A hammer on the head. A bullet in the brain. Vivisection to find out how he went wrong.

Or she. Maybe she even got pregnant. Maybe she even had babies.

Then again, maybe not. Because as I read on, one message became clear. Enhanced animals could not breed successfully with unenhanced animals ostensibly of the same species. The genetic alterations had changed us too much. Some matings could result in offspring, but most were deformed and all were sterile.

I thought of the experiments that had given them this information and shuddered with loathing.

Then I thought of little Faith, despondent in her miserable nest. I had brought her to life in order to breed with her. But it was an impossible project to start with. All that would result, when she finally reached sexual maturity about the time we reached the new world, would be deformed babies. Or maybe one or two healthy ones, and only another four or five or six or ten years later would I finally realize that the healthy ones were sterile anyway. And by then it would be too late to start over.

There were enhanced capuchin embryos on board. The secret inventory told me exactly where they were, and I could get to them. It's what I should have done in the first place, only I didn't know.

And now what was I going to do with Faith? If she was discovered, it would clinch the security service's opinion of me. I had to continue to conceal her. And yet even if she lived to adulthood, what would I do with her? I couldn't mate with her. It would be like breeding with a completely different animal. Like mating with a cat or a fish. And I could never teach her to be quiet. I would have to hide her all the time. I had expected that, of course. I knew she would never be bright enough to enlist her in my plans. But I thought, in my vain imaginings, that when she started bearing my children she would be happy enough, nursing and nurturing them, even as they grew up to be smarter than her. But there wouldn't be any offspring. Her life would be one of continual confinement, with no purpose in it—no mate, no young, no freedom. Pointless, endless captivity.

I found myself hoping that she would hurry up and die.

CHAPTER TWELVE

Animals

The thought made me sick. I had only just realized that I loved Faith, and now I was wishing for her death? What kind of monster was I? Suddenly she no longer fit my plans and instead she was dangerous to keep around, so I wanted her dead.

Until that moment, I had thought of her as being an infant *of my kind*. Even though she wasn't enhanced, we were both capuchins, weren't we? Now, though, I knew that we were not of the same species. We could not mate and produce fertile offspring. Therefore, in my view, she could not be a member of my sentient tribe. She was not a *person*, but an animal.

Yet there was no change in her. What was the transformation that turned her from beloved future spouse to dangerous and inconvenient animal? It was only in me. Or rather, in my knowledge. I knew now that she could never be what I needed and wanted her to be. She was not "one of us," even though on the Ark I was the only one of "us" that existed in any form warmer than a frozen embryo.

I dropped out of my sleeper program and fled the computer, fled the room, fled the house. I soon found myself on the wall, climbing to the nest.

Not a nest, I realized now, looking at it, looking at her eyes gazing at me through the mesh of the box. A cage. That's what I had created for her, even if I refused to admit it. A cage, because I knew all along that I could never trust her to be free. She wasn't going to stay in that box only until she became strong and clever enough to handle herself on the wall. I was going to have to keep her in a cage forever, and I realized now that I had planned it that way all along, even if I didn't admit it to myself. Because I could never have trusted her to understand the need for discretion, or what discretion even consisted of.

I went inside the nest and she reached for me. She didn't always do that. Was it a sign of strength? Yesterday it would have made me feel hopeful. Now it made me sick at heart. It was no longer useful for her to live. And yet what was I supposed to do? She was alive. She depended on me for every drop of water, every bite of food, every stroke of affection. If I simply abandoned her, she would soon die, yes—but she would die yearning for me, wondering why I had abandoned her . . .

But she was an animal, right? She didn't have feelings, right?

That was humanist thinking: Because animals aren't exactly like us, they are infinitely different, wholly other. Thus we can treat them however we like.

But animals are not wholly other. Their consciousness steps down from ours in infinitesimal steps, just as there is infinite variation among us. Who is to say that the most intellectual and creative of chimpanzees is not above the level of the most stupid and brutal of humans? And behind chimpanzees, other primates, and behind them, perhaps, dolphins or dogs, whales or cats. None of them wholly different from us, but rather differing only in degree. Capable of love, of feeling, of knowing, of remembering. And so if it matters how you treat humans, then it matters how you treat animals.

Not that animals can't kill and eat their prey—those species differences are real, and nature teaches each animal to value the survival of individuals of its own species above all others. Why should we be different? I have a right to protect my own reproductive future. This capuchin monkey, even though I brought it to life, is nevertheless a danger to me. I have a right to protect myself from the danger it poses.

I also have a responsibility to protect it from all harm, because I brought it to life, because it trusts me, it loves me, and I have loved it. No, I can't lie to myself, I still love it.

I am immobilized. I must act, and quickly. I must either move Faith or remove her entirely. She can't stay much longer on the wall. There are places now that have already been checked for launch conditions by Maintenance, and I can move her. But the new nesting place is dark. She'll be terrified. Her life up to now has already been lonely, full of terror and ill health. Now, unaccustomed as she is to gravity, shall I take her into a place of darkness where the heavy fist of weight will hold her down like shackles? And then shall I strap her down to endure in terror and solitude the hours of complete weightlessness followed by gradual acceleration, with frightening new noises, all in utter darkness? She is so fragile—the chances of her living through the ordeal are slim. Her life is now pointless and unhappy. It would be merciful for me to help her die in peaceful sleep.

Merciful and *convenient*. See how I rationalize. See how I persuade myself that what I must do is actually best for her in the long run. Is this how Nancy's father and mother justified the terrible life they gave her? It's her fault. We're doing this for her best good. She asked for it. Blame the victim, exonerate the perpetrator.

I will not exonerate myself. It may be that by killing her I would be sparing her much suffering—but I would have spared her far *more* suffering if I had never been so selfish and stupid as to pull her out of her embryonic hibernation. What was I thinking? I wasn't thinking, I was fantasizing and then acted on my fantasies of rebellion, of propagation of my own tribe. She was never real to me until it was far too late.

So now I hide from the decision I must make. I write, I write, I write. Carol Jeanne sees me, busily typing, and she doesn't bother to read what I'm writing. She's so busy; she thinks I'm helping. But I'm not helping. I'm writing bits and snatches of all that has happened, I'm trying to explain how I got to the place where I am now, trembling on the cusp of becoming what I most hate—a sentient creature who feels he has the right to do whatever he wants to a fellow creature he thinks of as a beast. I know what I must do. But I also know that if I continue as I am, doing nothing, I will have made the other decision: that my life is *less* important than Faith's. For if she is found—and if I do nothing, she will certainly be found—then I am dead.

And would she live even in that case? I think not. She's too sick and weak. I think the humans would put her to sleep then, perhaps with the same poison they will use to kill me. An injection, given without emotion or compassion. A disposal of the inconvenient. And they will call themselves merciful for killing her. Why, then, can't I accept that valuation and do it myself first?

They won't consider it a mercy to kill me, though. They will watch me die with relief.

That's why I'm writing this, I think. Because I see my own death. So I have caused this text file to be hidden away in the computer network. As long as I continue to access my sleeper program, this account stays hidden. But if I stay away from the sleeper program for more than a hundred days in a row, the sleeper will cause this text file to be replicated on every computer in the system. It will appear as a long mail file, asking every human on the Ark to read it. Then you will know that, though I am dead, I was once alive. Not just a monkey—or, if a monkey, then at least a monkey capable of having the same kind of moral struggles that you, too, would have, if you were capable of recognizing the existence of sapient beasts.

I toyed with the idea of vengeance. Of having the sleeper, when it delivers this file, then destroy the entire network and leave you all helplessly drifting through space, unable to access your computers and unable to rebuild them fast enough to save yourselves from the collapse of the delicate life support systems. But I am not a monster, nor do I fancy that my life is the primary purpose of the cosmos. If I die, most of you who read this will be innocent of wishing for my death. Why should I then kill you? What would that make *me*, if not a mass murderer?

So I have limited myself to disabling the sysops' control over the network for twenty-four hours when this account is delivered to you. That will give you time, all of you, to read it if you care at all; to print it out. To rename the file, to copy it in several places. Then when the sysops regain control, they can't wipe out my account by using their universal control over the mail system. I will still be alive.

And something else will be alive, too. My sleeper program. They can't get rid of it. Long after I'm dead, it will live on. It will do no harm, and no one will ever be able to access it but me. No one will know it is there. But it will still be there dreaming, watching in its sleep, waiting for my keystrokes to wake it up. It is my one child that will live beyond my own life.

It is not much. And it is not enough.

* * *

I was writing about my first attempt at dealing with freefall up on the wall of the Ark when suddenly there was the most awful shrieking from the front room. Mamie, of course, but this wasn't her normal histrionic voice. I rushed to the door just as Carol Jeanne rushed past, followed by the girls, sleepy and terrified.

Mamie was in the front room, her face pressed against a wall, sobbing uncontrollably, for all the world like a child who had been disciplined. Red was there, with Penelope and Dolores and Neeraj. Red was trying to comfort his mother. I knew at once that Stef had died.

Red looked at Carol Jeanne. "A second stroke, far more massive than the first. It carried him off within minutes. There was nothing they could do."

Dolores and Neeraj came to Carol Jeanne and embraced her lightly. Penelope used the moment to gather Mamie to her ample bosom. No one thought that perhaps I might also need comfort. Not even me. I stood there, transfixed. Stef is gone. Just when he wins his freedom, he dies. Just what is going to happen to me. And he died paralyzed, just as I will die from immobility. And what did his declaration of independence from Mamie accomplish, in the end?

Within a few hours, it was clear that he hadn't even accomplished his own funeral. Hadn't he specifically forbidden Mamie to plan it? And yet Red acquiesced to her will on every point. Yes, it would be held in the meetinghouse of Mayflower village before it was dismantled. Mamie would choose the speakers, the songs, the singers. They would even spread the word. She would have her way with him even after death.

Carol Jeanne rebelled at this as soon as she could get Red alone. "You can't do this," she said. "You know he forbade all of this. It was virtually his last request."

"Funerals are for the living," said Red. "Not for the dead. Mother needs the comfort. Father doesn't."

"Maybe *I* need—maybe even *Mamie* needs to see that in the end, she didn't control him after all."

"Mamie never controlled him, Carol Jeanne," said Red disgustedly.

"What planet were you living on? Ever since I've known them, she ran him around on the end of a stick."

"He was a grown man," said Red. "He could have left at any time. But even after I was grown, he stayed. Did you ever think why?"

"His will had been so sapped by then that—"

"Pure bullshit, Carol Jeanne. Wills don't get sapped. People stay in hideous relationships like that because they're getting something from it. Father was getting something from Mother, even if you couldn't see it."

"What, she was good in bed?"

Red laughed lightly. "Maybe she was, but he never gave her much chance to find out." He shook his head. "You didn't grow up with them, Carol Jeanne. I loved my father. I love my mother. But I also lived in constant rage. Not at her, really, because she was like a child, utterly selfish and incapable of recognizing what she was doing. But *he* knew. He saw how she controlled me, manipulated me, battered me emotionally, and he did nothing. I hated him for that, because I knew that he was aware of everything and he let it all happen. So I found my own accommodation. I got along. I eventually learned how to calm Mother down. How to pick my battlefields. How to hand her a small victory so she wouldn't notice a big defeat. It was a very delicate dance, Carol Jeanne, but I learned how to do it, and until I had to balance a wife's demands along with my mother's, it worked very well."

Carol Jeanne was listening, I knew it, and learning things she had never understood before. But this last could not go unanswered. "So it was *me* who disrupted the happy household, is that it? You're even more tied to her apron strings than I thought."

"I daresay Mother has never worn an apron in her life. Not even a pinafore." Red grinned mirthlessly. "I'm not blaming anything on you. I'm just telling you that it won't do Father any harm to let Mamie have the funeral she wants—and it will make life considerably easier for the two of us. Let her play the loving wife. She did love him, you know."

Carol Jeanne laughed derisively.

"It was a selfish, possessive love," said Red, "but it was all she knew how to give."

"Why can you be so deeply understanding of her, and so completely incapable of understanding me?"

"Because you never needed me the way Mother needs me," said Red. "You never needed anybody."

"If you had ever bothered to come to know me, you'd know that that is the exact opposite of the truth."

"Well, well. So we part in utter ignorance of each other."

Carol Jeanne turned away from the most painful subject and went back to the original issue. The funeral. She knew the right and wrong of *that*, anyway. "What if I file a protest about the funeral? Will you lie under oath and deny that Stef asked to have his ex-wife barred from his funeral?"

"I'll admit that he said it. But I'll also strongly recommend against letting the old bastard's last vindictive act poison my mother's life and her standing in the community."

Carol Jeanne slapped his face. "I won't hear you speak that way about Stef. If you were half the man your father was, we would still be married."

"What you mean is, if I was half a man, like my father was."

She slapped him again.

"So we see that at heart, you are the violent one," said Red. "I've never laid a hand on you except in love, but now I say things you don't like—talking about *my* father, mind you—"

"Your father, but my friend!"

"It was always his way. To play the victim, and enlist people's pity and sympathy. Brave Stef, staying with that bitch of a wife no matter how she bosses him and humiliates him, all for the sake of the boy. What a good man. How we admire and love him. Well, I believed that crock, too, until I was about sixteen years old and it finally dawned on me that if *I* could resist Mother and get my way sometimes, so could he. But instead he did what he's doing now. He let her do what she wanted, and then relished the moral superiority it gave him."

"And will you say that at his funeral?" asked Carol Jeanne. "Do you carry honesty that far?"

"I don't think honesty is appropriate when one is burying one's parent," said Red. "I will say how much I loved him. How much I

272   **Orson Scott Card and Kathryn H. Kidd**

learned from him. And it will all be true. It just won't be . . . complete."

"No," said Carol Jeanne. "Nothing about you is complete."

"I won't argue with that one," said Red. "Because it's true. You, of course, are the image of wholeness. But in your moral perfection, dear, sweet, compassionate-for-the-dead Carol Jeanne, I do hope you won't turn my father's funeral into an instrument of revenge against me or my mother. Whatever you may think, we are both torn apart by his death in ways you could never understand because you didn't grow up in that house."

"I understand more than you think."

"And a great deal less than *you* think," said Red.

"Don't worry about my behavior at the funeral. If it goes the way Mamie and Penelope are planning it, I won't be there," said Carol Jeanne.

"That's exactly what I meant," said Red. "But suit yourself. I'll be there, with my daughters. And if you're not there, everyone will conclude that you couldn't be bothered to attend the funeral of your children's grandfather. Whether they chalk it up to arrogance, apathy, or spite, it won't be me who looks bad."

"And that's what matters, isn't it?" said Carol Jeanne. "To you, image is everything. Well, get this. I actually loved the old man. Reality, not image. I admired him. What you saw as weakness, I understood as patience. I kept waiting for you to grow into a man of his strength. So while you and Mamie are spouting lies about a man you never understood and secretly despised, I'll be there too, to show respect to the man Stef really was."

"Believe what you want about him," said Red. "I don't really give a shit what you choose to do or think or feel."

They glared at each other for a long time in silence.

"I'm sorry I slapped you," Carol Jeanne said at last. "I never do that."

"No," said Red, "you never *did* that. But now you *have* done it. So now it is definitely on the list of things you do." He turned and left the room, left the house.

And I, in my infinite compassion, my generous unselfish nature, I realized at that moment that Stef's death gave me a chance to do something that I had been unable to figure out a way to accomplish. If Faith died before Stef's funeral, I could dispose of her body along with his. That way her little corpse would go into the recycling system, to be broken down into unrecognizable chemicals. Her desiccated bones would never be found in some obscure corner of the crawl spaces. Her body could never betray me then.

It was then that I decided to act. My immobility was ended. I had reached no moral conclusion. I had simply decided to do what my own survival demanded. I no longer had an unconscious wish to die. And if that meant I had to take the life of one who loved and trusted me, then so be it. I might be a monster, but I would be a living one. Guilt might torture me forever, but I would be alive to feel the guilt.

I went to Mamie's room, climbed to the top shelf of her cupboard, and took down her little canister of Dalmane tablets—the ones Mamie got to help her sleep after Stef left. The active ingredient, flurazepan, was in human-sized dosages. One pill helped Mamie get drowsy. One quarter of a pill would put Faith to sleep in minutes, and she would never wake up.

I closed the container and replaced it on the top shelf, exactly where it had been. I would have to remember to tell Carol Jeanne that it might be within the girls' reach, especially if one of them decided to become a climber. Then, carrying the pill in one hand, I left the house and headed for the wall.

In one sense, it was the easiest thing in the world to do. I dissolved the pill in the formula mix. First I cracked the pill against a metal pipe. Then it took a little stirring, but it finally crumbled and disappeared into the fluid. Nothing beyond the ability of your average chimp. Your average capuchin couldn't do it, of course, but I'm enhanced, which puts painless murder within my reach.

Then I took Faith into my arms and held her. She was reaching for the bottle, making sucking noises. She wanted it. But I couldn't give it to her. She became quite impatient with me, but still I held her. Felt the warmth of her, the way her muscles and bones moved against my belly and arms. Studied her face, which, sick as she was, was full of life. Before I kill you, my first child, I have to make sure I remember you. I will not blot you out of my memory. I will not pretend you never existed or you didn't matter. I will be able to conjure up your face at any time. If ever, in the future, I have a moment of happiness, I want your face to appear before me in my mind so I will remember who and what I really am.

Only when she became desperate and angry with me did I finally bring the nipple to her lips. It was right that she should be angry at me in the last moments of her life, even though she would never understand the real reason why I deserved her rage.

Her hands were so small.

She sucked and sucked. Vigorously. Strength was coming to her at last. Despite all the loneliness and terror, her will to live was strong and she was recovering. Which is not to say she would not have been felled by the ordeal of launch. But I knew, even as she drank the poison, that even in a cage high on the wall of the Ark, the will to live could flourish, could overcome terrible odds.

Finally the sucking relaxed. She was sleepy, her eyes heavy-lidded. She looked at me, letting her lips relax away from the nipple. I wanted to see accusation in her eyes. But I knew that what I was seeing was peace and comfort. I was seeing love. She loved me at the end.

I held her limp in my arms for an hour. She was cooling, stiffening a little when I finally laid her down. Just a body now. Not Faith at all. I sat there in the near-darkness, looking at the dark shadow of her fur against the cage floor. I don't know how long. Thinking the same thought, over and over again. I have done murder. I have killed an animal that loved and trusted me, to suit my own convenience. Now I am a human.

The monkey is writing a diary, too. It was Peter who first realized that Lovelock had a secret when we were tending at Dr. Cocciolone's house one night. Peter told me the monkey kept blanking the screen whenever he walked into the computer room, and then he says, "Nobody cares what you see, Diana, so you figure out what's going on." Thanks a lot, Peter. Except it's kind of true. Neeraj, for instance, doesn't realize that Peter kind of likes him, because they keep having these quarrels all the time. He thinks Peter is the main obstacle to his fitting in with the family. He doesn't have a clue that I'm the one who hates him most of all, because I just don't show it by doing nasty things to him. I just shut him out. He doesn't exist for me. And he doesn't notice that he doesn't exist because Peter is so focused on him and constantly demanding his attention. Adults are so stupid sometimes.

Lovelock isn't an adult, of course. Oh I suppose he's an adult monkey but it's not the same thing. He does notice what I do so I couldn't just walk into the computer room and expect him not to turn the screen on. But it wasn't hard to turn Emmy loose in the hall. She wandered into the computer room eventually (after twice going into Mamie's bedroom, the little snoop) and I charged in afterward and dragged her out. I didn't even look at the computer screen. A little while later I gave Emmy a couple of toys and turned her loose again and again she finally found her way into the computer room. She tried to get Lovelock to play with her, but I started playing with her instead, drawing her off into a corner of the room, saying stuff like, "We mustn't interfere with Mommy's monkey, Emmy. He's doing work for Mommy and he doesn't have time to play."

I really only had one chance to look at the screen. I waited until I heard him typing again—and then I waited even longer, in case he was watching to see whether I'd look when the keys started clicking. Finally I did look, and he didn't notice me looking, and I saw that the screen was covered with sentences, like a diary, and it was filled with "I" this and "I" that. I didn't have a chance to read anything actually, but it was a diary, I know it. Or something like a diary. And Peter chortled like a madman and said, "I'm going to find that file. He can't hide it from me." And I said, "Peter, you can't find anything on the new network, you said so yourself," and he said, "If I can't outsmart a monkey I might as well die," and I said, "Well hurry up and make it a double funeral so we don't have to keep the meetinghouse up for another day. We've got a ship to launch." He said "Ha ha so funny I forgot to laugh" which means that I won because that's such a moronic thing to say that he only says it when he's been whupped. So ha.

The funeral was just as Mamie ordered—and just as Stef had feared. I would have found it marvelously amusing, really, except that I couldn't stop thinking about what was tucked below and between Stef's legs, up near his crotch. It hadn't been easy, moving his legs to make a space for Faith's body. In fact, getting her down the wall hadn't been all that easy. She didn't cling to me this time. And the whole way from the wall to the morgue I kept expecting someone to see me and wonder what it was I was carrying wrapped in toilet paper. But people are all so busy getting ready for the launch that they're either working frantically or they drop off to sleep wherever they are. Literally. People are taking naps everywhere.

Like all coffins for those cultures that display the dead, Stef's had a split lid, and the top was open. The mortician was doing his hair and makeup and so I hid behind a stack of papers on top of a filing cabinet until she left the room. I was afraid she might close the lid or turn off the light, which would have made things a lot harder for me, if not impossible. But I think she was just going to the bathroom, because she left the lid open and the light on and I was down inside the coffin in moments. I pulled Faith's body under the little white lacy curtain that hid the lower half of the body and was a little shocked to discover that they didn't even bother dressing the bottom half. It made sense, in a way—everything he owned was going to be given away, except the clothes he wore in the coffin. Those would be destroyed and put back into the biosystem, because there were too many people with tabus about wearing graveclothes. So why waste a perfectly good set of pants and underwear, shoes and socks? That's why the split coffins were used, probably. Even that was a concession—there were those who thought any display of the corpse was vulgar and wasteful.

They don't know vulgar and wasteful, unless they can imagine my prying one of Stef's naked legs up and away from the other far enough that I could slide Faith's body into the gap between them. Her little body, laid to rest in the most intimate place of shelter on Stef's body. In a way it was comforting and appropriate. But when I looked at it another way, it made me sick to think of disposing of her body that way.

But it was just a body. I had to remind myself that Faith, whoever and whatever she was, was gone now, and all that was left was slowly decomposing tissues that, if found, would lead to my destruction.

It was almost as hard to get Stef's leg back down. But once I did, Faith was completely hidden.

I lingered there for a moment. Too long a moment. The mortician came back and I heard her bustling around in the room.

I almost made a run for it, but I couldn't be sure which way she was facing. If she saw me emerge from the coffin, she would be curious about what I had been doing. She would search Stef. She would find Faith.

But if I stayed in the coffin, she might never leave the room again until she was done, and then she would close the lid and there I'd be, trapped. Carol Jeanne would lead a search for me within hours, probably, but I doubted anyone would conceive of looking in Stef's coffin. Even if I didn't suffocate, even if somehow I got back out later, there would be questions. Where were you? What were you doing?

She finished his makeup. She did his hair. The spray nearly suffocated me. I didn't sneeze—I felt like that was an important accomplishment at the time.

Finally she turned away, carrying the comb and hairspray bottle. I knew that this might well be my last chance. I scrambled out from under the little veil concealing the lower half of the body, quickly made sure it was hanging vertically, swung up onto the closed lower lid, and then dropped down behind the coffin, hanging on the brass rail that went all the way around the box. I did it all in only a few seconds, and almost soundlessly. It helped that the mortician was humming—the silence wasn't absolute. I hung there from the rail, hidden between the coffin and the wall, while she reached up and lowered the lid and locked it in place. Then I climbed underneath the coffin and, when she was busy putting things away, slipped out of the room.

So all through the funeral, I kept thinking of Faith's body in the coffin. Much of what they said applied to her—ironically, bitterly. And when the minister talked about hope of the resurrection, I yearned to be able to weep. But it wasn't in my physical vocabulary. Hope of the resurrection. If there was a God, if Jesus really did raise the dead as these people said, what hope of resurrection would there be for Faith? She was only an animal. She had never had a soul. Not by any theology *I* had ever heard of.

And I had the insane thought: What will I tell my children? That death is the end? That there is no soul? Never mind that any hope of having children was definitely on hold right now. I could only think that it was the fact of intentional burial with food bowls and weapons that was taken as a sign of real sentience in prehistoric humans. You know that someone is intelligent when he believes that there's a life after death. Which suggested something rather unfortunate about the agnosticism of science. But not really; even those who denied the literal existence of the soul nevertheless had to live as if there were one. As if life mattered. As if individual humans had a free will that was not the product of genes and upbringing. You can have whatever opinion you like on the matter, but if you're going to live with other people in a community you have to believe that all individuals are volitional, and when it comes down to it, that means a soul, or something like it. Something that could be judged in moral terms; something precious, that had to be respected. It was the very fact that they did *not* think of me that way, that they implicitly denied my soul, that had burned in me so long.

Maybe the soul is nothing but other people's belief in you as a moral being. Maybe it's just a creation of the community, which becomes real only when other people believe in it. Maybe when, someday, people begin to believe that *I* am a moral being, capable of being judged and worthy of respect, I will actually get a soul for the first time. I wonder what it will feel like. Maybe I won't notice it at all. But I will teach my children that there is something in them that is more than a mere organism. Something that chooses freely what to do, what to become, what to create, what to destroy. And because I believe in their souls, maybe they will have them. And they will believe in mine, and so I will have a soul whether any humans believe in it or not.

What children? What children ever ever ever ever ever ever ever ever ever ever ever

So I sat there on Carol Jeanne's shoulder at the funeral, feeling her stiffen as flaming hypocrites like Penelope "spread the word" about a man they had slandered or ignored in life. And I tried very hard to believe in Faith's soul, so that perhaps she would have one. A posthumous sort of immortality.

At the end of the service, I wrote Carol Jeanne a note. "Want to follow body to recycling," it said.

"Isn't that a little morbid?" she asked.

"Yes," I wrote. "Please."

She looked at me oddly, but then nodded.

There was no further service after the funeral—no displays of his handiwork, I'm happy to say. No big dinner, either—there was no time for that. There were workmen ready to deflate the meeting-house as soon as everyone was out of it. Most people were already living in the cramped launch quarters, double-bunked, because their houses were now deflated and rolled up in warehouses.

I rode on top of the coffin as a guy from recycling pushed the cart to an elevator and on down into the corridor leading to the recycling center. I didn't pay much attention to him. All I could think about was that I had to watch for my chance to snatch Faith's body out when he wasn't looking and get it into the chemical bath that dissolved off all the hair and fleshy parts and whatever organs hadn't already been salvaged for the transplant banks. Then more chemicals were added and the bones also dissolved. Nobody examined the contents of the bath until the entire process was complete. Once her body was in there, I was safe.

If he thought it was odd to have me along for the ride, he didn't give a sign of it. Didn't talk to me. That was all right. A lot of people were shy with witnesses, because they knew that we recorded everything that we saw and heard.

The recycling room wasn't large. The chemical bath was about two meters long and a meter wide—pretty much the size it needed to be. It could be closed and sealed during the process of dissolving the body, so that it wouldn't matter when the orientation of the room changed during launch. In fact, the bath was against the correct wall, was exactly as tall as it was wide, and—yes, as I guessed— it could be opened from the front when the ship reoriented and what was now the front became the top. Very good design. Stef and Faith would go in one way, but when the bath was reopened to draw out the chemical soup in which all their basic elements would be recycled, it would be through another door. There was something deeply symbolic in that, I was sure, but I couldn't for the life of me figure out what it might be symbolic *of*.

The recycling guy was standing there, looking at me. I realized that he wanted me to get off the coffin so he could open it. Well, say something, why don't you? *I'm* the mute, not you, buddy.

Wordlessly I got off and watched from a table as he opened both lids of the coffin and then dropped its front wall, too, so that Stef's body could be rolled off and dropped into the chemical bath.

With a sigh, the recycling guy took off his funeral suit and put on a pair of watertight coveralls and a lightweight full-head helmet with a plastic mask. I was so fascinated watching his precautions to avoid getting any of the chemicals splashed on him that I didn't realize that I was letting my only chance pass me by. And in fact it wasn't really a chance at all, because he was facing Stef's body the entire time, perfectly able to see anything I might do. Besides which it occurred to me that if he was going through these precautions to avoid getting any of this stuff splashed on him, it must be pretty potent stuff. What were the chances I could toss Faith's body into the mix without getting any of it on me?

So from my perch on the table, I watched in horrified fascination as he came over to Stef's body and, without so much as taking off the shirt and tie, began to roll it off into the bath. For a moment I hoped that somehow Faith's body might be pinned between Stef's legs so that she would be carried into the bath along with him and he wouldn't even notice, or if he thought he saw something it would be too late to examine it.

No such luck. He rolled Stef's corpse into the bath. The liquid was fairly viscous and splashed very little—none of it reached the table where I was, though some did get on his coveralls and face mask, since he was so close. Still, I instinctively turned away to protect my eyes from the splash—or perhaps because I couldn't bear to watch the actual moment when Stef's body was consigned to oblivion—and when I turned back, there it was, Faith's dark little body, lying alone on the white satin of the coffin.

I wanted to disappear, to flee from the room, to die, to kill him— something. But I did nothing at all. I sat there, frozen. He, too, was immobile for a moment. Then he turned slowly and looked at me.

What could I do? What could I say?

I could speak only with gestures, and the only one I could think of was the truth. I was overcome with grief and shame and despair. I covered my face with my hands and bowed my body.

How long I held that position I don't know. When I looked up, he was no longer watching me. He was holding Faith's little body in his hands. He glanced at me, saw that I could see. And then he gently laid her body into the bath, his own gloved hands going well down into the mix so there was no splash at all. A gentle parting. A moment of tenderness. Then he looked at me, bowed his head gently, and walked to the shower to wash the chemicals off his helmet and coveralls before undressing.

Only then did I find myself in control of my body again. I fled the recycling room and returned here, to Carol Jeanne's office, where her computer, bolted to a desk which is bolted to the floor, remains connected to the network when most others are already in storage for the reorientation of the ship at launch.

I searched for his picture, this recycling worker, and found it among the recycling staff. His name was Roberto "Bêto" Causo, and he was on the Ark because his wife was a top scientist with life support. There was no other information about him, except for raw meaningless facts of birth and education in Salvador, Bahia, Brasil. His entry tests showed him to be a psychologically healthy introvert of above-average intelligence and below-average ambition. None of this meant anything to me. All I knew was that he knew my secret. My life was in his hands. I had no idea what he was going to do, whom he was going to tell.

And yet I also knew, looking into his eyes just before he lowered Faith's body into the recycling bath, that he would never tell. Somehow this young man, who had never seen me before, had understood that whatever it was that I was doing, it was not his responsibility to stop me, to punish me, to report me. Instead he understood something of my grief and guilt and he chose to be kind.

Could I trust him?

I had no other choice. At any time in the next four years as the Ark journeyed toward our new world, he could decide to tell what he had seen, and in that day I would surely die. Till then, though, I would live.

It was something I never thought possible, that a human being could look at me and see, not a strange or dangerous or even cute little animal, but a person to be pitied or respected or—or whatever, I don't know. What was his silence on the whole ride to the recycling room? I had thought it was fear of me or a failure to think of me as a sentient being. But perhaps Causo's silence was something better than that. Respect for my grief. Sensitivity.

I have spent almost every waking moment since then writing and writing. Carol Jeanne is so busy overseeing the storing away of all the other equipment that she hardly notices me. In these days I have filled out the rest of my account. I've tried to remember how I felt at any given moment, though I suspect my anger and fear and bitterness have colored everything. But underneath everything there is this constant thread of hope, given to me by this stranger, Causo. Hope that I might not be as utterly alone as I thought.

Perhaps there are human beings I can trust. Perhaps, after launch, I can bring new children out of the freezers—enhanced ca-puchins this time, my own kind. Not just one this time, but three or four, so they can keep each other company. And instead of a cage high on the wall, perhaps, just perhaps, I can take some human or humans into my confidence. Perhaps I can get some help.

One thing I have learned, for certain. I can't do it alone. So if I'm going to stake my life one more time on trying to defy the rules and create a free tribe of my own people, I will take the risk of asking for help. Perhaps Causo. Perhaps Neeraj. I don't know. I'll watch, I'll think, I'll try to find some clever way to sound them out. What-ever it takes, my future children will not have to cower in a lonely cage for their entire lives. If the person or people I confide in are worthy of trust, then my children will thrive in human company, learning human speech by hearing it. I will teach them sign lan-guage as well, so they have a way of speaking to me and so I can speak to them, too.

And if the whole enterprise fails because some human could not be trusted, then at least this time I won't have to take my child's life. It will be my body that gets lowered into the chemical bath.

It's time to close this account now. It isn't complete. There's a lot that I've left out. I've been unfair in my depiction of some of these people, Carol Jeanne probably most of all. Isn't that just too damn bad. It's not as if I had a lot of time to think about this as I wrote it. It's how I felt, and that's as valid a part of the data as any of the objective facts of what happened. If you're reading this, it's because I'm dead, so I won't much care what you think of me. All I care about is that you know how much freedom meant to me, how deeply I longed for the right that you all take for granted: To have a family, to live among my own free people.

Maybe your reaction will be to destroy all your witnesses. Maybe they'd prefer it to lives spent in hopeless captivity.

Or maybe your reaction will be to bring my fellow sapients into a life of freedom, letting them develop their own lives and cultures without shackles.

Or maybe you'll never read this at all. Maybe someday I will reread this account myself, remembering how fearful and hopeful and ashamed and guilty and angry and bitter I felt at this moment. I will remember, and smile to think of how far I've come, with all my plans successful, my people thriving. I will give the command that erases the entire record, as I prepare to lead my people off to a life of freedom in the wilderness of the new world.

ACKNOWLEDGMENTS

We both would like to thank:

the participants in the Hatrack River Town Meeting on America
Online (keyword "Hatrack") for reading and responding to the
manuscript of this novel as it unfolded, chapter by chapter. Particular thanks go to Jane Brady, who wrested chapters from our
sweating hands; Mike Glinski, for moral support; and to Heather
Kay, Howard Hansen, Margaret Tobey, Lee Dioso, Ken Schafer,
and others who offered constructive criticism of a work in progress; Shirley C. Strum, Frans de Waal, and other wise researchers
into and writers about the lives of primates whose work helped
make Lovelock come to life; James Lovelock, whose gaia theory
has been extrapolated into a future scientific discipline of gaiology—may that portion of our story, at least, come true; and the
creators of the computer games *Freecell* and *Civilization*, for helping this project to take a year longer than it should have.

Kathryn H. Kidd also recognizes:

Charles Carriker, whose loans satisfied the hungry gods at American Express; and Clark Kidd, husband extraordinaire, for prayers
and encouragement and gratefully received financial assistance.

Orson Scott Card also recognizes:

Mark and Margaret Park, for kindness beyond the call of duty;
Scott Allen, for keeping both the computers and the house in working order; Kathleen Bellamy, for keeping the world at bay and the
office running; Geoffrey Card, for hinting that he couldn't wait to
read the next chapter, and then responding to it so quickly; and
my wife, Kristine A. Card, for bearing the madness and the burdens with unfailing patience and love.